Silkie

To:

Sean

David Rothgery (uncle)

12/15/14

Silkie

World One, World Two

(a novel)

David Rothgery

Mill City Press
Minneapolis, MN

MiLLCiTY PRESS

Mill City Press, Inc.
322 First Avenue N, 5th floor
Minneapolis, MN 55401
612.455.2293
www.millcitypublishing.com

ISBN-13: 978-1-62652-759-1
LCCN: 2014903825

Cover photo of Makayla Ries by Joshua Daniels
Book Design by Sophie Chi

Printed in the United States of America

To my wife, Hsiao-Ching, and my children:
Andrew, Ian, Marc, and Rachel.

"How does your poem end?" he asked,
suddenly looking down.
"Or was it the end?"
[The Brothers Karamazov, *Fyodor Dostoyevsky*]

1. World One, World Two

The eagle—magnificent, regal, snowy crowned, yellow beaked, rich brown plumaged—was . . . in a box.

The box was the size of an orange crate—plywood and slats bolted to a metal frame strapped by wire to the top of a wooden pole. There was screening at the front . . . and a hinged door lift at the side.

It looked like a large rural mailbox.

Splendid though the plumage was, the eagle wore it like a suit stiffened by dust and time—with only the head sticking out and allowed to move. An emperor wedged into the barrel of its own body. It raised its head, the only move possible, to peer out at those peering in. But what did it gain from that?

A series of wooden hand-painted signs along a highway steaming in the hot Colorado summer had pointed us the way. One of them, dangling by rusty chains from a huge red and white Conoco Service Station, announced: "LARGEST BALD EAGLE IN AMERICA"

We needed gas anyway. "Can we get a Coke or an ice-cream bar too?" my older brother Toby asked.

The year was 1961. I was only eight.

On the outside, it was another pathetic little junk of a service station—with broken truck parts and abandoned cars on both sides, and nothing for the eye to see beyond it except flat dusty prairie. On the inside, though, it was a virtual department store of postcards, enamel-painted ashtrays, Indian beads and pottery and hand-made blankets. And, for the kids and greenhorn easterners, not the usual "pit of rattlesnakes" but . . . the eagle.

A skinny old lady, looking worn and bored and wearing a loose smock, pumped the gas and muttered, "Through the store, behind the building."

A $5 fee to see it. More hand-painted signs: "THIS WAY TO THE EAGLE." "ALMOST THERE."

We wound our way through the maze of wooden counters overflowing with candy, chips, plastic cowboys, Comanche arrowheads. Above and around us the walls and ceilings were blanketed with bear rugs, Hopi regalia, cougar and buffalo skins, elk heads, and Wild Bill Hickok and Will Rogers posters.

I was already picturing it. A majestic specimen—a snowy-white head, royal, flaming eyes—its talons gripping the highest branch of a tall tree inside a giant aviary. Maybe, a few branches below, there would be a red-tailed hawk—the sort you'd see in *National Geographic* swooping down and snatching at a sidewinder.

Toby pushed open the door. I crowded through behind him . . . to see . . . what? We were outside again. Two small wooden shacks—one a shed, the other an old outhouse—and a pile of rusted tools, pipes, and stacked empty soda and beer crates. Beyond that . . . absolutely nothing. Flat dry open space and a thin line of mountains stretched before us in all directions.

"So where is the damned thing?" my father asked.

"Hey, it's right here," Toby called out.

To my left, maybe six feet away, was that dirty old small wooden-crate-like box atop that pole. Screening wrapped around the front and fastened by nails crudely hammered sideways to hold it at the edges. The hinged door lift was for feeding.

Inside the box, mostly in the dark . . . the eagle.

We stood there. Silent.

"God!" my brother said finally, so quietly you could barely hear it. "How long's it been in there?"

I wondered too, but I couldn't speak.

The eagle was not even moving its head in response to our voices. Then slowly it turned toward me and . . . peered into me. *Through* me.

So strong was the impression, I turned to see what was behind me: Sky . . . everywhere . . . brilliant blue with nothing to break it except that distant chain of mountains shimmering like a mirage in the sun. I turned back to the eagle, but discovered I was still seeing that magnificent sky—stretched out behind me but now as though not from my eyes but his.

It became too much for me.

I let my head drop, closed my eyes, stumbled away, feeling very dizzy, reached out for something . . . someone . . . and called out, "I'm sorry," just before half lurching forward. I would have fallen had not my father grabbed me and pressed me tightly to him.

"Stephen!" my mother called out in alarm.

She told me later she thought I'd gone unconscious. I hadn't.

I was very conscious. The most poignant conscious I'd ever been. What I was reaching out for I didn't know.

It was sometime after midnight, and I lay curled up in the back of the car, half awake, listening to my parents' voices barely audible against the sound of the tires on the pavement, my head on a pillow pushed up against the side window—wondering if I should ask my father, "Dad, do you suppose they ever let the eagle out? How long you suppose it's been in there?"

"Is there any way we can call someone to complain that it's not right?" Toby had asked a few minutes earlier. "What if we went back and just smashed open the box?"

"That'd be breaking the law," my father had responded.

Of course, he was right. The law was on the side of the man who owned the store, owned the gas station, owned . . . the eagle.

"I'll get you out," I heard myself saying aloud, as though to the eagle himself.

"What's that?" my mother called back.

"Nothin."

It's been forty-four years since that day. I'm fifty-two. Somewhere during that time, but not all at once, I came to understand that I was living in two worlds. World One was solid, neat, orderly. The safe world. The world of certainties, morals by law and prescription. Boundaries, diplomas, policies, rules. There was nothing solid about World Two. It was elusive, chaotic, amorphous. Its moral parameters were cloudy. It was not so much a world as a universe. Full of aimlessness, inexplicableness, loneliness.

I was too young to conceptualize it that way on that hot day in Colorado when I saw the eagle, but if I had I would have said that World One was the world of the service station, the enamel-painted ashtrays, the mounted buffalo heads, the $5 fee, the wooden box, the screening across the front through which the humans gawked. World Two was my stumbling away, my lying curled up in the backseat of the car late that night listening to my father's voice, and recalling what I, as the eagle, had seen when it peered through me to the sky beyond.

I am a teacher. In my office at the college is a filing cabinet.

In it are the folders of my students. Their papers. Organized by class and term and assignment. The papers remain neatly tucked into their folders, which are in turn alphabetized in the drawers. When they are out of date, I toss them away. They are of World One.

Every year or so, however, a folder resists the confinements of the drawer, of the file cabinet. The papers in it—ragged, torn from notebooks of various sizes—seep over the edges . . . because they are of World Two. The world of the eagle's spread wings, its far-off gaze.

One of those folders was Silkie's.

The papers in it got out—spilled out onto the floor.

Silkie herself was of World Two.

And for that reason she could free the eagle. Perhaps she did. But if so, it was in a way I could never have imagined.

2. A Student from Somewhere

Whoever she was—apparently a student (not one of mine)—she'd just come in from the rain. Wearing a soaked and dripping faded blue cotton parka, her forehead and matted blonde hair glistening in the office light, she stood there, inside the doorway to my office, back by the bookcase.

My first inclination was to search for something with which she could dry herself, but as there was nothing to offer but a box of tissues on my desk, I contented myself with a look of sympathy and a quick glance toward the window to my right to acknowledge her plight.

It was a downpour—the rain beating on the glass with so much force it was streaking in all directions, even upward.

Quite apart from the storm she'd braved to get to the campus, however, I was in no mood to admit a new student. The class was already full, and she had already missed two meetings and two assignments. Besides, I was nursing a headache from not having slept well the night before, and at the very moment she had slipped into my office, there were three other students asking annoying questions.

"HOW LONG DOES THE FIRST PAPER HAVE TO BE?"

"DOES IT HAVE TO BE TYPED?"

If they'd taken the time to read the syllabus, for God's sake . . .

I fended off the questions with cursory answers, trying to hide my impatience.

"MY COMPUTER IS DOWN, SO CAN I DO THE ROUGH DRAFT IN PEN?"

"Yes, a lot of the students write more naturally in pen, in fact."

Between two of the students hovering over my desk, I took a second look at her—the young woman in the sopping wet parka. She was still standing near the bookshelves toward the back of my office. Silent. Her head slightly tilted to the side. Her eyes studying me with a peculiar intensity.

I was about to ask her if I could help her, but was obliged to continue responding to the others.

"SO THE FIRST PAPER IS DUE NEXT WEEK?"

"No, just the rough draft."

To my surprise the strange woman was taking down a paperback from the top shelf and opening it. Was she in my class? How could I not remember a student with such riveting eyes?

"Yes. Listen, most of your questions . . . you'll find the answers spelled out in the syllabus."

I saw my right arm and hand motioning them toward the door, and, embarrassed I had in effect banished them from the office, I apologized. "Sorry, I have a bit of a headache."

They were gone. I still had my headache. The young woman (who I was certain now was not a student of mine) was still there, saying nothing, in fact was reading from the paperback she'd taken down from the bookcase.

"Yes?" I asked.

She seemed to drag her eyes hurriedly through the rest of a sentence in the opened book, then, without closing it, looked up at me.

"I need to be in your class."

It was not a question.

She was thinner, younger-looking than most college-age girls—in fact, on first glance, might have been mistaken for a fifteen-year-old.

As I pondered how to answer, she began turning her head right and left restlessly in almost feral agitation, warily scanning the room like some kind of helpless animal. Her eyes seemed almost too large for her small frame. Had her hair been dyed red or her nose hung with two rings, her eyes would still have been what I remembered about her.

When her attention settled, it was on the rain pounding on the window behind me and to my right. Through it and well beyond. Then back to me.

"Which class do you mean? All my classes are full."

"Writing 121. I should be on your list."

"What is your name?" I asked.

"Marian Sanders. Silkie. Silkie Sanders."

I picked up the roll. Sure enough, there was her name—

"Marian Sanders"—crossed out.

"You missed both Tuesday and today. The first two classes. So I had to drop you. That's the policy. I've already added two new students from the waiting list . . . you know . . . those wanting to get in if someone doesn't show. That's how it's done."

She nodded, but with no indication she understood the situation or even cared. She continued to fix her eyes on me.

For some reason, an image flashed in my mind of a wolf cub I'd seen in a television documentary that week who'd strayed from its kind and was standing alone in a creek—hungry, tired—watching warily the man filming him.

"That's how we're supposed to do it," I said, wondering why my "how it's done" had become "how we're supposed to do it."

She continued standing there, saying nothing, *as though she were waiting for me to comprehend something.*

"You understand, don't you? Besides, there's the issue of your being already a couple assignments behind." I turned to the five-page syllabus on my desk (as much to escape from the discomfort of her gaze as for the ostensible reason) and laid it open on the desk before her. "You see on the calendar of assignments here that the first day in class each student did an in-class writing—a kind of inventory of him- or herself called 'Taking Stock'—and shared it, and we discussed the first real assignment—the personal narrative. I mean it's hard to catch up if you're . . . "

She took the paper and read it over carefully for more than two minutes—more time than necessary, given she wasn't going to be doing the assignments anyway—then looked up at me.

"My daughter . . . she's been sick. I took her to the doctor, the clinic. I had to make sure about . . . her. . . . She was crying. Otherwise, I would have been here . . . the first day. And today."

Her voice was softly sonorous and came from some far-off place full of certainty about where she had been if not where she was now. The kind you took in before responding.

There was now a look of exhaustion about her—one that went well beyond her having trudged through the rain to get to my office, beyond admission to the class, beyond even her daughter's illness—one bordering on despair.

"I'm sorry," I said, "I can't really . . . this late . . . and with the class limit . . . you know . . . and the department policy, let you back in."

"Yes," she replied. But there was no acquiescence in it.

She stood there, holding herself—grasping her shoulders tightly (a cold from more than the rain?)—then turned slightly to the side, her eyes full of quiet fury that seemed to go beyond just me.

"I'm sorry," I said again.

Still, she stood there. Not looking at me. Then, remarkably, "May I borrow this book?"

"Pardon?"

She held up the paperback for me to see. *Woman at Point Zero*. A novel by the Egyptian writer Nawal El Saadawi.

I was taken back. First removing the book off the shelf without permission (was my office the public library?)— then, without being in my class anymore, asking to borrow it. "Well, I mean, you're not . . . "

"The downtown library doesn't have it."

Perhaps it was the boldness of the request, or the novelty of it, or my being pleased she would want to read such a book, that got me. (Fewer and fewer of my students gave evidence of having read anything beyond the high school mainstays *Lord of the Flies* and *To Kill a Mockingbird*.) I smiled.

"I suppose, if you remember to . . . return it." It never even occurred to me she might not be a student at all and therefore not likely to be on campus anymore.

She nodded, then turned to leave.

"Listen, . . . Marian . . . "

"Silkie."

"Silkie, . . . *I'm sorry.*"

Even as I said it, though, I was aware my "I'm sorry" this time did not mean just for not letting her in, or for, accordingly, making her life more difficult. I meant something else. Beyond that. *But what?*

She left. With the book . . . and the syllabus as well.

As I drove home, I could think about nothing else except that exchange with her, that mix of despair, admonishment, expectation, fury in her eyes. "What was I to do?" I asked myself. "That's how it works."

Still I could not banish the feeling I'd failed not just her but myself in some profound way.

To my surprise, I discovered my headache was gone.

After dinner, I drove back to my office, retrieved the class list for Writing 121, and found her name: "Marian Sanders." For "Phone" it read: "None." For "Address": "1443A Gilchrist."

I went looking for her.

Why this decision? Guilt perhaps. The administrative policies for enrollment had always struck me as a little too rigid. Usually, one or two of the duly enrolled students disappeared in the course of the term, and so the total enrollment would not exceed the maximum. On the other hand, a student's missing the first two class meetings, for whatever reason, often signaled a student whose attendance would be erratic throughout the term. So, guilt does not explain my decision.

The "black spot" does.

Both—the guilt and the decision—emanated from it. The black spot in my brain. More precisely, my temporal lobe. "That's where it is," the neurologist had said, pointing to a tiny dark mark on my CAT-scan.

It was his explanation for my seizures, the first of which I'd experienced years earlier with that eagle in Colorado. A brain injury. The result of a concussion I'd gotten when, running around the side of a garage, I'd collided in a sickening head-on-head with Jimmy Meinhoff. Nothing to do with the eagle or its plight—except as the stress of the moment might have activated the injury, which could be seen clearly on the CAT-scan in the form of that black spot.

No problem. There were all these medications—anticonvulsants. Deaden the unruly neurons. Smother the spot.

Turned out, though, the doctor was wrong. The "spot" in the CAT-scan was not a concussion injury. It was a hole. A hole that was most likely always there.

I figured it out myself—with the help of an article I stumbled onto in the *New York Times* on the subject of brain injuries. "I feel like I have a volcano in my brain," a seven-year-old autistic girl explained to her doctor.

And that's my excuse for my enigmatic response to that young woman who'd come out of the rain and wanted to be readmitted to my class. For why I said, "I'm sorry." For why I went looking for her. A tiny volcano, which, with each eruption, took over more and more of my brain through the years.

There was no way the medication was going to plug it up entirely. The hole went down too deep. The problem went too far in. Too far back. To who I was before the eagle.

Volcanoes on occasion explode. They have seizures. But much of the time they are churning beneath the surface. That's how it was with that autistic girl. With me. Way down in. Churning. Never dormant. Always building up

. . . wanting to get out.

And that's what it was doing big time with that young woman Silkie in my office that day.

Maybe it was her eyes. The way she looked at me. Or her voice—soft and sure. But it was her taking down that book, too. I'd figured it out long before. All those books' writers— Hawthorne, Dostoyevsky, Melville, Hesse, McCullers—they had volcanos in their brains too. You could tell because their characters did—Hester Prynne, Ivan Karamazov, Goldmund, Billy Budd, John Singer. The people I wanted to be had volcanos in their brains. Some "God" impulse to figure it all out. I had it in me too. As a young Catholic kid, I'd envisioned myself as a St. Francis of Assisi or Albert Schweitzer. I was in desperate need of an "infinity settling over me," as Millay put it, or a "hallowing of an interval otherwise inconsequent," as Sylvia Plath imagined it. I needed one of my seizures to take hold of me in a way that would render me either mad or mystically enlightened.

But I hadn't ever and wasn't now doing a damned thing about it. The volcano was churning, but I was smothering it. Not only with the medication but with my life as I was living it.

I had no choice. I was a professor. My responsibility was not to explode. No, it was to light the spark. Plant the seed. Pass on the baton. Toss the pebble that starts the ripple. And surely I'd done that. Now and then I'd see it in a student's eyes. The connection: my soul with his; my mind with hers.

The problem was I was not the beginning nor the end of these chains in nature, in enlightenment. I was in the midst of them like everyone else. Another link in another chain. Another ripple in another sea of endless seas. In a system that just kept moving, I was unable to grasp more than what my senses bumped up against. I would hold on to a link, only to feel it disintegrate; point out a ripple, only to see it disappear. As they ceased to exist, so did their significance. Meaning got lost in the process of teaching.

I began to think of myself as a purveyor of symbols and marks on paper masquerading as ideas and wisdom. I'd give my students broken pieces with the lie they could build them into a whole. My teaching became more robotic and stale, but it didn't matter because I took home a check. My academic position paid the bills. I went to lectures, but visiting scholars did nothing to reinvigorate me—seeming to offer not so much new ideas as repackaged old ones. Their insights were always human-limited.

Whatever I'd been reaching out for with that eagle, I'd stopped reaching for. I'd been holding tightly to the solid world. I did what was expected of me—not only in my work but my everyday life. Made my meals. Cut my lawn. Had my trees trimmed, my car serviced. I visited my children once every few weeks [I had been divorced for four years]. They were living two states away, and that meant overnight flights, sitting in airports watching talk shows and political pundits on TVs, awkward greetings with my children followed by artificial "fun" weekends of fast foods, Disney movies, and Sea World.

Always the volcano churned. Crusted over by the medicine but never entirely smothered, it had become God to me. Not the God of my Catholic school days whom I had long abandoned, but a different one. To mollify this God, I didn't go to church. Instead I hiked on mountain trails, drove in the evenings listening to music—Cat Stevens or Rachmaninoff or whoever suited my mood—and on occasion ate out at the Greek restaurant on the campus where I usually ordered a glass of wine and a gyro and contemplated who I was.

On a more ambitious level—thinking it was the sort of task my new God demanded—I sought out work in the "developing world" and ended up taking a teaching job in Nigeria. Some notion I had told me vicarious suffering would satisfy. For two years there, I passed on to my students knowledge in the form of irregular verbs and Shakespeare. They, in turn, passed on to me enlightenment in the form of parched fields and tribal killing. The experience fed my volcano.

Returning to teaching at the university, however, I discovered the volcano, far from satisfied, had been reignited and was demanding attention. The intensity continued to build. It needed someplace to go.

And here was this Silkie. I knew it instinctively, without ever reading her essays or her journal. She too had a volcano in her brain. And, over time, my instincts were confirmed.

So maybe, in a sense, I was looking for Silkie—or looking to create one.

3. Gabriel

"God will get him out. Free the eagle. He is God. He can do anything. Keeping that eagle in the box isn't right, so it's just a matter of telling Him about it . . . praying."

At some point during the long night in the backseat of our car on that Colorado highway, that's what I was thinking. And about the Archangel Gabriel. I'd gone to a Catholic school. Knew all about the archangels. Especially Gabriel.

It was strange because, after a very hot day on that interminable stretch of road in Colorado, and as shaken and exhausted as I was by the seizure I'd suffered upon seeing the imprisoned eagle, I should have been sleeping. With the cool of the evening air seeping in from along the edges of the back door window, the peace of the midnight highway, I should have been able to fall asleep and forget how its eyes had looked through and beyond me. But I couldn't. I was just a kid. I'd remembered my catechism lesson. *What do our guardian angels do for us? Our guardian angels pray for us, protect and guide us.*

"Gabriel is your messenger to the Lord, so when you

need God to help you, pray to Gabriel," Sister Mary Frances, my third-grade teacher, had said, as though recently, in the archangel's presence, she'd been instructed to pass on this lesson.

She'd rewarded me once—for earning a 100 percent on an arithmetic test—with a small glossy color card displaying an image of him standing astride a mountain, magnificent whitish-gray wings outspread, his head turned toward the heavens. Young—eight--as I was when I'd first got it, I thought it was an actual photograph.

It was those magnificent wings that got me. He would need to do some flying for me.

First thing I did, then, when we got home three days later, a week before the start of school, was write Gabriel a letter.

> *Dear Archangel Gabriel,*
> *There's this eagle in a box. A very small box. He cannot move.*
> *Please get him out. Sincerely,*
> *Stephen*

I'd chosen my mother's blue pastel stationery and my father's expensive Shaeffer fountain pen. Because, if I made the letters very carefully—in the sacred-ornate fashion of those in the Bible—Gabriel (and God Himself) would have to take notice.

One night, I sat there at the little table in my bedroom,

with the stationery in front of me, determined to free the eagle the only way my situation—eight years old, a thousand miles away—would allow. Get God to help.

I reasoned it was a small request. Not a selfish big one for me like a new bicycle or a thousand-dollar bill.

But the task of producing such a letter was a lot more difficult than I'd anticipated, and I had to do it three or four times—crying because the capitals *A, G, S,* and *H* never looked anywhere near as good as those on the gold-leafed pages in the Bible. When I was done—imperfect as it was—I set the note in front of that colorful picture of Gabriel. Would it not have seemed silly, I might have knelt down and prayed the words of my letter aloud. Everything that needed to be said was right there—on the paper. I bowed my head and whispered, "Please do this for me. Help that eagle."

Over the next month I made personal sacrifices—as I did at Lent—so my request would merit special attention. I gave up eating Neccho Wafers—my favorite candy—and helped my mother clearing the table after dinner every day.

And each night, as I lay in bed, I pictured Gabriel gracefully descending and alighting atop the eagle's prison box in the middle of the night when no one was around and slashing through the lock with his heavenly sword.

I'll admit, though, I wasn't convinced. Unless we traveled back to Colorado, how would I know? In the end, I had only Sister Mary Frances' word.

And that, I would discover—months later on a day when

I got sick at school, and started to vomit, and Sister Mary Frances took me to the convent, called my mother to pick me up, and told me I could wait there—wasn't any good.

In that convent parlor, nothing was out of place. Flower vases perfectly centered on tables, white linen coverings hanging perfectly straight, chairs facing across from one another, pictures of Jesus and the saints on the walls, nativity scenes and little statues of Mary and Joseph here and there. On the table next to me was a large Bible and next to that a framed display of all three archangels—Raphael, Michael, and Gabriel.

I could hear, way back in the kitchen, the sisters talking in "thee's" and "thou's" (though I wondered if they weren't just having fun with me), so I took the opportunity to pick up the picture and examine it closely—looking for some clue to convince me my letter had had the right response. How could Gabriel open a lock with wings? Or swing a sword. So he had to have hands someplace.

"Those are the archangels," she said. It was Sister Mary Frances who'd come back to check on me. She startled me because I hadn't known she was there. Embarrassed, I hurriedly set the picture down.

"Feeling better, Stephen?" she asked.

I nodded.

"Your mother should be here soon."

She was walking back to the kitchen when I got up

enough courage to call to her.

"Sister!"

She stopped and turned. For some reason, in the dim light of the parlor, she looked very different to me from how she did in the classroom. Her nun's habit had slipped slightly back, and I caught a glimpse of the hairnet beneath it. Here, in the convent—which was in essence a large old stone house—she was just a little old lady. She was short, a little plump, and wore glasses, probably in her fifties. Being a nun meant she had some special connection with God, but she was, in the end, just a little old lady. So how could she know the answer?

I hesitated, but I'd already started.

"If you . . . if you pray to God, and it's for a good thing, He'll give it to you, won't he?"

It was the great and wise teacher in her that answered. "Yes, if it's a good thing."

For a brief moment, she'd banished the "just an old lady" image, and I felt better. I waited, expecting her to ask me what I meant. The specifics of my question.

But she didn't.

"Pardon?" I finally asked.

"If it's a good thing," she repeated.

She had her answer ready—perhaps for all such occasions.

That settled it for her. Adjusting the white cardboard habit, she smiled at me as though she were patting me on the head, then slipped her hands into the black fold of her gown.

"Okay, Stephen?" she asked. Maybe sensing something was wrong.

"Yeah, I just wondered because . . . there was this eagle. . . . It was in a box. . . ."

I told her all about it, and how I'd used the miniature of Gabriel she'd given me and written a letter to him for help. To my dismay, though, my story and all my efforts on the eagle's behalf—praying and copying over and over again the letter—didn't seem to make much impression on her.

"You know, Stephen, the Lord has enough to worry about with us human beings."

"Yeah, guess so." I nodded.

She must have seen the disappointment in my eyes then, because she repeated, "Yes, God grants prayers if it's for a good thing. For we human beings. Birds can't pray."

There was real certainty in her voice.

But when she bent down to readjust the position of the framed picture of the archangels on the table (I'd accidentally turned it too far to the left), her being so concerned about this reminded me of how my great-aunt, in her old house, used to dust the end tables and straighten the doilies covering them. And juxtaposing the two images—Sister's putting the picture back and my great-aunt's straightening the doilies— was what did it for me. The revelation. She *was* just a little old lady. A doily and picture straightener. Her mind could not get beyond that. She could not, therefore, have any special insight into God's plan.

The clunk in my brain was loud enough to hear. Seeing Sister Mary Frances that way became a whole new understanding of her. Yes, she was the authority. Firm but not cruel. Never lost her temper. She knew enough of geography and arithmetic and history and how it all fit together to be a proper teacher to eight- and nine-year-olds: "Africa is a continent. . . . Invert the numerator and denominator when you divide fractions. . . . Coronado discovered the Grand Canyon. Learn the catechism. Pray the rosary once a day to combat temptation. . . . Humans suffer because God lets Satan test us. . . . He created archangels to help those made in His likeness . . . but of course that doesn't include eagles." She came out of the mold a perfect specimen of what she was supposed to be. A nun who taught little Catholic children to read, write, and be good little Catholics. Someone *told* her about those things the same way she *told* us. But she didn't really *know* or *understand* in the way I thought she did. About super beings named Gabriel or Satan or about heaven or about what happened when you died.

She didn't know any more about it than I did. How could she say that eagles couldn't pray? My eagle could.

I'd meant to ask her about not just the eagle but also Norma Jean—because Gabriel was part of that too. Norma Jean was a classmate who had cerebral palsy. It was not a real obvious kind, but because of it she had a sickly look and wore her glasses down on her nose like a granny. None of us knew anything about CP at the time. All we knew was that she had that sick expression and was not a particularly good student. So she was made fun of—boys and girls both. Not openly, but she must've known. Harry Rutherford used to sit as far away from her as he could at lunch. Theresa Giddons let out a groan when she happened to get paired with her for a history assignment.

One day Norma Jean asked a boy by the name of Billy Burke for help with an assignment. Because he was with his friends at the time and didn't want to be associated with her, thinking about his reputation, he said something like, "Figure it out yourself. You retarded or something?" Didn't say it quietly either.

I know because I was with him at the time.

Why'd she persist? You'd think, being stung that way, she'd just walk away, but she didn't. Maybe to get him to retract it, or maybe she just believed he'd been joshing her. "Come on," she said, and you could hear the hurt in her voice, "don't say that. . . ."

"Go away!" he shouted, recoiling as though she had the plague, and when she didn't—instead began whimpering—he shouted it again—"Jesus, go away!"— and began rubbing his hands together and shaking them to disinfect himself of her because he'd gotten too close to her.

I saw what it did to her. "Why'd you say that?" I asked him. "Just leave her alone." He did, but when he walked away he muttered, "Why would I wanta help her anyway?"

Norma Jean had heard me stand up for her and must've got a crush on me because of it. Began coming up to me, asking me questions about assignments and taking a seat next to me in the cafeteria. The others saw it, and one day it was turned on me. During a touch football game this guy named Max Baird—always showing off how tough he was at football, though that was all he was . . . tough, rough . . . not really skilled at passing or catching—got into a shouting match with me just after I'd scored a touchdown. He said he'd got me with both hands, but I knew he hadn't, that he was just humiliated by the fact that I'd gotten free for a pass and scored and he'd looked clumsy slipping and falling into the mud when he'd reached out for me.

I walked away. "If you're gonna cheat, I'm not playin," I said.

He began taunting me. "Goin off to see your girlfriend Norma Jean?"

"Shut up, she's not my girlfriend!"

But he saw he'd hit the right button and kept at me. "Stephen loves Norma Jean!"

I don't know if I was so mad because of his taunting me or I simply didn't want it to get around that Norma Jean was in any sense my girlfriend . . . or that I had any girlfriend. Exasperated, I pushed him away and called out, "I told you she's not my girlfriend and I don't even like her," and then walked away. But as I did so, I happened to catch sight of her, in the handful of kids that had crowded around—Norma

Jean. Her expression frozen, her eyes sad-like . . . crying . . . not on the outside but on the inside. Like that of the eagle. There had to have been a clunk in her brain too—about other humans, about the treachery of words—just like the clunk I'd have in my brain about God and nuns a few days later.

For the whole rest of the year, whenever she saw me, her eyes got red, even when I said nice things to her.

I prayed to Gabriel about her too. Even wrote another letter to him (though without the ornate lettering of the "eagle" one). With it, a prayer: "Dear Archangel Gabriel, make Norma Jean feel better."

I told my mother about Norma Jean—what I'd done. She suggested I bring her a flower—in a pot. But I was embarrassed about what giving a flower to a girl would mean. She would tell her friends about it. I didn't want to hurt her, but I didn't want them seeing me as being sweet on her either.

As I said, I never got a chance that morning in the convent to ask Sister Mary Frances about Norma Jean. But it wouldn't have mattered. She would have said something that didn't mean anything. Years later, when I thought back on it, it occurred to me Sister Mary Frances was never really genuine about anything. Had she confessed how once, as a little girl, staring down at a dead bird on the sidewalk, she doubted God was all merciful, I would have seen her differently. But she never did. Those many more years she'd lived than I had didn't translate into anything that she might have said that morning to make me feel better—about the eagle or about who I was to want that eagle to be free.

She just walked away from me. In her mind she'd settled it. God had more important things. She walked away and took God with her. Maybe that's how it was. Maybe God too just walked away from things He considered too trivial to deal with. Eagles in boxes. Norma Jeans that get hurt.

Over the next month, I was able at times to forget that clunk of realization in my head about Sister Mary Frances and all the other sisters in that convent. Told myself the Archangel Gabriel really did swoop down and smash the box, and the eagle flew away into that far-off sky his eyes had burned into me that day.

At other times, though, it didn't work. What I'd learned about nuns rang in my ears like some ultimate truth. I heard again that robot-like response—a little like that of the skinny old woman in Colorado pumping gas ("Through the store, behind the building")—and said to myself, "God and Gabriel are too busy to worry about one little eagle."

4. The Search

I'd never done such a thing before—gone looking for a student at her home address. The strange girl named "Silkie" who'd asked to get into my class—she was the first. A curious sense of urgency was driving me. "1443A Gilchrist Street."

It was a little after 7 p.m. It turned out 1443 Gilchrist was an older two-story wood-frame house bordered on the right by a vacant gravel lot and on the left by a transmission repair shop. It was the only house in the block in an older neighborhood several streets from the center of town and several more from the campus. Except for a strip of grass along the sidewalks there were no lawns in this area. The only two trees on the street somehow produced wet dead leaves everywhere. Across the street was another old house with a "For Rent" sign in the window.

At the top of five stone steps leading up to the front porch was an ornately carved wooden fence post on which was nailed a small sign that read "1443A around back." That meant I had to stumble my way over stepping-stones half sunk into the ground on an unlit side of the house. And were it not for a security light from the transmission shop and the iron railing bordering the wooden stairway—along which were cleaning buckets, clay pots, and a mop—I might not have made it to 1443A. There was no light shining from within, but the venetian blinds were closed, so I knocked. No answer. I searched for a doorbell and pushed it. No sound. I knocked again. No answer.

I made my way back around to the front of the house and knocked on the door.

"Yes?" A woman's voice.

"Excuse me, I'm looking for someone. In 1443A."

The door opened slowly, but was held ajar.

A heavy woman—probably in her sixties, wearing a bathrobe, her gray hair held tightly in a net—peaked out. I could barely make out a man, maybe in his thirties and very overweight, seated in an armchair toward the back of the living room.

"Excuse me, can you tell me if a Marian Sanders, or Silkie Sanders, used to live here—in the back apartment? That's the address I have."

She opened the door all the way now—apparently satisfied I was no threat. I could see the young man more clearly now. Probably her son, he was seated so rigidly I decided he was somehow disabled—mentally or physically—and very likely dependent on his mother for his livelihood.

The woman looked me over and seemed reluctant at first to respond. "Well, yes. She did. But she's no longer here. She and her little girl . . . they stayed here only a couple months, then left. Are you a . . . relative?"

"No, I'm her teacher," I said to assure her. "I mean she was going to take my class at the college, and I just wanted to tell her . . . she could."

"Oh."

"Do you know where she moved to?"

"Well, I'm not really sure she moved anywhere. I mean she didn't really have the money to pay. Not near enough. I was nice to her, you know. Let her stay anyway. Two . . . no, it was more than two months, I guess it was. Didn't have a job or anything. Said she had to have a home to keep her little girl. Really cute girl. Had a strange name. She herself was a strange one. I mean the mother. You know?"

"She wasn't strange, Mother," the young man called out disapprovingly from behind her. "You think anybody different is strange."

"Well, you know when those people came to check on her and her little girl. Why was that?" she replied, turning back to her son to quiet him.

"That was nothing, turned out, Mother, you know that."

I waited for more helpful information, hoping perhaps the son would come to the door, but he continued to sit there.

"So you don't know where she went?"

She shook her head. "No. No. I don't. I gave her some advice about that. I was worried 'bout her. Like I say, I was nice to her. Told her to try the Mission—you know they take young women with no place to go. But I'm not sure if she did. Or to one of those other shelters. You know she might have a friend. But she didn't seem to. Unless she found work. Anyway, you might try the Mission."

I was stunned. Thinking how I'd been so bureaucratic with this Silkie. I thought back to her appearance. Her jacket had been somewhat soiled, but I'd attributed it to the rain. Her eyes—now desperate, now expectant and almost demanding, now despairing, now full of fury.

"You're sure she didn't say she'd be moving to some other place? I don't know where this Mission is. I guess I should but . . . "

"I'm really not . . . good with directions." She turned to her son for help.

"I can draw you the way," he said. He reached over to the table next to him and snatched a pencil.

"Here." His mother pulled a sheet of paper from a drawer and took it to him. He began drawing lines, though with some difficulty, then gave it to her. She brought it to me.

"Like I say, she may not be there."

"I'll give it a try. I appreciate it," I replied, and nodded and smiled to the son. He nodded back.

As I walked back to my car, I heard her calling to me: "I did let her stay for some time. Did what I could for her. That daughter of hers is a really beautiful little girl. Hope you find them."

I decided that her concern was not sincere. But then what

right did I have to judge? This woman had allowed Silkie to stay without paying. I hadn't even let the girl into my class.

I drove to the Mission, which was a place, as the lady had explained, where the homeless were cared for—the money probably provided by donations from churches in the city. By the time I arrived it was already dark, and a lot of men, and no women, were standing around—most of them by themselves, staring down at the ground—in a gravel courtyard adjoining a large one-story building inside of which was a lit kitchen and dining room with other men cleaning tables. It was fenced in with a cardboard sign of rules tacked up under an awning:

> *No hanging clothes on fence.*
> *No lying down in the courtyard.*
> *No smoking.*

A very short, completely bald man (so I couldn't tell if he was twenty-five or forty-five), alone, nodded to me without smiling. He reminded me of a strange guy I'd worked with years before as a graduate student doing janitorial work late at night in a hospital. We all thought he was mentally "slow" because he spent so much time cleaning thoroughly—scrubbing every wall, for a minimum wage of $2.25. I asked him one night as we got coffee from the vending machine who he was. He told me he was just there for the summer and needed work to pay his way back to school in New York.

He was a doctoral student in biophysics.

I nodded back and went inside the building. Against the far wall was a caged-in area with a line of men in front of it. Behind the screening was a very large man—tall and heavy—missing a lot of teeth, giving out tickets for laundry.

"Excuse me," I asked when he was finished. "I'm looking for a woman who might be staying . . ."

"Women are in the other building," he said, almost as though reprimanding me.

"Of course," I said, and felt stupid, given that up till now I'd seen only men. "Where?"

"Out the door and around to the right."

"That way?"

"Right."

"Thanks."

"Wait a minute, Mister. It's past eight. Men can't get in. Have to wait to the morning."

"Do you know if there's any way I can leave a message?"

"There's an office. If someone's still working."

"Where's that?"

"Next door. Out that way."

There was still a light on inside. I knocked.

"Closed till six—morning," a woman's voice called out. "Come back then."

"I just need to leave a message."

There was a pause and the door opened. A very tired

middle-aged woman, in a jacket and jeans and apparently about to exit for the evening, peaked out.

"Yes? What was that?"

"I'm a . . . teacher. I think one of my students may be here." [That "teacher" thing had worked earlier.]

"What's the message? Who for? I'll take it and check the names. A lot of women here, you know." She said it in a mechanical way, but not one entirely lacking in feeling. It was probably how I'd spoken to Silkie in my office the day before.

"Sorry, do you have a paper and pen?"

She sighed—more from exhaustion than impatience—then disappeared inside and came out again.

"I'm not sure if she's here. In fact, I don't know at all, but . . . " I wrote hurriedly,

> To Marian Silkie Sanders,
> If you still want to get into my class, you can. Come Monday morning to my office again.
> Stephen Mollgaard
> English Professor.

I left with little expectation she would be found there, and I discovered I was now, for sure, feeling a deep sense of guilt. My bureaucratic decision about not letting this Silkie Sanders into my class had become a matter not just of a nagging regret but of morally reprehensible behavior.

More determined than ever, I returned the following

morning. She was not there. "You might try Catholic Community Services—their food kitchen or some of the other shelters where they take in young girls . . . you know, runaways," a tall, sinewy woman—like someone raised on a farm—suggested, in an almost gruff voice, but as with the woman the night before, not without compassion. I appreciated her help.

It was Saturday, and I had most of the day.

Catholic Community Services was little more than a large cinder-block building with a huge storefront window revealing a large open space with racks full of clothes, tables manned by volunteers, cardboard boxes stuffed with odds and ends, and a handful of chairs with old women asleep in them. Outside, two young men were fixing bikes, and a line of ten or so people passed through a side door that appeared to be a soup-kitchen.

I asked a woman manning one of the tables inside if she knew a "Silkie or Marian Sanders." No luck.

Under other circumstances perhaps I would have given up, but I held out hope that Silkie was registered for other college classes, and I could obtain her schedule Monday morning. And if she had managed to get into a different writing class, I could still tell her I was sorry. Tell her that I'd tried to find her.

Somehow her knowing that was important.

5. Ruth

After my first class Monday morning, I stopped by the department office.

"Jan, you mind checking to see if there's a 'Marian . . . M A R I A N . . . Sanders' enrolled. And if so what classes she has. I . . . dropped her but I might let her back in."

As Jan logged into the registrations on her computer, I went to my mailbox. In it, along with a couple campus memorandums, was a somewhat beaten-up mailing envelope. I opened it to find several handwritten pages paper-clipped together—one the in-class "Taking Stock" assignment, the other entitled "Ruth"—along with a note on a page torn from a notebook:

> *Dear Professor Mollgaard,*
> *I did the assignments you said I missed, plus the one due next week.*
> *Are these okay? I will stop by today during your office hours again.*
> *Silkie (Marian) Sanders*

"Never mind," I told Jan.

I walked to my office and sat down to read.

> *"Taking Stock—Inventory of Me"*
> *Silkie Sanders*
> *I don't have much. No father. He went. No mother.*
> *Cancer. I was 14. No siblings. I'm my own. One daughter.*
> *Age 5. Her father went too.*
> *I have photographs. Dance and dancers—Ruth*
> *St. Denis. Greek Maenads. Sufis. Susana and Isadora.*
> *Those my daughter likes—buffalo in a blizzard, penguins*
> *waddling in a line. Fractals too—of snowflakes,*
> *cauliflowers, and African villages.*
> *Other photographs—the kind stuck in my mind.*
> *A little girl—deaf, a painful hurting tooth—sitting*
> *alone on the ground under a table in a Guatemalan*
> *marketplace. I can't do anything for her. A baboon*
> *in a metal cage in a zoo. I can't do anything for him*
> *either. Just the pictures—in my mind.*
> *I came and went . . . and took away the pictures.*
> *Last Tuesday I took a picture. I was on a bus. My*
> *daughter was with me. We stopped on the highway.*
> *All the cars were stopped—both ways. Pickup hit a*
> *doe. Her two fawns, mad from fright, were running*
> *in wild confusion back and forth across the road.*
> *A young man exited his car, swaggered over to the*
> *injured deer. Had the air of knowing what he was*

doing, knew about such things, how to deal with them, slipped behind the doe, grasped firmly her neck. One sudden deft wrenching, put her out of her misery, so that once and for all the fawns would just give up, go on their way into the forest. The people got back into their cars, went on to work, to school.

I don't have that picture. I have the other. The fawns who didn't go on their way . . . who went another way . . . not the way they'd been going. Maybe the people, but not the fawns. They lost the grace of deer, their bodies turning one way, their legs another, crossed, tangled, stiffened, one with the other, buckling in mind and body, running in horror from their own mother in too many directions . . . then . . . turned again . . . and went some way that was strange . . . not the way they'd come.

My daughter wanted to follow, and so did I, so we got off the bus. We needed to go that way too. The strange way. So we did. Followed the fawns into the woods. We took the picture without the camera, and talked about it. She wanted me to explain. I tried.

I have the photograph—the fawns.

Photographs from long ago too. I picked the wild strawberries and put them in the notebook paper I cupped for that. And then to the field beyond where I picked dandelions. And gave them to my mother. She always smiled then, her quiet way—stopping what she was doing, swallowing noticeably.

I do a lot of leaving buses. Following fawns. Picking strawberries. Catching snowflakes. Dancing. Taking pictures in my mind.

Then I read the personal narrative—the first formal writing assignment that was not due even as a rough draft till later that week. It was not messy, but a lot of words and phrases were crossed out with corrections written above and in the margins.

"Ruth"
Silkie Sanders
That day I got to cross the bridge again. My Aunt Camilla drove me because my mother was sick. "Tired," she said. I knew she was because she'd just sit there and say, "Fix your own food, okay?" But it didn't matter. I liked Frosted Flakes. I could just pour them into my yellow tin bowl. And get the cardboard container of milk with the picture of the cow on it out of the refrigerator. And pour it into the bowl. No sugar needed. I ate a lot of Frosted Flakes those days. My daddy wasn't living with us much, just now and then. He'd come and get me and bring Dots and chocolate Bon-Bons. Later I would come to hate them because he knew those were my favorites. He hadn't come for a while though. So my Aunt Camilla came that day and said I'd be staying with her for a few days.

My Aunt Camilla had a big flat cream-colored car with large fins, very old and rusted. When I sat in the front with her I was very small, could barely get my eyes above the dashboard to see the road in front, so most of the time I just looked down into my lap looking at one of my picture books.

When we got to the bridge, though, I could see the steel frames crisscrossing against the sky.

And that meant I would be safe again for a while.

My father would come to our house, but not to my Aunt Camilla's house, which was really my Aunt Judith's house. It was across the bridge and up and down streets with a lot of old houses. Hers was so old it probably went back to before WWI. But I didn't know about wars then. It had a basement which had a coal bin, and just walking by the door into that basement you could smell the coal from long ago—even feel it in your nose—even though now it was just a few smashed and broken pieces on the floor.

It had an attic, too. Where Aunt Judith stayed.

The room where Aunt Judith lived was not really the attic itself but a little cut-out cove on the stairway up to it which started behind what looked like a closet door in the hall between the kitchen and dining room. 15 wooden steps altogether. 7 steps forward, 3 steps to the left, 5 more steps back to the right again. Cleaning-fluid containers and pails along the way and so always smelling clean. Dresses hanging too because there was no real closet for them. 6 steps from the actual attic, through a doorway without a door, sat Aunt Judith usually. In a creaky old wooden rocking chair in a little room furnished with that chair, a small cot in the corner, and two or three tables on which were 20 or so religious pictures and icons. She would always be deep in prayer, her mouth moving, quivering with the words, her eyes closed much of the time, her fingers on a rosary usually.

When I first saw her I was frightened. Her skin so wrinkled and sagging, her cheeks especially—to both sides of her chin. Her hair gray and matted from perspiration from praying so hard. I heard Aunt Camilla tell a neighbor once she had no mirror so she could always see herself as young. On the smallest of the tables were three pictures. I thought they were all of her, but it turned out only two were. The other was of Ruth.

"Who is Ruth?" I asked Aunt Camilla once.

She hesitated then said, "She was your Aunt Judith's daughter. She looks like you, doesn't she?" I didn't think so until she said it then, but when I saw the picture on another day I remembered and thought, "Yes, she looks like me."

"Where is she?" I asked.

"She died when she was very young."

"What did she die of?"

*"Oh, it was just an accident. On a farm. A creek."
That was all she would tell me. She probably didn't
want me to think about death yet.*

*I knew my Aunt Judith wasn't like other people.
She stayed up in that room nearly all the time except
to come downstairs to go to the bathroom, and on
occasion to sit alone at the breakfast table and eat
cinnamon toast and coffee. She didn't use a toaster,
but put the bread directly on the rack in the oven with
butter on it, so that it was always a little soft in the
middle and crisp on the edges.*

*One time when Aunt Camilla took me up those
steps, my Aunt Judith turned to me and said something
like, "How is Ruth?" I didn't know what she meant.
"That's Ruth, isn't it?" I asked and pointed to the picture
of her daughter, and she said, "Yes. And this is Jesus.
Ruth loves Jesus." She showed me a picture of Jesus. He
had flowing blonde hair, very kind eyes, and had his
hand on his heart, which you could see glowing red
through his body. She pulled out another picture of him
from her drawer—a little card—and said I could have
it. I took it from her hands, trying to avoid touching
them because they were so bony.*

*"Is that you?" I asked and pointed to a picture of
her a lot younger. She smiled and laughed, but said
nothing.*

But Aunt Camilla rarely took me up there. Once

in a while I'd hear Aunt Judith yelling at Aunt Camilla about something, and Aunt Camilla would look very tired afterward.

My father did not come to that house. I knew it was because Aunt Camilla didn't like him because when she'd pick me up at my house, she'd say something like, "Where is he today? Off again?" Or something like that.

So when we'd cross the bridge I didn't need to worry about him.

But that day he did. I was out front blowing bubbles when I saw the pickup—a dirty red one—turn the corner. I froze at first then ran into the house. In the living room I stood wondering where to go, then remembered the attic. It wasn't Aunt Judith I was thinking about—just the stairway hidden behind the door. I don't know why I thought he wouldn't know about it. Maybe because it was behind a door and I was only 7, and I didn't know he'd ever been there.

So I opened the door, closed it behind me very quietly, then went up those stairs. And two steps from the top, behind and above me, I could hear the rocking chair creaking and Aunt Judith murmuring—talking to God with her little beads again. "Is Ruth here?" she asked suddenly. "No, it's me," I answered nearly out of breath." "Come to visit me," she said sweetly.

I waited. Maybe it was 5 minutes before I heard the door open and my father's voice. "Marian?" I didn't *answer. Aunt Camilla was arguing with him. He called again. I didn't answer.*

I heard him open the door, then his shoes on the stairs. Heavier than Aunt Camilla's. I counted. When he reached the 9th stair, one before the one that turned up to the right toward me and the open doorway into Auntie Judith's room, he stopped. "I have Dots for you," he said.

I shook my head. "I don't want Dots," I said.

"Come on, Marian. Guess what. I'm taking you to the zoo this afternoon."

I shook my head and pulled myself backward into the room and between two dresses hanging on the wall. But I heard more creaks on the stairway. Solid, heavy.

"Don't make me come and get you," he said.

"Marian!"

His voice just above me, he pulled the dress aside.

I ducked down, but his hand reached in and took my elbow roughly. Suddenly, I heard the rocking creaking of Aunt Judith's chair behind me become silent, and before I could figure out why, heard it being scooted, dragged violently across the floor and my aunt's voice sharp and high-pitched. "You don't take Ruth, you hear!"

My father let go of my arm.

His voice didn't sound so strong now. It was quavering. "Ruth? You mean Marian. You crazy woman. Ruth is dead."

"Marian is not a Christian name. This is Ruth," she screamed, and I could see between the dresses she'd half raised herself from the chair, her torso bent toward him and rigid like a weapon.

My father was, to my astonishment, frightened. He didn't move. "Listen, Marian—Ruth—whatever—is my daughter. She's coming with me. We're going to the zoo."

He reached for me and in that same second I heard my father yell out with pain and fall backward. One of the dresses was over my face but out of the corner of my eye I saw a kitchen knife in my aunt's hand, and her arm and head stiff in defiance.

"Ruth is mine," she said.

I now heard other footsteps on the stairway and Aunt Camilla's panicked voice. "What happened?"

My father turned away and rushed down the stairs holding his arm, which had a long bright red mark. He half brushed, half pushed Aunt Camilla out of the way and was gone.

And so it was I learned I was sometimes Ruth. And that when I was Ruth in that old house with Aunt Judith, I was safe.

And for almost two months that's how I was. When Aunt Camilla would call me to dinner, "Marian," I would tell her I was Ruth. "I'm not dead. I'm Ruth."

But I knew that really I was . . . dead.

As I returned to my office I saw her. She was seated, her back against the wall near the door, on the floor in the hallway, her arms wrapped around her upraised knees.

I smiled. "I got your papers. Come in," I said.

It felt very comfortable saying it to her.

She said nothing, just followed me in. I motioned for her to sit in the chair, but, oddly, she chose to sit on the floor, her legs crossed. She was wearing an old sweatshirt with a faded print caricature of some sort on the front, a shirt hanging out from under it.

"They were very good," I started. "What you left for me—the 'Taking Stock' and the narrative—in the envelope. Even before that, though, I'd decided to let you back in . . . to the class."

She nodded, but continued to sit there, saying nothing, just looking up at me, her eyes revealing neither surprise nor gratitude.

"You don't know this but I spent all of that evening and the following morning trying to find you. At the address in your file. The lady there said you'd moved and didn't know where you were."

"Where did you look?" she asked, more with curiosity than alarm or embarrassment, and with a hint of appreciation.

"She thought you didn't have much money. Told me to check shelters. Made me feel guilty."

She continued to stare but said nothing.

"Where do you live . . . now, I mean? I guess I shouldn't

ask, but . . . "

"A friend."

I waited for an elaboration, but it didn't come.

"Well, anyway, I was feeling bad and . . . I guess it doesn't matter. You're in, if you still want to be."

She nodded.

"It was unfair of me. Your daughter being sick. Your child is more important than anything we're doing in this class. In any college class. I should know that."

It felt as good as anything I'd said to anyone for a long time.

She continued to gaze at me. It was more than curiosity, I realized. She seemed to be actually studying me.

"I should have . . . Anyway, what's the problem with your daughter?"

"She's . . . was . . . sick."

I waited. Hadn't she told me more than that already? But again she didn't elaborate. *It was crucial that she be truthful to me about her.* A half minute passed before either of us said anything. I was determined to make her fill in the silence.

"They took her away from me, but . . . I have her now."

Her eyes bespoke both anger and frustration when she said this. *Was she including me in her frustration, because all bureaucrats were part of the same institutional mind?*

For a few seconds I was speechless. Hadn't I just broken the rules for her? Hadn't I told her I'd searched all over town for her—costing me many hours? What other teacher would do that? Perhaps I was being too sensitive—reading her inflections wrong.

"Then what you said about her being sick . . . ?"

"She's . . . okay . . . now." She turned her eyes away and was nervously, aimlessly, dragging them about the room.

"Is everything okay?" I asked.

"Yes."

"Well, then you'll be in class tomorrow?"

"Yes."

"Do you have any questions about the rest of what's on the syllabus? Besides the papers you already gave me. I went over all of it in class the first day."

She shook her head.

"Then we should . . . "

"Did that girl die?"

"Pardon?"

"That little girl in the picture."

She was staring at the photograph I'd hung above my desk. I'd copied it from a book of famous photographs of the twentieth century. Omayra Sanchez, twelve or thirteen years old. Only the upper half of her body visible because the rest was held fast by a river of lava, muck, debris from a volcano in Colombia in 1985. Dry mud smeared all over her face, which was shimmering and chalky white. The photographer caught it all. Her hands grasping a wooden pole of some sort. It was out of focus, but you could make out—in the mass of mud—a piece of white cloth (a dress?) and other metallic and wood objects less clear.

"Kind of riveting, isn't it?" I responded. "I guess it's in the eyes. They hold you. They're . . . so much at peace. Imprisoned in the earth like that. Very tired, but . . . remarkably. . . not despairing. The way she looks back at you . . . no struggle. Just a profound acceptance. Some of her family. . . four of them, I think, were swallowed up the first day of the eruption. They were actually gripping her ankles at the moment you see here. But . . . to answer your question . . . yes, she died. An hour, a few hours . . . I forgot what it said in the caption. . . . After the photographer snapped this picture . . . she just . . . let go . . . and the earth . . . took her in."

Silkie sat there gazing at it. "That's sad," she said finally. "I mean, why couldn't they get her out?"

"They tried. For several days. Television cameras there too. Some screw-up in getting the equipment there in time."

"Her just accepting like that . . . I remember reading somewhere . . . someone who writes about science . . . that right at the point of going away . . . dying . . . the pain is gone . . . for animals. The lion has the gazelle at the neck. The gazelle just . . . gives himself over. Like the girl there—in the photo."

I recalled that another student—Julia Scott—had asked me about the picture the previous term. Julia was one of those students who was certain about everything because she'd gotten As in high school and always put her thesis in the first paragraph and restated her main points in her final paragraph. She'd been challenging me in class at every opportunity. Looking up at the picture, she summarily concluded, almost reproachfully, "They should have gotten her out"—as though it had been my personal responsibility to rescue her. I shrugged, and when Miss Scott finally left it was clearly with an impatience with both me, because I'd had the bad taste to hang such a photo, and with Omayra for dying that way.

I left it up, though. It's still there. I am in love with Omayra because of those eyes. One of the few things in my life that tell me it may come out all right. All this mess. This detritus. The truth is, if it were 1985 and I could go down to that scene, not just to gawk at the carnage around her, a voyeur of her personal life-and-death struggle, but to help her, I would. I would be that photographer—sharing my own story. I'd buy a plane ticket to Colombia before I'd hail a cab to go ten blocks to a church service.

I was glad Silkie asked about her that day. I wanted to tell her Omayra's story.

"Oh, I should tell you—your papers. From now on, submit them in a manila folder . . . like this one. In fact, keep all your papers and your journal in there. At the end of the term you'll be turning in everything that way—your portfolio of what you wrote for me. I think you can get them in the bookstore for twenty cents. Do you have any questions?"

She sat there staring down at her lap, and finally, too thoughtfully, almost imperceptibly, shook her head.

"Incidentally, your 'Taking Stock' paper . . . what you wrote . . . was very unusual. I liked it."

"I . . ."

I waited. She was silent but did not get up. I should have said "okay" or in some way dismissed her, but I didn't. I know now I wanted her to keep sitting there. Even if there was nothing more for either of us to say.

Finally she shuffled to her feet. "I apologize," she said quickly, "that I missed class."

"Here," I said, seeing an extra folder on my desk. "Right here, . . . I have an extra one. Take it. For the papers you submit. You won't have to go to the bookstore to buy one."

She took it, stood there staring down at it, then turned to leave.

"I'm sorry," I heard myself saying. Just as I had her first visit to my office.

Why? I didn't know at that moment—only that, as on the first occasion, it had to do with something quite apart from the syllabus, or the class, and I hadn't meant to say it out loud.

"What?" she asked.

"Nothing. . . . I didn't mean . . . just sorry about . . . your daughter."

6. The File Cabinet

The folder I gave Silkie, almost two years ago, for her papers—that's the one student folder that now sits in the bottom drawer of my file cabinet at home.

All my current student folders are, of course, in my office at the university. I save a few student papers every year as models of good writing, but not any one student's entire portfolio of submissions. Silkie's was the exception—all her papers for the four classes of mine she took and her class journals, collected in a very fat folder which now sits in the bottom drawer of the file cabinet in my bedroom.

The very first term I taught Silkie, though, her folder was still in my office—alphabetized with those of her classmates.

Files—whether in a computer or a metal piece of furniture—provide a necessary order. Alphabetical. By name. By subject. By category. Composition class folders here—in the front—Intro to Literature folders in the back. Nineteenth-Century American Lit folders in another drawer. Administrative folders in still another drawer.

The problem was, Silkie's folder gradually resisted that order. It was too messy. Its contents too chaotic. And after two terms—its edges and creases weakened and torn, swollen with hundreds of handwritten dog-eared notebook papers not even assigned for that class—it needed two rubber bands to keep it all together. So that when I tried to jam it into its alphabetical place, it pushed back, and closing the drawer crushed its unruly pages, flattening the edges over the index tabs of nearby folders.

It didn't fit.

I had to lay it flat in the back of one of the drawers.

In time, I took it out. Brought it home.

Had its messiness been only a spatial one, a physical one, an administrative one, I wouldn't have. I would have eventually disposed of it—as, eventually, I did with all past student folders. Its messiness was, however, a far more profound messiness. One that qualified it for being preserved in a very special place: the bottom drawer of the file cabinet in my bedroom.

It is, at the present, only one of two folders in there.

The other one never swelled to the size of Silkie's. In it were seventy-four newspaper accounts and two letters. Most of the accounts were very brief—usually no more than a paragraph—and a few weeks ago I removed both the letters and twenty or so of those accounts and put them in a jar and sent them on a very long journey.

The two letters were those I'd composed to Gabriel—about

the eagle in the box and Norma Jean. I never threw them out. Of course, they were just "receipts" of a sort—the paper evidence of the real things—the silent prayers I'd sent to the archangel. Thinking about that now, I'm not sure where those prayers went at the other end—Gabe's end. God's end. Stuck in the bottom of some dusty file cabinet somewhere in the cosmos, perhaps. If they got filed at all.

Over the years I got pretty bitter about it.

Tell me, Gabe and God, do you guys in heaven have a system? For keeping track of all those prayers circling up that way. Maybe you don't need a file cabinet. Maybe you just file it all in your memory. Omniscience must include memory, no? Even so, I'm thinking—with all those thousands of nuns and priests urging their flocks to pray to the archangels . . . to God . . . there's got to be some kind of filing system. By year? Generation? Pre- and post-Crusades? All those born in the reign of Pope Leo XIII? By type of request maybe? Animals in boxes that need to be let out. Children whose parents were slaughtered in genocides wanting them back. Does your system include slush piles too? For the requests you just don't want to bother with. Counterpart to badly written novels. Maybe that's where my two prayers found their final resting place? A slush pile.

Anyway, I still have the original letters. Ultimately, they ended up in that folder in the bottom drawer of my file cabinet. Along with those seventy-four news accounts.

The whole story of Silkie is in a way the story of the bottom drawer. Of that file cabinet.

I was twelve or thirteen when I got it.

"Stephen, give me a hand with these things!" It was my father calling to me from the driveway. The trunk door of the car was pressed tightly over an old piece of wooden furniture by way of ropes securing it to the bumper. He was a big man—much bigger than me and stronger—so he didn't need my strength. When he was younger he'd worked in a warehouse receiving room. But what he had in the car trunk was for me, not him. It was, in fact, an old four-drawer wooden file cabinet he'd picked up for ten dollars when an antiquated educational administration building was shut down in a nearby county.

"It's for you," he called to me as he undid the ropes. "Thought you might be able to use it."

"You mean for school papers?" I asked.

We began lugging it up the stairway to my room.

"I don't know—see what you need it for," he responded.

If he had something more specific in mind, it didn't register with me. I took it that he'd come upon a nice piece of useful furniture at a good price and didn't know what to do with it so decided to give it to me for now. The fact that he might have made a special trip to that old school building just to get it didn't occur to me.

I did use it—but only as a repository for school binders

and books, cigar boxes full of baseball cards, my Monopoly game, and comic book versions of classic novels like *Mutiny on the Bounty*, *Robinson Crusoe*, and *Twenty Thousand Leagues Under the Sea*.

One morning, though, I saw my father in my bedroom staring into one of the half-opened drawers of the file cabinet. He had just come home from work—late night at Bell Telephone—and I'd just come out of the bathroom to dress for school. He closed the one drawer and peeked into another, but almost absent-mindedly. He seemed to be staring off into space as much as into the drawer.

He was healthy at that time—as far as I knew. He was only fifty-seven. As I said, a big man, some two hundred and twenty pounds, with a full head of hair. And he rarely if ever missed work. In recent months, though, he had an air of being sick. Walking more slowly, his mind somewhere else. On several occasions I'd had to ask him something three times before he heard me.

It was unusual for him to just come into my room like that too.

"Dad, you can have it for your work, for . . . you know . . . your stuff . . . anything you need it for," I offered. "I'm not really doing much with it."

"You might want to . . . for other things besides these," he answered, nodding down at the baseball cards and comic books I'd tossed in carelessly.

"Like what?"

"I don't know . . . things you write for your teacher. School assignments. The ones you want to save because you spent a lot of time on 'em. And if you cut out anything—pictures, stories, from magazines . . . that you want to keep." He shrugged. "Someday those things will mean more to you."

"Yeah, I suppose I could do that."

A couple other times, I remember, he asked me, "Making good use of that file cabinet?"

I don't recall how I answered, but he was persistent and one weekend brought home for me a stack of file folders, which I dutifully slipped into one of the drawers, not yet sure what I'd use them for—though it occurred to me they might be an easier way for me to organize some of the clippings of sports articles and magazine photos I'd been pasting into scrapbooks till then.

I never knew exactly what kind of work my father did at Bell Telephone—just that he was a technician. He never thought it interesting enough to share with Toby and me.

He never got a college education, but he liked to read. Zane Grey westerns and Agatha Christie mysteries but a lot of heavy stuff too—like Will and Ariel Durants' *History of Philosophy*, Dostoyevsky's *The Brothers Karamazov*, everything of Mark Twain, Gibbon's *The Decline and Fall of the Roman Empire*. Collections of world-famous short stories. I know because once in a while he'd read aloud, with some passion, a few lines from one of them to me—usually when he'd been drinking beer and I was at the dining table studying. I'm not sure what he thought I'd get from his extemporaneous interpretive readings—out of context and out of nowhere like that—but both the words and his sharing them with me left an indelible impression on me.

He liked searching through the stacks of secondhand-book stores for memoirs, journals, and other such first-person accounts—especially those related to the two world wars. I figured it was because he had himself served in Europe from 1943 to '45. But he never talked about that either. Except one time.

I was just exiting the kitchen with a snack of some sort, when he came in with a very large black book tucked under his arm.

"Going somewhere?" he asked.

"Just upstairs."

"Look here. I just got this from the library. Collection of photographs from the war. Europe. The Pacific. Pretty old—1944." He lay the book on the kitchen table, flipped through the pages, and stopped finally halfway through and pointed to a small photo in the upper corner of the page. It was of a bombed-out church or monastery with a lot of destroyed buildings in the background. "This is Mount Cassino. Before we marched in, our planes did this. The Allies." Then he pointed to a picture on the opposite page of victorious American soldiers walking past a group of women and children in a newly liberated small town in Italy.

"I was part of those," he said thoughtfully, staring down

at the photos. "Sicily too."

I wanted to know more, but, as on other occasions when there was any mention of the war, he responded with a curt "I'll tell you sometime."

He must have thought I was just going to go outside or change the subject, but I didn't. I sat down at the kitchen table and began leafing through the pages myself.

"Did kids come out and cheer you guys like liberators or something all the time?" I asked.

"Most places they were quiet. In Italy. Depended on the place. Some did. Look at the picture of what was left, though. How could they?"

I nodded, turned some more pages.

"There was this little boy," he said, casually, with a smile on his face, almost as though he were going to tell a good baseball story. "Some small Italian village we were stopped at for a couple days. He was eleven or twelve, I guess. Real dark thick hair. For some reason he walked over to me and said in broken English, 'Now it will all be very good. I will have a good life.' Something like that. Like he was telling me a secret he knew about and I didn't. It was almost defiant, but not to me defiant."

He smiled and shook his head, and I saw the smile was more one of puzzlement than amusement. "He didn't know. Things were going to be bad for a long time. He was too young to understand how it goes with conquered countries. I think that was one of the things I wrote home about—that kid."

The few times he did allude to the war, it was always in terms of this quiet kind of scene. Never about battles, beachheads, buddies being killed, Germans being dragged from bunkers—the sort of thing I pictured. Instead, about twelve- and thirteen-year-old German boys—"Hitler Youth"—being marched past as prisoners, some crying; parents rummaging through war-torn buildings looking for food; framed family photos still hanging on walls in parlors in which everything else—tables, chairs, chandeliers—was rubble; women and children pulling carts of household goods along the road going somewhere else; soup lines. Never a full story about a battle for a village or bridge. Always just these snapshots:

> "There were these German soldiers—prisoners behind barbed wire—actually smiling as we took a picture. They knew the war was over for them. They'd made it."

> "There was this little girl—two or three years old maybe—blond hair and curly like Shirley Temple . . . crouching . . . looking like she could have been out in the playground."

> "They would organize the town's women to clear the streets, get rid of the rubble and debris. The men were all gone. Their husbands and brothers and sons. The women were frail but surprisingly hardy. Doing something constructive. So . . . working with grim but defiant faces."

"These men in thin, dusty dress suits cooking
food in small pans on the streets . . ."

He must have seen dead bodies, must have killed, but
never talked about it. If he started going that way with a
story, he'd stop . . . right in the middle. "The Russians were
brutal . . . what they did to the Germans who lived there . .
. terrible things . . . even to the women . . the chil . . . but of
course, if you knew what they themselves had been through
. . . for their families . . . the four or five previous years . . . it
was not so . . . ." He'd take a drink from his beer mug. Never
teared up. But his eyes got glassy. Or I imagined they did.
Because at the end he seemed to be talking to himself, and,
when he stopped, his silence was intense.

Once, when I saw him reading to himself from the
published diary of some soldier who had been a prisoner in
a German camp, I asked if he'd kept his own journal.

"For a couple months," he told me. "But it got so gooked
up . . . muddied and damp from sleeping outside in the rain
and from the snow melting into my pack . . . you know . . . it
was impossible to keep it up. I remember trying to write on
the dampened paper . . . through the wet . . . but three days
later couldn't read it . . . just a smear of letters . . . and then
the pages started sticking together. . . . That was frustrating
and even what I was trying to say . . ."

The way he explained it, though, left me thinking he
was just trying to dismiss the subject. "Do you have any of
it still, Dad?" I persisted.

He set his book face down on his lap and stared at it, like he didn't want to look at me . . . or was ashamed about something. "I should have kept some. I think I did. It may be somewhere. Nothing much in it that is readable anymore."

I said nothing, sensing if I remained silent he would go on.

"You're right . . . it was a mistake. I should've kept it anyway. Kept going anyway. Even if now I could only read a word or two . . . my mind . . . memory could fill in the rest. Anyway . . . I . . . quit. Besides, seemed like I was just making lists . . . everything—things like what we had to eat that day, and where we were and when we'd be moving out. Monotonous. Then when things really got hot, and there was really something to say, I saw how pitiful it was. What I was writing. The words weren't doing what I wanted. Wanted for them to do. Tired me. Some things you can't just say like you're talking about a TV show or a field trip. But . . . maybe someday I'll look and see if any of it's worth showing you. The pages that didn't get smeared. Okay?"

I nodded, wanting to ask him what he meant by "words weren't doing what I wanted," but I didn't. Maybe because I already had an idea.

I probably should have pushed him a little to open up, and it was in the back of my mind that someday I would.

Just like not being able to go to college, his not having kept a detailed journal of his World War II experiences seemed to bother him. That he'd failed himself and maybe me somehow.

A few months later, he began piling books on me. First it was Stephen Crane's *The Red Badge of Courage*—the "Classic Comics" version of which he'd seen in one of my file drawers. "Read the real thing," he said and tossed it onto my bed. I did and found myself increasingly fascinated with both the way Crane got into the mind of the frightened Henry Fleming character and the Civil War itself.

> *Once he thought he had concluded that it would be better to get killed directly and end his troubles. Regarding death thus out of the corner of his eye, he conceived it to be nothing but rest, and he was filled with a momentary astonishment that he should have made an extraordinary commotion over the mere matter of getting killed. He would die; he would go to some place where he would be understood. It was useless to expect appreciation of his profound and fine senses from such men as the lieutenant. He must look to the grave for comprehension.* —Stephen Crane, *The Red Badge of Courage*

Soon I was checking out of the local library one after another the whole series of Joseph Altsheler books for young boys—each one centered on a different battle in the Civil War.

Then it was Jack London he was giving me—*The Call of the Wild* and *White Fang*—and Jules Verne—*Around the World in 80 Days, The Mysterious Island*—and Mark Twain's *The Prince and the Pauper* and *Pudd'nhead Wilson*.

"Look what I got for just $20.99 . . . twenty-one bucks," he said to me one morning. "Near the hardware, there's a small shop. The man there has old books in the back." He put a stack of identically bound books on the table in front of me. "A whole set. Six of them. Thought you'd like real-life adventures. He went everywhere, this guy did. India. The Sahara Desert. Lowell Thomas. I guess you've seen him on TV doing the news." He handed me *With Lawrence in Arabia.* "Here, start with this one."

The next day I did.

On my fourteenth birthday, he gave me two books. He'd wrapped them himself in white paper—the only time I recall him doing any kind of gift wrapping—as though they were a kind of heirloom. The first one did not surprise me because he had mentioned it to me as one I would like—*All Quiet on the Western Front.* It was the other one that threw me. It was T.E. Lawrence's *Seven Pillars of Wisdom.* "T.E.," it turned out, was for "Thomas Edward"—the "Lawrence" of Arabia.

"Is this some kind of philosophy book?" I asked.

"Not really. In a way. Lawrence wasn't just a soldier, he was a scholar," he told me. And added, "You might try to read a little of this each day."

I was honored he thought I could get something out of it, and I nodded in a way that let him know. It pleased him, I could tell. And more and more he began turning his attention to me rather than to my brother, who was into fixing up old cars, not books.

The more I read, the more he took to reading aloud to us—from writers like Thurber and Gallico and Twain. I think I was the only one who looked forward to it when he would get into those moods—which were often fed by his drinking a bottle or two of beer. Blatz was his favorite.

Drinking was something he did a lot of. He wasn't a "drunk" in my mind and rarely went to bars unless a friend from work invited him. But some Saturdays he would go through five or six beers. And when he returned from work each morning—when Toby and I were at school and my mother was at one of her various part-time jobs—he drank a couple to get himself to sleep. I saw the cans in the trash. I often wondered why his friends had a beer belly but he didn't. He never really lost his lankiness.

The fact is most of the time he lived a separate life from us. If I had any after-school activities, he would be gone to his night job before I even got home. Most of the time—depending on whatever job she'd been able to land—Mom would come home to an empty house and see my father only when he crawled into bed in the late morning.

I'm not sure but I think it was less the not seeing him because he wasn't there and more the not being with him even when he was there that bothered her. There was an elusive discontent about him. Maybe it was the war experience. Or, like I said, that he'd never had the money or opportunity to go to college, and held in awe those who did. Or that he hadn't himself written anything noteworthy about the war as Robert

Leckie had with his *Helmet for My Pillow*. He talked about Leckie's book a lot. "It almost makes the horrors worth it if you can describe it to others like this," he said.

He was at work when he had the heart attack. It turned out he'd been smoking a pack of cigarettes a day at work. Surely the beer didn't help. A co-worker called the ambulance and attended to him but well before the ambulance arrived he was dead. He was only fifty-nine.

I was only fifteen.

Years later, when I happened to see a photo of him from three months before he died—taken at a retirement party for one of his fellow workers—I realized that at fifty-nine he'd looked like seventy.

We had a memorial service for him instead of a funeral. And I recall very distinctly only three things about it. First that, amidst all the dark suits and dark dresses and whispered "I'm sorry"s and people introducing themselves to me as co-workers or as older cousins or great-aunts whom I wouldn't remember because I was "so young then," there was one guy, balding, medium height, not frail in the body sense but brittle in some way I couldn't at first figure. He was looking a little lost, like he didn't know anyone else there and was confused as to what was the right thing for him to do. Now he was stopping to look more closely at a flower arrangement, now stepping outside and smoking on the walkway, now strolling out onto the hillside near the cemetery, now coming back in and picking up one of the church bulletins and pretending to read it. I was one of the greeters, so I went up to him and sensed in his eyes some greater confusion beyond the service and his place in it.

"I'm sorry," I started, "but I don't . . . know who you are."

"I was in the Italy campaign with your father," he said. "The war. For almost two years . . . till the end."

His name was Harry Epstein, and he lived two states away—in Illinois. I found out later my mother had seen his name in our old address book and remembered he and my father had exchanged Christmas cards for three or four years after the war. She'd called, left a message about my father's death and the particulars of the service with a woman who said she was a younger sister. She hadn't expected him to come from so far.

I would have tried to get him to share memories of the war, but by then the ceremony started, and I was one of those who had to talk. As I spoke I saw him standing at the rear. At the reception after, I looked for him but he was gone. I felt guilty about that and didn't know why.

Perhaps my guilt contributed to the second thing I recall about the service. During the reception I had the urge to go away and knew I couldn't. In some confusion I found myself slipping out into the hallway and sitting down on the floor, in my suit, against the wall at the far end of a rack of the guests' coats so I couldn't be seen. I sat there alone for twenty minutes until my brother came looking for me, asking if I was all right. I nodded and went back into the reception.

The third thing I recall is what I said when I gave my talk about my father: how good a father he'd been, how he'd worked hard all his life, served in the war, made sure his family had a house and food on the table. I told them about a couple fond memories—the rainy day he'd picked me up when I got lost coming home from school in the second grade; the morning he'd given me a scorecard of a baseball game between the Indians and Braves with five autographs on it, including Bob Feller's and Lou Boudreau's. But I didn't mention what would be his greatest gift to me—the file cabinet, and those books.

Because I didn't know yet what part they would play in my life.

7. Drawer 3

In the weeks following that service, even with the life insurance, my brother and I had to take jobs after school. Toby managed to find one at his friend's father's mechanics shop changing oil and doing grease jobs. I cut grass and did other yard work. My mother took on a couple jobs—answering phones at a car dealership on weekends, and on weekdays looking in on old people who couldn't afford to live in nursing homes.

Eventually, though, we had to move to a smaller house. That's when I made the discovery. My mother and I were cleaning the attic of our old place for the move, and I stumbled onto two old cardboard packing boxes—taped shut. When we opened them we found sixty or seventy newspaper clippings–some entire front pages—all yellowing and brittle, the corners frayed, going back to the 1930s. Some were accounts of major events with big bold headlines: "Will Rogers, Wiley Post Dead in Crash." "Roosevelt in Landslide." "The 'Babe' Dead at 53." "Rosenbergs Executed." "Truman Fires Macarthur." "Russians Put Man in Space." "Kennedy Assassinated. Johnson Takes Oath."

But a great many of them were of less momentous events. One I remember was a story about a teacher at his high school who got fired for an "immoral act" with a male student. It was a science teacher he'd liked because he'd given my father his first slide rule as a gift. My father had told me the story—about how the teacher had been let go—"because of a lie," he said.

I pulled out all these old newspapers and clippings from the two boxes, folded them neatly, taping them where they were ripped, and removed extraneous pages from whole newspapers he hadn't bothered to discard, saving only the accounts of the key events.

I thought of my file cabinet—the one he'd brought home for me—and the empty folders, and I began categorizing all those clippings and filing them in the top drawer.

Not long after, I too began saving news articles. At first it was just doing what he'd done—cutting out accounts of the major events: the assassinations of Bobby Kennedy and Martin Luther King, the Apollo 13 drama, the McGovern nomination, the Watergate stories.

It became an obsession, and before I knew it I had hundreds of clippings from papers and magazines.

It required a system. Labeled, categorized folders: "Africa," "Middle East," "Entertainers," "Science," "Sports," "Writers," "Politics." With time I refined them. "Science" became "Physics," "Space," and "Medicine." "Middle East" became

"Israel" and "Egypt." "Human Interest Stories" I divided into "Local" and "National." I even had a folder for "Deaths," so that when Roberto Clemente died, I had to decide whether to put it in "Sports" or "Deaths," and when John Steinbeck died whether it should be in "Deaths" or "Writers."

My little newspaper museum kept expanding until I had most of the two top drawers—Drawers1 and 2--filled.

A few months later, I found myself adding an altogether different kind of clipping. One Tuesday my high school English teacher stopped me as I was about to enter the classroom.

"Stephen," she said, "just go to the library the rest of this week. We'll be doing grammar drills and going over topic sentences. You know all that. You'll be bored. I don't want to waste your time. Do some reading on your own."

The next week she told me the same thing, and because that class was the last of each school day, I usually stayed in the library beyond the final bell. Those two weeks, I discovered Dickens by way of *David Copperfield,* and Hawthorne by way of *Twice-Told Tales,* and even the first book of Hugo's *Les Miserables.* The librarian recommended *Up from Slavery*, which I read in a day and a half. Then it was Wright's *Black Boy.* Then *Grapes of Wrath* and *Le Rouge et Le Noir.* Particularly taken by certain passages, I began copying them. From *Les Miserables*:

> "Ah, there you are!" said he, looking towards Jean Valjean, "I am glad to see you. But! I gave you the candlesticks also, which are silver like the rest, and

would bring two hundred francs. Why did you not take them along with your plates?"

Jean Valjean opened his eyes and looked at the bishop with an expression which no human tongue could describe.

From Hawthorne's "The Minister's Black Veil":

"If I hide my face for sorrow, there is cause enough," he merely replied, "and if I cover it for secret sin, what mortal might not do the same?"

From *David Copperfield:*

I am born. Whether I shall turn out to be the hero of my own life, or whether that station will be held by anybody else, these pages must show . . .

In consideration of the day and hour of my birth, it was declared by the nurse, and by some sage women in the neighborhood who had taken a lively interest in me several months before there was any possibility of our becoming personally acquainted, first, that I was destined to be unlucky in life; and secondly, that I was privileged to see ghosts and spirits.

These literary passages, however, were not "News" and so did not fit in the folders of the top two drawers—which I'd labeled Drawer 1 and Drawer 2—so I gave them their own section ("A") in Drawer 3. More and more passages went into that drawer, including poems whose lines I memorized:

From Matthew Arnold's "Dover Beach":

> *The Sea of Faith / Was once, too, at the full, and round earth's shore . . . But now I only hear / Its melancholy, long, withdrawing roar.*

I got into Richard Wright from *Black Boy* and read *Native Son* and then *American Hunger,* and from that one discovered he believed the only way to find meaning in life was to "wring" it out of "meaningless suffering."

I'm not sure I could have told you why I was copying down and filing these passages. Just that I liked them enough to save them. Maybe it was that these writers and books were *speaking to me personally*. Teaching me something I had to hang onto. Purposeful in that way.

But it was more than that. Those pages from literature, along with all those news clippings, were my way of *ordering* the world, the universe, making sense of it. History taught us what societies and countries and leaders had done right . . . and what they had done wrong. Writers taught us to think clearly, profoundly, and thereby to act ethically, compassionately; taught us to confront dilemmas, sort out moral quandaries, seek out beauty in nature and art. They *taught me. Me.* I drew from them the necessary wisdom to live as I should.

I was *ordering* my existence by way of that file cabinet.

Years into my professional teaching career, I began adding to Drawer 3 a whole different category. One afternoon, riding on the bus, I began jotting down the names of students I remembered from previous classes I had taught. I don't recall what got me suddenly doing this—only that I was curious as to which students they would be—what common factor would be at work. Before I exited the bus, I'd written down seventeen names. The number grew over the next week into thirty-seven. Next to each, in parentheses, I began to list the one or two salient qualities about that student that was the reason I remembered him or her. For some, I ended up writing two or three paragraphs. I was interested less in physical qualities (though I had to admit that attractiveness was a key one for some of the women) than in intellectual or experiential factors. To my surprise, though most of them had performed well in my class, it was not their high rank which was the salient factor. Over my years of teaching at three different schools I had taught in excess of 175 individual sections, thousands of students, yet most of the top students in those classes had slipped from my memory. What was it about these students that made me remember them? For many of them it was an unusual paper they'd written or something about their life they'd revealed to me in one-on-one student-instructor meetings in my office.

Sierra, for example.

SIERRA. *One of Sierra's papers, a very defiant one, revealed she'd run away from home because she was attracted to women and she knew her parents would not accept that. Her final paper—which was to be a classical* *argument—made the case that argument itself always led to confusing perceptions and assumptions, and contradictory facts, and thus to a sort of disillusionment. The final paragraph, preceded by an extra space, seemed to be from some other paper or subject or story altogether. For no apparent reason that she offered in the paper itself, she suddenly described a scene in which she had been sitting in the college union at a table and saw a man go to the coffee machine and insert his coins. But the cardboard cup tipped, and by the time he'd righted it, it was too late to catch any of the coffee. He fished into his pocket and came up short. Shaking his head, more discouraged than angry, he walked away. Not long after, a young woman put in her money. This time the cup did not tip. And the girl walked away with her cup of coffee.*

This "saga" of the coffee vending machine constituted Sierra's final paragraph. She gave it no overt connection to the rest of the paper.[**Drawer 3B**]

I liked the ending. Yet I could not have defended its inclusion in the paper to another writing teacher—at least, not to his or her satisfaction.

For some of the students, the description was brief. As with Oliver.

OLIVER. *Oliver was in my WR 121. His first paper*

was supposed to be a narrative from an incident in his life that was significant in some way. What he gave me was not a narrative, though it had to do with the death of his kindergarten classmate. More a reflection, in poetry, of the elusiveness of life, it started: "About Joshua, I can say that in life he died, in death he lived. His brain was a man's, his body a sickly boy's. I wonder then, is there more to a brief life than writing about it in a sad story, a tragic play? Is life more than an inspiration to art . . . more than the beginning of an inevitable end?" [**Drawer 3B**]

For others, a much lengthier description was called for:

HASSAN. *He was my student when I was his fifth form teacher in Nigeria. Form 5B. Form 5A had the brightest ones. Still, even to get into a government college he had to pass a stiff exam, and he was one of those who made it. Probably, barely made it—because in Form B, he was among the slowest.*

I taught his class literature, one of five required subjects, in preparation for the West African Certificate Exam. The Saturday of that exam he sat far to the rear in a spacious hall with about fifty other students. A handful of them would do very well and go on to universities all over the world. More than half wouldn't do quite as well and would end up in one of Nigeria's teaching training colleges and ultimately in primary school classrooms. *Those who did poorly would be channeled into the commercial stream as secretaries in bureaucratic offices. Very likely he scored in that lowest group.*

But in the greater test of humanity he must have done very well. Much better than his classmates. I am sure of that, though I knew little of his life outside the school. I knew only he was Hausa, not Yoruba. Muslim, not Christian. That he was from Katsina, not Ibadan. Of his family I knew nothing. My conversations with him were limited to studies. I should have asked him at one time or another whether or not he tended goats with his father, or planted groundnuts alongside his brothers, but I didn't.

What I remember most poignantly was that he always sat in the front of the room to my left in his school uniform—white trousers, white jacket. And when he went to town he'd wear his sparkling white kaftan and white cap. At such times he was like all the other students—walking straight and proud and confident. A scholar among the many poor and uneducated in the marketplace.

In class, though, he had no confidence. He held his head rigidly forward, entreating me to teach him what he needed to know. In his eyes was an anguished intensity of frustration that he couldn't get it. Couldn't master the literature of Shakespeare, Keats, Austen—the writers whose works would appear on the test. Wole

Soyinka, who would one day win the Nobel Prize, and Chinua Achebe were not on the syllabus. Nigeria had been independent for many years by then, but not the minds of their educators.

His eyes burned with a fervor to learn I had never then, nor have since, seen in a student. A fire burning to succeed that he knew would be extinguished by the West African Certificate Exam he would take at the end of the year. Unless, as a teacher, I could work a miracle.

His eyes were begging me to perform it—the miracle.

The other teachers—British, Canadian, one Arab from Sudan, two Nigerians—had no sympathy for such as Hassan. They looked only at ultimate performance. "He's a slow one. Not up to snuff in this material. He's not going to pass even one of the subject tests," a teacher from Wales remarked with a rather disdainful smile to me, knowing I would certainly concur.

I couldn't work the miracle.

I tried, and I could tell he appreciated my efforts, my attention to him. He saw reflected in my eyes the hurt and agony in his. In the end, though, I failed.

He was a very kind student. And determined. But, like many in the world, he was not up to his aspirations. A painter who felt the pain of van Gogh but couldn't be one. [**Drawer 3B**]

There were two students who had written to me long letters long after they'd been in my class—one from a bar in the middle of the night in New York City, the other from atop a mountain in the Bolivian Andes. Both were thoughtful and had expressed a desire to keep in touch with me over the years. In my descriptive paragraphs, I included passages from the letters.

Over the years, many students made it into my file cabinet. The front of Drawer 3 became "Section A" and was for my literary passages. The back became "Section B" and was for my interesting students. Ninety-three in all.

If you wanted to know who it was I would become, who Silkie stumbled onto two years ago, Drawer 3 would have been a good place to start: the passages from books and poems in 3A, the memories of my special students in 3B.

The bottom drawer, though—Drawer 4—is the key to understanding why my relationship with Silkie developed as it did.

8. Drawer 4

The story of that drawer began with a simple discovery. A realization. That there were news events which were different in some essential way from all the others. Literary passages so stark that rather than enlightening me, they profoundly unsettled me. Personal experiences that deserved more than a journal entry.

One morning when I was a senior in high school, I was eating my breakfast—a bowl of Cheerios—with the newspaper open next to me. On the second page was the "News of the World"—the section with a series of brief accounts of national and international events that deserved many paragraphs or pages but were boiled down to just a few lines because the editors had deemed them not worthy of more column space.

"Mexican Girls Murdered" was the heading on one.

The single-column, fourteen-line story told of three young girls, aged nine, twelve, and fifteen, who had set off across an unspecified desert in Mexico to find work in the city to support their family which had no money because the father was dead and the mother was raising not only her children but also her sister's. The three girls got lost and, set upon by bandits, they were raped and murdered.

It was their age that got me. These weren't "women." They were girls. Girls looking for work. I thought about how poor the family must have been . . . and how hot it must have been in the desert. And I thought about how it had been grown men that murdered them—just three little girls.

Unable to continue eating, I sat there with the spoon in my hand, but doing nothing with it. Thinking about that article. So much between the lines—those fourteen lines. How it must have been. The scene carved nightmarish images into my brain. I forced myself to imagine all the details as happening at the very moment I was imagining them—their hearing the car in the distance, the sound of the oncoming car's engine on the isolated dirt road, and seeing what that car looks like (an old Ford, rusted, dented? Red, black? What does it matter?) . . . the faces of the two or three men who get out (young men themselves desperate for work, perhaps?), the girls knowing right away these men are not there to give them a ride, the oldest girl (why did the newspaper not give her name?) telling her sisters it will be okay, but knowing it won't . . . that if there is a God he's not around today, at some point, being laughed at threateningly, finally roughly grabbed, and their fighting desperately, screaming, and without being aware of it are on the ground clutching at dirt as though they can dig themselves into the earth . . . maybe into the universe itself.

That night I cut that brief account out of the paper. But where was I to file it? It wasn't a major historical event. Did I have a folder labeled "Mexico"? Even if I had it wouldn't have seemed the right place. It wasn't so much about a geographical or political region as it was about a universal phenomenon . . . a metaphysical madness. It wasn't about Mexico. So Drawers 1 and 2 were not appropriate. But it wasn't a passage from a book either. It wasn't the great literature of Dickens or Hugo, inviting me to think deeply about philosophical and moral dilemmas. Drawer 3A wouldn't work. It was just a brief account. Of rape and murder. Perhaps the girls were students, but very likely not, and, of course, not my students, so Drawer 3B wasn't right either.

In the end, I slipped the clipped newspaper brief into the bottom drawer of the file cabinet. Drawer 4. In no folder. I would ponder where to file it later.

It stayed there that way for days, weeks. I forgot about it. Months later, it found its folder. Because it found a partner. I had been finishing a school assignment—a paper on the civil rights movement—and came across a book in the city library about the Jim Crow era. In it were ghastly photos of lynchings from the early part of the century. For one such account there was no photo. A woman named Mary Turner. 1918. Georgia. She'd protested the lynching of her husband. A white mob decided to lynch her too. She was pregnant at the time. They hung her upside down, doused her with gasoline, lit her, then cut open her abdomen so her unborn child fell to the ground.

I photocopied the article to use in my report but intended, as well, to file it with my newspaper clippings in my cabinet. As with the three Mexican girls, however, it didn't seem like it belonged there. I had a folder labeled "Civil Rights," but inserting it there would have been inadequate, even wrong. Like placing a little boy's sad poem about his father's dying of cancer into a folder labeled "cancer." It didn't fit. It belonged elsewhere.

It was that night I determined to have a very special folder. For the bottom drawer—Drawer 4. In it would go: the photocopy of the Mary Turner lynching account; the newspaper clipping about the murder of the three Mexican girls; and the two letters to the Archangel Gabriel.

Over the years—until just a couple weeks ago—many more news accounts got put into that file. Some I cut out a key part of them. Some I put into my own words. There was one about Duaa, for example:

> **DUAA.** *"When the shooting ended in Karbala, a holy city 60 miles southwest of Baghdad, the killing began for the family of Samira Jabar. Emerging on April 6 from two days of hiding from U.S. bombing, Jabar took her daughter Duaa Raheem, 6, to fetch water. Duaa happened on a black plastic object shaped like a C-cell battery attached to a white ribbon. Curious, she picked it up and brought her discovery home to*

share with her two sisters. On the concrete floor of their tiny kitchen, she cradled the object in her lap and twisted a screw. The explosion it triggered ripped Duaa's body in half, killing her and severely injuring her sister Saja, 8. 'We thought we were safe because the bombs had stopped,' says Jabar, 30, a farmer's wife. 'My daughters were stolen from me.'" [Time, May 3, 2003] **[Drawer 4]**

And Imam:

IMAM SALIH MUTLAK. *Her older sister said she was usually alone and didn't have friends. They read the Quran and watched television together. The younger sister liked sad Egyptian movies.*

The other day she left a note for her parents that she planned to be a martyr. They lived in a very conservative Iraqi village where women are not permitted to leave the house without permission. She did that, and thereby lost her honor. As she approached a group of American soldiers, with grenades in her hand, she was shot dead. [AP, May 31, 2003] **[Drawer 4]**

Was she a hero (a martyr) or a very unhappy human being? And Carlos:

CARLOS CACERES. *I read in the paper today a UN worker named Carlos Caceres was one of three pulled out of a hotel in West Timor and murdered by* *a mob led by militiamen. He'd asked to be evacuated but was assured the local Indonesian soldiers would protect him. He had three doctorates, had studied at both Cornell and Oxford, and spoke five languages— including Russian and Czech, which he learned while on assignment in Moscow. He was a lawyer who did not, as his mother wanted, choose the easy life of a practice in Miami. [September 8, 2000]* [**Drawer 4**]

And Saartjie:

SAARTJIE ("SARAH") BAARTMAN. *"Freak" and prostitute Saartjie Baartman's remains were honored in a solemn ceremony in Capetown, South Africa, yesterday. She had been displayed like a freak in Europe two centuries ago and died a penniless prostitute in 1816. Poets, musicians, politicians—altogether some one thousand people—paid tribute. Did she come? [August 9, 2002]* [**Drawer 4**]

I guess I could have put in hundreds more, even thousands. Gathered together the newspapers of the world and kept cutting. All the letters written to archangels and saints and priests and gods too. Would have required a million file cabinets. Those few had to serve. One folder. The bottom drawer. Drawer 4. Not momentous historical events. What to call it?

Drawers 1 and 2 I had labeled "News"; Drawer 3, "Literature and Students." But because I never gave that folder in the bottom drawer any label, I never gave Drawer 4 a label either. If I had, it would have been "Outrage." Or maybe just "Rage."

I began to think of it as my "Rage" drawer but never labeled it as such for fear I'd need to explain to my mother what it meant. It was beyond what I could explain. In my mind it became just "Drawer 4" or "The Bottom Drawer." Rage? How many years can rage live? Rage against the owner of a roadside carnival who stuffs an eagle in a box, nails the box to a post, and extorts $5 from you to participate in the crime. Rage against the nun who claims to have the eternal answers she doesn't have. Rage against . . . He who has all the power but looks away—away from a woman being lynched and three little girls being raped and murdered.

My rage lived. Thirty-five years. But, stretched out over so long a time, "rage" is too strong a term. Perhaps . . . "quiet fury"? How long can a fist stay clenched . . . before it atrophies?

So what was the point of saving those "rage" clippings?—in an everyday manila folder whose index tab gets bent back and weakened with time . . . in a bottom drawer that gets stuck and makes a grating noise if you don't press down when you pull it out . . . in an old wooden filing cabinet.

You see, it turned out that folder full of "rage" didn't molder into oblivion. It got out. It went to a very distant place. With someone's help. Silkie's. And now her own folder has taken its place. The bottom drawer. Drawer 4.

9. A Strange Sickness

"Just so you know," Silkie said, "I have a sickness. A mental disorder. Schizoaffective something or other."

She was wearing denim overalls—with wide shoulder straps—over an old sweatshirt.

I shrugged.

"I just wanted you to know."

It was the third week of the term.

I was startled not so much by what she was telling me as by her deciding she had to tell me at all. And her sudden appearance in my office to do so.

Since the awkward episode of my readmitting her, I had not spoken with her one-on-one. There had been no need. In class, though she rarely volunteered a response or a question and did not mix with classmates, she was always there doing the work as required. It was true, however, that she often seemed very distracted, unfocused, sometimes with her eyes down, sometimes restlessly looking out the window then back at her book, and I hesitated to call on her during discussions of text readings for fear I would humiliate her because she was not paying attention. Where was her mind?

Still, even when unfocused, her eyes were intense, and I wondered if what I saw was not so much from lack of interest in the discussion as from thinking too deeply and painfully about it.

Now here she was sitting across from me, leaning forward more with her eyes than her body—eyes alert, revealing what?—an intense desire to understand something, or maybe, the opposite . . . to be understood. It was the latter, I decided—seeking "to be understood." Perhaps even that first day she'd shown up in my office, that desire or need had been there. But what was it she wanted me to understand?

This seeming to insist I be attentive to her—I might have dismissed it as my imagination if it had been a one-time phenomenon. But it wasn't. Along with it came this queer sensation that she was *expecting* me to do something which I wasn't doing. And if she was just studying me, why was it not as from normal curiosity? Why was it with so much intensity?

It struck me once, just as she'd exited the class with her eyes on me, that most people blink or turn away when you look right back at them—because she didn't. An unbroken gaze. Like that of a little girl. Not embarrassed to be staring at me. Studying me.

And why was it now she wanted me to know about her "schizoaffective something"? I'd noticed nothing remarkable about her behavior that suggested a mental illness, except perhaps that restlessness of movement that hinted at some anxiety, and a tendency in her writing to skip a little too much from one focus to another—usually between paragraphs, though sometimes even between and within sentences. She was careless about her appearance. Her hair had been soaked that first day, but even when dry it hung in the same quickly brushed fashion. (Of course, she had been and perhaps still was homeless.) She liked to wear a scarf in her hair, and she wore beads on occasion—colorful and conspicuous. Shell-necklace beads most often. But there was nothing wild or crazy about her. Well, except maybe that intensity in the eyes.

"Thank you for telling me," I said. "Do I need to know?"

She shrugged, smiled. Then got up and left.

I determined to look it up—"schizoaffective disorder." What I discovered was a confusing terrain of clinical description: "constellations of behavior traits causing either significant impairment or social or occupational functioning or subjective distress." What especially caught my attention were these: *"often there is a belief one has a special relationship to some other person as a way of coping," "associated features may include anger, social isolation and seclusiveness, eccentric behavior,"* and *"anti-psychotic medication usually has limited results—delusions and anxiousness may decrease but rarely disappear entirely."*

Whatever peculiarities I had observed about Silkie, they were not of the extreme order suggested in these clinical descriptions. Why had she, in effect, warned me?

One day toward the end of the term, I got an answer, of sorts.

It was a class discussion on a short story entitled "Night Women" by Edwidge Danticat about how a poor Haitian woman, forced into prostitution in order to feed her small son, fabricates for him tales of angels to explain the strange men coming to her in the night. Silkie was, as usual, seated in the back, quiet, but looking somewhat agitated. She was bent over her notebook writing or doodling, seemingly paying no attention to the discussion, both her eyes and pencil boring into the paper to a degree that alarmed me.

I continued to call on other students. Silkie had put her head down on her desk. I became concerned, and if she did not raise it soon, I decided I would walk over to her and, in a whisper, ask if she was okay or needed to leave the room. Perhaps the agitation had resulted from the story itself, so that it was not so much that she was not paying attention to the discussion as that she was *paying too much attention.*

"Even in this country. . . especially in big cities, there are women . . ." Laura Wilcox was saying.

She'd stopped because a murmuring was coming from somewhere in the room. Silkie. She was muttering something, although it was not clear what. Something about a "she" and "middle of the night" and "bus stop." Silkie had raised her head, half risen to her feet then slipped back down, and, pounding her desk with her fist, was speaking in a voice that gathered strength and bitterness with each breath, from some long-ago pain. Broken thoughts searching for expression in broken phrases—"like it's not one thing over here . . . her kid and love over here and what you may be doing over there . . . she was crying . . . I was there . . . with their fuckin pious churches fucking anyone who needs a drug to get through it all—this shitty world we live in. . . ." Her right arm was flailing now, her hand clawing and grasping in all directions, her long blonde hair falling half over her face, her one uncovered eye darting here and there, aiming at scattered random targets—and finally settling on me and not turning away, as though directing this all at me—charging me with these crimes, or with not having done anything about them . . . or maybe the *responsibility to make them right*. What was it I was to make right? "One in the morning!" she continued. "One . . . two . . . in the morning . . . my own little girl . . . at a bus stop! Why should they care? Jesus! Institutionalized? Who decides?!" Then in more smothered agitation, an expression of smoldering hatred, staring down at her desk, she finished more to herself, "What do they know? What does anyone . . . know?"

I hadn't dared to cut her off. None of us had. It was the kind of thing you had to let play out. Because it wasn't so much a loss of control as it was a necessary release. To how things were—in her world . . . or in the whole world.

I, the supposed instrument of calm authority in that room, let the rage have its say.

It had come from someplace I'd been to myself.

She stopped, trembling and holding tight to her desk. The class had frozen in their seats—stunned by the suddenness of her tirade cutting through prescribed classroom protocol.

She'd said no more than ten sentences in the six weeks of that class. Till this day. Till this.

Now there was only silence.

Laura was looking at me, wondering what I was going to do about it—Silkie's obscenity-laced tirade.

I said nothing. Did nothing except take a couple steps closer to Silkie.

She didn't apologize. Just glanced down at her notebook, which I could see now had no words on it—just a series of geometric figures in intricate detail.

Jason, because he was sitting immediately to the left of her, saw it too. Jason, a very average student, a basketball player, average even as that I'd heard, at a moment of what I now regard as remarkable insight, reached over to her desk, pointed to the drawings, and asked, "What are these?"

"Fractals," she answered, barely audible.

"What?"

"Fractals." I recalled her "fractal photographs" in her "Taking Stock."

"What are fractals?" he asked.

Somehow catching her breath, she pressed her hand to the paper, her mind to the fractals, as a way of freeing herself, then, turning to me uneasily, asked softly, with a hint of contrition, "Can I . . . use the board?"

"Go ahead," I said, smiling, not just relieved, but amused by the sudden transformation of mood. Of role. Unruly student become teacher.

With a piece of chalk too short for what it was called on to do, her right hand and arm shooting off in all directions, she was attacking the board like that of a passionate sculptor on stone. Then, getting more methodical, she stood back, saying nothing, erased a line here and there, stood back again, drew more lines . . . until she'd produced some intersecting circles, which became parallel parabolas or just spirals.

"They are like . . . solar systems," she said, almost to herself, then repeated it in a stronger voice, "intersecting," at the same time starting in on another figure that looked to be a cross between a flower and an explosion . . . and still another appearing to represent nothing even approaching a form, much less a "fractal." For those three or four minutes, there seemed to be no one else in the room to her. Finally two somewhat completed figures stared back at the class, teasing the other students to ponder their meaning.

Out of breath, now, she aspirated, as much to herself as to the class, "They're like . . . snowflakes . . . seashells . . . you know . . . leaves, you know? . . . I mean the patterns . . . a different kind of geometry . . . but worth it . . . now and then . . . to look at . . . figure out."

Becoming aware of the class, then, she seemed to realize she'd lost them and began walking back to her seat but was stopped by a male student's question: "If it's another kind of geometry, these fractals could still be described . . . by formulas . . . mathematical formulas. Right?"

Silkie thought about it, then turned back to the board. "Yes, I suppose, except then . . . you couldn't . . . put yourself into them . .. because there's no formula for. . . ." Her voice trailed off, and we could not hear the rest of what she said. She nodded to that student and went back to her seat.

If she'd been embarrassed about any of this, she didn't show it. She had her head down, pondering something. The mystery of the fractals? Something much beyond them? When she finally looked up there was a curious mix of peace and fury in her eyes.

"Thank you," she said to me and went to her seat.

We went on with class.

I wrote in my journal that night.

> *Today Silkie startled all of us. Erupted. Like a dagger. An anguished spirit tearing through the curtain of classroom etiquette. Composition 121, room 223. Out of the world of syllabi, assigned persuasive essays and prescribed morality, and into another—more universe than world. To break free of it, she explained fractals to us at the board. Jesus!*

I would write about her a lot after that.

10. "Madness?"

One of the passages I had copied down years earlier from the book my father gave me—T.E. Lawrence's *Seven Pillars of Wisdom*—was this:

> *Sometimes these selves would converse in the void;*
> *and then madness was very near.*

"Mad" is not a term we use anymore to describe the mentally ill. Nor even "insane." We say, "He is a schizophrenic," or "She is very unstable, you never know what she's going to do." And most of what I came to discover about Silkie over the weeks and months that followed would surely have fit nicely with such a description. "Silkie is mentally unstable."

If, instead, I say, "Silkie is mad," then, I romanticize her. It's the literature teacher in me—the Lear, the Hamlet, the Don Quixote, the "yellow wallpaper" woman. So I will not say that she was "mad," but rather that she was in life what madness is in art. Michel Foucault wrote, "[T]hrough madness . . . a work of art opens a void, a moment of silence, a question without answer, provokes a breach without reconciliation where the world is forced to question itself."

Silkie was a work of art who opened a void.

How could I claim so remarkable a phenomenon for her? Certain it is that, had it been only her telling me she was "mentally ill," or her "fractals explosion," I could not.

She was, in most respects, during the four terms I taught her—two composition and two literature classes—a normal student. She wrote papers on activist issues in my composition classes—the mistreatment of animals in the meat industries, abuse of foster children, poverty in Africa. She earned A's on most of them either with the first submissions or their revisions. In my literature classes she favored the strong women writers—Dickinson, Plath, Chopin, Rich. Her attendance was on occasion erratic, and when she did attend she rarely spoke up and often seemed distracted, but her few responses to the stories and poems were thoughtful, sophisticated in perception, analysis, and command of language.

Was it possible that, despite her homeless condition, she was a reader? That first day taking down *Woman at Point Zero* from my bookshelf. "The downtown library doesn't have it," she'd said. Perhaps even an avid reader?

My suspicion about that was confirmed when, one day as I was dropping off some clothes at a St. Vincent de Paul store, I came upon her thumbing through the used paperbacks. She had on a backpack, jeans, and her faded blue parka from the pocket of which she had just snatched a handkerchief to stifle a sneeze. Somewhat to my surprise, I could see that one of the two books she was holding and thumbing through was Dostoyevsky's *The Idiot*.

"Silkie."

"Hi."

"Do you come here a lot?"

"They're only fifty cents each here," she said.

Far down the aisle and seated on the floor looking at children's books was a little brown-haired girl who had turned toward us when I appeared.

"Your daughter?" I asked.

Silkie nodded.

"She likes books too, I see."

She half smiled, then sniffed. "Sorry, runny nose."

"What's her name?"

"Maheza."

I looked puzzled.

"It's African."

When I left I thought about Maheza. Not just her hair but her complexion, which was much darker than Silkie's. Was her father black, then? Was he himself African?

I thought again about Silkie's explosion in class . . . her "my own little girl! . . . at a bus stop!" What was that all about? Some real event or something in her mind?

She was alone much of the time. In class she always sat by herself, and I recalled only once seeing her conversing with a classmate. On two occasions while driving in town, I happened to spy her walking—once by herself, once with Maheza.

I did romanticize her. I admit it. Silkie was a quiet loner;

a reader; a thin, almost skinny homeless, mentally ill young girl, who fixated on fractals in nature and who wrote about being some long-dead "Ruth." And add to that the abnormal way she had of looking at me.

At times, I wondered, though, whether the madness was as much in *me* as in *her*.

My response to her from that very first day—driving all over town to find her, admitting her to a class that was already full, repeating to her "I'm sorry" on two or three occasions, and not knowing why—suggested some imbalance in *me*, not her. Some deep-seated, unexplored need that, if not irrational, was at the very least curious.

But then, why was *she* the one who triggered this sort of response in me? A "why" that was only one of many I would ask myself about her over the months I knew her, taught her. "Whys" deriving partially from behavior of hers I can characterize only as occasionally bizarre.

There was that November morning, for example, when I entered the classroom somewhat earlier than usual, and spied her—seated way in the back, seemingly unaware of my entrance or the presence of the other two or three students on the other side of the room—very still. Her right arm hovered above her desk and her left rested flat on the desk. She had the appearance of a mime who'd frozen her movements. A dancer poised to start in on a performance.

I set my lecture notes down and stood there taking in the silent spectacle.

I wondered if it was just my imagination. If she was just deep in thought. This position? This long? The other students—engaged in conversation—were paying no attention, and after what I guessed had been close to two minutes she pulled out of it.

What was that? Had it been not so much an anomalous trance as some ritual habit—one necessary for her?

She apparently hadn't noticed my attention to her, and when class began I could see that she was as she always was: very quiet, her psychic separation from the others in the room perhaps a bit more pronounced.

I began, as I'd planned, talking about the Rogerian Approach to argument.

Discovering, however, that my pedagogical focus was distracted by my too-keen awareness of where her eyes and perhaps her mind were, I was not very coherent and ended class a few minutes early.

She remained seated.

As the last of the students were exiting, she rose, stood by her desk pondering something, then began to turn half of a slow-motion pirouette. Graceful, almost spiritual. It was very brief—maybe only twenty seconds. So quiet and inconspicuous, it might not have been noticed even if the whole class had been there.

But I saw *it*. An "it" that was meant for me.

Or was I just hoping it was?

She turned to me and caught me staring at her, stood

confused at first, then gathered her papers and books and slipped past me, nodding as she did.

All that day I pondered the meaning of that pirouette, that mime-like trance—if indeed they had any meaning beyond just a Sufi-like balm for the soul. Why did I want them to mean more? Indeed, why didn't I ask her?

Already I'd come to regard her as a mystery. Who was this strange woman Silkie? This girl who told me she had some delusional disorder and whose eruption in the classroom finished with a lecture on fractals at the board? This student who became rigid like a mime and then pirouetted as though there were no one else in the classroom? Who wrote a narrative about being a dead person named Ruth.

A few days later, she was dropping off her folder with two revised papers in it. She had a tendency in her compositions, where her ideas and images rushed together in intensity, to interweave them without using the proper construction and punctuation. More poetry than prose. More lyric than expository. And I'd noted those places.

She was wearing a wrinkled white blouse with very worn denim overalls again, and was playing with a blue ribbon in her hair that wasn't doing its job, so she'd pulled it away and it was dangling in her hand.

"I made the corrections you suggested," she said. She turned to leave but abruptly stopped and stood there, saying nothing at first. Then . . . "Did you like Ruth?"

"Ruth?" I didn't immediately recognize the reference.

"Oh, your . . . narrative? Yes, I did. The ending . . ." I opened her folder, searched for it, took it out of the folder, and read from it. "'I would tell her I was Ruth. "I'm not dead. I'm Ruth." But I knew I was—dead.' I didn't quite understand it. I mean, I did . . . in a literary way, but . . . it doesn't matter. I'm not sure I'm supposed to. I liked it."

I'd gone to the trouble of pulling it out and reading aloud hoping it would get her to explain. She didn't. Just stood there with a puzzled expression. More about me than her writing, it seemed.

That was the first time I became aware that my eyes were on her with more than a teacher's gaze, and I cast them down again to the paper. The inscrutable in her. The way she had of seeming to study me, penetrate me. That unblinking gaze. The vulnerable alternating with the expectant . . . even, at times, the fierce. Yes, the fierce. How else to describe her eruption? An eruption she'd mastered only by attacking the board with fractals.

She nodded, but then, surprisingly, sat down and continued to study me silently.

I decided to make good use of the opportunity.

"That day . . . in class . . . when you . . . let go like that . . ."

She squirmed a little, and I redirected my approach. "I mean, even in your writing . . . it's like you have a lot you want to say. Too much. So you . . . in effect . . . lose control of some of the sentences. You need to direct . . . the passion . . . the force . . . so it's effective."

She looked down, then up again at me. Some of her hair had fallen over one side of her face. With her small frame and overalls, she had the appearance of a twelve-year-old boy who'd just come in from a fight.

But then her gaze all of a sudden shifted, and I realized they were no longer on me but rather . . . through me . . . a long way off . . . and perhaps, paradoxically, inwardly . . . at herself. It stayed with me . . . that shift of her gaze and where it had ended up. Through me. Back into herself. Then through me again, pondering something much deeper than both of us. *The eagle. The eagle's eyes.*

The most perplexing manifestation of the elusive nature of Silkie's mental state was yet to come, however.

Her journal.

I require that students keep a journal in all my classes—a minimum number of entries based on responses to readings in the text. But, except for asking them to read aloud in class occasionally an entry or two, I do not read the journal as a whole till the last week. And, typically, a student's twenty entries fill up less than half of one of those black-and-white stenographer's notebooks. Silkie's, however, was jammed with additional pages in the form of papers torn from other notebooks with frayed and smeared edges, in different colors and patterns (blue, pink, lined, unlined)—folded in halves and fourths. Inside the front cover she'd written a brief note to me:

Professor Mollgaard
The entries for your class are where the corners are
bent back. Ignore others. Sorry.
Silkie

These "others" filled up the whole first half of the journal and included entries that seemed to have been written long before. But even on some of the "bent back pages" were entries with "months ago" or "years ago" scribbled along the left margins. Nor was it a typical eighty-page stenographer's notebook, but one with a hundred and fifty pages—all of which was filled with writing.

Certain that my curiosity would get the better of me and I'd peek at a couple of the other entries, I nevertheless set about focusing on the required ones, and opened her journal at the first bent corner, which was well into the notebook:

1/19 I caught a dragonfly once. I was six. Enclosed it in my hands and spoke softly to it. A pet. I would be nice to it. Slowly then I opened my hands. It did not move. Its wings seemed stretched along skeletal web-like lines and with this a long dark tail with yellow heart shapes along it. I stared at it so long, wondering that it did not fly away, that I became the dragonfly. Saw myself looking down. Wondered long and hard. And flew away. And was the better for it.

1/21 What if what we wrote we knew would be the last thing we would write? That we would die the next day?

1/27 They are within us. Screams. They are not just down the hall or down the street. The screams. Not just today but yesterday and years ago. Tomorrow and years to come. Not just in my brain. My heart too. Gripping it so tightly it screams out. Down my arms and into my outstretched fingers. Screams. Can they be heard by that woman walking her dog? That man with his briefcase? That little deaf girl under the bench in the marketplace in Guatemala?

Her next entry started on the same page, and was the first to have "years ago" scrawled in the margin. Finding it was descriptive of her homeless life, however, and therefore promised to be more interesting than the class entries, I read it and, when I'd finished, others of the same sort. The dates were not chronological, and they seemed to be from different years.

1/29 One night I decided to just notice. The world outside my own. Through the gate that was my front door . . . from my little alley. There was a grate out there in the street, and from out of it was this spiraling fountain of steam.

And sounds—I could separate them as just sounds— roaring engines, truck horns, a woman calling her cat in an upstairs window, a meter incessantly clacking, the grunt of a forklift, and the solid ringing crash of plywood onto the sidewalk. Or it was all a discordant ensemble the ear tries to shut down until . . . a scream would punctuate the almost night. Did the scream itself shut down the noise? Strange how it could do that. Then I would hear the train. At first it just hissed, but it set off the bells, the clang at the street. Then I could see it. Cars passing, lights on inside but not many people silhouetted inside.

2/12 Junkheads pass by. Mostly young men, but here and there a woman with them. Somewhere out there is a dancing dragon. And it's me.

2/28 Once a month the Baptist Church had a waffle feed. You could partake if you sat through the service. My friends Boots, Kelsey, and I never missed it. A real and free breakfast. They knew who we were. The others who came and didn't expect us to be giving anything back. But this morning Boots got sick. Ate too much. She'd been hung over. Still had that look. And having morning sickness too. Right there in the parking lot—a pothole toward the far corner—she crouched down to let it come out of her—every part of her. Vomit. Some shit too. Almost fell face forward. Some kids saw her, then others. All just stared. Eating as they were and seeing that. I stood by her. Stood in front of her so they couldn't see. Like a sentry. Daring them to say anything. Kelsey and I helped her away. Cleaned her up down the street.

Boots' home was half tent, half cardboard box—weighted down with bricks. She used to look forward to those waffles. Once a month.

3/2 He slapped her. Slapped Boots when she was pregnant. We saw it. The rest of our "family." She and I had known each other for almost two years. She used to dance, strip, but lost her job. Right after is when I met her. I used to help her hunt for cigarettes big enough to enjoy. Up and down the blocks. Anyway, one day, guy began saying vicious things to her. I think she knew him long ago. But we saw it, and saw him slap her hard. She fell down.

We didn't do anything right then. Boots wouldn't tell us what it was about. But we saw the same guy two days later and watched where he went. Todd and Wilson came up behind him. We got him down. Shoes, knees pressing on him. I swung and kicked at him too. Then they just held him, and I sat on his chest and slapped him like he did to her. Over and over again. So hard it hurt my hand. So loud I couldn't hear anything else.

3/6 I was lucky. Being only 100 pounds, so skinny and I could squeeze through the padlocked iron gate into the alley. I was protected at night. It was only partly an alley because a stone wall at the end connected the two buildings. It was too high for anyone to get over it. I was safe. It had a couple large dumpsters but they were only for cardboard so there was no bad odor. And most of the time the door to one of the buildings was unlocked. There was nothing inside the back room there except discarded furniture from when the place was an office supply. No longer in business. So when it was very cold, I could slip inside with my blankets and some of the cardboard.

3/14 Today I saw death—again. It is somewhat common and yet never common. The strangeness that death is . . . it's quite amazing in how it depends on the situation. Sometimes it is sad, horrible and daunting. Other times it is a laughing matter, absurd justice, and at times it just makes everything clear. Today though—I saw him go down the street. He was whispering—louder and louder.

5/24 Several weeks ago Maheza was drawing a cheetah she saw in a magazine at the St. Vinny's. The cheetah in the magazine was chasing a springbok. She held it up to me. The head with the ears was especially good, and she had 5 or 6 spots. She tried to make the body sleek but widened it to get enough spots in. "It only has 3 legs," I said. She stared at it. "I mixed 2 together," she said. She took it, put it back on the floor and started to draw in another leg, but then stopped. "This one has only 3 legs," she said. "Oh," I said. "What happened to the other one?" "It doesn't have that one." "Oh." "It's a special one." "A special cheetah?" She nodded.

3/15 When I did something wrong, when I was bad, I hid. In shame. Behind the chair. Under the table or bed. In the doorway of an old building. But these bad men hide in the open . . . behind badges, in business suits, with smiles, under permanents and comb-overs. Behind religion and reputation.

I would sit on a rooftop, an angel looking down at them below—these bad men. I would be thinking, "They walk slowly and with confidence and pride. But they cannot see what I can see. Because I am an angel. Up here that is my status."

4/1 It was this date 7 years ago. I was 15. I'd been staying with friends, sleeping on the couches. At other times by the river. The cold and the fear and lonely feeling of rejection were slow suffocation. A beautiful and gentle woman I met helped me find a girls group home, but she couldn't keep covering my expenses. She didn't ask me to leave. I saw how it was, though, and skipped out early one morning and ended up in stranger's apartment. A 21-year-old from L.A. She was hard. Mean. For some reason she took a dislike to me. Said she had a friend who had an empty apartment. Turned out he was a meth dealer, and it was just a vacant room full of beer crates and broken bottles in a house condemned and boarded up because of a heavy mold smell and rot. It was creepy but I threw down my blankets for the night, planning to leave next day. During the night it happened. 5 or 6 guys—all in their 20's and 30's. Locked the door. The window was already covered with plywood. Yanked away my blankets. "Show us what you have, girl," one of them said, "or you don't get it back." I cried. One of them laughed. The others smiled. "If you don't, we'll help you," the one said. For a second I felt like I was in a classroom full of taunting teenagers waiting for me to answer a question they knew I couldn't answer. My crying turned into shaking—all over. I hesitated then began slipping my sweater over my head. Showed them what they wanted to see. A lot of hoots, cheers. They yanked the sweater from me, and kicked my backpack to the corner. One especially ugly guy—short, fat, very large round head—a snowman of skin—held out my sweater, but when I jumped for it to cover myself, they closed around me and pushed me into the corner. I tried to find some hair or cloth to tear at, but it was all air and they hit me. The fat one was first. Then—one by one—they used me. I passed out. When I woke I was half-wrapped in my blanket. Had I done it or them? But I was alone. Then the door opened again. Three of them had returned. Pulled me up. One of their hands covered my mouth—pushing so tight it made my teeth cut into my lip. Pushed me to a car outside. I could hardly walk, so they held me up on one side while my foot dragged along the ground on the other. Held me down in the back seat. I could taste blood in my mouth and it almost choked me. Took me to the park. Very dark. The whole thing again. I forced myself to find another world. They left me there. I heard the car motor in the distance. Then it was very silent. I began crawling. A long way. Hands and knees. Maybe two or three hundred yards. Out of the park. Finally stood up. Held onto whatever there was to hang onto—a light pole, a fence, a tree. Finally pounded on a door—again and again. Man answered. Lifted me. Carried me like an infant. I never came down from his arms.

This grisly account—what did it mean? Maheza? How old was Silkie now? Twenty-three, twenty-four, perhaps. Maheza five or six. So was she the result of. . . ?"

I found my hand shaking, and I accidentally dropped the whole journal. Out fell two wads of onion-skin pages folded over once. I opened the first wad to find four pages of—"fractals." The first page seemed to be an illustration of what she had been doing on the board—starting with simple geometric shapes then with successive drawings, overlaying them with other geometric shapes, making them more and more complex and intricate. On the last page were pictures of a fern, a great spreading oak tree, a snowflake, and a rose, which she appeared to have cut from magazines and pasted down. Along the margins of these pages she'd written notations like, "best I can do, but not bad" and "Not chaos but order" and "Algorithms! What are they?"

I opened the other wad of pages—folded in half—that had fallen out. Pasted photos of dancers. Three of them—black and white and old. Under each she'd printed a name—"Ruth St. Denis," "Maureen Fleming," "Pat Hall Smith." At the bottom of the page she'd written: *My Ruth is a dancer too. Her body is a woman's. Mine. Not as men see a woman's body. She dances. Along the river. Her feet on the wet earth.*

I closed her journal, slipped it into my backpack, determined to read more of it that night. After supper, passing on watching the evening news, I propped myself up in bed and opened the journal at a random place near the beginning . . . and was astonished at what I found written there.

> *8/14 Fixtures in the market place. Beggars with their empty bowls and sealed eyes line up against the blackened walls like statues bronzed in dust. Some implore "El Dios" for their lives to be better. The tourists from the U.S. and Europe take their pictures. Usually not asking because if they do the beggars hold out their hands.*
>
> *One beggar is very different. He lies sprawled in the dirt near where the market opened into a park. A crazy man. Cannot even shape his mouth to say anything. Just moans. Very loud as though it could hook onto a passer-by and make him see. Drools so much there is a rope of saliva from his lips to his contorted fingers,*

which he can't close to hold a bowl. He cannot sit, so he leans forward as if suspended in a fall. No one pays any attention to him. Apparently he's here every day moaning so loud so continually, everyone ceases to hear except the tourists. And he frightens them. I spent my days wanting to offer him something, and finally I gave him an orange and a bag of nuts and a small amount of change. Immediately—but for just a few seconds—his moaning ceased. His twisted fingers raked the orange and nuts into a small cloth bag. And the entire market turned to watch us. They watched until he began to moan again and I left, embarrassed and confounded. His moan was a daily fixture which I had not lived there long enough to become accustomed to. Only his silence could serve to stir those around.

What country was this? "Tourists from the U.S.," she writes. Where had Silkie been?

As I read through the journal there were more of these perplexing entries which seemed to describe other places in the world.

8/16 The blind, the deaf, the crazy, the retarded—commonly—in these countries—they are chained in the house, abandoned on the street or simply left at home. Like a table in the corner or a foot stool. All day they stare into space. The deaf girl—age 6 or 7—is left at the orphanage every day while all the other children go to school. We are together so I'm allowed to know her. So brilliant she is. She draws pictures on the notebook pad I give her. The Guárico tree down by the river. Branch by branch. The goat. The eyes she draws again and again, frustrated she cannot make them just right. In the end she gives up. But the next day goes back to the same picture. The eyes.

6/14 The people have no water, so neither does this crocodile. His scaly body is dusty and dry, as is his mouth. The gully next to him has no water. He just lies there, not moving. Encrusted in the dry earth around him. There is a fence surrounding him that allows no more than 10 feet or so in any direction..

The baboon sits drooped over. A child tosses some peanut shells and a piece of wrapper from a cigarette package. Around him are hundreds of the peanut shells, cigarette wrappers. He does not even raise his head to look at me who is there just to see him. There is nowhere for him to go.

2/2 At the end of this alley in the souq a woman sits huddled in the dark. A baby's head peaks out from her robe. She holds out her hand to me with entreating eyes. I give her a 100 dirham. "You can't give to all of them," Abdul tells me. I nod. "Why are there so many?" I ask. "It's a problem. The king is working on it," he answers.

Were these entries some sort of creative writing? Based on photographs or documentaries perhaps? Or copied from some other sources? What countries were these? She had differentiated them from ours. The "tourists" were from the "U.S. and Europe." A crocodile with no water. A baboon? A zoo somewhere? The "blind, the deaf . . . in these countries." Did the name—"Abdul"—mean some country in Africa or the Middle East? The "El Dios"? Mexico? Central America? And what of these peculiar lines: *He does not even raise his head to look at me who is there just to see him.* And *I was allowed to know her.* "Allowed" by whom? For what purpose? From where came these strange experiences? Silkie was barely in her twenties and had spent much of life homeless—in poverty—as her other entries made clear. Where and how could she have lived abroad? Even if, indeed, the allusions were just vicarious . . . secondhand . . . the details were such as to suggest she'd had some experience comparable to what she described. How could she have traveled to such faraway places given her homeless condition?

Then there was this entry—tied to "Ruth" but equally inexplicable.

> *4/4 Till yesterday, Ted was the one who came. Every Tuesday with his horse "Caleb" and the wagon to pick up our garbage. It was a smelly old wagon, and Ted stopped at each house, climbed down, picked up the garbage and threw it in. He was tall and thin with a*

gaunt face and dark brown hair parted neatly to both sides like a little boy's. Mother had me run out with all the garbage wrapped in newspaper and bread wrappers very early in the morning before Ted got there, which was usually just before I left for school. He always called out to me if he saw me leaving, "How is school, Ruthie?" But I never knew how to answer. Just smile. I felt bad for him because sometimes I heard people say, "You'll be like Ted the garbage man, if you don't study and work hard." Yesterday morning, though, it wasn't Ted. It was somebody else, and when I tried to find out why, nobody would tell me. Then Charlie, my brother's friend down the street, grinned like he had a big secret and whispered to me, "He got fired. They found out he's not really a man. He's a woman. His name probably wasn't even Ted."

Surely this was the same Ruth that had been in her story. But what year? A horse-drawn garbage truck?

I determined to ask Silkie about these strange entries. Where she had written "Long ago" in the margin, was it to keep me from reading them or to be certain that I would understand the correct placement in time if I did read them? Even the one about the rape?

"I have a problem."

 I looked up from my office desk to see Silkie standing

there with Maheza. It was the second week of the next term. My American Literature survey course.

Maheza's eyes were just as expressive as her mother's but deeper, more haunting. Alone, she could have been judged to be of any of many ethnic mixes. Her hair chestnut-colored, her skin a smoother, softer version of the same, and her features perfect, she had a beauty only very young children can possess.

She was wearing a worn hooded ski jacket, which came down to her knees, and lavender jeans thin and frayed from many washings.

Her eyes were sizing me up.

"What problem?" I asked.

"I don't have any place to put her this afternoon. Can she sit with me during class? I brought a book for her to read."

I shrugged to say it was fine with me. It happened on occasion—a father, a mother, bringing his or her little boy or girl to class. I'd done it myself in graduate school. Some professors frowned on it, but I never had a problem allowing it.

"How do you spell her name?"

"M . . . a . . . h . . . e . . . z . . . a."

Maheza stood there, staring, seemingly puzzled by me. "Just like her mother," I thought. "Studying me."

"Hi, Maheza." I reached down and took her hand and shook it. It embarrassed her, and I regretted playing the adult's expected role.

"You . . . have children, right?" Silkie asked. "You

mentioned in class once about them?"

"A boy and a girl. She's eleven, he's ten. They don't live with me here in Oregon anymore, though. Corrine and Paul."

"Do they live nearby?"

"No. California. Long way. I fly down whenever I can."

There was an awkward moment, when Silkie was looking down but appeared about to say or ask me something, and indeed she started to: "You are . . . I mean . . . are you . . . ?"

I waited. "Pardon?"

"What's that picture of?" Maheza interrupted. She was pointing to the brilliantly colored cover of a world literature text on my desk. She was asking her mother, then turned to me and flushed—maybe afraid I would think she was directing the question at me.

"It's a painting," Silkie said.

"A guy named Chagall did it," I added. "He liked to make everything look like dreams. Animals flying. Isn't that what it looks like? A dream? You dream, don't you?"

She didn't say anything.

"There are other paintings in it too." I opened it to show her how many had been worked into the literary selections to represent different periods. "See all these other paintings?" I pointed to a Renoir portrait of a little girl in dark hair holding a cat.

Maheza stared at it but still said nothing.

"You can have it, if you wish," I said, thinking it was really her mother who would appreciate having it.

Silkie glanced at me curiously, so I explained.

"Publishers send us these books free hoping we'll order it for our classes. I just got this one today—it's a new world literature book—but I'm not going to adopt it. Someday she'll be able to read it."

Maheza hesitated, then took it in both arms.

"It's pretty big, isn't it?" I said. "Do you still want it?"

She swung it away from me in answer.

"Thank you," Silkie said and turned to leave.

"Wait, I'll walk with you to the class. I wanted to ask you something—about your journal."

As the three of us exited the building I started to put it to her, then remembered the rape entry. Perhaps she really hadn't intended for me to read any but the entries marked with folded corners. Still, how could I stop now? Focus quickly on the strange ones. "I . . . I've been wondering about some of the entries. The ones that look like they came from other notebooks. Sorry, but I took the liberty of reading some of them. The ones where you talk about being in other countries. At least, I think you are. Were you really in those places, or were they just some creative writing you were doing?"

"Yes."

"Yes what?"

"I was."

"Where? When?"

"Years ago."

I waited for an elaboration, but it didn't come.

It was always this way—my having to probe to find out anything about her. She was content . . . more comfortable . . . with leaving the pictures unfinished, the photos blurred.

"I mean, why and which places were you in?" I was not willing to let this one go, certain some helpful or at least interesting revelation would come out of my persistence. More than with any other student, I wanted to know more about her.

"A long time ago."

"Well, I'm thinking you must have been . . . "

"Ruth."

"Well, yes, that one. Ruth."

"She goes when she wants and . . . where. Maybe they're just dreams. Vivid ones. But I'm not always sure."

"Pardon? I'm not following . . ."

"I can describe them . . . I have to . . . just because they are so . . . vivid. Being there in a way."

"So you mean . . . "

"Can we talk about it some other time?" She lowered her eyes. Maybe it was because Maheza was present and some of what she had written would be disturbing to her daughter.

"Well, okay."

I was disappointed, though. I had wanted to ask at least the one very crucial question—about this mysterious "Ruth."

I would ask some other time when she was more open to talking.

"Maheza, it's cold." She was bending over her daughter

to button the top of her jacket.

"Here, let me hold her book," I said, trying to be helpful.

I was left feeling more puzzled than ever about Silkie, and I wished I hadn't chosen a time when she wasn't able to, or willing to, answer fully.

A few minutes later, in the classroom, Maheza lay on the floor on her stomach next to her mother's desk. She had opened the book I'd given her to some other colorful artwork page and was tracing her fingers over it. I found myself studying her—wanting her to raise her eyes so I could read them—discover what of Silkie's mysteries were lurking there as well.

It wasn't till that evening that I recalled the awkward moment in the office and Silkie's stopping in the middle of a sentence: "You are . . . I mean . . . are you . . . ?" What? Meant to be a statement or a question? I inserted possible endings, but there were too many. A fact which caused me to regret even more that I had not followed up on it as we'd walked to the classroom, and asked her, "What were you about to say, Silkie? And why did you not complete it?"

The following weekend I would visit my children. One week later would come the mystery of the phone call. A few months later the mystery of the jar.

And I would have to deal with "madness"—hers and mine—in a whole new way.

DAWSON FAMILY. *On Wednesday the house of the Dawson family in Baltimore was firebombed. The mother, Angela Dawson, and all five children—Carnell, Jr., 10, Juan Ortiz, 12, twins Kevin and Keith, 9, LaWanda, 14—were killed. The husband is in critical condition. The family had crusaded against the drug dealers in the area. They were constantly threatened, but stuck it out. They refused to be bullied. [October 16, 2002]* **[Drawer 4]**

11. Paul and Corrine

It was both madness and dance the night of the divorce. Seven years earlier. Me. Four-year-old Corrine. Three-year-old Paul. Metropolitan Park at midnight. Dodgeball, one of those large balloon balls that are hard to throw with any force unless you are close up.

Children look different by the park lights at midnight. Their faces glow. As they run their long hair cuts through the dark like fire flashes. They sound different, too. Their laughter emanates from unseen places.

The exhaustion and breathlessness of the wild chase was an antidote to the court proceedings earlier that day.

> *"Infidelity or mental cruelty. Has to be one or the other."*
> *"Mental cruelty then."*

What if they had been there—in the courtroom? What if during the questions establishing "grounds for dissolution of the marriage," we—Paul, Corrine, and I—had chased each other around the attorneys' table and into the hallways and back again around the judge's desk?

"Describe the mental cruelty."
"Well . . ."

It wasn't like I'd been habitually coming home at 1 a.m. in a drunken stupor or abusing her verbally. "Mental cruelty" is a pretty elusive thing. In the end, my wife failed to make her case. I struggled to make it for her. Actually, it was a fairly subtle thing. How it fell apart. At some point I began withdrawing into myself. Yes, there was another woman—a colleague—but no affair, just a fascination with her peripatetic, neurotic lifestyle. Yearning, alternately playful and sad eyes. Nothing more.

"Well . . ."

As best I could, I made the case—for my wife.

"I've heard better," the judge said and granted the divorce.

What did he expect? Who can explain what happens to the human brain and what it does to a relationship over six or seven years?

Had she—my soon-to-be ex-wife—been with us that night . . . the four of us in the park . . . we would not have understood any better . . . but we would have realized that not all had been lost.

But she wasn't. So the sweet madness of midnight dodgeball dissolved into the routine of the "visits." Weekly. But, then, when she remarried, monthly, bimonthly.

I congratulated myself on my decision: I would go to see Paul and Corrine unannounced. I'd planned my regular visit to them for two weekends later, but my short experience with meeting Maheza made me feel especially lonely for my own children, and, that longing requiring some sort of serendipitous relief, I resolved to fly down that Friday night to surprise them. Besides, having to fly "red-eye" through the night fit my mood. I would have to wait three hours at the airport before calling them, but that was okay. It was the unexpected that I wanted.

It was Paul who answered the telephone.

"Hi, son. This is Dad."

"Hi . . . Dad. Yeah . . . "

"Hey, I'm in town. Flew in last night. I was in the mood for seeing you. Not waiting another two weeks. I thought I'd surprise you and your sister. I can drive over and pick you guys up right away and we can spend the day together and take a motel tonight. Like last time."

"Really?" No excitement in his voice.

"Just getting up? Maybe I called too early. . . . I can give you a couple hours and meet you somewhere if it's okay with your mother."

"What are those sounds? You still at the airport?"

"Yeah. Just got in. Announcing planes at the nearby gates. Lot of early flights."

"Dad . . . "

"Yes?"

"I'm in the Explorers now. It's a group, meets once a week and we do things. You know . . . go places. Kind of like the Boy Scouts . . . 'cept we do a lot of different kinds of things. I don't like the Boy Scouts."

I waited. "So is there a problem with . . . ?"

"No, not really. It's just that today we're going on a field trip to an old mine. We're camping out at night in the park nearby. It's kind of cool."

"Oh."

I waited for him to add, "But, hey, I won't get to see you again for another month, and I can see the mine anytime. Maybe even with you, Dad." He'd always exhibited a fierce devotion to me in the midst of the breakup. Would always admonish my wife if she said anything too sarcastic or disparaging about me. "He's not always like that, Mom." But he'd grown into a new scene, a new set of friends and responsibilities. That's just how it was. What else did I expect?

"But, listen, Dad, I can . . . What about later or tomorrow?"

"No, that's okay. I was hoping you'd have a soccer game or something I could go to. I've been planning on seeing you. Your mother says you're very good. Get a goal most every game."

"Yeah, we're in second place."

I waited for him to go back to insisting on finding a time to see me, but he didn't.

"Anyway . . . I guess I should've told you I was coming," I said, my voice dropping. It was good for him to hear the disappointment. My son was choosing a mine over me. When my visits were so few. I remembered then that it was "Doug"—his "new father"—who had encouraged him to become an Explorer. It was his sort of thing. He'd probably earned Eagle Scout status himself. "Next time then. Or maybe I could just pick up Corrine . . ."

"Okay, Dad. Is that all right? Sorry. Dad, here's Mom."

"Hi, Paul was just telling me about . . . his field trip. I just felt like coming down this weekend. Is Corrine there? Maybe I can spend the day with her."

A lot of silence.

"Corrine's in the bathroom. Listen, Stephen, she and I are getting ready to go shopping. Some sales today for clothes she's been needing for school. It'll probably be late afternoon. I suppose then . . ."

"No."

"Pardon?"

Corrine was becoming a young lady. Clothes for school were a big thing with her now probably. I'd foolishly persisted in seeing her as the devilish little tomboy of three years earlier. The result of looking too often, too fondly, at a photo on my bedroom wall of her on my shoulders pressing my hair down over my face.

"No, no. Forget it." It was easier to be pissed with my ex-wife than hurt by my children, but it came down to the same result. Explorers, sales on clothes. I'd feel guilty for changing Corrine's plans. New clothes . . . I knew how that was. Then we'd have to rush to have a good time later. And it wouldn't be a good time for that reason. Besides, no Paul at all. A day I had looked forward to lift my spirits—one I'd remember long after for its spontaneous nature, the madness of the inspiration and last-minute decision—would not even involve one of them, and would be for the other an artificial, to-please-Dad thing.

I could have asked their mother to let me talk to Corrine, but that would have put my daughter in the position of worrying about hurting her father's feelings if she went with her mom shopping or hurting her mother's feelings if she didn't.

"Well, you'll still have the evening and . . . you flew all the way down here . . . just for them."

I thought to say, "Shit, yes," but I didn't.

"No, it's okay," I said instead. "Really. I should have let you know. Tell them I'll see them in a couple weeks. As planned. Okay?"

"Okay. Sorry."

My plane wasn't flying out till Sunday at noon, so I had all of Saturday free and decided to take a taxi into the city.

The driver was a college-student kind—a Middle Eastern guy—and probably earning money to go to school. Not the boorish sort of taxi driver you usually get. This driver was young and wore glasses. Quiet, sensitive manner.

"Where to?"

"Anywhere in the city is all right. I have all day to kill."

The driver nodded his head. "So maybe near the train station? Or maybe . . . "

I was sitting in the backseat and leaned back to make myself comfortable—planning to just gaze out at the sights of the city.

It was just as we pulled on to the freeway, though, that I felt the "aura." The word neurologists used to describe the feeling that signals an oncoming seizure. *It was going to happen.* It *would happen. A seizure.* I'd felt the aura even earlier—at the point of putting down the phone with my ex-wife—but I'd suppressed it then. Now it was reawakening.

The rejection that day by my children had done it.

It was all freeways from the airport into the city, and certainly, therefore, not a good time for *it* to come.

Still *it was going to happen. How long could I hold it off?*

I found myself focusing on a billboard about Sprint. A pretty girl smiling at one end holding a cell phone, a young man in a sport coat at the other, a phone in his hand. The Los Angeles skyline as a backdrop.

Just had to stave it off. Stall it for a while. Get into a conversation. Screw my mind into some "sticking place" which did not admit of the sort of thoughts that were bringing on this seizure.

"You a college student?"

"Sorry?"

I raised my voice over the sound of the traffic. "You go

to college?"

"Oh, yes. Yes. I was. But I'm having to work . . . you know . . . awhile to earn enough again."

"What are you studying?"

"Studying?"

"What field. What classes?"

"I was planning on . . . maybe engineering . . . but . . . takes too long . . . too expensive. So . . . don't know."

"Yeah. I know how that is."

"You. What do you do?"

"I'm . . . a professor."

"Professor. A teacher." [He sounded really impressed.] "What do you teach?"

"English. Writing. Literature. Not here though. In Oregon."

I should have known what to say next, but couldn't hold on to a clear sense of anything anymore. *It was coming.*

It would feel good . . . breaking free from the despondency that had been weighing me down for months. Even if it was a poor substitute for the more wonderful breaking free by way of a mad romp with my children. A small eruption in this taxi. A temporary release not unlike Silkie's eruption in the classroom. When would it come? Did I have that much control to choose a time? The precise moment . . . so as not to cause an accident?

"Listen . . . sorry. . . I don't want to . . . alarm you but . . . I'm going to have a seizure."

"I can't hear you. You know . . . all this traffic. Even this early. You believe it?"

I had glanced at the license and picture pasted on his visor and saw his name was Omar. It would be best to talk to him as "Omar" and not "taxi driver."

"Omar—that's your name, right? . . . I'm . . . going to have a seizure."

"Seizure?" Oddly, Omar didn't respond at all at first. The panic I expected didn't happen. "You mean like . . . what is it . . . you said a seizure . . . you mean an epilepsy thing?"

"Yes."

He took a quick worried glance at me. Then—

"I can't stop here. You want me to take the next exit?"

"No, actually I don't. I'll be okay." I was having trouble breathing right and making myself heard because of it. "I can control it so it won't be bad enough you'll have to help me or anything. Just wanted you to know. It'll sound . . . may sound . . . bad. But I'm okay. Just keep driving. Happens a lot. I won't hurt myself. These things happen sometimes. I don't go unconscious. I know how to control them. You know?"

"Okay. Sure?"

"Yeah. You know. They actually feel good." I was trying to make him feel less anxious. "Kind of like getting drunk. Letting go when you're down."

He looked puzzled. But then, to my surprise, he became solicitous.

"So . . . then . . . you're depressed?"

"Pardon?"

"You said 'down,' didn't you? Depressed."

"Yeah. Big way."

"Sorry for that."

"Thanks."

My breathing and ability to talk were getting more constricted. I stiffened to brace myself, and I saw him bracing himself too and glancing anxiously into the rearview mirror.

"Don't . . . worry, please. I'll bang pretty hard against the door maybe. Lock them, okay. I'll miss your seat . . . keep it all back here . . . can control it that much . . . just the force, you know? I'll direct it."

"Okay. So these things are a little crazy, no?"

"Yeah. You got it. Little crazy. Ten-second high."

I didn't know if he understood that, but I saw him through the rearview mirror half-smile.

"Then when you're done, tell me how to do it."

"Will do." Feeling as I did, I liked his sense of humor. He'd accepted my version of all this.

Finally, I put my head down into my hands and . . . let go.

It was very explosive. It had to be. And it felt good. The only thing you could do.

When it was done, I lay on the seat, breathing heavy, smothering a need to cry.

Omar looked back over his shoulder at me. "Okay? So . . . not all good, is it?"

"No, it is," I said almost breathlessly. "All good. You'd be surprised."

I sat back then, letting the aftershock dissipate.

He glanced at me again and saw me with my eyes half closed, and apparently decided to let me rest. When I opened them again he was pulling off the freeway, but we weren't downtown yet. He stopped in front of a convenience store and went in. A minute later he came out with a Sprite and gave it to me.

"Back in Lebanon," he said, "when I was only ten or so, there was this small boy. Only seven or eight. I knew his brother. The boy had these things—seizures—all the time. Tried to go to school but didn't work. He took some kind of medicine but it didn't work, so he just stayed at home all the time, you know. Seemed like they just ignored him except when he had seizures . . . then they held him. You know? Just to give him his meals. His food. Like an animal. Really bad. No, sad. I come into their house, and he is just sitting in this chair in the corner. He'd look at you, but we'd just do things . . . like he wasn't there. Lived that way for a long time then hit his head real hard and that was it. Dead. Killed him. I used to feel sorry for him. Seemed like no one did anything . . . things . . . for him."

I thanked him for the soda and we headed off for town again.

Oddly, the seizure and his sensitivity to me made me feel a peculiar bond to this Omar.

"You can pick a place to let me off."

"Okay."

"I don't know Los Angeles very well. Only been downtown

a couple times."

"What are you doing in town? Business?"

"My kids live in the area . . . . I see them once a month or so. When you divorce your wife you end up divorcing your children."

"That's not good. That's sad."

"You try to keep it going, but it becomes take 'em to a ball game or mall or something. Not the same anymore." I didn't have much breath but I began, in the wake of the seizure, to feel the rush, the high, the way you talk too much when you're drunk. But at some point I was just talking to myself. I was just muttering. I don't know; maybe he got some of what I was saying, but it just kept dribbling out. "It's been five years—playing that weekend father business. Awkward stuff. Especially with a new 'father' around. All in the name of stability. Real father becomes 'stranger.' Awkward getting-acquainted-again sort of thing. 'Well, they don't mean to be that way, it's just that being away from me for two months, they've had new experiences,' I tell myself. So there are going to be those artificial do-I-take-them-to-a-movie-or-to-Sea-World-or-Disneyland dilemmas. Where would you like to eat? What movie would you like to see? Oh, you've already seen 'Aladdin.' With your mother? Oh, with your mother and him (fuck him anyway). Well, how about . . . Oh, that's not up anymore, is it?'"

I'm sure he didn't catch half of what I said or meant, but I wanted him to hear my tone—the way I was saying it—anyway.

Strange who it is you want to talk to in this world . . . and when.

"My friend. He drives a taxi too. He's divorced. A kid four years old. Same thing."

"The fact is the times I remember most fondly with them have never been the designed ones, the expected ones. The sum in meaningful memory of all such times with them over the years I could store in one half of a neuron. But now and then there've been these . . . what I think of as 'mad moments'—unplanned things . . . you know. I'm playful by nature, so sometimes I like to harness it in a constructive way. First time was just a few hours after the divorce was made final. Well past midnight. They should have been in bed, but there we were running wildly around a large oak tree in the park. By the river. Exhausted. Didn't stop till two in the morning. Spontaneous madness. Unplanned. Like I said."

"Here's the train station. Look all right here?"

"Sorry. I was talking too much."

I gave him a $20 tip.

"Nice talkin to you," he said. "Feeling better?"

"Yeah. Lot better. I wish you well with your studies. Engineering."

I felt a Funeral, in my Brain, / And Mourners to and fro / Kept treading—treading—till it seemed / That Sense was breaking through—

And then a Plank in Reason, broke, / And I dropped down, and down— / And hit a World, at every plunge, / And Finished knowing—then—
[Emily Dickinson, # 280] [**Drawer 3A**]

FRED. *Fred sat in conference with me. He was a Vietnam vet who had written on his post-traumatic stress. In front of me was the very dry, clinical paper he'd crafted. Full of facts, but no personality. I asked him what he thought of it. "Terrible," he replied. "Why?" I asked. "I'm not in it," he said. "I can't. If I relive those episodes, psychiatrist says I will go into a relapse." But he insisted he wanted to continue on that topic. "What shall we do then?" I asked. Ultimately, I proposed he leave the paper as it is, but sandwich in between paragraphs (in italics) scenes from his own war and after-war experiences which illustrated the clinical facts. But that as soon as he was unable to continue with any of those* *personal stories, to stop right where he was. Even if it was in the middle of a sentence or a word. "Just put three dots," I said. " Let the reader fill in the rest." He tried it. A paper full of broken-off vignettes. He read it aloud in class. The students, overwhelmed, were in tears. Three years later he returned to visit me. Told me they were using that technique as therapy for other PTSD's.* [**Drawer 3B**]

WITCHES BURNED—INDIA. *Between 400 and 500 women in a small region of India— Bihar—have been burned to death as witches. Fewer than half the people in this region are even literate.* [**Drawer 4**]

12. The Phone Call

In the near darkness, the flashing red light on the phone was the first thing I noticed.

I recalled that I'd seen it flashing before leaving my office but, in a hurry to get to class, had ignored it. Now, tired from teaching my students, who seemed especially apathetic that morning, I should've just ignored it again until I was more in the mood. Silkie had missed class. I was depressed she hadn't shown because she was one of the reasons I looked forward to starting my Mondays, Wednesdays, Fridays. Besides, it was a cold and rainy morning, and the class met in a building across campus, so that by the time I returned to my office, not only was my jacket damp but my fingers were a little numb, which was the reason I couldn't turn on the light before spilling my books and papers all over the desk. Cold and depressed as I was, I considered putting off listening to my phone messages.

I sat there, in the dark, and closed my eyes. When I opened them, there was the persistent blinking red light. I reached for the receiver, punched in my voice-mail code, and heard, "You have one new message. To listen to your message, press 1." I did. Nothing but silence.

Then, in a thin, quavering voice, which I thought I recognized, a young woman was saying,

> *"I'm sorry. Silkie won't be . . . in class today. She's . . . dead. Her daughter . . . her daughter needs to be fed. I'm . . . I'm sorry."*

With the final "I'm sorry," the voice trailed off, the receiver perhaps held outward. There followed some fumbling and then clicking sounds, and then nothing.

I wonder now, as I think back upon that moment, why it was I did not feel immediately the great horror and shock that should have followed from such a call, and I can only protest that it was because the voice was immediately familiar to me—that of Silkie herself. The quality, and that poignant reluctance to speak which somehow always cut into me. Besides, authentic reports of death about students do not take so strange a form as this did.

I replayed the message. Was there some key word I'd missed to belie its dreadful report?

> *"I'm sorry. Silkie won't be . . . in class today. She's . . . dead. Her daughter . . . her daughter needs to be fed. I'm . . . I'm sorry."*

I'd heard it correctly.

But surely that was her, Silkie--she herself. That somewhat

hesitant, more-comfortable-not-having-to-speak voice. Some very bad joke here. But why would she joke this way?

And what was this "daughter needs to be fed" business?

I played it back a third time.

I froze. The unmistakable word "dead" had by now eaten all the way through me.

I sat immobile, still holding the receiver—indeed, unable to move for several minutes. The image that so often came to me in such nightmarish moments struck again—opening a strange door and tumbling down a dark stairway into an even darker cellar. As I sat there, though, immobile, in that chair, in that cellar, struggling to process the apparent tragedy, I knew instinctively that whatever awful truth was inherent in the call, it was not just *about Silkie*, but, in some way, *about me*. Because surely it was Silkie's own voice. And so if I followed it to its source, I would not find her corpse but rather her hand reaching out to me . . . taking me some place—somewhere I'd never been before.

Now, today, when I recall the confusion in my brain, the entangled threads of thought, at that moment, I realize it was because I was processing *three distinct messages*. One, the literal meaning of the twenty-one words and five short sentences. Two, the apparent contradiction of that meaning because the voice was Silkie's. Three, the unspoken "This, Stephen, is for you. Listen." Strangely, in some way, it was the third one, the least tangible one—perhaps because it was born of the other two—that was strongest.

I released my hand, which had locked over the receiver, and, taking a deep breath, leaned back in my chair.

What is happening here?

I should get up, do something.

What?

Think it through. Take hold of what I do know for sure. Concrete facts.

She was not in class. Need to follow up then on the call. Find a phone number. Call the family.

What family? What phone? She doesn't have them.

Of course, yes. I would do something like that. Immediately. It wasn't just any student. But what? How to get truth clear here! How?

Not knowing how to act, how to find out, I just sat there.

I could not produce a clear thought about how to do the reasonable things.

The form the message took was all wrong . . . whatever the nightmarish nature of its purported meaning.

I simply could not get up from my chair. Frozen as much in time as in space—if not in the usual sense of fear or even paralysis.

It was some other form of petrification—like finding yourself in a new dimension and not knowing what to do in it. Opening a door to an unexpected, never-experienced dimension. Only this time, I sensed, the *opening*—the "cellar door"—*had been . . . was for me alone.*

It was nine or ten minutes before I began to respond in the rational manner such a grim call demanded. When I did, it was to retrace my steps. For sure, yes, the message light had been on even before I'd gone to class. And because this was the only message, it had to have come very early—perhaps even in the middle of the night.

I played it back, thinking it was still possible I hadn't heard some quintessential phrase which would have unmasked the real truth of this almost cabalistic configuration of words. "Dead," though, remained the key one, no matter what the "daughter needs to be fed" suggested.

> *"I'm sorry. Silkie won't be . . . in class today. She's . . .
> dead. Her daughter . . . her daughter needs to be fed.
> I'm . . . I'm sorry."*

I had only the voice itself on which to pin my hopes. That thin, quavering voice. Yes, for sure, that was hers, Silkie herself. But then how could it have been? So *maybe not. My God, if not!* She said she was living with "a friend." Another young woman? A teenage girl? But if it was not her, not Silkie on the phone, then . . . was it true?

These speculations turned desperate and themselves were entangled into and then strangled by the horror of the audible signals that defined the entire ghoulish phenomenon. "*She's . . . dead.*" Jesus . . . God! Silkie dead?

Yes . . . yes . . . not in class that morning. I was always

very aware when she was there and when she wasn't, and the truth was she had missed only one class that term.

This call, though, reported that Silkie, one of the most unusual students I'd ever taught, and whom I'd taken a very special interest in, was . . . dead?

Still . . . the thing about feeding her daughter . . .

It made no sense. If this were she herself, Silkie, why would she joke like this? It was not her nature. A friend perhaps calling about the tragic result of some lover's argument that turned violent? Did Silkie have that sort of boyfriend? Or any at all? The father of Maheza? Maybe he was some guy who'd taken off . . . someone she hadn't chosen well. My students' papers often alluded to such things. Their dysfunctional pasts. Their abusive parents. Their junkhead brother.

But Silkie? Then again, she was mentally ill. Would this have anything to do with it? Her daughter needed feeding? Why couldn't the person calling feed her? And why did that fact matter above everything else if she were dead? Who was this person if not she herself? If her friend . . . or a relative . . . she could certainly do the feeding herself.

Still, I sat there—incomplete, broken thoughts flooding my mind, crowding out rational response.

I got up. Stood staring out at the gray sky, the barren trees, its branches now still, now quivering in the wind. Students were half walking, half running to get out of the cold. A scene now empty of meaning.

It had to be a hoax.

That direction—the possibility of a hoax—unfortunately, entailed even more unlikely motives fueled by malicious intent. And such a possibility didn't mean there wasn't still *some serious event behind it all*—a certainty that pushed away a more refined analysis of possibilities I'd embarked on. Why would anyone think to call me at such a time? In the early hours of the morning. So calmly stated. Why would *attendance at a class* carry such weight in the face of death? Why did the caller not identify herself? Once, four years earlier, one of my students had died of a sudden illness, but I was notified by the department office which had received a phone call from the family of the victim. That was how such things worked. Not like this.

I acted. Finally. Checked the computerized class list for a phone number. But what had that gotten me the very first time—when I'd first admitted her to my class? No phone number. No real permanent address.

I called telephone information for the name "Marian Sanders" and was told there was no such listing. How about "Silkie Sanders"? No such listing.

I sat there immobilized again. Was she not taking at least one more class? Maybe it was the same day, and if she showed up it was simply a matter of seeing for myself.

I went to the department office and had them check her schedule. Yes, it turned out she was in a class that met that day in the social sciences building, but it didn't start for an hour. An hour during which I knew I couldn't just sit there and wonder.

I returned to my office and sat. Reverse the film and erase the message. The nightmarish call goes away.

Was Silkie . . . *really dead?*

But as I sat there, that odd sensation I'd felt earlier—in the first seconds after the call—returned. That the import of this strange event was not just in what had *the previous day or night possibly happened to Silkie*, but in what was *at this moment happening . . . to me.* And maybe in this same way to her as well. If she was still alive.

An hour later, I went to her next scheduled class.

She was not there.

I panicked. Began walking the hallways of that building. Past classrooms, some of the doors open with the teacher's lecturing audible and then not, abstract paintings on white walls, bulletin boards next to offices. Everything in order. Back around. Again.

Finding in motion what's lost in space . . .

I found myself saying that over and over. From "The Glass Menagerie"? So if I just keep walking and not stopping to think . . .

And suddenly. . . there she was. Coming alone toward me, the way a girl who is always alone in body and spirit looks—eyes cast down at first, then up at me, but in some realm way beyond both of us, and evidently tired to the point of being haggard.

Again her hair was carelessly half over her face, and complementing it was a cheap-looking, wrinkled wrap-around skirt hanging open enough to reveal her left leg. Maybe it was the mixing of that image with the other images of death that were plaguing me—those attendant to a brief foray into the unnatural, a world not dictated by mores—that caused me to be drawn to her sexually for the first time.

That startling response, one I had not felt for her till now, quickly gave way, though, to the wonderful relief of knowing she was indeed all right. So much relief that I had to press my arms rigidly against my sides to keep from hugging her. Especially because there was nothing about her to suggest the panic I'd been experiencing.

She stopped, not saying anything—her eyes betraying the surprise of seeing me in that other building. Then, "Oh, you. What are you doing here?"

"You missed class."

"Yes, I'm sorry, I had this . . . "

"The phone call. What was that?"

She eyed me with a kind of confusion, a fixed gaze—askance and upward. "Which one?"

"The one that . . . I got a message on my phone about you. That you . . ."

She waited for me to finish, clearly perplexed at my question, my being there, the panic or at least exhaustion that must have still been manifest in my whole manner.

"I'm sorry, you don't know what I mean?"

She shook her head. "No."

"I thought it was you. Your voice. Wasn't that you? Calling me."

She shook her head.

"I guess not, then. You're okay?"

She nodded.

I waited for a possible explanation, but it didn't come.

"Listen," I said, "someone called . . . I thought it was you . . . called and said you were . . ."

I stopped. Maybe it was remembering her mental condition, which I'd never quite understood. Whatever . . . I stopped. Just stood there. She in turn was looking back at me with that fixed gaze—askance and upward. One of perplexity, yes, but only partly so—because there was in it, also, as on other occasions, a quiet admonishment I didn't grasp.

I was still shaking. The phone call's third, unspoken *"This, Stephen, is for you"* message was only stronger now.

"I guess it's not that important. I'll see you in class . . . when? . . . Friday."

I left. Took a few steps down the hallway, then turned. Gazed back at her. She had stopped and was looking back at me as well.

"It's okay," I said. "Don't worry about it." I went back to my office. Sat. Unable to mark papers. To read. To think clearly about anything.

I went to the window and gazed out as I had done earlier. This time, though, there was comfort in it. I was alone. The only one in the universe gazing out at these very special gleaming black branches. These hurrying students at this particular moment in time.

And . . . she was fine. Nothing wrong. If it was a hoax, she was okay. If it was something to do with her sickness, she was still okay. It was all over. Whether it was the one possibility or the other—hoax or sickness--wasn't the crucial issue. The being okay or not being okay was the issue, and therefore my discovering she was, indeed, okay should have ended it.

But it didn't. Something else had happened. To me myself. Something much beyond the particulars of this call. And I suspected whatever had happened to me had happened to her too. Did she know? No—she appeared very confused about my searching for her. At least . . . at first. So what was that . . . that kind of admonishment in her eyes when I questioned her? Was she really unaware? Of course. Why should she have pretended?

I sat at my desk in a catatonic state through my office hours and past lunch, hoping Silkie, having thought more about it, would come in and explain. Or offer anything that might be helpful in clearing up the mystery. She didn't.

DEBORAH. *Conferencing with me about her research paper, Deborah told me she could not decide whether to do it on (1) the demise of the industrial complex, (2) language, or (3) computers. So much for "limiting your topic"— staple advice for first-year writing students doing research papers.*

As she conversed with me, it struck me she was unusually intelligent. That there was something in her subconscious connecting the three huge topics. That it would be a very original paper. "Do all three," I said. She looked at me incredulously. Always been told to limit her topic to what she could focus on. "You'll limit it. You've got something going on in your mind. I don't know where you'd be going with it, but I suspect something very interesting will emerge."

Indeed, her final paper was not only very well-researched and profound, but very entertaining. One of the key metaphors was a cat's litter box. Toward the end, she quoted Derrick Jensen's A Language Older Than Words: *"There is a language older by far and much deeper than words. It is a language of bodies, of body on body, wind on snow, rain on trees, wave on stone. It is a language of dream, gesture, symbol, memory. We have forgotten this language. We don't even remember it exists."* [**Drawer 3B**]

13. Mick and Rafael

The archangels, nuns, and priests failed me miserably when I was a kid. Counselors, psychologists, and psychiatrists failed me later—in college, graduate school, and marriage. I had friends, certainly, among my teaching colleagues, but none that I felt comfortable opening up to about matters such as that of the phone call. Because they always had answers without understanding the questions.

The question I needed understood late the afternoon of the phone call was, *What happened to me? Why did I feel the phone call was as much about me as Silkie?*

Only nature and art come close to understanding a question without the need to ask it. In desperation, then, I aimed my car outside of the city and along the river, listening to a CD of Marian Anderson singing old folk songs. So ethereal a voice. So infinitely blue the evening sky.

Even nature and art failed me this time, though. The long drive afforded me too much time to think and to become increasingly bewildered, even alarmed, by the degree to which the call was affecting me even after I'd discovered Silkie was not dead. *What happened to me?* became *What did the call mean?* A "mean" that included me as much as Silkie.

I turned the car back toward home.

In the course of my life I've met only a handful of people who would not, if I were to recount to them the incident of the phone call, and then ask why I was obsessed with the feeling the call had been as much about me as about Silkie, provide a World One answer. In my case, that handful was composed, not of fellow faculty, but of ex-students.

Rafael and Mick were two of them. When I needed to be who I really was, I called on one or the other. They were both still undergraduates, though no longer in my classes.

Mick was the older of the two—just three years younger me. I phoned him, let it ring a long time. Gave up.

On this day, I needed to talk to someone.

I tried Rafael. Rafael was much younger than Mick. Only twenty-two. International Studies with an eye to going to medical school and working in Congo or Uganda someday. He'd led a full life already. Had biked down the coast, through Mexico and into Guatemala. Lived in someone's garage that he fixed up so he didn't have to pay any rent. Worked his way through college. Had no TV or computer or car. Played the violin—but mostly for himself and his friends. His papers in the two classes I taught him had a sardonic complexity that was a joy to get entangled in. He was a reader. He wasn't really a "seeker" in the spiritual sense but wanted his life in some way to address the big questions. He'd attached himself to me by visiting my office frequently, and we'd gotten into long discussions about philosophy and education.

"We're playing down by the campus near the bookstore. On the corner near the east end of the quad—bunch of us—told 'em I'd join them. Want to come?"

"When?"

"I'm leaving right now. Takes me twenty minutes."

"Maybe. Sounds interesting. I might come later."

"Do."

My get-togethers with Rafael were mostly one-on-one over bread and tea, so I wasn't sure whether I'd go or not.

Maybe I'd just bike.

Too late I discovered I was in hyper-perception mode. The effect of the call—a subconscious numbness—had transformed itself into a too-conscious awareness. Of everything. In each thing I beheld was some clue I should have been picking up. The fine rain, the stores, salons, cafes, parked cars, alleys, empty lots, No Parking signs, the street-cleaner with his power blower, the man on the motorcycle with the cigarette hanging out of his mouth, a distant siren. Some clue . . . to what? The phone call?

Lines from a Sylvia Plath poem I'd taught—"Black Rook in Rainy Weather"—came back to me: Something about "not . . . expect a miracle" but just "some back talk" from the "mute sky." Whatever my eyes attempted to fasten on failed me—like fireflies I would take hold of only to discover that in doing so I extinguished the light. The continual dancing away of some insight I thought was there, but wasn't, began to wear me down.

Still, the bike ride—up and down the darkening back streets, the wind on my face, the cold of my hands on the handle bars, the lights and human activity around me—was preferable to a quiet nature drive which permitted a too sickly dwelling on the phone call.

I headed to where Rafael said he and his friends would be playing. It was almost an hour since I'd called. Four guys and a woman—two violins, a flute, a guitar, and some African drums—were working feverishly on some piece I half recognized as a Paul Simon composition. All were dressed in white shirts, with sloppily strung ties and dark jeans to give the effect of tuxedos and chamber music. The flutist even had on some sort of top hat.

I parked my bike in the rack on the corner and sat myself on the curb—close enough so Rafael could see me—and nodded a greeting. Fortunately, the rain had stopped.

Only the woman on the one violin and the man with the guitar appeared to have professional skills, but the music was lively and they'd drawn a small crowd.

It was for the joy of playing only because there was no open music case out front.

I was glad I'd come. Content to sit there and listen.

Later the guitarist, a delicate-looking young man, played a solo—a quiet piece I recognized as coming from Bizet's *Carmen*. Listening to him would have made the whole evening worth it.

Rafael, skinny with rather long hair, looking absurd in his too-small suit coat, came over.

"Hungry?" he asked. "We're headed to my place to make some soup. Bread already rising.

It made me feel young biking behind them down the back streets. Rafael's "place" was more than a mile beyond the campus where there were houses built in the 1930s when the land was rural. Rafael, as I said, lived in a converted garage behind a large farmhouse that was itself rented out to a bunch of college students.

There were no chairs—just cushions against the wall.

Except for the shower and toilet, enclosed in the back corner, it was all one room.

The one woman in the group didn't look much older than the guys—small, delicate features—but she had an air of being older, more mature—maybe thirty-one or thirty-two. Dark hair, shoulder-length, and dark eyelashes. She smiled with a glow as though she were genuinely happy. Enjoyed other people. Finding out who they were. When she took off her makeshift tuxedo blazer and undid her tie, I saw that her white shirt was really just a cotton sweater. In that and the jeans, she looked a few years younger, and I wondered if sex wasn't more of what I needed than talk.

She and Rafael worked together over a very old sink and an adjoining table—both apparently brought over from someone else's kitchen. She was cutting a lot of vegetables and dropping them into a large kettle. He was shaping and preparing bread that had already risen.

The three other guys from the band all knew each other and had a lot to talk about. All of them probably students—Rafael's age. They attempted small talk with me, to be polite, but I didn't encourage it. Leaned my head back to let them know I was comfortable just resting, remaining silent.

At one point, Rafael bent over and whispered to me, "Sorry." He must have sensed I needed to talk, and this wasn't the scene for it.

The next day, Saturday, I called Mick again. We arranged to meet at two at the Willow Café.

With nothing else to do, I set out early.

The Willow was crowded: a mess of college students and middle-aged yuppies in jeans and parkas with laptops and steaming coffee concoctions. I chose a table in the back and ordered Red Zinger tea.

To my left at one table was an older man in a well-pressed blue dress shirt and dark tie, and with close-cropped hair, and at another a student with a ponytail which fluffed out like a reddish honeycomb. He was staring at the screen on his laptop. To my right, a young, round-faced man was apparently being counseled because he kept repeating as though he felt guilty, "I haven't yet accepted Jesus in my heart. I've been reading the passages . . ." Whomever he was talking to had his back to me, so I couldn't make out what he was saying. I could hear only one side of the conversation. "What you told me to read . . . Paul . . . and I think it's going to happen but I'm not sure."

Two tables away were three women, one—much older than the others—with very kind eyes. She was a nun known all over the city for her charity work with prisoners. I'd met her once years before, but she wouldn't remember me.

It hit me I was once again *searching for some clue*. In these people around me. What? Some opening perhaps.

A very quiet slippage from the world I was in and into . . . what? The same world but different. More of the Plath poem came to me: something about "a certain light" leaping "incandescent" from a chair.

"Incandescent" . . . understanding. A different perception. I put my head down on the table, ignoring my tea.

Mick, a high school dropout in his late forties, with no professional background, just now starting to pick up college courses at night, showed up wearing a long untucked work shirt and jeans. He leaned forward, his long reddish beard actually touching the table, and shoved a paper across to me.

I'd met him in a freshman comp course I was teaching

four years earlier. "What is this?" I'd asked myself. At least six-five, a just-out-of-the-woods rawness, long beard, and eyes that peered at you with a queer mix of mad and gentle. A cross between a nineteenth-century Mormon preacher and John Muir.

"For your first assignment," I explained to the class, "write a narrative of some significant day in your life. Confine it to a day or less and just one place so you can focus on the details of that one event or moment. Three or four pages."

What did this strange-looking guy named Mick bring in? Something called "For the Almighty's Consideration." Twenty-one pages. Divided into the chapters or "periods" of his life: "hippy," "hell-raiser," "musician," "dockworker," "draft-dodger," "carpenter," "hobo," and "lover" (of too many women who gave up on him). The whole of it started with, "When I was fifteen years old I woke up one morning and walked out of my home carrying an army-surplus duffel bag crammed with clothes and a battered briefcase." A narrative, yes, but more poetry than prose. Walt Whitman compassion and humility. Allen Ginsberg cynicism and rage.

My mouth fell open when I read it. I called him in. Told him if he insisted on staying in the class instead of testing out of it, he could devise his own damn assignments and I'd read them for him. No, Mick replied, he'd go along with the syllabus and maybe go off a little on his own now and then, if that was okay.

He took another writing class with me later and two

literature classes, and I was reading everything he was writing, learning how to write from him. We became friends and began exchanging each other's stories to critique.

"Drank once with Vonnegut," he told me once with pride and a smile. Told me too that on occasion he had serious bouts of depression.

Now here he was, pushing a paper across the table to me. "Take a look at this," he said. "I made the mistake of signing up for a class on . . . 'Personal Communication,' it's called . . . as part of the general requirements. Couldn't get into anything else that fit my work schedule. Found out too late this imbecilic prof's into some kind of scientific way to assess pedagogical success in his class by dividing the learning into 'discrete measurable bits of knowledge.'"

He gave me a wry "Can you believe it?" look.

There was beer on his breath. Not much, but some. Enough that I would be careful what direction I drove his mood.

"I made up this to help him," he said. "What do you think?"

It looked like a typical bureaucratic form except typed on a typewriter, not formally printed. The heading said, "Assessment Form."

"It's a way for all teachers to keep track of how many 'Pellets of Knowledge' they have 'deposited' into students' heads for that week. I gave them a couple examples of a 'pellet of knowledge'—so they know what's legitimate to count.

I read his examples: "James Baldwin was a homosexual,"

and "*Comma* without one of the 'm's' becomes *coma*." Below that was a blank line, indicating the "Average number of pellets deposited per student" and "Average 'half-life' of each pellet."

"I thought he might like this as a model for easier grading."

"You're not really going to give it to him," I said, smiling—knowing he might. "He's not going to appreciate your sense of humor."

"I don't appreciate his moronic sense of education," he grumbled back.

"Do you have to take him?"

"We're already well into the term."

"Wait till you've got your grade."

"If I'm going to be graded this way I don't want to see it."

He was one of those who when he spoke you listened . . . because he cut out the dead words, and the ones he left in always had a sardonic edge.

I looked around the room, beginning to sense that what I needed to vent required beer, not tea. Some loosening of my brain cells. Problem was Mick had been a heavy drinker when he was younger. A dockworker in Oakland. A Bohemian somewhere in the Midwest. Educated by and in life. The consequence of which was he didn't think too much of it. Life.

Now the only time he drank was with me. And that was rare.

Probably I was the only one who regarded his twenty-five or so wild years worthy of envy. I was his way of remembering and taking pride in how it had been. I was his way of bringing his two very different lives together.

He was my way of connecting to a world I'd wished I'd been more a part of. Besides, he was almost a genius. His deftness with the language, his biting cynicism, his attention to the details of everything around him. When I recommended him to a colleague for his class, the colleague was pissed with me. "The guy's fuckin brilliant! What do you expect me to teach him?" The truth was Mick wrote better than most of the faculty in the university.

Once a month we met somewhere. For coffee. Or one beer each.

I picked up his "Pellets of Knowledge" form.

"It's a matter of control for us teachers," I said, smiling. "Knowledge is too messy. We can't get hold of it. This way we've got something to feel safe about for grading purposes. The way it is. But, yes, moronic."

He was silent. There was something on his mind too. An elusive something. And this paper—this "Pellets of Knowledge"—he'd shoved across from me was part of it.

I was starting to feel guilty about why I'd called. He had worse problems than I did. I wondered why he'd felt the need to have a beer or two before coming. Problems at home?

"Anyway—other than this one—how's it going? The other classes. Still sticking with anthro?"

He shrugged. "Yeah, but I prefer the urban kind. Big cities. Not the Trobriand Islanders, Samoa and Margaret Mead."

I smiled. "I see you more at the other end. Being studied."

It struck me odd that here he was in his forties and he'd done pretty much everything but now had to get out a book and read about it or take notes on it.

"It's not so bad. Except . . ."

"What?"

"What am I going to do with it?"

I glanced over at the young man being counseled—the one who hadn't yet "found Jesus in his heart." His counselor, or the minister, was getting up to leave. "It will happen, you'll see," he said. The young man smiled. "Right . . . I'm sure about that." But he just sat there staring down at the table after the minister guy left.

"Gotta pee," I told Mick.

When I came back, I came out with it. "Listen. Reason I called was I got this strange . . . almost ghoulish . . . phone call yesterday morning. About one of my students."

I recounted the whole thing.

"I still think . . . it was her . . . herself . . . who called."

"She didn't show any sign that . . . anything was wrong?"

"No. Besides . . . there was something else about it all. I . . . jumped at it. Lost it. The whole experience. Like it was something momentous for *me*. *My* life. I didn't react like I would have . . . at least I don't think . . . if it had been any other student."

He looked at me like he didn't follow.

I shrugged. "She's got a mental illness. She told me about

it. Still . . . even with that . . . it was something else. I freaked out—not only for the hour before I discovered she was all right, but ever since. Till now."

We sat in silence for a minute, then he got up to order another cup of coffee. "How about you?" he asked.

"No." Under the table my hand was shaking. I was afraid I'd spill a second cup. He was right next to me and the beer odor was more evident now.

"You okay?" I asked. I'd learned never to allude directly to his drinking.

He gave me an emphatic nod. I read it as a warning.

Then again maybe I was being too sensitive. I'd asked him to come. He'd usually been the one to encourage these get-togethers.

"You brought some of your writing?" I asked. "You've been promising. The one about your growing up in Florida."

He pulled out a handful of pages folded in half lengthwise from his shirt-jacket pocket.

"You carry your stories around like that?"

He ignored my question and set the wad in front of me.

"Can I read some of it now?" I was still needing some closure on the telephone message—the reason I'd called on Mick—but I could work into it.

"That's why I brought it. Wonder if you think I can submit it to the university literary magazine. It's set back in the old South I grew up in. Seffner, Florida. My grandma didn't want me having anything to do with blacks. Especially this one old guy I liked because he'd nod to me when I'd pass. Something about his way of being told me he knew a lot about things far away in time and place. To her, though, he was just another 'Darky'—a whole different sort of creature. She used to drag out how she said it--the 'ar' part--a spooky, hushed way."

He left to get the coffee.

Alone now, I sensed the broken pieces in my mind could be made to form a mosaic—an image. The "pellets," the "messiness" of knowledge, the phone call. Yes—all just a matter of images.

I began reading his story.

It wasn't long—-five pages—so when he returned he was silent, and I kept reading.

"These parts," I said, and began to read out loud.

> *. . . but my grandmother gave me a sharp rap on the head. "He's a Darky . . . Why would he want to talk to you? He's not like us . . . and doesn't want to be."*
>
> *I was crushed . . . because I hadn't had a chance to talk to the Darky . . . hadn't been allowed to bridge the gap of age and race and place and time. I wanted to tell the old man about my capture of a beautiful black and orange grasshopper, which I killed in a gas can and grieved about for weeks. But he was a Darky—not one of us.*

"And the end.

> *It occurred to me that everything dies. My grandmother,*

my mother, myself. The Old Darky would die. The sun, the sand, the very air would certainly someday die. And angels would wait and watch, and waft away on wondrous wings the detritus of death. I fed them to my fear, one quivering morsel at a time, as I passed each silent sentinel. . . . I fed them till I was full of fearlessness.

"You have fun with words. But they come out beautiful. Better than anything I can do. Submit it for sure." I slid the pages back across to him.

"No suggestions?"

"I could read it more carefully, but I doubt I'll come up with anything to make it better."

I put my head down. For almost a minute, it seemed.

"The call?" he asked.

"Call?"

"Phone call. The girl being dead."

"Yeah."

"What are you going to do?"

I thought about it. "Your story there. The last scene . . . you—a little kid—passing in front of those vultures on the fence posts—what did you say? . . . 'Black-beaked . . . silent . . . motionless . . . wings drooping' . . . whatever. The way the scene affected you. And all you were doing was passing by. And your regrets about not being able to talk with the 'Darky'—as your grandmother called him. Because your grandmother warned you not to. You were a kid. But you knew there was some special . . . truth in those fence-post vultures, and the Darky. Something your grandmother didn't have to give you. Think about that. All those years of schooling, of learning formally, even of working and training and whatever, and that scene is what you go to. But what did you learn from it? Nothing you could describe, anyway." I stopped.

He waited for me to continue.

"The girl in the phone call—Silkie. Like the Darky in your story. You sense that's where you should be going. That there's something there for you to listen to. Some different truth."

"That's why there's art."

"Yeah. Art. But I mean even beyond that. You know the movie *Ordinary People*? Heard it won an Academy Award or two, so I picked it up at the video store. It was okay. Not great. Anyway, there was this scene in it . . . lodged in my brain. The father character played by Donald Sutherland is jogging along on the sidewalk in a city park with a friend from his office—some sort of investment house. His friend is doing all the talking—prattling on about potential stock deals or something, but all the while Sutherland's character is becoming increasingly disoriented. His son's been having psychiatric problems and his wife is very insensitive to him—the kid—and all the tension in the house and his disillusionment with his wife . . . is really eating away at him. That and something even more existential that the scene itself makes . . . stark—the triviality of his friend's concerns about stocks, good deals on them.

"Suddenly he stumbles . . . but instead of righting himself he *goes with it*. Like he *intended* to stumble . . . or rather that he has to . . . because he runs off the sidewalk madly, in panic, and falls into the leaves on the ground and begins burying his hands . . . his whole self . . . into them. Like he's had a seizure.

"The scene got me. I was with him. Needing to do that. Just jump off the sidewalk and dig myself into something more tangible. Something that is out there somewhere and I've been ignoring it. Knowing even so that you can't be doing that. That in this world it's safer to stay on the sidewalk where you know what's what. Solid. Certain. Not messy. Uncertain. Like what your grandmother said. Stay away from the Darky. *'Why would he want to talk to you?'*"

Mick was gripping his coffee cup in both hands and was staring at the steam coming up.

"So . . . what's this to do with the phone call?"

"The point is . . . with that phone call . . . the way I responded . . . that's what I was doing . . . jumping off the sidewalk."

"What I've been trying to do is get *on* the sidewalk. Not off it. I've been off it all my life. Look at the mess I made of it."

"But it's an honest mess," I retorted. "It's not like that form there you made up. Certain knowledge. Safer. But not real. Not true. Not how it is. Just safer."

"There's a balance."

"I guess. But the sidewalk isn't it. Yeah, it's solid there. If

I stay there I know what's what . . . know where I'm going. The world I live in every day. Rules, boundaries, schedules. When my classes begin and end. 'Your papers are due Friday, class. Make sure you revise them—use your handbook.' I add the points to determine grades by . . . whatever . . . the syllabus . . . list scores by the last four digits of Social Security numbers. You know—professional standards . . . ethics . . . expectations. My relationship with my students is defined that way. Right? I call it World One."

"Your world's more than that. Teaching. You actually educate people. There is such a thing as real knowledge. Even real wisdom."

"To a point. The department objectives lay out the core of it. Rhetoric. Communication. Argument. Thesis to be supported. 'Affirmative Action does not work because blah blah . . .' or 'Pot should be legalized because blah blah.' To get them to think about something besides pot and abortion and capital punishment, you give them an article from the newspaper to discuss, respond to. They learn the process. What the thesis is. How to develop it. Research it. Who's your audience? Organize the paragraphs. For most students that's as far as it gets."

"What else are they supposed to get?"

"Trouble is if you ask them, 'Why?' they answer only how they're supposed to. They say, 'Because critical thinking is essential.' Right? Objective reasoning. Why? To write a coherent essay. So what if you do? They don't answer that it's to find Truth. Because it can't. Wasn't it the philosopher Arendt who said something about the eternal—and I read that as eternal Truth--can only be glimpsed outside our normal human activities?"

"If there is such a thing as Truth. Besides, what has this to do with your sidewalk story and the phone call?"

"And your story."

"Yes."

"Because most of us don't even get beyond having a thesis sentence. A good argument. Never wrestle with why you bother to argue passionately. And even those who do—philosophers, great religious leaders, whatever—even they should not always be listening to their sacred books, their rhetorical arguments, their grandmothers' strictures to stay on the sidewalk and away from the Darky. Now and then . . . *sometimes* . . . they should be jumping off the sidewalk, or sitting down with the Darky. Checking out the other world. World Two. The messy one. The world, the way that doesn't seem to make sense. Because you can't pin it down, and when you do—pin it down too much—there's no truth left in it that you haven't squeezed out. Because . . . it's messy."

"The only way we can keep going is not to let the messiness get to you," Mick said.

"But that's why professors come up with things like your . . . 'pellets of knowledge' to sort it out. And 'Limit your thesis.' Because if you don't confine it, it's cancerous. Gets everywhere. It's best, safer to stay on the sidewalk where you can see what's what, not what else it may be. Otherwise, you bury yourself in art or nature or drink or drugs and hope for a mystical experience. Otherwise, like in your story, you're walking alone at night, a frightened kid, with vultures all around you, and you discover you learned a whole lot more from them and from the Darky your grandmother told you to stay away from."

Mick looked away.

"I think," I said, my voice quavering, " . . . I think . . . Silkie's my Darky."

He turned back to me. "Do yourself a favor. Do something that's not in your nature. Even if it means . . . ethics be damned." He shook his head and grinned to let me know he might not be serious.

"Which ones?"

"Which ethics?"

"Yeah."

"The ones that have to do with this Silkie."

I could see now he was serious.

"She started to ask me something the other day— something like 'You are . . . are you . . . ?' But she never finished it. 'You are . . . who?' How would I have answered? 'Let's see: My name is Stephen Mollgaard. I live in the safe world. Each morning, get out of bed, shower, dress, retrieve the newspaper from my porch, read the news and sports while I eat my Grapenuts with fruit. Go to my office. Prepare my classes. Go home. Eat. Watch the news on TV. Mark papers.

Go to bed. Oh, and I try to read at least one new book every week—a new novel by Coetzee, or a poetic rendering of the universe by a physicist. Says to me I'm educated, that I have an inquiring mind. I'm concerned by how I see myself being seen by others. That's me, Silkie. World One."

"So what?" Mick looked impatient with me. Almost angry. Was the beer kicking in? "Look at me. Most of my life . . . drunk in one form or another—and I don't mean just liquor drunk. I didn't even care where the sidewalk was. And here I'm going on forty-nine trying to figure out how to help my wife pay the bills. Sometimes you need to know how to get back to the sidewalk." He shook his head.

"Anyway—that phone call freaked me out."

Mick went to the restroom, and I found myself feeling ashamed I'd directed the conversation as I had. So intense. So selfish. He didn't need that in his life. He and his wife and their adopted kids were barely making it.

When he returned, I was determined to say nothing. Let him direct the conversation.

"You know, someday you're going to crack," he said. He wasn't smiling.

Then he fished around in his jacket and pulled out a worn pocket spiral notebook, flipped through the pages full of scrawled notes till he came to a blank one, tore it out, and set it on the table. Then he searched another pocket and pulled out a broken pencil.

I wondered if he had just remembered something he was

supposed to do. But instead of writing any words he drew a dark line from the top of the page to the bottom. His hand was shaking noticeably.

"Say you have a wall. Between your World One and World Two. On the sidewalk. Off the sidewalk. This is that wall . . . a stone wall. And you're over here on this side of it. The left side. That 'World One' you're talking about." He put a number "1" there. "You're walking along the sidewalk over here. Or jogging. And you know there's more to the world than your side, but you don't know how to get to the other side . . . of the wall." He put a number "2" on the right side of the line. "There's no opening, as you say. Tree branches grabbing at your jacket and hair as you run. Snagging you. Forcing you to keep thinking about that other world on the other side. If you suddenly smash into it . . . into the wall . . . or clamber over it, you risk losing everything. Risk injuring yourself or not being able to get back. But it doesn't matter. Then one day you stumble onto what appears to be an opening. At least you think it is." He turned the pencil the other way and erased through the line at one point before going on. "Maybe you quietly stop. Take a closer look. Carefully try it out—the apparent opening. Silent like a . . . like a wildlife photographer. Or maybe you're afraid it'll go away and you find yourself rushing to push . . . plunge . . . through. Not even hesitating. Instinctive. Fueled by years of frustration. Push through the tangled branches . . . dig your hands into the leaves on the other side. I'm thinking that's what you did with that phone call. Sensing maybe it was an opening. But if it wasn't you *were going to make it one*."

He drew a bold arrow from the left side through the erased opening to the other side, then gave me the paper.

I shrugged. "Maybe. Maybe that's what I was doing."

"You're still doing it."

I stared at the paper a long while.

Mick's line on a paper—representing a stone wall separating the two worlds—was okay. There, in the café, it was all we had. I prefer, though, the image of a shoreline. The Pacific Coast. The one world—One—is the land. Solid. Safe. Certain. The other—Two—is the ocean. Liquid. Treacherous. Mysterious. But the demarcation is elusive, illusive. It is not straight nor is it the same from moment to moment—what with tides and waves overflowing the banks, eroding the beaches, cutting away at the rocks.

Or maybe the abstract is a better way to think of this. If the side of the wall I live on day to day is Life, then maybe the other side is Death. Or it's where everything wrong on this side is made right. Or everything incomprehensible—the eagle in the box, and Norma Jean, and those three Mexican girls—is made comprehensible.

The going back and forth from one side to the other, then—that's best left to the angels and God. Or to the mystics. Or the ones taking the visionary drugs.

As for me, tuck my existential rage into the bottom drawer

of my file cabinet. On this side of the wall.

Best to not even get too close to it—that wall. Rumor is if you go there, you might be afforded a very brief moment—a glimpse—of *how it really is*. But it will cost you dearly. Your sanity . . . your safety. The artists, the writers tell you what will happen. If you get too close to the wall. If you try to find an opening through it, or get over it. The citizens of Ursula LeGuin's "city of happiness" found themselves walking "into the darkness"; Kate Chopin's Edna found herself walking into the ocean and drowning.

That day of the phone call, I was still on the left side of the wall . . . just as Mick said . . . but I'd come to be somehow walking along it, looking for an opening, and, not finding one, frantically pushing up against it. Not just that morning but for the year or so preceding it. Well before Silkie had shown up that first morning soaking wet from the rain and demanding I take notice of her, I'd begun to allow the richest part of my consciousness to feed on moments that had no apparent value to me . . . to my life. . . my career, my tangible achievements. I was carrying around inside me an intensity I didn't know what to do with but which was, very gradually but very surely, pushing me closer and closer to that wall, bidding me smash through it, or scale over it, to discover what might be on the other side.

14. Ombeni

My emotional collapse was precipitous.

Whoever had made that call that morning, whatever its meaning, the effect on me was crushing. So much so I wondered if I wasn't just guilty of some uncharacteristic histrionics. But then, didn't that mean the effect on me should have been fleeting?

It hadn't been. It stayed. With time, cut deeper and deeper into me.

My teaching deteriorated a little more each day. In her class because I couldn't seem to direct my teaching to anyone except Silkie. In my other classes because I discovered I couldn't muster together the energy, the perspicacity necessary to ensure the dynamics that made teaching satisfying.

For about an hour that day, death had been on the line. Not classes, not points for a paper, but death. The death of someone whom I was very fond of. Death not by way of a car accident or an illness, but an eerie call in my office from God knew where. Institutionally prescribed behavior aside, conditioned professional response had no role here. I no longer had any rules to guide me.

Not only had my relationship with *her* become transformed, but so had my relationship with *everything*.

Several weeks before the incident of the phone call about Silkie, I received in the mail a letter from an organization called Children Forgotten. On the envelope was the picture of a little girl—dark-skinned, black hair in disarray, half starved, dirty, eyes vacant. I'd received many letters from other overseas charities, Save the Children and Christian Children's Fund among them. I'd sent checks but never sponsored a child. I hadn't even opened one for months. On some impulse, however, perhaps growing out of my own loneliness and the recent encounter with my children, I opened this one. "Sponsor a needy child for just $35 a month. . . ."

I sent in my name.

Two weeks later, I received a whole packet of information about her—a little girl named Ombeni who lived in Tanzania—introducing me to her family and history. A picture of her was attached in the corner. On separate pages were the description of the sponsorship and the formal agreement to be signed, the latter stating that I would send $35 each month, which would be used for her needs. Her biography revealed the appalling conditions in which she had been living—a victim of extreme poverty. With parents for a few years. Then father essentially abandoned family. Mother had to work far away. On the streets for several months. Taken in by grandmother who was very sick. Lived on the streets a few more months. Sexually abused age eight. Back with grandmother. But starving. Her situation reported to the agency by someone.

The letter added that I could also, if I wished, especially at Christmas, send her additional money or a gift.

Admitting to myself that there was a selfish element in my decision—that this sponsorship was to a great extent to make myself feel noble—I reasoned that, even so, I would be the instrument of a change for the better in a child's life.

I sent in my check, and a few weeks later the agency wrote back thanking me for my sponsorship, telling me what my $35 each month would be used for: food, clothes, a school uniform. Folded into that letter was a smaller page with a note handwritten in what I assumed was Kiswahili, translated, and addressed to me, from Ombeni herself. "Thank you for the money you are sending to help me. I am going to school now." The message seemed stiff and designed to keep me sending my dollars, but I sent back a brief reply even so: "I'm glad you are doing better," and "Let me know if you need something else."

Perhaps, because I was frustrated by the bureaucratic exchange, or because this unsatisfactory reply had come just a couple weeks after *the phone call*, the next time I sent my check I included a short note to her—a question I hoped would help me to know her a little better. I would keep it simple but design it to be open-ended. "Tell me, Ombeni, a little more about who you are. What has made you happy in life? What has made you sad?" I expected the agency would translate for her.

They did, and her short response was included in their next update of her situation: "Thank you for asking. It makes me happy to play with my friend Sero. And when she leaves it makes me sad."

Jesus! I needed more. Much more. I was feeling very, very lost without Paul and Corrine in my daily life. And this was all I was to get in the way of more meaningful correspondence with Ombeni?

A little over a month later, however, I was surprised to see a letter in my box that had a return address ending in "Dar es Salaam, TANZANIA." It was in care of some "Owolo," not the agency, and was handwritten in printed letters. The envelope, which opened at the long end, was of the blue-and-red-edged sort that used to mean air mail. I withdrew two pages of lined yellow paper written in pencil in the same hand as the address on the envelope, except that it was in Kiswahili. It began:

> *Jina langu ni Ombeni, ninamdogo wangu mmoja, ninampenda sana. Ninapenda pia kusoma lakini siwezi kusoma sana kwasababu mama mdogo wangu ni mdogo . . . .*

I assumed, at first, this too had gone through the agency, even if it was odd it hadn't been attached to their own translated version in one of their envelopes. As I pulled out the handwritten letter, though, it was clear the agency had nothing to do with it, and maybe knew nothing about it.

There was no explanation, yet the letter had gotten to me. Problem was I couldn't read it.

I resolved to find someone who knew Kiswahili—a student from Tanzania or Kenya very likely–and get it translated.

What had Ombeni written me?

It was now several weeks since the Silkie phone call incident, but my overtures to Ombeni were, I sensed, just more of that exploration of the *wall* between the two worlds. The Silkie whom I'd see sitting in the back of my classroom three times a week and the Ombeni whom I'd never seen, became joined in my mind. Not as being in any way the same person, but rather two persons who held out for me the same promise—of finding an opening in that wall.

I was reaching out to both of them.

Ombeni because she was more of that World Two on the other side of the wall than I was. Silkie because that grisly phone call had put her—for one hour—in the land of the dead, another name for World Two.

One morning very early, at the university, before anyone was around, I had a seizure—just outside the restroom down the hall from my office. I pushed tightly up against the door frame—my shoulder and head—starting slowly and sliding up till I could squeeze out of me whatever it was that needed squeezing out.

MARI. Mari, *a very unattractive, pathetic-looking young woman—who always wrote about calculus and science, and who despised religion, and who always walked alone on the sidewalk, but who, years later, asked me for a recommendation letter—recently won a prestigious scholarship. I was very pleased.* [**Drawer 3B**]

ADAM CZERNIAKOW. *Words to Outlive Us by Michal Grynberg is the record of Holocaust Jews—twenty-nine of their writings found scribbled in attics and basements of the Warsaw Ghetto. Themes, sometimes of "immense moral complexity," thread through the scraps and diaries. The "terminally eloquent language" tells of a hope that was mostly shattered by SS officers, one of whom casually shot a little boy trying to pull a carrot from the Aryan side through a hole in the fence. Adam Czerniakow, who, in hopes of getting immunity for some of the Jews, did the bidding of the Nazis, eventually in despair killed himself. He was one of the twenty-nine. [October, 2002]*[**Drawer 4**]

15. About the Seizures

The seizures came—one after another.

From out of the black spot.

The interns who diagnosed my epilepsy some forty years earlier showed it to me on the CAT-scan. The black spot on my temporal lobe. Where'd that come from? Maybe that concussion I got at age seven. Running around the barn ran smack into Jimmy Meinhoff. I heard the crack and felt it at the same sickening moment. That must have been it. I mean, an eagle in a box can't put a black spot in your brain. Nor could the rape and murder of those three Mexican girls. Anyway, because of that collision, over the years the doctors kept plastering over the black spot. Drugging me with every kind of anticonvulsant. Smothering the potential explosions. The pills worked—I never, physically, hurt myself or anyone else.

The black spot was still there, though. The volcano was always churning. And with that ghoulish *Silkie is dead* phone call, it began acting up in a very big way.

My regularly scheduled appointment with my neurologist was coming soon. Problem was, my regular doctor—Dr.

Williams—had just retired and I was to meet with his replacement—a Dr. Kadzinsky—whom he'd introduced me to the previous session. Kadzinsky was much younger—early thirties at the most—and therefore not as experienced. More significantly, what he knew of my epilepsy would be confined to the clinical records. He knew nothing of the peculiar nature of some of my seizures, which I'd alluded to, though somewhat misleadingly, in my sessions with Dr. Williams. And, of course, he was not aware of the recent traumatic event in my life—the phone call.

It would be a routine session. "Auras"—those elusive sensations signaling oncoming seizures—only two or three and not very strong. Seizures—none at all. He would schedule a lab test to be sure I was in "the acceptable range" of convulsion control that I could drive a car. He would update my prescription.

But what if I were straight with him? What if said, "Doc, you and I need to jump off the sidewalk and talk about what's been happening to me." How would it go? Dialogue for a tragicomedy.

[SCENE: Patient's room. Large photos of mountains and streams on the wall. An exam table. A counter with a sink. A small table with health magazines of various sorts. The doctor is seated on a stool. I am seated in a chair.]

"How have you been doing since your last visit with Dr. Williams?"

"Fine."

"So you're not having any seizures?" [The doctor is very self-assured. Records show I haven't been an alarming case.]

"No."

"Auras?" [Very professional. Reading my chart and taking notes. Medical style.]

[Shrugging] "Sometimes, but nothing that leads to anything."

"Like?"

"To unconsciousness. Nothing I worry about."

"How bad are they?"

"Not bad."

"Mind if I go over your history? Have they changed over the years? It says here the epilepsy began when you were . . . what, seven or eight? You've been on several kinds of seizure medicine. Were some of them not working well?"

"No, just side effects."

Dilantin made me dizzy. Depakote made me constipated. But Keppra's just right. [Sounding like Goldilocks and the Three Bears.]

"So, even though you still have auras, you're satisfied. I mean you're not having seizures?"

"Not . . . not the kind you mean. Some of it's good for me."

"Good? Auras or seizures? How can they be good? In what way?" [Starting to wonder about my psychiatric as well as my neurological state.]

"Letting a little air out of a balloon that gets too . . . full."

"A release. Interesting metaphor."

"*Yeah, a release. Have you heard of that sort of thing before? From other patients?*"

"*Well . . . not really. Depends on the power of it. Maybe that's not the right word. Maybe you need to explain a little. Describe an example. A time when you had . . . that sort of seizure . . . release.*"

[Taking a deep breath]"*There's actually something mystical about it. I don't mean really mystical . . . but the feeling of it. Just in walking. A constant sort of thing. Pressing on me. An awareness, maddeningly elusive, of a new way of understanding. The sense that everything around me—the other day it was a picture in* National Geographic *of a young girl carrying water . . . and once it was a young man playing his violin in the second row of the orchestra . . . and a very long time ago when I was a kid . . . this eagle that was caged in a small box . . . that they were a doorway, an opening. To some other side. If not a doorway, then a wall. Just slip between these two stones—through this narrow crevice—and it will all appear different. You will understand in some . . . new way.*"

"*I'm not really getting what . . .*"

"*It's become a need with me. Not an obsession because that implies some cognitive element. No, it's a force within me. What I mean is my seizures have come—to me—to be more than just neurons misfiring. Actually, somewhat . . . mystical. My very first seizure, for example. I wonder about it. The way and timing of it. I was bothered by this eagle stuck in a box. I don't want to go into the whole story because it just might*" *bring on another seizure right here and now and that wouldn't be good, would it? But as I say . . . I wonder about it. Why it had been at that very moment if the convulsion were not being driven as much by spirit as by brain? You follow?"*

"Not really."

"The other day I was telling a friend I feel like I'm running along a sidewalk and I have this urge to just break away from it—fall on the ground. To stumble off into the leaves, to dig into the earth. Seizure-like. You know? Or perhaps to just lie there. Fact is, Doc, sticking to the sidewalk is getting tougher and tougher for me. I'll be biking to school . . . or walking down the hallway to class or . . . or riding on the bus home . . . and discover my brain's so ragged . . . so jagged. . . that along the way it's continually snagging itself on something I can't get past—the vacant stare on the face of an overweight female student alone outside a classroom, a news article on a mass slaughter in Congo, a dead possum in the road. What I'm saying is, a lot of times I find myself wanting to ride some sort of a seizure, and in fact a couple times I let myself fall against the bookcase in my office and half-collapse—the closest I can come to plunging into leaves. Or to banging up against that wall."

"What wall?"

"Sorry. The one you have to get through or over or under . . . to get to the other side."

"What's all this to do with seizures?"

"It's the letting go part of it. The release. From how everything is."

"I don't get you. Aren't these different issues? Emotional needs, not . . ."

"Let me explain. A long time ago I read in the newspaper about this young autistic girl. She said she felt like she had a volcano in her. I used to wonder if she let it explode now and then. And if it came out of a black spot like the one in my brain. The black spot you can see on my brain scan. I like that image, don't you?—A volcano. Me needing to explode. The 'needing' is key here. That's why sometimes it's another picture. Did you ever see that play The Miracle Worker? *Helen Keller pawing the air wildly to finally reach the world that the word 'WATER' promised? Well, sometimes it's me flailing wildly—trying to reach out to something. It's just that I can't find it, reach it, or . . . it's not really there to reach.*

"I'm sure you never thought of it like this. My affliction, I mean. To you there's only the black spot. No volcano. No flailing. So you prescribe medicines. For the black spot it works. I won't drive my car into a guardrail or go catapulting down a mall escalator before the eyes of horrified shoppers. You're covered by law.

"What you don't know, though, Doc, is that the Dilantin, the Keppra, didn't . . . doesn't deal with the volcano inside me which began fulminating three or four years ago. When I feel the aura telling me they're coming—the eruptions—I don't smother them the way I used to. The way you want me to. Because with the medicine I could do that. Keep control because most of the neurological stuff was in check. But now

I know for sure—I'M LETTING THEM HAPPEN."

"Letting them happen? Why, for God's sake?" [He's close to exasperated.]

"I don't know why. The volcano, the flailing—those images didn't come to me right away. Just a frustration—a need to flail out, push out, explode. . . . I don't know. Sometimes a human being has to just let go, Doc. Has to do that. Push out against everything at one moment, no matter how embarrassing, how humiliating. Has to stumble off the road he's running on and plunge into a pile of leaves and dig his hands into the dryness of them on top, the wet and muck of them below, and the very earth itself and just lie there. Like trying to get hold of the entire universe at one moment. To understand it. To demand answers.

"There was a time, Doc, that drink—beer or more—was the relief I sought. The problem was always it took too long, and I'd get sick first.

"Besides, with drinking I'd only shrink inward. Not explode outward. Did you ever think about it? Seizures make that sort of violence respectable. If you swing out with your fists into a wall or smash a vase or throw a chair across a room, it isn't acceptable. If you bounce off a wall and gag, it is. A seizure is a phenomenon you have to accept. 'The man is down, frothing and choking. Help him.' If you pounce on someone else to kill, people condemn you. If you pounce on yourself to kill, people feel sorry for you. In my seizures, it looks like I'm pouncing on myself, but, in actuality, I'm pouncing on

the universe. For a few seconds I have a stranglehold. And no one else knows. To others, I'm just in need of a pillow . . . a pill. A doctor. A psychiatrist.

"And now it's worse. A lot worse. You see, I got this phone call. From this Silkie. So that black spot is a lot bigger. The volcano fulminating inside it a lot more powerful. And the medicine isn't going to do it. It'll smother it for a while, but in the end it ain't gonna work. There's only one thing that's driving my neurons right now. And it's not a chemical. It's a person.

"So here I am, Dr. Kadzinsky. Do you understand? Understand who I've become? I'm some other kind of creature, Doc. I'm living in World One, just like you. But I've set up camp along the wall . . . and I'm waiting. I already know something of what's on the other side. It's a very different world. On my wall there's a picture of this little girl named Omayra—stuck in lava—going to be dead in an hour or so . . . it's her world.

"What I'm saying is, certainty itself has become a big lie to me."

But it wasn't like that, of course. My session with Dr. Kadzinsky the next day was routine. "No worrisome auras, Doc, and certainly no seizures. Nothing to be concerned about. Medicine is working fine."

I would deal with the seizures myself. The kind he didn't know about.

"The effect of the ghoulish phone call on me will pass," I told myself. "Emotions being what they are, even as the immediate shock passed within a day, so too the aura of mysticism about the call will dissipate before too many days."

It didn't.

Not only that, it had taken on a new form—heavier, sicker—a troubling in mind and spirit that seemed to build with time.

It was clear to me why. Death. Silkie had been, for me, for that hour, dead.

"Well, just give it some more time," I continued to assure myself, "and all but the memory of that day will have vanished. The drama of a phone call was just that—the drama of a movie scene. It will wear off."

I fixed my attention on my classes.

Halfway through a writing class a few days later, however, I began fumbling through the text to find a page I'd already marked. My hands began trembling, fear of a possible seizure occluded my thoughts altogether, and—unable to finish the class—I apologized, gave them their homework assignment, went straight to my office, and shut the door.

It didn't satisfy—my way of explaining to myself the effect of the call on me—the *quantitative* difference a la "It's just that I'm a bit too drawn to her (*more* than to others)." No, it was a *qualitative* difference. My emotional needs or attractions were not the whole story here.

The truth came at me with the force of a revelation—late one night as I lay in bed, not able to sleep.

Silkie had actually become *another person* to me.

The same . . . but not. Perhaps it was because when I questioned her in the hallway–"The phone call. What was that?"—her look of bewilderment left me no place to go. She made no attempt to offer possible explanations as to the why and who of the call. Indeed, didn't seem to know anything about it. Only answered "No" and then seemed to watch me. Assessing how I was responding. *As though the crux of the entire event was my dealing with it.* Not helping me with the rational basis of the occurrence, she left me alone with a nagging question: Was it because she really didn't know or because she chose not to reveal what she knew? And—the follow-up question to either possibility—why would that be?

My relationship with her was no longer teacher and student. But then what was it? Father-daughter? Brother-sister? Son-mother? Living-dead? Or . . . lovers? No, none of these. Or, rather, maybe all of them so jumbled in my brain, I couldn't sort them out. I couldn't see her as I'd seen her before.

Something had changed. What?

Everything about her took on new proportions. Her eyes, which had before always looked at me with so much expectation, curiosity, now emanated a . . . what? . . . sensitivity . . . sensibility . . . that seemed to swallow me. The mystique of her mental illness, perhaps? Worse, I was judging myself through her eyes. My own sense of self was on trial. I suddenly couldn't afford to be a failure to her—not just as a teacher, but as a human being. *What I thought of myself hinged on how she responded to me. What she thought of me.*

Silkie had, with the phone call, gotten sucked as an entire entity out of the world that was neat and institutional—World One— and dropped into the one that was chaotic and existential—World Two. And there I'd have to deal with her. On the other side of the wall.

JOURNAL (Nov. 20)
Events like this define their own universe.
From its very start to its end, that lone meeting in the hallway has implanted itself in my psyche as somehow fated. THIS WAS SUPPOSED TO HAPPEN. MY LIFE IS NOW LINKED TO HERS. THIS IS INSANE!

CHRIS. *Chris—who paid his way through college by working in a bakery, spent several weeks volunteering in a clinic in Uganda, and ultimately studied medicine in Israel—once wrote a paper in my class entitled "Yelling at Bulldozers" that began like this:*

"Trees are pretty, especially old, big ones. Isn't that a nice comment? Sadly, that is as far as I'm going to take it. No epic descriptions, dripping

with gratuitous adjectives, trying to do justice to soaring boughs or to leaves gently whispering the song of life. No, if you like to look at them, they are rather nice. If you get sick of looking at them, depending on your personality, you can either cut them down or climb an especially big one and jump out. That will be that. If you start cutting them down they will lose any beauty that they might have had, and you will start to picture them as boards with leaves on them. If you jump out of a big one, you will have other things to worry about."

Years later, he sent me thoughtful emails from Uganda. One started like this:

"One of my people died, I don't feel comfortable calling her my patient. I am not yet a doctor. It is the most scarily profound thing that ever happened to me. I am not at all a doctor, but for this girl I was the only hint from the outside world that ever took an interest and offered anything. She had sickle-cell anemia—the type one is born with. She was five years old, but looked like she was at the most two. I was taken to the small house (mud, grass thatch, no windows), where she was lying in the corner. A tiny child, breathing so laboredly. . . ." **[Drawer 3B]**

16. A Break

"Wanta take my place?" he asked me. He was in his early forties and out of breath from just running a punt all the way back.

Damned right I did.

It was a pickup touch football game. I didn't know any of them by name, but I'd recognized two of the young men playing as graduate students and another two as colleagues in some other university department. They seemed to be part of a large gathering because on the far side of the field behind them were fifteen or so men and women standing around barbecue pits in one of the park's covered, raised picnic areas. I'd just been driving by, saw them in the distance, and decided to stand and watch along the sidelines.

Close enough they'd see I wanted to play.

On the other hand, I was older than the guy dropping out by ten years probably and the rest of them by twenty. So when I ran onto the field I could see their doubtful looks.

I'd show them. Yeh, my legs would give out when I ran too hard, but I was reasonably trim and agile and could cut and catch passes with no problem—especially if they didn't think I was worth blocking.

We were on defense now, though.

"Who's your man?" I called to the guy I'd replaced.

"Zone. Anyone on that side," he called back.

The other team's quarterback, who looked a lot like Terry Bradshaw, tried my side on the first play but underestimated me, and I batted the ball away when the receiver broke in front of me. Next play he broke again, suckered me in, then took off down the field, but the quarterback overshot him. Good thing. He was five yards past me.

When they finally scored, it wasn't around my side, so I counted myself lucky. So far, holding my own.

Their kickoff squiggled toward me. I picked it up and stood there. Waited till one of them was about to touch me, then nimbly stepped aside like a bullfighter and managed to scamper ten yards down the field. (It really was a scamper, not trudge.)

That surprised them, and they gave me one of those patronizing "The old guy's still got some steam in him" looks.

That was pretty much it, though. I caught a very short pass later, but most of the rest of the game I just kept up.

Even so, it felt good. I figured I could brag to somebody somewhere about how I cut around that guy and ate up the ten yards.

And, for an hour I forgot all about Silkie.

17. Obsession

She would come in to see me. I was sure. The nature of the phone call was such that it was reasonable to expect she would. To discuss the possible explanations. Was there not a great mystery to this terrible phone call? One that needed solving? Even if she knew no more about the call than her silence in the hallway that morning indicated, she would certainly have the same curiosity about it that I did. Surely she had some knowledge that would point in some direction. To some likely person. And if that person were she herself, she would come to me, confess it.

But she didn't. Almost three weeks had passed since the call. During that time she missed one class. When she was there, her attention wavered.

My curiosity about it all became a frustration, and even a sense of betrayal. I had for one hour panicked. About her. Surely she owed me some gratitude.

Not only was there her perplexing silence about the phone call, but the bewildering effect it had on me.

In some desperation, I did a class exercise that I'd often

employed as a device for encouraging discussion: each
student was to choose from the readings that term a sentence
or short passage that he or she found especially memorable
or powerful or meaningful. I knew she would not volunteer
so I deliberately started at one end and went around the
room one student after another. Passages were read from
Dickinson, Hughes, Douglass, Twain. When it was Silkie's
turn, she did not even look up at me. She'd already opened
her book to the page and was staring down at it.

How tired she looked.

She flicked back the hair hanging over her left eye, and
began reading. It was from the final lines of Whitman's "Out
of the Cradle Endlessly Rocking"—a much longer passage
than the others had chosen:

A word then, (for I will conquer it,)
The word final, superior to all,
Subtle, sent up—what is it?—I listen;
Are you whispering it, and have been all the time,
you seawaves?
Is that it from your liquid rims and wet sands?

Whereto answering, the Sea,
Delaying not, hurrying not,
Whisper'd me through the night, and very plainly
before daybreak,
Lisp'd to me the low and delicious word death,
And again death, death, death,

Hissing melodious, neither like the bird nor like my
arous'd child's heart,
But edging near as privately for me rustling at my feet,
Creeping thence steadily up to my ears and laving me
softly all over,
Death, death, death, death, death.

She was reading it dispassionately, almost robotically, but in so doing was dredging up a poignancy in the lines that might have been swept away in a more affected passionate rendering—much like the actor who holds back and thereby conveys the truth of his words more powerfully. But now, with the next few lines, she seemed to draw some force from within her, her voice turned sonorous, and she was soaring somewhere.

Which I do not forget,
But fuse the song of my dusky demon and brother,
That he sang to me in the moonlight on Paumanok's
gray beach,
With the thousand responsive songs at random,
My own songs awaked from that hour,
And with them the key, the word up from the waves,
The word of the sweetest song of all songs,
That strong and delicious word which, creeping to
my feet,
(Or like some old crone rocking the cradle, swathed in
sweet garments, bending aside,)

The sea whisper'd me.

When she was finished she continued staring down at the book, then looked up at me for just a second (asking for approval, or forgiveness?), and then down again. With alarm, I discovered what surely I already knew: I'd become obsessed with her! Love? If so, why was the sweetness so poisoned with dread. Not only because I was a teacher and she my student, nor even because I was more than twice her age. But because there was a desperation in me that had already been destroying me, and somehow she was now part of it. I needed someone with whom to share my intense world. Someone to help me bang up against that wall. And with that phone call, *someone* had offered Silkie. The dread was for both of us.

Months later I would wonder if it hadn't been the other way around—not that I was pulling her into my world, but that she was pulling me into hers. Perhaps that we were already both in the same world (World Two?) and stumbled onto each other.

I needed her. But what would I do with her?

18. Letting Loose

"How's the thing with the phone call—that Silkie—going?" Mick asked.

I shook my head. "I think it hit me from the wrong angle or something."

"Isn't it possible you're overreacting? That in the most normal sense, you've 'fallen' for her?"

We were sharing a Panini for lunch in a booth at Spirits, a student burgers-and-beer hangout near the campus a couple days after my neurologist appointment.

"I suppose. Maybe. But what does *fallen* mean here? If it is, it surely isn't the 'fallen' I've known before this."

"Don't you need something like that about now in your life?"

"You mean a sort of antidote to my dreary single, middle-aged existence?" I smiled. "But even if I did need it, the age disparity is a problem, no? Not to mention the student-teacher relationship no-no."

Mick shrugged. "Do we always have to live by the rules?"

"I feel like God's having a laugh at my expense," I said.

"That damned phone call. Did a real number on me. In her class, in all my classes, even beyond the school. A very strange young woman comes into my life—not only out of the rain, but out of everything I've known. Did I tell you how she showed up the very first day? Pouring outside. She was soaking wet. Two classes late. Missed the whole first week. Then looks at me like I'm the one."

"What one?"

"Like . . . she's waiting for me to do something . . . has this look in her eyes . . . and when I don't . . . weeks later, a phone call. The whole thing a little too eerie . . . supernatural. A guy a little too bent that way. A guy looking for an opening. God steps in, but the path he shows the guy leads to a greater oppression. And, you know what? This is the crazy thing. Silkie. When she comes in, I feel very comfortable. A peace, a comfort that seems to be what I've been reaching for. Yet, I can't touch it. Touch her. I don't know—maybe you're right. I need it.

You have too many scruples. You fall for a girl and your conscience sees it as an indiscretion. Even just to have the emotions. You're an English teacher so you make it into a stage drama, a short story—a midlife crisis in literary dress. An interesting girl, a mysterious woman, takes some peculiar interest in you . . . with eyes you can't fathom . . . and you don't . . . go for it."

I had to smile. "Go for it?"

He got up to go. "I'm going to be late for class."

"Go. I'll get it this time." I walked over to the bar to pay, but stopped, called back to him. "I decided something this morning."

"What?"

"I'll let you know. But if I'm going to get through this term I have to do something."

What I'd decided to do was to take hold of it. But not the way Mick implied. I had an actual plan. Get cold with her. Be very critical of one of her papers. In my comments on it. Slap it on her desk without even looking at her—indifferently. To let her know I wasn't pleased with her performance. She'd get the point. That it meant disappointment with her in a lot of ways. Her schoolwork—for sure, she'd been less focused. But more than that. We had a mystery to deal with, damn it, and she wasn't doing her part.

I did it. Wrote at the end of her paper: "You don't seem to be putting in enough time revising anymore. Jamming your sentences together again without taking the time to punctuate so it gets read right." When I returned it to her at the end of class, I set it in front of her without making any eye contact.

At first, it seemed to work. At the very least it jolted her. I felt immediately satisfied. In effect, I'd spoken both to her and to me. Put my relationship with her back where it should have been—teacher to student. I'd found her fascinating, interesting, and, yes, it felt very comfortable sitting with her. But that was all. The phone call would not have its way.

I'd underestimated the mysterious (mystical?) power the phone call had over me, though. It reasserted its dominance with a decisive strike.

When the class was over I stood answering questions, keeping my attention steadfastly on the students in front of my desk, but found myself weighed down almost immediately, precipitously, by some unfathomable and powerful guilt and confusion accompanied by disturbing images that escaped before I could hold onto to anything about them except that they were in some way connected with my "rage" folder. In the midst of this phenomenon, I was watching Silkie out of the corner of my eye so that I could know both the result of my ploy and the moment when she'd left the room. Convinced she was gone, I looked up and discovered to my dismay she was standing there, in the doorway, her eyes fixed on me. It was more than curiosity, I was sure of that. It was a *wondering* about me. It was that first day I'd met her all over again—me working with students about questions I had no interest in, and she standing, waiting, off to the side. It was her in the hallway the day of the phone call. Some meaning lurking in those eyes that I could not fathom. Only feel.

My eyes caught hers, and the lines of our gaze hooked and hers began to pull at mine. At that same moment, I felt my brain crash and plummet by some cable that yanked the rest of me downward. Confused almost to the degree I'd been disoriented by the phone call, I found myself just standing there, stupidly staring at her.

Did she understand? That moment? The whole damned thing? *What did Silkie understand?*

When she was gone, I found myself following behind her. On the sidewalk outside, I called to her.

"Silkie, wait."

I would confront her directly. Talk to her. About what? Say what to her? Something between what I'd just tried and Mick's "Go for it."

For some reason I didn't care what. Just wanted to sit her down in front of me in my office and see what would happen. What would come of it. Come out of her. Come out of me. I could say something constructive about her last paper. Or just that she hadn't been engaged in her work as she had before the phone call. That would at least move us toward exploring that mystery.

She turned and waited for me.

"I was just wondering how you're doing. Are you all right?" I asked. A good beginning. The sort of question any teacher might ask a student he knew well—why she'd seemed listless, not well, the previous week. And, of course, ostensibly, that's what I'd asked.

But it wasn't.

The real meaning of my question was, "Am *I* all right?" How could she, Silkie, have an answer to whether *I* was all right?

"I'm okay," she said.

I stared at her with what she must have seen as a look of phony concern, not knowing where to go next.

"You want me to walk with you? To your office."

"If you don't mind."

As we walked, I noted she did so with her head forward, with a very measured gait and quiet purposefulness.

"You know, Silkie . . . that phone call of three weeks ago . . . it disconnected a lot of my circuits and when I'd reconnected them nothing ran the same anymore. Even now." The metaphor was intended to lend levity to my rather blunt acknowledgment of the effect she was having on me.

She seemed to laugh, but it was a nervous one.

"What was it again?" she asked. "That phone call. Did you . . . ever really tell me?"

Right! I'd never explained. Did she really not know? I'd forgotten that perhaps, in fact, she didn't. And if she didn't, what good was asking?

"Is now a good time?"

In response, she said nothing—only half turned toward me, her eyes askance, studying me, not embarrassed. As she had that morning in the hallway.

There was an empty bench ahead. We sat down.

"I'm just wondering if maybe . . . since the day of the call . . . you seem not really focused. I want to be sure my response didn't . . . " I stopped, shook my head at my phoniness, idiocy, cowardice. "Listen to me." I looked down as though the weight of what I had to say was too much to put on her, and a voice pushed through from within me with an intensity that startled me. "Listen, you are a very special kind of student." It was the safer thing to say. Even at that moment I knew what I meant was, "a very unusual human being." "I don't know what's happened here, but I . . . "

Her eyes were on me intently, unblinking, waiting to see where I was going.

Where I was going was wherever I needed to go. Mick was partly right. My mistake had been trying too hard to be discrete. I had to let loose if I was to free myself.

"I . . . don't want to be . . . responsible for . . . in any way . . . making you into more than . . . who you are."

What did I mean by that? But it felt right. To say it that way. Still, what the hell *did* I mean by this? How was I in any way "making her into" anything that she would have any clue to? I began grasping for something to render what I'd just said plausible. "I hope you weren't bothered by my overreacting to that phone call. I did . . . didn't I? Haven't I?"

I took a breath and in that moment glimpsed where I was going. I was determined to make her open up to me. I was going to drive to the center of this as the words came to me, and letting whatever sense she wanted to make of it take care of itself. How else could I do it . . . without crossing lines teachers should not cross with students? What, after all, did I mean by "what's happened here"? What indeed had *happened* here?

I became silent—forgetting (because she wasn't answering)

I'd just asked her a question. I had this distinct sense of my disillusionment with everything—what had happened to my marriage, my abortive plans on my last visit to my children, all the way back to the eagle in the box and the three Mexican girls—at this moment pressing down on the back of my head and neck.

I wanted to cry.

She seemed moved, not disturbed, by the passion pushing through my rambling—a passion that a discussion of her school performance did not merit. Her eyes were on me—rigid, thoughtful, but saying nothing. Again with that look of watching me as from a distance. *Surely she knew. Surely I didn't need to explain.*

I continued. "Listen, . . . teachers . . . just like students . . . need to . . . communicate with others. What's inside them. To know someone wants to listen to them, to the ideas they are feeling so passionate about. Groping to understand. You too. You're groping, I think. Especially in the case of people dying or, possibly dying, as with that phone call the other day. We are in a world that can be pretty shitty sometimes to too many people." The "pretty shitty" was to shock her about what I was trying to tell her. "Younger people like you who've had a rough time in life . . . who are groping, we need to listen to sometimes. I . . . need to learn from you too. So I don't want anything . . . to harm that possibility."

Where the hell was I going with this? She could read right through it, I was sure. She knew all this didn't mean what I was so stiffly trying to make it mean. So why didn't it seem to alarm her? She didn't squirm. Right before her eyes I'd acted out a veritable seizure, spilling out my desperation, and . . . she didn't say anything. Perhaps even wanted me to feel comfortable. I don't know. But my spewing out, so incoherently, what I was trying to convey to her—it felt . . . *very all right*. A catharsis. Almost spiritual.

Did she know that?

"Thank you," she said. She lowered her eyes and was silent for close to a minute. Then, without lifting her eyes, she said again, "Thank you." She was trembling.

I nodded, and she left.

Alone again, I discovered a sense of exhilaration in me— purged of all that had been weighing me down. I'd failed to draw her out, yet, it didn't matter because I had drawn something way down in me . . . out.

And I remembered some line from some Toni Morrison novel about there being a kind of loneliness that "rocks" and "roams" because it is "alive on its own."

RACCOONS. *Last night, driving home, I suddenly saw two animals in the lights of the car in front of me—one squirming as though hit, the other frantically scurrying to the other side of the road. Two baby raccoons. The car that hit one of them went on. The raccoon kept* *spinning, half-dragging itself. Then stopped fighting. (Silkie's "gazelle . . . giving himself over"?) I pulled to the curb, put on my hazard lights, and walked back. By then a man in the house across the street had come out with a shovel. The one raccoon was no longer moving at all. The other was gone. "Babies," he said, and slowly scooted the dead raccoon across the road to the curb with his shovel. "The ones that have been bothering me," he muttered. Then, having gotten it across, he remarked, "Poor thing."* [**Drawer 4**]

19. The Train Dream

It was perhaps that night or the next that I had a dream.

I was walking alone at night. It was cold, and the ground very hard. It seemed there was no light anywhere—no stars, no lit windows. Only one structure whose shape I could separate from the rest of the darkness by virtue of its closeness to me. A small house maybe. I walked toward it and discovered it was some sort of old train station in disrepair. Nobody was there. Decaying wood, broken planks. Along the front of it were apparently abandoned tracks. I walked along them for a while. Suddenly I heard a train coming. For some reason it did not arrive gradually, but at one moment was very close, and another moment still far off, then close again. Only a handful of cars. I backed away to watch it pass. But as it did, it slowed down. Stopped. In front of me. Passenger cars but none of the windows with any light or silhouetted heads inside. A door opened right where I stood, bidding me to enter. Even . . . perhaps . . . commanding me. It was meant for me alone or it would not be on these tracks, stopping at a station no longer in use, nobody getting on or off. I walked up the steps into the car. It was empty. Except—down at the far end of the car on the right so I could barely make her out—Silkie. I didn't know where to sit. If too far away, I was being unfriendly. If too close, I was coming on to her. She was reading a book on her lap. She looked up at me curiously, then back down at the book. She said nothing.

I felt the train starting up again and I grabbed onto the seat to keep from falling. Where was it going? What was I supposed to do? What was she supposed to do? Oddly, I didn't walk toward her, didn't sit down. Just stood there hanging on. It felt okay to do that. Even in that—the standing there, saying nothing— there was something sacred.

I woke up. Knowing how quickly dreams dissipate in our memories, I started to write it down. Not a complete paragraph. Just phrases. So I wouldn't forget.

CELESTE. *She told me she liked Emily Dickinson's poetry. I asked her after class why. She answered me in her journal entry for that week "I always feel very alone. But I realize I'm not alone when I read Dickinson. Because she is alone too—even, I suspect, in death. She reaches out to me by writing me her poem, telling me her story. She is thereby less lonely, and so am I."* **[Drawer 3B]**

20. This Is How It Is

Three days later, unable to sleep, I went out into the night. It was in my head to drive to the downtown area and walk. Not slowly, thoughtfully, but with a lot of kinetic energy. Reinvigorate my survival self and in the process stomp out the sickly self-absorbed self. Too often, I'd chosen to drive alone on back roads listening to music, or walk through the campus reflecting on things I could do nothing about. The campus was where I'd spent too much of my time. It was, after all, an oasis from life. A place of reflection on quiet tree-lined walkways and enlightenment in library stacks. It was an unreal world where *being* had nothing to do with *living*, but only with thinking about it. Even the structures were different. They were grand buildings for all time. When they aged they grew ivy and became richer, like wine. Off the campus were dress shops and groceries and auto parts stores, more functional than aesthetic or durable, and, when they aged, they were left to rot and were ultimately boarded up—because they no longer served any real purpose.

She—Silkie—came from that world. From off the campus.

Being so very reflective herself, she'd crossed over to the more reflective world. I needed to cross over the other way. From the world of libraries, halls of learning, and sickly ruminating to the world of lube shops, convenience stores, tattoo parlors, and frantic existing.

It was in panic that I slipped on my jacket and started for the door. Even in that state of mind, though, I grabbed a yellow tablet and pen. I needed to walk, but I also needed to communicate to someone what was inside me. With the tablet, though, I would be ready. It would be my way of not looking too lost if I ended up sitting alone somewhere. To others I might be writing a letter, a story, a poem, a novel.

I got into my car and drove. Aimlessly. At first along the edge of the campus. Boutiques, bookstores, bike shops, pubs, and fast-food restaurants. It was late, so there was only an occasional student or two. I passed a secondhand clothes store . . . a yogurt shop . . . a falafels and gyros place with outside tables . . . a Chinese take-out . . . a Starbucks.

I parked the car on a quiet street, then began walking—off and beyond the campus—finally cutting down the main cross street and then, at a vigorous pace, continuing for several blocks.

The plan was only half successful. I was exhausted. Enough to sleep, perhaps. But there was still that need to communicate.

On the edge of the campus once again, I came upon Spirits, where I'd had lunch with Mick a few days earlier. I liked its smart brown oak exterior and small golden replica spire because it looked not like a tavern but almost like a little church. A place where students congregated after night classes or a long day's studying. Even on weekdays it was open till midnight to accommodate them.

I would sit down. One beer. Think what to do, whom to talk with.

It being a Wednesday, it wasn't crowded—just a handful of students—mixed male and female—around two tables. But noisy. A TV suspended from the ceiling was blaring out an ESPN commentary on the weekend's upcoming basketball games, another showing a rerun of *Seinfeld*.

I hesitated, decided I would sit down anyway, and chose a table in the corner.

The waitress came over. Latina. Obvious accent. Early twenties. Dark eyebrows. Friendly eyes. Long dark hair—swirled and bound on top of her head. Would have been more attractive hanging down. Some health regulation, probably. She was dressed in jeans and a dark blouse, no uniform. Very campus scene. She was cute. If she would sit down across from me . . . I would tell her all about it. What? But of course she wouldn't, couldn't, and I couldn't either because . . . I was too old for her, she had to work, and . . . it would take too long.

That the thought had even crossed my mind was worth a chuckle.

I ordered a light beer. She brought over a small dish of

salted nuts too. I thanked her.

At the center table the conversation was getting louder and, even with the TVs shouting, I could make out some of it. A heavy-set guy in a dark turtleneck and sport coat was making a case for university athletes being paid. "Jesus, you know how much was the take from that one game? You think we'd even have a girls soccer team. . . ."

"You turn them into professionals and see what you get," a small girl bunched up in an iridescent ski jacket and bent over the table responded as though to herself.

"What? *What* is already the way it *is*, isn't it? It's already big business."

An hour later, I sat staring at the yellow tablet on which I'd begun jotting down broken thoughts—none of them moving me closer to where I needed to go. *Somewhere closer to that other world. World Two.*

When I looked up again the conversation at the nearby table was *Seinfeld*.

"Yeah, on the surface it's just shit they laugh at. The obvious. Pissing in the shower stuff. But you look at who all these people are—that's what *Seinfeld*'s all about."

"What?"

"Schmucks. Losers. George Costanza. The schmuck."

"That's what I'm saying."

I stopped listening.

As I sat there—more than an hour—in Spirits, all was World One: a cacophonous mess of sounds emanating from the sort that wasted a weeknight drinking beer instead of studying . . . the incessant, too amplified, inane sports commentators from the upraised TV . . . the maddening flashing neon Heineken signs reflecting off the glasses stacked behind the bar.

I was unable to fix on any of it . . . or the yellow ruled tablet in front of me with the scribbles and scrawls of broken ideas.

It was the wrong time to be so alone. So alienated from everything and everyone around me.

I needed desperately to tell someone *the thing*.

"Reina!" one of the men called to the waitress.

I thought back to my high school Spanish class. "Reina." With an "e" or an "a"? Meant "princess" or "queen." Except to serve me the two beers and bring over a bowl of peanuts and do the expected "Do you need another?" twice, she'd shown me little attention, directing most of it to the other, younger customers at the two tables in the center of the room—who seemed to be regulars by the way they joked openly with her. Young men.

She blended right in with them in a way I didn't. Maybe she was a student too, just working her way through school. I certainly didn't look the professor in my old pants and sweatshirt. Or maybe I was looking just a little too lost this night.

Still—there was the yellow pad. The one on which I'd been scribbling the broken thoughts. Had she wondered what I was writing? One of those times when she'd come over because my mug was empty, she'd stolen a glance at the pad. "Yes, another one," I'd answered, and for a moment, her eyes still curiously eyeing the pad, I thought she might ask what I was writing. She didn't.

The yellow pad . . . the pen . . . the scattered World Two thoughts in the form of unreadable phrases, indecipherable meanings—something professorial in that. Here on the table in front of me.

No. Probably to her I was just another old guy coming in to ogle young girls in student hangouts. Truth was I'd taken notice of how her blouse tended to slip off her right shoulder—a rounded shimmering in the soft light of the bar. Even that release, so sweet and short . . . or just the prospect of such . . . would have been something [*existential fulfillment in the form of beautiful shimmering shoulder*].

I'd stolen glances at her—that was all—as I sat there at that back table during those two or three hours . . . becoming increasingly aware of my need to talk to someone . . . increasingly alarmed about . . . the pressure inside my head . . . the auras signaling the black spot was acting up . . . the volcano coming. Two beers—no good for guy with epilepsy.

I paid. Left. To keep the volcano from coming. Walked to my office. And sat there, slouched in my chair. Perhaps for twenty or twenty-five minutes I stared at the scribbled notes on the yellow tablet.

The slouching became a slipping—downward until I'd

let myself literally drop to the floor where I lay, curling up fetal-like, letting my mind wander off to some peaceful place. To sleep?

How long did I lie there? I don't know. A kind of meditation that did its work. Told me what to do.

I would write her.

With a yellow pad and a pen, I sat myself up against the back wall near the bookcase. Upright in the desk chair was too artificial, too official.

I put the pen on the paper and began writing feverishly some of the broken thoughts I'd had in Spirits:

> *Dear Silkie,*
>
> *. . . only when you are writing something you don't expect anyone to read, you are sincere. Anne Frank's diary. Stuck it in a drawer. It got out.*
>
> *. . . in my office . . . woke from dozing on the floor, Silkie. Couldn't sleep at home—long*
> *walk and couple beers at Spirits . . . now here*
>
> *. . . urge to write . . . necessity*
>
> *. . . perhaps in morning won't feel this way . . . now do*
>
> *. . . have those people in your life that you say <u>the real things </u>to. When you <u>have</u> to say*
> *them. Even when you're not actually speaking aloud, you're still saying it to them in your   mind. They're the ones you picture doing that with. Things inside your head you have to   s a y.*

In life. The little sad things. The big ontological ones. Questions with answers that   don't come. So you throw them out there. To the one who might listen.

. . . somehow able to make sense of the intensity I exhibited toward you the other day.

. . . didn't initiate this, . . . someone else did.

. . . the phone call—from somebody—saying you were dead.

. . . way I saw you forever changed . . . way I see everything—things bothered me from long ago—got out.

. . . maybe, then, you, the call, excuse for what was already there.

. . . trying to understand this.

. . . but apology further from sincerity—way to pull you close—sincerity tainted. Does acknowledging that make it more sincere?

. . . don't expect response from you

. . . you being one who lived a lot of life—"on the street" and in your mind.

. . . this letter a "pulling back" or a "reaching out"?
. . . too confused to be certain.

My God, what was I writing?

I stared bleary-eyed at the paper. I was stumbling all over myself. I could start all over. Or just edit it. Leave it as it was because in that form it expressed not only my thoughts but my mood, my distracted state of mind. No, throw it out altogether. It was too rambling, too honest, too . . . yes, distracted. I couldn't give her this. Here I was her teacher stressing the power of direct communication. Efficiency of words. What was this mess? No, I couldn't give her this. Maybe a watered-down version of it. A "safer" letter—one centering only on an apology for overreacting to the phone call that day. Tell her there were "walls—necessary walls between teachers and students"—especially when the teacher found the student "appealing in some way," and that on that day I'd "jumped over the wall between the two of us and found myself unable to get back to the other side anymore." That the situation had "fed into a psychological state" in which I was seeking a different kind of relationship. And thus my intensity on the bench with you that day.

I dropped the tablet in front of me. I was exhausted—physically, mentally, and most certainly spiritually. This giving her a letter—I would have to sleep on it.

I'd started with a reawakened purpose and ended with a discouraging disillusionment.

I went home. Slept.

The following morning, before school, I set my incoherent version aside and wrote on my PC a shorter, less rambling, less dangerous version. For the last line I wrote, "Perhaps I shouldn't say this, but you are good for my soul." I thought about it, but then deleted it. Before leaving, I typed it in again.

I slipped the letter inside her journal during my usual biweekly check of entries. As I did so I recalled a phrase from a story by James Baldwin—"all have sounded empty words and lies."

MATTHEW. *Matthew began one of his journal entries: "Once, when I was twelve, I delayed my entire Boy Scout troop, making us all late to an Eagle Scout ceremony, because I became entranced by river otters at an indoor exhibit in Toronto. I sat for four hours watching them swim and dive, dive and swim. Apparently the staff paged me several times over the P.A. I remember hearing the crackle and pop of the speaker, and perhaps a nasal drone, but I never heard my name.*

"Years later I sat for three hours and watched sugar ants making their way towards a puddle of honey on a plywood table. In the sweating July kitchen, with no sound save the buzz of the refrigerator's compressor, I watched them march." **[Drawer 3B]**

SARO-WIWA. *Nigeria exhumed the body of Saro-Wiwa, the activist executed seven years ago for speaking out against the inhumanity of the oil companies. [February, 2002]* **[Drawer 4]**

ALI. *Ali showed up in my Form 1 class in Nigeria the very first day. I'd called the roll, and when the name "Zanna Abello" came up, there was no response for several seconds. Then—"Here!"*

I went on with the names, but when I dismissed class, a student walked over to me hesitantly, quietly.

"When you called my name, sir, someone else answered."

"Pardon?"

"Someone said they were me."

"Why didn't you answer yourself?"

"I'm sorry . . . the way you said it . . . you are an American . . . you didn't pronounce it like English . . . from U.K. . . . so I didn't recognize it."

"Oh. What is your name?"

"Zanna Abello."

"Yes, here it is." I turned to the class. "Hold it! Which of you answered 'Here!' when I called out the name 'Zanna Abello'?" A half minute later, a boy, looking very guilty, slowly walked up the aisle to my desk.

"I did, Sir."

"Are you Zanna?"

"No."

"Then why did you say you were?"

"Forgive me, sir, but I want to go to school.

I thought I could just come. I got on a lorry. I thought I would wait till you said a name and no one answered. I would say I was that boy."

"But you can't just do that. Lie."

"Pardon me, sir, but I scored highest on the test in my village. But the chief sent another boy because he is Christian. I am not."

"You're Muslim?"

He nodded.

"What is your name?"

"Ali __"

I reported the incident to the headmaster, and Ali was paddled by "the Sergeant," as was the rule, for lying.

But I felt sorry for Ali and took him into my house. Tried to get him into some other school.

In the meantime, the department of education scolded me for "rewarding" him for lying and told me I had no right to keep Ali in my house. I said, "It's my house." (Strictly speaking it was a government house, so I was careful about my tone.)

In any case, eventually I found him a school run by a mission some fifty miles away.

Ali had stayed with me three weeks, during which time he listened to my Paul Robeson "Spirituals" record over and over. [**Drawer 3B**]

21. Again—No Reply

"I'm having trouble with my final paper," she said, seating herself across from me in my office.

Her hair was, uncharacteristically, neatly combed and held back by an olive green printed scarf tied in a way that made her look like a Russian peasant girl. Indeed, there was a refreshing bloom of one who'd been working outdoors in a garden. It was a way I'd never seen her before. And it was the first time I said to myself, "She can be . . . beautiful." I'd always until then regarded her attractiveness as coming from her strange way of being, from her habit of restlessly looking side to side, and at other times that steady gazing at me, unblinking, studying me. She had this morning a beaded necklace from which hung a tiny silver seagull. I'd noticed it before hanging from her backpack.

Her head was down. Had my note embarrassed her?

I waited for her to say something about the letter I'd slipped into her journal, but she didn't. I'd been worried about that final line—"Perhaps I shouldn't say this, but you are good for my soul." *How had she taken that?* As coming on to her? Well, wasn't that what I was doing? But not in that way. No, not really, just stating the truth. That her distinctive take on the world was what I needed right now. Distinctive? What did I mean by that? Her mental illness? It meant what it said. Truth was truth. Its own defense.

The letter had been a kind of rope bridge. Inviting her to come across. After all, she'd already thrown to me a rope bridge. With that phone call. If indeed it was *she* who called. But . . . to what purpose?

Still, here she was saying nothing about it. Asking about her final paper only.

I began reading it over. It had to do with Dickinson's poem "I Felt a Funeral in My Brain." In it she argued that Dickinson's "funeral" might have been a mental illness. Even epilepsy.

Still, she was saying nothing about my note. I became more and more disoriented in my replies to her questions. Barely able to concentrate on the sentences I was reading.

Halfway through, I realized I was not able to focus clearly enough to make suggestions and abruptly handed it back to her. "Listen . . . Silkie. Were you all right with my note to you?"

"Yes."

"I was afraid it was . . . too strong."

"No, it was . . . good . . . nice. It's just that it's more than that. It's . . . ineluctable. I just learned that word. In a story I was reading. I'm not sure I'm using it right." She took a deep breath. "Anyway, it's like that. Like what . . . what is . . .

may . . . happen . . . I don't know. I would be scared but . . ."

Abruptly she stopped and rose, smiled, waved good-bye. "I have a job now. They sell beads." She lifted the beads and seagull hanging from her neck for me to see—in case I didn't accept her excuse, I supposed. "I just remembered. I'm late. Really."

"Enough hours?"

"No, not yet. Just when they need me."

"Wait," I said. "I just want to apologize if my letter . . ."

"No, it was okay. But . . . there's more." She shook her head, to tell me she didn't want to talk anymore. She smiled before leaving.

What was this "ineluctable" and "scared" and "there's more"?

> **JEANIE.** *Jeanie wrote an argument paper the thesis of which was we should rid the world of love—parent-child love, husband-wife love, boyfriend-girlfriend love—because it hurt so much. Another student came up to me after class and said, "That poor girl!"* [**Drawer 3B**]

22. A Blinding Snow

It had the effect of a rejection. Her nonresponse to my letter. I'd gone too far. She'd seen my obsession as nothing more than the emotional vulnerability of a middle-aged man who would be advised to return to his proper professional stance with regard to her.

The appalling depression returned that Friday night, and I would fly down to see my children except that the following day an unusually heavy snow fell, and the planes were grounded.

Gazing out from my front window at the glistening white everywhere, I was reminded of my childhood in Ohio trudging off to school with my older brother. There was comfort in the memory. Very early Sunday morning, then, as the sun was just rising, I plunged into the whiteness, cloaking myself in a robe of magical abandonment.

The snow was not only blinding but almost two feet high in places, and with my head down I dragged my feet through it, paying no attention to where I was going, as I found my mind fastening on my train dream of days earlier—on how it had seemed to be for me alone. Trying to hold on to what had seemed to be sacred in it.

But it was to no avail.

With her nonresponse to my letter, the dream had lost its force. And the whiteness I'd enfolded myself into was bitter cold and cutting.

From feeling "chosen" in any way, I'd come to feel foolish. Silly. Dirty.

I found myself slogging through a veritable blizzard. I could not see more than four feet in front of me. Too late, I discovered I was lost. Had gone too far. Everything was dizzyingly white. The road was, to the eye, inseparable from the sidewalks and lawns. The street signs were covered. Except for the nearly buried parked cars, I could not tell even if I was on a street. More alarmingly, in seeking out the snow's power to heal my soul, I'd forgotten its power to freeze my body. I'd not dressed warmly enough. I had a hood but no ski cap to pull down to my eyes, and the icy snow and wind on my face felt like a block of ice pressing against my brain. That icy ache began to build, and I frantically wiped it from my forehead, to shield it and keep it dry, but in doing so I could not see where I was going and, stumbling like a blind drunk, was forced to attend to it only intermittently. Worse yet, I'd apparently strayed too far into a newly developing community up the hill and onto roads winding into construction areas with streets not yet named. There were fewer cars, no traffic lights to get my bearings. I became disoriented.

I panicked. One wrong turn cost me another fifteen minutes in the frigid cold.

When I managed to find my way home, I struggled to remove my clothes and fell into bed. My arms were shaking, my hands trembling. Rolling into a fetal position, I wrapped myself in my blankets, but it did not work, and I wondered if the cold was not so much from the ice and snow as from the realization I had allowed myself to be, yes, the victim of a diabolical joke played not by Silkie, but by God. I had been His buffoon. Needing to find *Meaning*, I'd made an ass of myself. And the crowning glory of this joke was my letter to Silkie which she had rejected.

There was no mythical train, and even if there were and Silkie was on it, she was an unwilling passenger. God was playing with human vulnerability. Human need. Silkie had not so much rejected my letter as demur at what I was doing, wonder about me. She was not partaking of this mystical sense of things that I'd foolishly adopted. There was no *Fate*. No *Meaning* whatsoever to all that had happened. Sacred indeed. The phone call was only that—a phone call. I was any man in some normal stage of human development. Which theorist was it? Ehrlich? Sullivan? Maslow? Which later stage of life was I in? Reevaluation of one's life? Disillusionment? Revisiting one's idealistic youth?

I determined before going to school that morning, before the week was out, to redeem myself with her. To that purpose,

I decided I would do immediately something I had entertained weeks earlier. The next time I saw her I would give her a copy of the short story written by Isabel Allende about the little girl Omayra, whose picture was above my desk and about whom Silkie had questioned me that very first day in my office a year earlier.

I photocopied both the story, from a collection of short stories I had once used as a text, and the final photograph of Omayra —those eyes so accepting of death. I sealed them in a manila envelope.

At the end of class that Friday, I set it before her. "A story I said I'd give you once," I whispered.

That evening I felt good about it. With the gift of that story, I'd slipped quietly back into my proper relationship with her: a teacher who'd taken a special interest in her educational and literary development. And it would remind her of how I had been so thoughtful of her when she'd found herself dropped from the class. It was friendship—that was all. I'd crossed the line, and she, in her own way, had let me know. I got the message.

Still, I needed her reassurance we were back to how we'd been. I waited.

It didn't come. She continued to attend class regularly, but she did not stop by the office to visit.

Until the very last day of the term.

TIJUANA CROSSING WOMEN. *Across the border in Tijuana they swarm around the American cars, flock to us like pigeons around some bread thrown on the ground. Carrying, in their arms, boxes full of cheap soap and candy. Babes on their backs. Women crowded about my car entreating, "Not much. Buy one!?" A man shouted in the right side window that he could fix our car cheaply—smiling as though it didn't matter whether it needed any fixing. The women did not smile. Their faces were without expression. Anguished, desperate.* [**Drawer 4**]

23. The Truth

"May I have one?"

My office, very early in the morning, which is when I do most of my class preparations. I did not see her enter. When I looked up she was nodding with her head to the candy jar on my desk. It was a cheap glass jar, cylindrical, its charm residing entirely in its contents—wrapped chocolate kisses.

A great rush of sweet gratitude overtook me. The despair I'd been feeling in the days following her last visit—the fear that my letter had frightened her away—had been banished in the matter of a few seconds with the four words "May I have one?" Here she was again.

Her scarf seemed to have been tied somewhat carelessly—under rather than over her hair on the left side. I wondered about it because it would have taken but a second to fix it, so her hair would have fallen off neatly to both sides.

I reached into the jar for one of the wrapped chocolates and gave it to her. "Gives me energy, but I tend to eat too many."

She took one—almost snatched it—and then unwrapped

it. And like a little girl, didn't say, "Thank you." Instead, just sat in the chair to the right side of my desk, enjoying the candy and saying nothing.

Something wasn't right about her. Tired perhaps. Or just distracted . . . worried?

"Are you all right?"

She looked up and nodded.

She wasn't going to tell me. That's how she was.

It didn't make her uncomfortable, apparently, to continue to just sit there.

The silence was too long this time, though.

"Shall I just continue with my work?" I asked with a half-smile that winked at the awkwardness of her not announcing why she was there.

She seemed to not hear me, though she was looking right at me.

I bent over my syllabus, too aware of her eyes on me to accomplish anything.

Tempted to once again open up to her inappropriately, I redirected my mind to take hold of something more in tune with her school work.

"Do you remember that paper you wrote last year about Congo . . . how rape was being used as a weapon of war? There was an article in this morning's paper about it. If you can't get a copy I can bring it . . . next term."

Even as I was saying it, I was embarrassed for, once again, drawing upon such intense subjects to share with her.

Especially knowing *it had happened to her.*

I, too, became silent. Wondering where to go next.

She closed her eyes, then slowly dropped her head into her right hand.

I waited. *Was she, perhaps . . . crying?*

"Are you sure you're all right?" I asked again. "I shouldn't have . . . brought that up? I'm sorry."

Still, she said nothing. In fact, did something I hadn't seen her do since the incident of the fractals—literally put her head down on the desk and covered it with both arms for some thirty seconds. Then, very quietly—in what was almost a whisper—

"I was the one who called you."

If she was waiting for me to respond, I was unable. She would, of course, explain. There she was, sitting there.

She didn't.

In truth I felt no need to ask why. To pursue the subject. But she sat there. Perhaps she wanted me to . . . ask. Wanted to talk about it.

"Why?"

She shrugged, shifting uncomfortably in her seat now. "I don't know. Ruth. Maybe it was Ruth." She lifted her head but stared fixedly at her lap. "Is it okay if I don't . . . say anything else? I don't really know. . . . Is that okay? . . . For now?"

I nodded. "Thanks for telling me." Then I added, "I'm sorry."

There it was again. That *"I'm sorry."* Not knowing from

where it came or what it meant. This time there was in it the possibility of a seizure too. Right there. One I needed to have. No, I wouldn't let it go—at that moment—wouldn't even let it build. But it was there. The need.

I reached into the jar of chocolates again. "Here, have another one," I said, smiling. "Wait, no take the whole thing. I tend to eat too many. Give some to Maheza."

I handed her the jar.

"She'll like them," she replied. "The chocolates. Even the jar."

So spontaneous a decision, so insignificant an act—giving her the jar. How could I know that one day the jar would carry not candy but a great cosmic weight?

Before I left for home, I went to my file cabinet and opened the drawer in which I kept copies of some of my students' papers. I hunted through the folders and found Silkie's from the first term I'd taught her composition. In it were all the pages of her journal. Not the original. I'd given it back. Unknown to her, I'd photocopied every page.

Now I drew her folder out, set it on my lap. My hands were shaking as I turned the pages. Her narrative. I read it again—the "Ruth" paper. "*I would tell her I was Ruth*," she'd written. Ruth had made the call. She, Silkie, was Ruth. She had made the call herself.

But why?

JOURNAL (Nov. 25)

Today Silkie revealed the truth about the call. She put her head down on my desk and covered it with her arms. When she did, an image came to me—from the movie Little Big Man. *Little Big Man, the character played by Dustin Hoffman—over a hundred years old—being interviewed by a young journalist. His skin is shriveled and sagging, and he himself very tired with all of his many years, his sad eyes able to look inward only, he lays his head into his hand and seems unable to grasp the superficiality of the questions the young reporter is asking. It is not so much that he can't remember all the details of his remarkable past as it is that he is overwhelmed by them . . . to the point of existential exhaustion. The journalist only wants his story . . . and he gets it . . . but at the end all the old Indian wants to do is lay his head into his hand . . . and say nothing.*

24. An Empty Chair

The next term, to my dismay, she did not come. She was not in any of my classes. She did not stop by my office to visit. Was she still a student? Had she dropped out for a term? She'd confided in me once she was not even sure of her major.

Of course, if she were not enrolled in any of my classes, why should I see her? A student visits her teacher about assignments. That's all.

I checked with the department secretary to look up her schedule, using as an excuse that I had to return her folder of papers. Silkie was not enrolled this term.

Something was wrong. Something to do with "Ruth," perhaps. Or something to do with me. That final revealing that she was the one who'd made the phone call signaled something I hadn't picked up on. Or was it just the circumstances of her life? Homeless again perhaps. No money to go to school. She could have told me. Then again, why should she have? I was not her father or her boyfriend. Just her teacher. Rather . . . former teacher.

 She was gone. No longer even a student. And I had no

way of finding out where she was . . . to see if I was in any way the cause, or if I could just help her to get back in school.

I am often beset by recurring images. From books. Movies. Photographs. Memories. Omayra. The eagle. At first they fasten onto me, but then, compulsively, I fasten onto them. To where I'm *inhabiting* them. Knowing thereby who I am.

During this time when Silkie was no longer there, and I didn't know where to find her, or why she'd chosen to separate herself from me, the image was . . . a chair. An empty chair. Sometimes it was the chair across from me in my office. The one in which Silkie had sat many times. But just as often the chair was another one. From long ago.

My father would get free tickets to the Browns' games in Cleveland and afterwards take me to a dark little restaurant called Toby's Place in an area under a bridge called The Flats. It wasn't the kind of place you'd go if you were looking for fine dining or sightseeing. In fact, there was considerable crime in the area, but in the daytime it had the flavor of a Carl Sandburg poem or a Studs Terkel vignette. There was a bar at one side and a handful of tables at the other. My father would have a beer there with his friends on occasion, but he liked their sandwiches, and so did I, especially the hot roast beef sandwiches with mashed potatoes, the whole smothered in dark gravy. I was only thirteen, but it made me feel grown up when I sat there alone with him across the table from me. He would have a Blatz, and I'd have a root beer. We'd talk about the game—Paul Warfield, Leroy Kelly, and other great players of that time—and we'd get on to discussing school and what I was going to do in life and even writers like Jack London and Mark Twain. I felt very close to him at these times. And when he died just a couple years later, the memory of those after-game chats, across the table, took on a deeper cast.

A year after his death, I happened to be at the downtown library, and I stopped off at Toby's on the walk back to the bus stop. Sat at one of the tables. The chair across from me was very, very empty. My father would never again sit there. Milan Kundera had written about that: how Man, who can't embrace the one "infinity"—the universe itself--can almost reach the other "infinity"—love. But even that is finally lost. He was speaking of losing his father.

For me it was in the form of an empty chair. The one across the table from me at Toby's.

And even as only my father could fill the one, it came to be that only Silkie could fill the one in my office. But it was neither of those chairs that came to obsess me. Rather it was *the empty chair*. Nothing fancy about it. A glorified straight-back kitchen table chair would have done, of some dark wood, perhaps. In some dimly lit little restaurant-tavern anywhere. A beer and a sandwich.

Someone to take that chair. Across from me. Just the two of us. A very comfortable, quiet intimacy.

I suppose I could have gone to a bar, as I had that night

at Spirits, drunk real beer, and found myself a woman—an honest-to-God date—to sit across from me. I've had girlfriends of a sort. But they were not the ones for that empty chair. There was Marta. Dark-haired ex-student but just a few years younger than me. Divorced from a surgeon, no less. Two children, one a teenager. She talked too much. About how her husband began to laugh less with her over time and more with his friends, scorned the "touchy-feely" to the point he didn't do much of either. It was clear my being a professor was a promise of the opposite. Talked about modern poets to impress me. Tried not to talk too much about her children. But it wasn't that she had two children that bothered me. It was that I had two children, and they had to be my focus. Besides, she was too sure about how things were supposed to be in life. I wasn't.

Another had been my yoga instructor—Tara. I tried it out for just three months. She took me on as a client. I needed to meditate more. Walk in nature more. "You can't even carry your own luggage, much less everybody else's," she said to me. "My suitcase is overloaded with things of little value," I replied, smiled. If she only knew. I found her physically attractive. Interesting. Not much more.

I admit to occasionally imagining what it would be like if the one in that chair were a literary character—Styron's Sophie, Shakespeare's Viola, even Hawthorne's Hester—sharing a bottle of pinot noir with me.

A perfect stranger might do. Of a certain kind, of course.

A Silkie sort. Are there others like her?

The chair remained empty, though. More empty than ever. Silkie had disappeared.

At the same time—perhaps because I had no one to share it with—that intensity inside me that I didn't know what to do with was building ever stronger.

GARY. *Gary stopped by my office the second term he had me for composition. Asked for my advice about his possibly leaving his parents for a year and traveling—said he needed to experience life. I told him to do what he felt the need to do but talk it over with his parents, one of whom was a teacher. A year later I got a letter from him (writing at 4 a.m. in a New York tavern) talking about his abortive stay in Florida and his hitching north. A few months later I ran into him in the university library. He was clutching three books which he heartily recommended to me.* [**Drawer 3B**]

25. A Needed Race

I tried to shake myself free from the pall that began to envelop me. The second weekend of the term I flew down to California to see Paul and Corrine. It was a scheduled visit. No showing up unannounced.

This time the surprise would take another form.

I would approach them with the quiet recognition that I needed something richer in meaning. I would not push my way through the "getting to know you" awkwardness that comes when they haven't seen me for several weeks. I would not reach out to them. They would have to "acclimatize" themselves to my presence their own way. *My* mood. *My* thoughtfulness.

Most times I brought them presents: a Transformer or tennis racket for Paul, maybe, a scarf or poster for Corrine. This time, I brought them books: a biography of Crazy Horse and *White Fang* for Paul, a biography of Madame Curie and *Their Eyes Were Watching God* for Corrine. Probably that decision in itself signaled to both of them this visit would be different.

"Well, here we are doing our thing," I said as we drove away. "Listen, what if we don't go to a movie or the mall this time?" It wasn't really a question.

Both of them shrugged, somewhere between anticipation and listlessness.

"What then?" Paul asked.

"I got it—we'll just walk in an enormous circle around the entire city and come back here." I could tell Paul didn't know if I was serious. Corrine was smirking.

"Let's eat and we'll talk about it," I said. "Where to?"

"There was a Dairy Queen back there."

"That's in the mall. Okay, but I'm not going to spend the whole time there."

"I've been wanting to see that Eddie Murphy movie. It's up here at the mall," Paul suggested.

"Dad said he didn't want to do that this time," Corrine countered, but very thoughtfully. She was reading me.

"Well, maybe later. How about this evening? Not now, though. We'll see how we feel."

After eating, we walked out to the back of the mall where I'd parked the car, and Corrine happened to spy an old church in the distance.

"Can we go see that old church?"

"I guess. Why?" I asked.

"Isn't it really old? It looks like one of those pictures of old Spanish buildings from the eighteenth century."

"Could be. I'm not sure we can get over there from here,

though. It's on the other side of the highway."

"Can't we just walk over?" Paul asked, suddenly interested in the prospect.

We explored the possibilities and found ourselves traipsing in the hot sun to the far back end of the parking lot and down a hill to a stream that ran behind the mall and under the freeway overpass. It was a longer distance than we'd anticipated, and the sun's laser-like rays had begun to cut into us mercilessly. The stream and the dark and coolness under the bridge seduced us into just resting there—under these huge stone and steel arms rising up on either side of us—buttressing a four-lane freeway above our heads. As we sat there Paul started flinging a few pieces of broken concrete into the stream and then to initiate a "rock, paper, scissors" contest—round-robin style—to see who won the most.

We forgot the church. Maybe it was because we didn't want to go back out into that sun, or maybe it was the quiet and the echo of our voices, but we began reminiscing about things that had happened long before. And now and then I'd catch them eyeing me inquisitively. Paul was especially thoughtful and content to gaze into the creek. His were kind eyes—always. Hers deep and strong, suiting her tomboyish personality. And she was still reading me. It hadn't ceased the entire day.

The topics meandered from one memory to another, most of them drawing upon the distant past when there had been four of us.

The reminiscing filled up almost three hours, and I had to remind them about the movie. Oddly, there was some reluctance.

It was near dark when the movie was over and we were walking to the car.

"Wait. Where's my purse?"

"Did you have one?"

"That small one made in Ecuador. I got it at an import store two weeks ago."

"Did you leave it in the theater?"

"No, down by the underpass, I put it down. I don't usually carry it."

We set off back down toward where we'd been hours earlier—along the stream behind the mall. Fortunately, the purse was still there, by a shrub, and we began walking back. The other side was grassy and banked up to a small park we'd avoided earlier because it sported only one or two trees for shade. But now it was more inviting.

I'm not sure exactly what happened to me—why I felt a seizure coming on. Perhaps because we'd had a good time and I was losing them again for weeks. I didn't want them to be alarmed, though, so I went with the force inside me and transformed it into something else. "I'll race you to the top of the hill!" I called out suddenly and began rushing wildly up the bank. It caught them both by surprise, but they ran too—Paul with his reputation at stake against his own father, and Corrine to let us know she could mount a challenge to either or both of us. Having gotten a head start, I beat them both, but then Paul shouted "Race you back down!" for his pride, and took off while I was catching my breath. I was still feeling the adrenaline and tore after him. It turned into an unending madness. All three of us. The losers in each case not allowing the other the victory. Up and down madly.

It was dizzying, exhilarating. But what Paul and Corrine didn't know was that, at the finish of each mad dash, I would close my eyes and picture that wall between the two worlds. And if I ran hard enough I could smash through.

We drove to the motel where I had reserved a room. Neither of them talked about the movie. It had been a disappointment to all of us. In fact, they didn't talk about anything. They were silent. It was close to midnight when we unlocked the door to our motel room. I'd brought a deck of cards and a couple of games, and it turned out they both wanted to learn poker. We used Fritos for chips and didn't go to sleep till well into the morning.

Just before we turned in at almost three, I showed them the picture of Ombeni. Told them who she was. As their father, it was the sort of thing I wanted them to know about. How it was in much of the world with others their age. An awareness I wished I could share with them more often.

There had been a spontaneity about the whole day's quiet adventures that satisfied me, but even before I dropped them off with their mother eight hours later, I'd begun to feel despondent because I wouldn't see them again for two months, and we'd have to start the attuning to one another all over again. Next time it would be without the benefit of the cool creek under the overpass or the wild races along the bank or the 3-in-the-morning Fritos poker.

They'd filled the empty chair—but only briefly.

AIDS VICTIMS *in Africa who quietly wait to die probably don't care that George Will wrote in his column today that "modern science in the service of religious fanatics" is a "distinctive terror." They do not care that Martin Heidegger once pointed out that the Holocaust was bad but so was "mechanized agriculture." Nor does the mother who left her already dead infant wrapped in a green Santa Claus sleeper by the side of Interstate 70 in Colorado in November of 1993. "A single pair of stockinged or shoeless footprints leading from the [snow bank at the base of a tree] suggested [the mother] was an indigent."* [**Drawer 4**]

26. A Rich Discovery

When I returned home I discovered that the chair was more empty than ever.

In my office one afternoon, it was not the metaphorical chair, but, across from me, the very real one that I sat staring at. On an impulse, I once again drew out Silkie's folder, including the journal, and took it home with me.

I'm not sure if it was because I thought I might read over some of it again, or if I just wanted it nearer to me, but I felt some trepidation even when I just set it, unopened, on the desk in my upstairs bedroom.

It stayed there throughout the week until the weekend, when I ventured to open it, and a couple of loose pages fell out. Quickly I put them back in, deciding nothing of the folder's contents could comfort me at this time.

I sat on the bed, the folder on my lap, unwilling to just replace it on the table. Spying the file cabinet, I decided I would keep it in there for now.

But as I did so, I found myself going directly to the bottom drawer. Therein was the photograph of Ombeni, the accompanying biography, and her brief note—all of which, upon returning from my visit with my kids, I'd deposited in that drawer—Drawer 4.

Sliding forward both Ombeni's folder and the one containing my "Rage" clippings, I slipped behind them Silkie's folder.

Instead of just shutting the drawer, however, I stood there staring into it.

I understood. Perhaps all along I had. Just not cognitively—until this moment: The three items were of the same world. World Two. The more authentic world. The world I'd gone looking for that very first time I'd set out to find Silkie to tell her she could join my class.

More significantly, though, I came to understand what I needed to do if I was to make it through that term. That drawer, indeed that whole file cabinet, would serve as my surrogate Silkie for the empty chair. That nagging sense of a mystical relationship with Silkie—exposed as some chimera of human foolishness and frailty by the revelations of the end of the previous term and by her disappearance from my life—was not altogether dead. Nor the *Meaning* in it. And in some way I could not explain, the *Meaning* was still surviving—in that file cabinet. The *me* that had been knocking up against the wall to World Two was alive in the passages I had extracted from the minds of the greatest writers, in Ombeni's letter, and in my "Rage" folder in the bottom drawer. That's why Silkie's journal, her writings, belonged there too.

The queer mixture of intensity and comfort that overcame me so often when I was in her company, the secret to that phenomenon, was the *me* in my file cabinet.

I would write every day in my journal—about all of this. The journal entries too would go into the file cabinet. The bottom drawer.

CRIPPLED GIRL IN HOLOCAUST. *One of the scenes in the film The Pianist showed a crippled girl carrying a birdcage, wandering alone and crying amidst the Jews about to be hauled off in boxcars. I believe it was a real memory of either the director Roman Polanski or the pianist himself—Wladyslaw Szpilman.* **[Drawer 4]**

27. Ombeni's Stories

 The very next day, the "Ombeni" component of my plan took a turn of its own.

I found two letters in my mailbox. One was regarding a parking ticket I'd disputed. It had been in an unfamiliar county, a portion of a street not clearly marked: $25. I'd protested by mail. Refused to pay it. The letter was returned with only a "$10 late fee" stamped on it. The $35 would have paid for Ombeni's food for a month. Maybe even her schooling.

The other letter was from Ombeni, the letters printed as capitals, some of which were difficult to decipher except by their pattern with the other letters in a word. I was addressed as "MR. STEPHEN." I opened it, withdrew the letter from its envelope, and found three pages of crinkly paper with uncertain printed letters in ink. In Kiswahili.

I set it aside, angry with myself because here was a second personal letter to me and I not only hadn't responded to the first but had not even found someone to translate it. I would still have to get to it—to find out what it was she was writing.

I read over the parking ticket letter again then threw it

on the table, annoyed with its contents—thinking to actually drive down to the next county and talk face to face with the robot who had written it. I snatched the letter, rushed to my car, backed out of my driveway, and was two blocks down the road before it hit me: I didn't know where I was going. Certainly not thirty miles to argue a stupid parking ticket. Very agitated, I kept driving, deciding that it would settle me down.

Several blocks later, though, the agitation still had not left me; indeed, had somehow insidiously transformed itself into a despondency that had to do with not only having to throw away $35, but with the degree to which something so insignificant had taken hold of me. Within the brief span of several minutes I found myself trembling.

I turned down a side road and drove very slowly. Glancing down at the seat next to me, I saw Ombeni's letter.

Instinctively I knew it was what I was needing. A surrogate Silkie. Ombeni. I didn't care to sort it out. She just was.

A mystery about both of them, perhaps. They both had a secret. I would discover both. For now, Ombeni's.

With this second letter from her I knew there was one—a secret. The first letter had been a curious thing. Perhaps just a response to my question to her about a sad and happy moment in her life. I'd therefore not made it a priority to find a translator.

"What if," I asked myself, "she is saying something she's needed to say all her life, but nobody was really interested?

Why, after all, was she one of those children the agency had decided was in need? Apparently there was no family who cared enough for her . . . or had enough time or money to care . . . or even to feed her. So, to the agency, she is only a victim. No other status. Yet, look at this. Somehow she learned to write . . . to print a few letters to say something. And somebody translated my request to her. Did they know she would actually answer? Who helped her write this letter? This response to me? The agency doesn't know anything about it, I'll bet. Well, I'll listen, Ombeni. If I can get the damned thing translated."

It became a real conversation with myself, and then an argument:

"Yes, you'll listen, Stephen, but think about it. Here you are sending this girl money for her meals and schooling and clothes. And you read her letter. The letter from a little girl of nine from a distant country—a girl who must have gone through hell. But she's just one of millions like that. So what does it matter if you make a big deal about reading her letter? Listening to her?"

"It matters. Matters if three or four or three hundred or four hundred of those little girls do finally get listened to."

"Maybe . . . if you say so. You're certainly supposed to think that way. The truth is, though, it doesn't change how things are in this universe. Caring is a hit-or-miss thing. Most of the time misses. The meaninglessness of it . . . randomness of it all doesn't go away because you answer a letter. Besides, what good could it do for her? She is thousands of miles away."

"So. . . I should ignore her altogether?"

"That's up to you. Just so you don't think there's more at stake here than your silly conscience."

"So, according to you, since the grand design of everything is that there's no design at all, maybe I should kill myself."

"Suit yourself."

I don't remember how long I carried out this absurd dialogue in my head. But I remember, at one point, waiting at a traffic light and deciding—with a shrug and a playful smile—that, yes, I would kill myself. The world was what it was. Couldn't keep ignoring that fact. "Sorry, Ombeni, that's just how it is. A lot of eagles in boxes and a lot of little girls like you with little prospect for a decent life." Besides, the best time for doing away with yourself was not when you had experienced some great loss, but when you figured out it didn't really matter whether you did or not.

"Okay, kill myself. At least I won't have to pay the parking ticket."

In the end, I decided to answer Ombeni's letter.

The obvious place to look for a translator was the African Studies Center at the university. Wouldn't African languages—Bantu, Hausa, Kiswahili—be part of it? Surely there was a student from Kenya or Tanzania on the campus if not an actual teacher.

I drove home to pick up the first letter, hoping to get both of them translated right away.

It turned out an entire wing of one of the buildings had in it the offices of part-time instructors of various languages—Farsi, Arabic, Chinese, Japanese—and a whole room for "African Languages."

I was directed between rows of students working on computer language programs to the rear of the room where the lab director, "Camara" something or other—a very dark-skinned woman, short hair, intense eyes, probably in her thirties and wearing an unflattering smock-like dress—was standing by her desk talking to an anxious female student. She nodded to me, then went off with the student to the latter's language-tape station and listened in on her earphones, changed some setting, was returning to me, but was intercepted by another student—this one a male—and went off to his station.

I decided this Camara was one of those very energetic, dedicated, conscientious, firm yet gentle teachers you come across every now and then—usually in elementary school—whose whole lives are the students they teach. I felt somewhat guilty disturbing her at a time when the language lab was so full.

"Sorry to bother you. My name is Stephen Mollgaard. I . . . teach in the English Department and need some help with a personal project that needs a translation. I have a letter—actually two letters—that are in Swahili, I believe. Can you tell me if you have any student here studying or speaking Swahili who could translate it? Someone from Kenya or Tanzania?"

She smiled as though mine were a welcome disturbance from her duties. "Hi, I'm Camara. Do you have the letters with you?"

I started to hand them to her but another student came up to her desk needing assistance, and again she got up. It would happen a couple more times in the course of my conversation with her.

"Letters? Can I read them?" she asked when she was finally able to sit down.

"Here. I'm not sure what she's saying. A little girl named Ombeni I've been sending checks to. In Tanzania. One of those charities where you sponsor a child. They gave me her."

She withdrew one of the letters.

"Maybe I should explain," I added. "At first the agency just had her send me brief notes of thanks, telling me how my money was being used—you know, for her schooling.

I found that a little . . . well, not enough. So I asked her to tell me something about herself that made her sad and something that made her happy. I didn't really expect what I got. I assumed the agency would translate my request and enclose some brief note, some response the next month. Instead I got a letter that looks like it was directly from her. I couldn't understand it. But it was in Swahili—Kiswahili, I guess is the correct way to say it. Anyway, I set it aside planning someday to get it translated but never got around to it. Then today this second letter came. I'm curious. She's only nine or ten years old."

"Which of these was the first one?"

"That one."

She withdrew it from the envelope and read over it. Then she slipped it back into the envelope and pulled out the other one. This one she read for a much longer time and gave a puzzled look.

"I think two or three of my students could do it—enough of it."

"That would be okay, I just would like . . ."

"What if I do it myself?"

"Well, I didn't want to bother you. I could pay a student."

"No, no, I'd like to. But I need a couple days. Do you have a phone, an extension, or e-mail so I can reach you when I'm done. I promise to get to it tonight or tomorrow."

When I left the building it was with an unexpected sense

of exuberance.

Well, maybe fate or destiny was still at work with me—the phone call Silkie made to me, my letting her into my class when I shouldn't have. Now, with this second letter coming when it did, and the instructor herself—this Camara—wanting, even eager, to help me. Perhaps, indeed, there was some Providence in this.

As quickly, though, I rejected the notion as absurd. Did Ombeni believe in that sort of thing? Destiny.

The next afternoon, Camara called.

"I've got the letters for you," she announced. "You have time this afternoon?"

We met at 4:30 in the Student Union cafeteria and took a table. She sat down without removing her jacket and laid the letters and translations in front of her.

"Tell me again why she sent you these. Why did she write such things to you?"

I shrugged. "I just got annoyed with the way the agency takes over. You know; you send in a check every month and they tell you how the kid is doing and that he or she thanks you for the money and it got used for this or that . . . so I just . . . for the hell of it . . . asked her to tell me more . . . about, like I said yesterday, sad or happy things in her life. That's how I put it. But I thought it would still be translated for me. Through the agency."

She nodded.

We ordered coffee. While we waited, we talked about what courses I taught, how long she'd been in the country (just one year), where she was from (some fifty miles from Dar Es Salaam). She was sitting bent forward somewhat too rigidly, never leaning back comfortably, and now and then she would glance over at the open letter very thoughtfully, almost as though disturbed.

"Is there something . . . troubling about it?"

She looked up, puzzled at my question apparently. "Troubling?"

"The letter . . . what's in it . . . is it . . . ?"

"No. I'm sorry. It's just that . . . "

She was staring at me, but more through me. Did I see some moisture in her eyes?

The coffee came. She stopped to pour in some cream.

"What I mean is . . . she's trying to say. . . not easy . . . difficult things. Well, maybe not difficult. But for her. She probably hasn't had much schooling. How old is she?"

"She was nine when I started this, but I think she may be ten now."

"She must be really smart. She says . . . about school and wanting to be a teacher. The other one's more complicated. About her brother. He died. And . . . well . . . she says he came back. They believe that in some places in East Africa—that you can die and come back."

She became silent. I could see her eyes were, for sure,

getting moist.

"Sorry, it's just some of this . . . I've got my own memories. So . . . I hope this is okay," she said, and slipped across the counter three typed pages, attached to which were Ombeni's original letters and envelope. "I translated . . . as best I could. Both letters."

"I really appreciate the time you took."

"No, that's all right. I enjoyed doing it. Listen, I had to fill in some . . . pieces of it. She doesn't know enough words—I mean how to write them."

"I understand."

"I'm glad you had me do it. If you get any more I'll be glad to do those too."

"Do you think she will?"

Camara shrugged. "I think she may. For sure if you write her in Kiswahili. I can do that for you. Tell me what you want to say."

She seemed to be conveying to me something beyond just the answer to my question.

"I'd ask you what they're about but I suppose I should just read what you came up with. Take more time with them. So if I want to answer, you can help?"

As soon as I got home I set the translation on the table, made myself some tea, and read:

> LETTER 1
>
> *My name is Ombeni, I have my sibling, she is younger than me. I love her so much. I also like to*

study, but I can't study much because I have to take care of my younger sister. I live with my grandmother in the village. My mom works far away from home, so I have to look after my sister when she is gone. My grandmother is sick too.

I like so much to go to school, when I grow up, I would like to be a teacher. But my dad who lives away from home thinks that I'm dull because I'm a child and he believed that I will get married very soon because I'm a girl so I can't get to the University level. But I believe that I will be a good teacher.

My friends laughed at me because I failed mathematics. I scored 5 out of 100. I did not know that I failed, I thought I passed, and my friends wanted me to show them my paper. I felt so ashamed, but I couldn't get time to study because I had to take care of my sister. And during nights I'm tired and in the village there is no electricity. I had no time to study.

LETTER 2

The saddest day in my life was when my brother died. He was only four and had a fever. For two nights my mother and uncle stayed up with him. But he died. One week later he came back. My mother said he came to her. But I didn't see him. I was with my friend. We were playing by the stream. I was supposed to be home so I didn't see him. I am sorry I disobeyed them. When

*I was home he was gone again. I waited for him for
many days, but that was the only time.*

I set the letters out on my dining room table. All that
week they were the most important thing in my life. In effect,
Ombeni was sitting across from me in the empty chair. I
needed her there.

The second weekend of the term, there was still no Silkie.
I began to worry that, indeed, she'd dropped out of school
altogether. Not just for one term.

I put Ombeni's letters in the bottom drawer of the file
cabinet and drew out my own journal. For the rest of that
term that journal would become a dialogue between me
and Silkie, me and Ombeni, me and myself, me and God,
me and World Two.

28. Journal Entries: Grappling with Loss

JOURNAL [Jan. 10]

Fate has its own "truth." The recognition of which means I now have to sort out the difference between "professionalism" and "Truth." Professionalism as in "Thou shalt not as a teacher . . ." and other such institutional precepts. World One. Truth as in . . . that wall and . . . World Two. The two worlds are not of the same stuff. Suddenly there is this "Silkie" complicating my life as though she were at the center of it or the meaning for it. And if I were to test out the meaningfulness, the validity of any reading of events as involving some sort of "destiny," then there can't be any game-playing, no dissembling, only honest submission to what happened. In other words, I have to be excessively honest with her. Even to the extent it might humiliate me. Get me into trouble.

But does that mean I am now bound to disregard "professionalism"? Go out into the world of shelters for the homeless, the world of Ruth and fractals, and . . . find her. Put it to her. What? Didn't I do that . . . miserably? She couldn't make sense of it.

Or is that disregarding of professionalism just what I want to do? That I <u>want</u>, <u>need</u>, something bigger to be going on here, period.

JOURNAL [Jan. 11]
Yesterday, a woman two ahead of me in a checkout line at the grocery store caught my attention. Most likely in her fifties, she was very short and for that reason and that she was wearing three or four old coats, without any regard to their respective lengths, I could not tell if she was very thin or actually overweight. If she was not homeless, she at best seemed to be barely making it. Yes, it was cold, but I'd seen the woman on the street several times wearing the same number of coats—even on hot summer days—and I'd wondered at the time how she could bear it.

Those other times I'd always spotted her from my car. This was the first time up close. The checkout lady was running her items over the scanner, when the woman suddenly stared down at the counter in some confusion, "Oh, I was supposed to get something else. For Minnie." The checkout lady waited. But the woman could not seem to remember and finally muttered to herself, "I can't seem to focus . . . right now. I'm sorry." There were two people behind me, and the one immediately behind me sighed loudly. "I'm sorry, I'll remember," the woman said again. "Oh, yes. Bugler. She wants some Bugler . . . for cigarettes." It turned out "Bugler" was tobacco and had to be retrieved from another checkout lane. As she did so, the woman behind me—well-dressed and in her late sixties—remarked sarcastically, "How is it I always get the right line?" I turned to face her and saw that she'd raised her eyebrows to punctuate her despair. The woman behind her smiled sympathetically.

Unfortunately, when the checkout girl returned and scanned the "Bugler," she discovered the woman was "8 cents short."

"Oh" the woman said in the voice of a little girl, "Can I have them anyway?"

"No," said the clerk, "I'm afraid not." I heard the two women behind me move restlessly.

"I've got it," I said, and reached into my pocket for a dime.

"Thank you," the woman said to me with an embarrassed smile, then pushed her cart with her cloth bag full of groceries out through the electric doors. Once outside, she removed the bag from the cart and carried it in her right hand.

I was tempted to follow her. To see where she went. Did she have a home like me? A family? Who was "Minnie"? A daughter? Sister? Friend? If so, what was their life like that she wanted to buy tobacco for rolling cigarettes with the last of her money?

That childlike way she spoke. Very likely she was mentally deficient or mentally ill.

What disturbed me most, somehow, were the raised eyebrows.

JOURNAL [Jan. 13]
I heard on the radio yesterday an inspirational story from Africa.

A Rwandan woman who was brutalized in 1994 by Tutsis. Her husband and all her 5 children were killed, and she was taken away and raped for a month. When she discovered she was pregnant by the rapes, she planned to kill the child, and at first hated it when it was born. But when it began to smile up at her, she came to love it even more than her other children. They were all each had in this world.

JOURNAL [Jan. 15]

Need Silkie. 3 weeks. Not even see. Of course, not even enrolled. I've crashed again. For quite a while. Had to delay going to a faculty meeting three days ago till I drove around for half an hour. I came on too strong last term.

Comfortable sitting together. Those few times in my office—in the chair across from me.

My teaching is suffering. Sick leave?

JOURNAL [Jan. 19]

I saw a woman, overweight, tired with her two children by the hand—a girl of about 10 and who was overweight also and walked as though she knew it, a little boy in a tanktop. They were all carrying grocery bags. No car. No husband.

JOURNAL [Jan. 20]

If anyone had the WORD, it would be a ghost. Someone who has died and come back. Right? Who else? It's only necessary then to find one, reach through some slit into the other side *and grab him, or her. Make the thing do your bidding. For answers. That Italian writer, Dino Buzzati, imagines Einstein looking for some such "slit" that opens into a world were not supposed to know about.*

JOURNAL [Jan. 22]

Walking back from the grocery, I could see this old man, looking older by the unkemptness of his beard, the humped-over, seated position as he waited on a bench for a bus. Suddenly in front of him, from my left, ran a very tall, trim, erect man, wearing white tennis shorts and a white T-shirt—very much the health-oriented yuppie. His eyes were very much straight ahead, and therefore very much on himself, and thus, as he passed, he did not even notice the old man seated to his left.

JOURNAL [Jan. 24]

I came upon this quote the other day from Chekhov's "Lady with the Dog." Is this not me?

"He explained that, too. He talked, thinking all the while that he was going to see her, and no living soul knew of it, and probably never would know. He had two lives: one, open, seen and known by all who cared to know, full of relative truth and of relative falsehood, exactly like the lives of his friends and acquaintances; and another life running its course in secret. And through some strange, perhaps accidental, conjunction of circumstances, everything that was essential, of interest and of value to him, everything in which he was sincere and did

not deceive himself, everything that made the kernel of his life, was hidden from other people; and all that was false in him, the sheath in which he hid himself to conceal the truth—such, for instance, as his work in the bank, his discussions at the club, his 'lower race,' his presence with his wife at anniversary festivities—all that was open."

JOURNAL [Jan. 27]

A newspaper article reports that some Oregon man was trying to buy property to save some 37 dogs, 100 cats, 2 ferrets, and a couple of chickens that he has been caring for to keep them from being put to death by the Humane Society. Thus far he has kept them on some rural land, but the money others have promised to buy his own land hasn't come through. He "spent all day Tuesday in the hills . . . loading a 48-foot trailer with sacks of dog and cat food, personal belongings and hand-hewn animal cages, trying to meet a midnight deadline for vacating the property he had hoped to purchase. . . . 'The problem is, I don't have anywhere else to go—I don't know what I'm going to do,' the 62-year-old-carpenter-turned-animal-advocate said. 'But I know I'll never give up . . . .'"

JOURNAL [Feb. 1]

Yesterday as I drove by the high school, I saw a student seated on the curb with her backpack slung on her back. The odd thing was she was bent over—her head almost all the way to her knees tucked under her. When I drove past a few minutes later, she was still in that position. Was she meditating? If not, what makes a teenager become so unaware of those around her that she doesn't care? Just needs to hang her head.

JOURNAL [Feb. 16]

I catch the trees, the mountains, the sky before they go to sleep for the day. It's at night they do their thing. Before humans wake and rule everything. And that means I have to do my driving in the very early morning—5 or 5:30. Being so early it's to <u>me only</u> they speak. Cars coming the other way—coming out of what I'm going into. Their occupants have to get to the next city for business, perhaps, or to find an all-night restaurant for pancakes, bacon, and eggs. Mine is a different purpose.

I alone am going the other way. Into a world that will lord it over the universe only an hour more. And I will make the best of it. It's the one time I can ask for, hope for, search for what at any other time will be counted irrational . . . absurd. I am part of a world that doesn't include anyone else. At 5 a.m., while the dark shapes of trees are still speaking, the irrational might be rational, the impossible possible, the absurd perhaps not so absurd.

JOURNAL [Feb. 24]

Yesterday I had an explosive seizure. I'd been standing at the kitchen, a piece of celery on my cutting board as the prelude to some well-meaning plan to make vegetable soup. I hadn't been eating healthy and was determined to put together something

I could draw on day after day so I wouldn't, in my atrophy each time I returned home, end up going to a restaurant or just frying eggs.

But the celery wasn't being cut—just being stared at it.

The truth is I'd begun to feel ashamed of myself. Embarrassed. Concluding, yes, it had been my making a fool of myself with Silkie that made her disappear. I might even have been the cause of her dropping out of school. If she had. Maybe it was just for a term. The combination of despondency and shame are becoming too much for me.

And yesterday I was really feeling that way big time. I knew what would have to happen. That I wanted it to happen. Her fractals explosion in the classroom long before. Only now it was my turn. I would give it permission. She'd found her release in words; mine would come in movement.

JOURNAL [Feb. 25]

I caught a glimpse of her as I drove near the campus. A woman, in her thirties perhaps, half walking, half running along the sidewalk, her head down. She might have been any student late for class except that something about her was different. As I passed, I was curious enough to look into my rearview mirror to get a better look. Her expression was one of a young girl frightened about getting in trouble, paying no attention to the other students around her, some waiting for a bus. She was running now in a stumbling way that you could see was how she always ran, her body bent over somewhat, her eyes straight ahead. Confused, mentally slow most likely. Running, stumbling, so conspicuously not graceful or normal. Alone.

JOURNAL [Feb. 28]

Driving to work each morning . . . too many times I'd felt frightened, disturbed about something. What? I didn't know. Only that it carried all the way into my office.

I closed the door. Maybe I shouldn't have done that. Maybe if I had joked with a colleague in the lounge once in a while I could have pulled myself out of it. But I didn't want to.

JOURNAL [March 1]

Friday in my composition class, we were discussing an article called "War on Trial" which traced the significance of the Nuremberg decision for all future wars. I challenged the class: "Does this trial–this 'crimes against humanity' principle—have any implications for us today. Or for Vietnam?"

No hands went up. I'd figured out that most of them had never even heard about Nuremberg except from the essay, and now only two or three of them seemed interested in my question.

Quietly, I lowered my head and closed the book.

The need to go somewhere had been in me for some time. Perhaps only as a quirky notion responding to a temporary frustration. The kind of "why do I persist in this?" impulse when you've just had two or three classes go badly.

Just that morning, I'd been sitting in my office, my door closed, feeling nothing, not even the inspiration to cry, when that notion of needing to go somewhere took on a real urgency. Go far away. From teaching.

Duty prevailed, of course, and now I stood before all these bewildered expressions.

They waited. My having closed the book meant something unexpected was coming. So what would I give them? I could not stand there forever. I had to speak what I had no inclination to express . . . maybe because it couldn't be expressed.

"So no implications for our contemporary situation in this essay?" I asked quietly. "What is the value of it then . . . or any of these essays?" No hint of exasperation or even frustration. "Assignments. That's all they are. I assign them. You do them. But why? What value does it have for anything . . . for the problems of the world? It gets me a salary and you your credits. That's all, right? The writer of this essay—that's not what she intended. Certain people were meant to read this. But they won't."

I regretted using the phrase "problems of the world." Sounded so artificial. So phony.

They must have thought I was leading into a class discussion. Instead I just stared at them and said, "So, if you don't mind, let's just stop. Forget class. In recognition of what none of this does for the world." There it was again: "for the world." What did that mean, anyway? Chickens? Penguins? Bolivian farmers? Weeds? Small-business owners? The people Amnesty International tries to help?

I gathered my papers from the desk and started to walk

out, but then—seeing how stunned they were—dismissed the class, explaining that I wasn't feeling well.

JOURNAL [March 5]

I went for a ride. A long way in a direction I'd never driven before. Down off Camus Way. Arlo Guthrie's "The City of New Orleans" kept me company. And a violin piece—"Just a Cottage Small" I'd recorded from an old LP. And then . . . I don't know what. My CDs were a queer mix of types and times.

A road sign caught my attention. One showing what appeared to be the outline of a beetle with legs too long and too bent and which turned out to be a warning of a road suddenly circling around and other roads spoking off from it. It produced a sort of mysterious and peculiar excitement in me, but I dismissed it with a "Rides are rides. Late-night drives are just that. And it's only when you write about them you can turn them into something more than what they are—which are lit streets and neon lights and black trees silhouetted against dark blue skies streaked with ghostly clouds." Road signs are just that—road signs. Except that at night they don't materialize until they are there for you. Your headlights awaken them like tombstones in a cemetery unmarked as such. And the solitary teenage boy shuffling along the road—his head down . . . baseball cap . . . cigarette . . . distraught over his parents' divorce, his father's desertion, or his girlfriend's betrayal, and angry at the world because of it—is not thereby, just because his figure emerges by the headlights of my car at midnight, a more profound phenomenon than a middle-aged woman shopping in a mall at midday.

Nor am I myself because I drive alone down these dark empty streets.

JOURNAL [March 7]

> *Dear God,*
>
> *Okay, God, this is how you work. Ruth. You played it out. Your practical joke. Silkie as Ruth. No problem for you. Two sides of a personality. Delusion. Whatever. No harm done. Simple matter of the guy going on with his life now. SHIT!*
>
> *I'm not going to blame it all on Silkie, God. Even before the phone call, even before her explosion in class that ended in her standing at the board explaining fractals, I was a friggin basket case. It's that Mercutio thing. Do you remember him, God? Do you ever go to movies? I suppose not. You're too busy playing jokes on poor schmucks like me or young Mexican girls crossing deserts alone. Well, let me tell you. He was Romeo's friend. "Romeo" of Shakespeare's play. Do you even read? This Mercutio . . . in the movie version . . . he got himself stabbed in a street brawl and his friends didn't know it. And he didn't tell them. Just turned his final minutes into a flamboyant boisterous tribute to the final joke. Play-acting. Carrying on as though he'd been stabbed. It didn't matter to him if anyone else knew it*

was for real and so they laughed with him—his final comic statement to a world that didn't care.

I just happened to remember it in a dream. Was that your doing too? It was the elusive familiarity about it. A reckless youthfulness that felt right that morning. I sat on my bed pondering what to eat for breakfast, and that's when it came back to me. The dream. That Mercutio was the "me" I needed that morning. I'd come to realize I didn't know anymore who I was, that I'd already, out of need . . . out of desperation . . . allowed myself to slide closer and closer to this other me in some other universe, just waiting to be yanked into it by some unexpected act, from some unexpected place.

I blame this on you, God. It went a long way back. Long before and over many years, I was stabbed . . . just like Mercutio . . . and began play-acting.

You gave me Silkie . . . then . . . whisked her away. Thanks.

> *"The white man came and asked us to shut our eyes and pray. When we opened our eyes it was too late—our land was gone." [Jomo Kenyatta]*

29. Reaching Out

At the time—which was 1:45 a.m. Monday, March 14—it seemed like a spontaneous decision: I would give out $100 in tens and twenties to random homeless people. Partly for the altruistic satisfaction, partly to halt the downward spiral of despondency which had overtaken me since Silkie's disappearance. But it was anything but spontaneous. Why had I been out walking the downtown streets in the middle of the night anyway?

The truth is it had come as the culmination of five days and nights of restless sleeps and aimless walks.

It started very late Thursday afternoon, March 10. My colleagues in my part of the building had all left. I sat staring at a stack of papers on my desk to be marked—dreading to start in. "I have to," I told myself and thought to reach out and pull the top one to me. The title was "Playing God: Abortion, Euthanasia, the Death Penalty." *I could not.* It was not just that I did not want to. *I could not.* There was comfort for some reason in not moving. In sitting there frozen.

I finally got up, slipped the papers into my backpack,

and walked across the campus to the Student Union. In the cafeteria, I bought a bowl of soup and a roll and sat down at one of the tables.

"Something is very wrong with me," I remember saying to myself. "Something very bad is going to happen if I don't . . . If I don't what?"

I ate. Drove home. Home. It had become more a surrender than a haven.

I decided to sleep, hoping in the morning my state of mind would be more conducive to marking papers.

I went to bed at 7:30 p.m. When I woke it was the middle of the night. My watch said 2:37 a.m. It was Friday.

I'd left no light on—not even the nightlight in the bathroom—and the effect of the total darkness on me was immediate. I began sweating, trembling.

The sense of elusive dread I had experienced in the office when I couldn't reach for a paper to mark had not yet abated; in fact, was now infused with a sense of real horror.

I tried curling up and burying myself in the covers, but the panic only fed on the tightness of my position.

I made myself a cup of tea and considered reading. I'd been reading here and there from *Dreams of a Final Theory* by Steven Weinberg, but it was too heavy. I was not up to the concentration. I searched for a video to drug me, ending up with the Zefferelli version of *Romeo and Juliet*—just to see, not Mercutio, but Olivia Hussey. When I'd first seen the movie her beauty had overwhelmed me. That had been years ago, so maybe it would be like seeing her anew. Not to be.

Watched for an hour or so and finally conked off, with the film still running.

That night was the same. Unable to sleep. Almost 3 a.m. Saturday. Pulled out another video tape. This time a not-very-well-known 1950s movie entitled *All Mine to Give* about a Scottish immigrant family in Wisconsin. When both parents die of some disease ravaging the area, the oldest son, only twelve, has to find homes for his five younger siblings. When I'd first seen it I'd been not only very moved by it, but, because it was a true story, inspired by it.

I watched it through the end but fell asleep on the couch soon after and didn't wake till eleven in the morning, feeling groggy, restive. Half the day—Saturday—was wasted. I went grocery shopping.

That night I finally slept through. I struggled with my students' papers most of Sunday and fell into a deep late-afternoon nap.

But my waking-sleeping schedule was so screwed up that Sunday night I could not sleep at all, and decided around 11 p.m. a good walk in the air would help.

I remember telling myself that I would go just four blocks to the corner convenience store. Instead I walked a couple more blocks to the next main cross street. Then just to the high school stadium. Then to the campus. But I didn't stop. Into the downtown area I walked. Past a parking garage. A Good Will store. The bus station.

I began to feel more exhilarated, defiant about what was happening to me.

It was close to 1 a.m., and the only people I was passing were men. Young men smoking. Old men, exiting taverns. Three of them huddled in a large office-building doorway, with coffee cups.

One was fairly young—maybe in his thirties. He had thick curly blonde hair and he was walking two dogs with separate leashes, but both were also pulling a small four-wheeled homemade cart he'd stretched a small sheet over. A miniature covered wagon.

At one point, I don't remember exactly when or where, I came upon a red-haired man in some sort of religious robe, a Bhagavad Gita or Bible under his right arm, thumping his forehead repeatedly with the heel of his left hand and muttering something unintelligible. Seeing him reminded me of "Tabi Sahlei"—a schizophrenic I'd come across regularly when I'd taught in Nigeria. "Crazy Sahlei." Uttering gibberish, he wandered the streets half-naked in filthy rags. Most ignored him. A few gave him scraps to eat—a mango, a piece of bread, a yam. He'd been normal till his late teens, but one day woke up crazy. The story was he'd been cursed.

This guy—with the robes and the holy book—was most likely a schizophrenic too. What brought it on? A family tragedy? Drugs? A curse? Did it matter? Went over the edge.

And what about me? Was I on the edge too?

It was just about then—about 1:45 a.m., Monday—I got the inspiration. Give out money.

It had always been a fantasy of mine anyway. But this

time for another reason: I would need to come up with some criteria for deciding whom to give it to and how much. I smiled at my cleverness. It would take two or three hours to do it well, and I'd surely be tired by the time I'd given out the last dollar.

I headed for the nearest ATM, remembering there was one only two blocks away.

I withdrew $100—five twenties. That meant delicious decisions. Would I give five people $20 each? Or maybe some more deserving person the whole $100?

I slipped the five bills into my pocket, then recognized my stupidity. What if I were robbed, and I lost all of it? Maybe even to the very first person I handed a $20 bill to? Ultimately I folded two bills into one of my socks, one in my wallet, two in my pants pocket.

I came upon two homeless men drinking coffee. On the walkway in front of them was a large can with a fire burning inside. One had long dark hair that was graying; the other was younger with a handlebar mustache. I gave them one of the $20 bills.

Neither was menacing, but the very fact they were two and I was one reminded me of the danger. I would search for loners. Or women.

In the park under the freeway bridge I spied a group of transients wrapped up in sleeping bags and blankets, their heads buried, but I decided it was no good to wake them. And, again, a little dangerous. Nearby, however, a very old bearded man in a knit ski hat, passed me and nodded. I gave him the $20 from my wallet.

And maybe that would have been it. The others I came upon were the sort that for sure would have used most of my money for drink.

Abandoning my fantasy (it was now 4:15 a.m., and I was exhausted), I circled back home. But I was on a street I was not very familiar with, and I was passing shops I'd never frequented. They were in old structures with tiny alleys between them. One was a costume shop, another a bicycle repair. Another had the carved head of a clown that hung over the front door.

It was just as the morning sunlight was descending gently on some of the wider more exposed avenues of the city that I spied her. A woman by herself. Wearing a too-large hat with ear-muffs and so heavily bundled in sweaters and coats she looked lumpy, she was sitting on the curb, just rocking back and forth. She didn't even seem to notice me. Next to her were two cloth sacks, a blanket tied to one, and various items in paper bags and cloth pouches. Around her neck were three or four necklaces with large beads.

I recognized her. She was the woman I'd encountered in the grocery store who had been eight cents short to buy the Bugler tobacco for someone named "Minnie."

Had I not seen her so many times walking around town, I would have regarded it coincidental at the least, fateful at the most.

What if I greeted her?

"Hello," I said.

"My sister is coming today," she replied, as though we'd already been having a conversation.

"Your sister? She . . . I mean . . . you haven't seen her for a while?"

"No."

"Where is she from?"

"My sister?"

"Yes."

"I'm not sure."

"Where is she now?"

She thought awhile. Then, "I don't know. She's home, I think."

"So you live with her?" I was hoping she'd say she did.

"No, no."

"Are you . . . homeless?"

"Sometimes."

"I mean is your sister going to take you . . . with her . . . somewhere . . . to her house?"

"I'll ask her."

"You don't remember me, do you?"

She looked up at me. "No."

"I was the one . . . oh, don't worry . . . it doesn't matter. Could you use some . . . money, you know, to get something to eat?"

"I have some."

"Do you have enough?"

She fished in her outer coat pocket. It was all change—maybe a little more than a dollar.

"Listen, you can use some more. Here. . . ." I pulled a $20 bill from my pocket. "Take this."

"My sister is coming."

"Well, then, until she gets here. You just . . . wait."

"Why not?" I thought, and pulled off my shoe and sock and took out the other $40 and gave it to her.

"Good-bye. Maybe I'll come back and see you some other time. What is your name?"

"Francine."

It felt awkward, just walking away. "I like your necklace . . . necklaces," I said. "They're . . . pretty. Where did you get them?"

"These? I have a friend. At that store. They have all kinds of them there. The clown store. She got me this one."

"Well, good-bye."

As I turned to leave, the image of the clown head I'd seen earlier flashed back to me.

It hit me. Beads! Hadn't Silkie mentioned that very first term that she had a new job? When I asked her where, she'd said something about "beads." Was this the place?

"Wait, you mean that store that has a clown head? Do they sell beads? Is that the one over that way. Near the university . . . by the campus?"

"I think so."

"A wooden clown head?"

"Yes."

I walked back that way. I too had thought it was a clown's head. But it wasn't. A closer look showed me it was a wizard, his hand outstretched and holding colored marbles or beads. Above the head, painted black script letters against a wooden white sign spelled out "The Bead Game." Was it a reference to Hesse's *Glass Bead Game*? It was too dark to see much through the windows, but the displays were manikins decked out in colored jewelry.

The building itself was old enough that I decided it must have housed one or more other businesses before this—perhaps a secondhand bookstore or maybe a cleaners. On one side of it, with a narrow alley of weeds between, was a lingerie shop with manikins scantily clad in red undergarments, and on the other a New Age novelty store displaying posters of Che Guevara, Jimi Hendrix, and Marilyn Monroe.

I peered through the window of "The Bead Game," on the chance it might somehow give me some clue as to the likelihood Silkie worked there. Way too dark to see much. Then I turned to the door; "9–5, Mon–Sat," it said.

> *The faint figure behind seemed to shake the pattern, just as if she wanted to get out. [Charlotte Perkins Gilman, "The Yellow Wallpaper"]*
> **[Drawer 3A]**

CAITLIN. *Caitlin was a student in the most remarkable composition class I ever taught. Her narrative was entitled "Sweetened Speed"—a memory of her experience working as a "carnie." It began with, "The Masters of the Elephant Man, Siamese twins, and giants of the traditional carnival have, years ago, unlocked the gates of their cages and with only stolen biscuits in their pockets the alienated 'freaks' staggered away from the sordid streets of their work. Alienated for their abnormalities but emancipated, now, from an iron display case, the human cruelty could cease." It ended with, "Black omnipotent men, stiff under pink teddy bears and blue bunny rabbits. Law and order surrounded by the music of carousel horses going up and down. Men thinking about survivors and casualties beneath dim pink lights."*

Two years later she would write me in the middle of the night from South America about the "vast and vacant . . . treeless and dry" Altiplano in the Bolivian Andes. [**Drawer 3B**]

30. Oasis

I did not have class till ten that morning, so I got in three or four hours of sleep.

At 3:15, I left campus and drove directly to the Bead Game, reasoning that, if she was there, I could claim I just happened to be in the city looking for a birthday gift for Corrine and passed the store and remembered she worked there. If she bought the excuse, fine. If she didn't, so what? She probably didn't even remember telling me about her working there. If indeed this was the place.

Of course, she may have moved out of the city altogether, or quit her job, or not be working this particular day, and it was those possibilities which I feared, not the fear I might have of coming off awkward if she were there. In truth, I didn't care how she interpreted my coming.

Nor did I think less of myself for whatever weakness my behavior was revealing. I could easily allow my mind the rationalization that "Fate" had decreed my path from the moment of that long-ago phone call to the moment I stumbled onto the Bead Game the night before.

I stood just inside the door. It was a larger store than I'd imagined, stretching a long way back past tables of glass-encased jewelry, and behind them many more tables covered with egg trays full of metal, clay, and crystal beads, flanked on both sides with walls full of necklaces, bracelets, macramé, and colored string. Two older women were staring into the glass cases in the front and a teenage girl was modeling a string of beads farther back for her boyfriend.

"Good afternoon," someone called out. A middle-aged hippy or gypsy, with long dark hair streaked with gray and hanging in two pigtails down the back, was smiling and approaching me. She was all in black down to her sandals with brightly painted clay beads around her neck.

I swung around to the other end of the table—pretending to be interested in some gemstone baubles—to get a better look. Right then I caught a glimpse of a little girl playing with beads on the floor through a doorway in the back of the store.

"Are you interested . . . ?"

"Maybe, but . . . actually," I interrupted, "I may know someone who works here. A girl named Silkie?"

"Silkie? Yes, she's right back there now. You want me to call her?"

"If she's not busy."

Moments later Silkie appeared from the rear doorway, in jeans and a sweatshirt, with eyes that seemed to be gazing out over the ocean. She said nothing. I nodded. She smiled. That was all.

By the time I'd picked out a necklace (I'd begun to think about what Corrine would like), she was helping Maheza on with her coat and hood and gathering up the beads from the floor. She herself was slipping on her own green hooded jacket. I set the necklace back down.

"I'm leaving now, Connie," she said to the girl.

"Okay, see you Wednesday."

She pulled Maheza's hood over her head, but Maheza yanked it back down with an "It's not raining."

Silkie let it go.

She turned to me. "We'll go with you."

I tried to remember—Had I asked her to? Go where?

As we exited the store, Silkie—holding Maheza by the hand—led the way, purposeful in what she was about but distracted in some more profound way.

"Do you have your car?" she asked me.

"Yes." I had no idea what was happening. I'd meant only to find out if she was still in town, still attending school, and had a place to stay.

"Aren't you supposed to be working?" I asked.

"No, I was off at three. I was just playing with Maheza."

"What are we. . . ?"

"You've got a little time to take us somewhere? I promised her—Maheza—I'd buy a . . . it's a special kind of roll she likes."

She turned to me briefly, but then away before I answered. Her tone had been deferential, but more as to "how" I would help her rather than "whether" I would. I hadn't yet said anything and would likely have been stupefied were it not that I had been accustomed to her mysterious ways and very much pleased by the turn of events. Till this moment, though, I'd attributed the bizarre nature of our relationship more to my response to her than hers to me. What was happening at this moment was different. And as we reached the car, she said something very curious: "I hope you don't mind. I think it's good this happened."

I was bewildered by the nature of the remark. "It's okay. What do you mean . . . ?"

I had meant to finish with "by 'this happened,'" but Maheza interrupted right then about her shoe hurting the back of her foot. I looked down. They were ragged tennis shoes she was wearing. And by the time Silkie had apparently fixed the problem, the question seemed irrelevant, so I let it go.

Now, reflecting back on Silkie's behavior that day, it occurs to me she never once apologized for the inconvenience. It was to her as if it had been an appointment of some kind. Even taking up as it ultimately did almost three hours of my time. The truth was, she seemed not to have considered how inappropriate it was for a teacher to be driving around a student as though it were his duty.

Perhaps it was that, without any of the social niceties that should have accompanied that presumption, *she knew it was the very thing I needed to do.*

On the other hand, she did apologize, later, for my not

having change to put into the meter, and therefore having to park two streets away where it was free, to get to the bakery, and then for her not having money when we were at the bakery to cover what Maheza wanted to buy.

It was a small bakery with an Eastern European accent. "There—over there," Maheza announced, and both she and Silkie rushed across the street even before the "Walk" light, while I waited.

"She likes this poppy-seed roll. . . . A friend took us here a few months ago," she said by way of explanation. "A lot of different kinds of bread and rolls here." Maheza was staring directly at a whole loaf with black poppy-seed swirls.

"She wants a slice of this," she said to the young woman behind the counter.

"Sorry, you have to buy the whole loaf."

"Oh, I thought . . . the last time someone here cut it for us. You can't just . . . ?"

"Maybe because it was the end of the day, and it was left over, you know?" She struck me as a new employee, unsure of herself.

"How much is the whole thing?"

"$4.75."

"I'll get it," I interrupted, feeling almost as good about it as I'd felt letting her into my class.

Silkie nodded. "We can share it then." Again, she didn't thank me. That's how it was with her. She rarely made use of everyday expressions—"Thank you" or "You're welcome" or even "Good-bye." Why then should I expect her to apologize for what the three of us might end up doing for two or three hours on a Monday afternoon?

As for the *this* of her earlier remark that it was "good this happened," perhaps it was all part of whatever was *happening* from the beginning—from that moment of the eerie phone call. Maybe even from her unusual entrance into my life— soaked, anxious, demanding.

No sooner had we left the bakery than Maheza called out, "Mama, can we go see the rabbit jeans? That red one we saw the other day?"

"I don't think it'll still be there," Silkie protested weakly.

"Can't we just go see?"

"I have time," I said.

"Even if it's there, I don't think we have enough . . . to get it."

"It's okay," I urged.

We drove down eight or nine blocks looking for the store that had had in it the "rabbit jeans."

"They're actually overalls," Silkie explained to me. "There was a patch of a bunny sewn on the front—she likes rabbits."

When we got to the right store, after two wrong turns because the street we wanted was one-way the wrong way—the overalls were no longer in the window. Three dresses only. It was a secondhand clothes store.

"Doesn't look like it's here anymore," Silkie said.

Maheza was undeterred. "We can ask, can't we?"

I shrugged.

"You used to have some denim overalls in the window with a rabbit patch . . . sewn onto the front. They looked like they would fit her," Silkie explained to the young woman clerk.

"We only had that one, and I'm afraid we sold it right away. Sorry." The clerk began flipping through the clearance rack anyway.

"Do you have anything else close to it?" I asked, surprising myself.

"Maybe. The children's jeans are over here," the woman said, and pulled out a couple other overalls. One pair was an emerald green with a bright orange marigold on it. Maheza tried them on and came out smiling.

"See, they fit," she said.

"How much are they?" I asked.

Silkie appeared to be somewhat embarrassed.

"$24.95. They're actually a new pair. We get some. Some slight defects. Irregulars."

"I can get it," I said.

Again, there had been no thank you. Not even a "Maheza, did you thank him?" And there was Maheza, beaming, already wearing her new overalls, which she'd slipped over her T-shirt, carrying her other clothes in a store bag.

The formality of her saying aloud "Thank you," I suspected, would have been the problem. It would have suggested a forced situation. Which somehow none of this was.

I admit it. I was happier than at any time I could remember in recent months. Perhaps Silkie too. It appeared it was the sort of thing she hadn't been able to do for a good while. And I was the one who was making it happen.

"How did you know where to find me?" she asked as we walked back toward the car.

I might have tried lying, telling her it was only by chance, but I knew she wouldn't believe me, and her opinion of me would suffer.

"You told me one time you had to get to work . . . and said something about beads. Besides, why do you assume I was looking for you?" I smiled.

"I wanted you to know."

I pondered that response in silence, wondering if that was the best way to get her to explain further, but she didn't.

"Actually, there was this woman. She's homeless, I think. She was sitting on the curb with all these beads on her neck and said a friend had given her them from the 'clown store.' That's what led me to where you work. Maybe you know her." I was thinking, in some simplistic way, all homeless people in the city would be acquainted.

"What did she look like?"

"Short, dumpy. Wears all kinds of clothes. I see her here and there—walking around."

"Fran."

"Pardon?"

"Did you get her name?"

"Francine."

"Fran. I just know her like everyone else does. She's always, like you say, walking by herself. Everywhere."

"She's homeless."

"No, she lives with some other woman. But Fran is the one with the disability checks. So she pays a lot of the rent. She's not . . . normal. She goes out by herself all the time. A lot of people say hi to her. One time she almost got beat up by some teenagers, and a couple men came along and chased them off."

"Teenagers beating up a woman?"

"Happens."

"So . . . the beads. . . . Did you . . . ?"

"We have some that don't sell, and they gave a handful to Maheza. We"—she nodded to Maheza—"decided to give a couple of them to Fran."

We began walking somewhat aimlessly—twenty to twenty-five minutes. Up and down side streets. Staring down at cracks in the sidewalk overrun by weeds. We must have said something, but I can't remember what or if we even did. Nor am I sure if it was me leading or her or Maheza. It just seemed to happen.

We were almost to the car when Maheza called out, "Look, the train's coming. Can we go see?"

She was pointing down to the end of the street where red lights were flashing and the gates were coming down.

Silkie looked over at me questioningly, and I shrugged, put more money in the meter to cover the rest of the pay time till 6 p.m., and we set off down toward the trains.

Maheza ran ahead of us in a sudden spurt. Silkie didn't seem worried about her, even when she dashed across the street.

It was a slow freight train. Silkie and Maheza sat themselves on an old concrete block wall and watched car after car drag by.

Maheza called her mother's attention to the graffiti painted all over the boxcars. "How come people draw on them?" Maheza asked. "Do they get into trouble?"

"If they get caught. They do it when no one's around."

"You want to write something on one of them?" I asked with a slight grin, and sat myself down a couple feet from Silkie.

Maheza stared at one of the boxcars parked by itself to our right, and I was afraid for a second she would go for it. In the end, though, having thought about it, she shook her head.

The sky was gray, and evening was closing in.

The train passed, the gates went up, and we found ourselves all alone. Almost no traffic. Only an occasional auto slowing down, crossing the tracks, its headlights jumping up, then down, as it did, disappearing down the darker roads on the other side of the train yard.

Maheza went up to the tracks and began dragging her feet over the ties.

"Mama, the pieces of wood . . . here . . . on these train

tracks . . . they're so old. See the funny lines in this one . . . and this one." She actually began to trace the lines of the wood with her finger now.

"Those tracks have been here a long time," I called to Maheza. Probably just because I wanted to say something to her.

She looked at me shyly then bent over and stared down the length of the tracks with her head upside down.

"How many ties do you think there are?" Silkie called out to her.

Maheza stood pondering and looking into the distance. "A lot of them. Must be a thousand. Thousand thousand."

"Maybe more."

"More?" Maheza responded, seeming to question that. She turned to stare into the distance measured by the number of ties. "Do you think they go to Maine? All the way there?"

"Probably." Silkie turned to me then, explaining, "She just read a book where a little girl lives in Maine."

This was the first time I'd seen Maheza acting like a little girl. In my mind till now she'd been a small adult, a small Silkie. Subdued by my presence. Quiet. Elusive the way Silkie was. Even watchful over her mother as much as Silkie was of her. Indeed, she suddenly ran over to her mother and asked, "You took your pill, right?" Then began combing her mother's hair.

In a few days, I would discover she had a tendency to seesaw back and forth with alarming suddenness between that vigilance of a parent and the heedlessness of a child. But, this particular evening, it was the little girl in her that dominated. Over the next hour she explored everything near us: a trash bin behind a restaurant; a menu encased in a small plastic window on the side of the restaurant; posters of coming or past local musical groups stapled to a telephone pole; the letters of license plates in parked cars in a lot to our left. She turned the gravel surroundings into a playground: climbing the iron steps up the back of an abandoned shop; throwing stones at a rusted Stay Off the Fence sign; running up and down a dirt hill; and, until her mother stopped her, pulling herself up the ladder of one of the track semaphore signals.

Silkie and I were saying almost nothing. And it struck me odd how comfortable that was for me. Just sitting there by railroad tracks watching Maheza. Glancing over at Silkie watching Maheza.

I kept thinking about what Silkie had said two or three hours earlier when we'd first gotten into the car: "I hope you don't mind. I think it's good that this happened." It had been a statement, not a question.

We sat there in silence for some time. It was Silkie who broke it. "I didn't do well last term. In school. So I took off this term. Next term I'll start in . . . try . . . again."

"You did well in my class."

"That was the only one."

"What else were you taking?"

"I have to have a job. Teaching someday. Maybe in another

country. I took two education courses. I didn't like them. I wasn't learning anything. Or I couldn't get interested in them. The way they were teaching them. Lesson plans. Too . . . orderly. No, that's not the word. I don't know. I don't know the word. I don't know what I mean. Maybe it's just me."

She didn't seem to want to talk about it anymore.

"Will you lose your financial aid?"

"I have another term. Probation or something. I'll do better next term. I . . . worry about Maheza."

So here we were. A half hour already. Sitting here. Silkie pondering something so deeply that several times I felt compelled to answer Maheza's questions myself. About when the next train would come. About whether she could ride a train someday.

A half hour later, when they got back into the car, I asked, "Where do I take you? A friend's house where you stay? Is that what you told me?"

On the walk back to the car we passed an overweight woman in a motorized wheelchair. Silkie seemed to know her and they chatted briefly—about who I was. She smiled and nodded to me. I nodded back, and we went on our way.

It turned out the friend's apartment where Silkie had been staying was in a two-story converted motel or small office building at least ten blocks from the campus and four or five from the downtown area. She went up a metal stairway on the driveway side up to the second door and along a wood-railed veranda. "I'm just here temporarily," she remarked as she took Maheza's hand and waved to me.

UNHAPPY TEEN GIRL *She was short, noticeably heavy. When she was still a middle-schooler, I suspect her classmates would have added "dumpy." Like a lot of teenage girls I pass on the street or even have in my classes, she was unattractive in most every way. As a result, she had, over the years, withdrawn within herself. A knowing, confident, alive personality might have won out even so. But it was never given any water or sun. So now she has that most overwhelming of handicaps: unhappiness. She walks with her head down. No defiance in her against the universe, or against God. No spark of youth. No anticipation of boys looking so she does not look back in curiosity. An old woman at seventeen or nineteen.* [**Drawer 4**]

31. "Promise Me"

What I said to her the next day I did not plan to say.

When I think back upon it, the events of the previous day should have been enough. I'd found out why she hadn't come. She had not been taking classes this term. And, more significantly, she had chosen for some reason to spend close to three hours with me. I slept well that night.

The sense of desperation in me was gone.

It was late, and I was trying to find a book on the shelf in the back of my office that I needed to preview before going home. I found it and was turning back to my chair when I saw her standing in the doorway, her hands thrust into her parka pockets so much she was stretching them downward.

Why was she here? She did not even make the excuse of saying it was to thank me for the previous day, the overalls and roll I'd bought for Maheza. She just stood there.

"Hi!" I said. "Come in."

As I took my seat, however, I discovered my lips were quivering and I felt a little light-headed. The desperation and despair of the previous weeks pushed up from inside me, and, feeling powerless against what was happening, I gripped the back of the chair and slid down into the seat.

At the same time, the rush of the release transformed itself into a comfort so poignant I began to tremble.

"Would you mind closing the door?" I found myself asking, and wondered what I was doing . . . or even what I was going to say.

Almost too eagerly, she complied.

I had my eyes going in every direction except on her.

"Listen," I said in some unfamiliar voice from deep inside me. "I'm sorry. This will seem strange to you. I need some help. Yours . . . your help."

Hearing no response, I turned to her.

Her eyes were on me, revealing some alarm. Recognizing, apparently, something was very wrong with me.

I saw her alarm, which almost too easily became one with my own. Wherever I was going or what I was going to say, I could not stop it.

"I . . . would like you to promise me something." I began breathing heavier and felt myself to be entering some sacred place. It was not a seizure but close to the same feeling of necessary release. My eyes fastened on hers. "When you're gone from here. From this school. Out in the world. Married. Or whatever you're going to be doing or where you are . . . whenever you're down, depressed, alone, or feeling lost, . . . write me, will you? It would make me feel better knowing you will . . . that you might, anyway . . . do that. It doesn't matter how many years from now."

She was leaning forward, intent, overcome by what I was saying. But the alarm in her eyes was gone. If indeed that was what it had been.

"You won't get . . . in your life . . . many requests like this," I added, finishing with a half-smile intended to ease the intensity of the moment.

She shook her head to say that I was right. She wouldn't.

"Would you promise that? Even if you know you probably won't . . . that years will go by and you'll get caught up in other things . . . me too . . . even if you and I know that . . . still if you'll promise me anyway, that would help me. Right now. At this moment it would."

My God! What was I saying? Why did this come out of me?
She nodded. That was all.

I tried to lighten up again. "I'm sorry to hit you with this. Maybe that phone call affected me a lot more than I thought." I needed some rationale for this other than, "I've gotten too emotionally involved with you because you've got some mystical hold on me." A metaphor was the way: "As I told you before, a lot of circuits got disconnected and when I tried to reconnect them, nothing seemed to be running the same way. Even my teaching. I know, this is a lot to put on you and maybe I shouldn't be . . . well, I hope you enjoyed our walk yesterday. With Maheza, I mean."

It didn't work—this attempt to go back to where I knew as a teacher I should be.

"I . . . I'm sorry. For some reason, in my mind you get connected to all these other things . . . that have been weighing on me. Things that have really nothing to do with you. Other places in the world. The shitty stuff that happens to people. Anyway, I'm sorry."

I stopped, took a deep breath. She was silent.

Finally she got up. "I'll stop by again," she said quietly. "Soon."

JOURNAL [March 14]

Where did that come from? What I asked her to promise. I couldn't sleep most of the night. It came from nowhere. She'd agreed, even seemed, briefly anyway, overcome by it, but . . . isn't it possible it was just because I myself had been so overcome? That she'd consented more from the passion of the request than from the request itself? And therefore, wasn't it possible that the request itself had not come as a surprise to her at all?

And what did that mean?

Now that I think about it, why was she even there? My request caused her to forget, perhaps?

I biked early this morning, trying to collect my thoughts. It was still very dark, and some of these homeless people have bikes with no lights on them. I came upon this guy whose bike was sideways across the bike path, and he was standing next to it packing in cans. Guess he didn't expect anyone to be coming so early. I almost hit him broadside and had to spin wildly off to the side into the field. It was his fault, but for some reason I felt guilty.

Found this quote in a short story ("Araby") by James Joyce—"If I go," I said, "I will bring you something."

LINA. *Lina volunteered to put her Paper IV (argument) quandaries out there for the class to ponder. She even came to the front of the room to take over. I retreated to the rear, pleased that a student would be so willing to put herself on the spot. Still, I was a little anxious for her. She was a good writer and profound thinker, but often struggled with putting together her disparate ideas and mind wanderings in a coherent fashion. Those struggles, which were her strength—ensuring depth of perception, complexity of exploration, and even spontaneity of style—she exhibited physically. Whenever she labored over sorting out ideas and moral dilemmas, she tended to gesticulate wildly, turn and twist in expressions of pleading and frustration to punctuate her perplexity. To some in the class—the run-of-the-mill 19-year-*

olds—*she was very bizarre, a borderline schizo.*

And so she held the class, explaining her "Iraq" paper—her moral misgivings about our own hypocrisy, our treatment of the civilians after major bombing strikes, our oil motives. She answered their questions, responded to their objections to her extreme liberal perspective. Now and then she resorted to her gesticulations and wild body movements to express confusion about how to sort out the ideas. And now and then I would direct the questions to the process—to the way she was approaching the paper and what it meant for writing all such papers.

But when she was finished, I sensed her frustration with the class, with the way they seemed to see her as crazy, on or even over the edge. They seemed to react more to her than her paper.

When the others were gone, I saw that she was crying quietly. Another student stood after class and talked quietly to her. I had not expected that he would be the one that would assure her that she should be proud of what she had done, not dismayed at the response. [**Drawer 3B**]

32. A Strange Request

Winter and spring terms of 2005, it seemed like every one of my classes had a student who had a relative fighting in Iraq or Afghanistan. One very early January morning, when I was the only rider on the city bus I took two or three times a week, the driver told me his son was in Iraq. "I don't even support this war," he said. "I was in Nam. Wasn't so sure about that one either."

"I'm not sure about much of anything anymore," I responded.

"There are facts," he responded. "The TV, the reports, you know, didn't always get 'em right . . . didn't want to. Hid a lot of 'em. Now too. But there are facts."

He was right. You could always be certain about facts. That winter, these were some of them:

> Deposed Chinese leader Zhao Ziyang, who'd publicly expressed sympathy for the Tiananmen Square students, died.

Nobel Peace laureate Shirin Ebadi refused to obey a summons to appear in a Tehran court, even though it would mean her arrest.

Martin Luther King, had he lived, would have been seventy-six.

I visited one weekend the home of a university colleague who taught religion and philosophy. He and his wife lived a self-sustaining existence, conserving the earth's resources in every way, on $3,000 a year. I was impressed. Acknowledging it was a poor excuse for my own lack of active commitment to saving the planet, I admitted to not being able to get beyond God's indifference to the universe as a whole.

Johnny Carson, talk-show host and comedian, died.

Arthur Miller, author of *Death of a Salesman*, died.

Hunter S. Thompson, author of *Fear and Loathing in Las Vegas*, died.

February 21 was the fortieth anniversary of the assassination of Malcolm X, a hero of mine.

In early March, a schizophrenic "bag lady" well known by both students and faculty because she'd lived some thirty years on or near the campus, was struck and killed by a car.

Time magazine did a special issue on remarkable individuals throughout the world who had "made a difference" in relieving suffering. I wondered how it was so few of us knew any of them.

A relative of Van Gogh—who had made a film condemning the brutal treatment of Islamic women (the film included the portrait of a young woman beaten savagely and then left to die with words from the Qur'an painted on her body)—was stabbed to death as he rode his bike to work one morning.

I wrote a recommendation letter that helped a Lebanese student get a $15,000 scholarship to medical school.

I stumbled onto a documentary on Chiune Sugihara, of Japan, who saved some 1,268 Jews during WWII against his government's policies.

Edgar Ray Killen, age eighty, a Klansman involved in the killing of the three civil rights workers in 1964, was just now coming to trial.

On a cold Sunday morning, I drove sixty miles east into the mountains to stand gazing from a small wood-plank walking bridge at a waterfall that was half ice.

It was the first Tuesday of spring term—late March—so

early I'd had to use my own key to get into the side door of the building. I was setting my backpack on the floor in my office when I looked up to see Maheza standing directly in the doorway, with Silkie behind her.

Maheza was dressed very neatly with her brown hair combed back and held in place by a bright green plastic band—the kind made to look like a ribbon. Under her jacket was the pair of overalls I'd bought her.

"You are very dressed up," I said with a smile.

She stood there quietly, shyly, eyeing me, holding a soiled, matted white stuffed animal.

"Is that a rabbit?" I asked her.

She nodded.

She was comfortable with me now.

Silkie was wearing her parka and jeans, and her hair, just like Maheza's, was combed back. Except hers was longer, silkier, and a muted golden.

"How did you get in? Wasn't the building still locked?" I asked, smiling, pleased she would come so early to see me.

"The security man. He was just opening the door when we came. He said it was too cold for us to wait outside."

"He doesn't usually open it this early."

"He's very friendly, isn't he?"

"He's always pleasant. Doesn't say much but . . ."

" I . . . ," she said slipping into the chair across from me. "I . . . need your help."

"Pardon?"

"I need your help."

I pulled my chair out and sat down too. "Something wrong?"

I remembered our afternoon together. Her expectations for me then had been implicit. This, apparently, was to be explicit. But both presumed the result. My willingness. She should have been hesitant, given the oddity of the request, maybe even have faltered. Instead she came right out with it like she was asking if she could be a little late with a paper.

"I'm going back to school again. A night class. The woman I expected could watch Maheza won't be able to."

I waited.

"I need someone to watch Maheza."

I waited. "You want me to ask if anyone in my classes does babysitting? Do you have . . . enough to pay . . . ?"

"No, you."

"Me what?"

"You do it. Take care of her for me."

What was this? A student asking a teacher to babysit as though it were a reasonable request. As though I shouldn't be surprised, should even have expected it.

"Me?"

"You have children, you told me . . . Paul and . . ."

"Corrine."

"But they're not at home, right? You're alone at night."

She blushed right then, perhaps realizing she'd presumed too much about my private life. But she added no qualifier.

In fact, her expression wasn't one of entreaty, but of expectation again. A kind of "This is just how it is."

"Yes, but . . . me? Why would you . . . ? Your daughter . . . doesn't know me that well. Besides, isn't it a little strange to . . . you know . . . ." I wanted to say, "strange to be asking your teacher to be doing it?" but stopped.

She was waiting.

 I wondered if I shouldn't respond very directly with something like, "You think I don't have papers to mark . . . that . . . alone as I am . . . I still have some life?"

But if I was bothered by her having, in effect, demoted me from professor to friend, to babysitter, I had to admit I'd already lowered (if that was the right word) myself with her on numerous occasions. The adventure in town. My own strange request for her to call on me in the future. Yes, that gave her the right to be that familiar with me.

"You drive around at night. You told me once. To think. The whole class you told. So why is it strange? You like children. You like Maheza, don't you?"

"Yes, of course."

"Will you try it just one time? Tomorrow night?"

It was so outrageous, I suddenly began to see the charm in it.

 "Tomorrow night?" I shrugged, half laughed. "Why not? Might be fun to try. Are you . . . staying in the same place? With your friend? Where I dropped you off that time?"

She nodded. "I'll tell you. Give me your phone number,

just in case. The class starts at seven, so maybe at six thirty?"

Was this a come-on? Her place. I shouldn't even be considering it.

I was, however, already looking forward to it.

> **GEORGE.** *George, a staunch Catholic and ex-con, is in his fifties now. He not only began to write, really write, in my freshman comp class but became obsessed with it. And he read books. Far into the night—night after night—he would be reading and writing. Most of it philosophy. He gave me credit for being "the one who changed his life."* **[Drawer 3B]**

> **CALIFORNIA FATHER** *A man in California, distraught about the breakup of his family, killed his wife and three children ages six to fourteen, huddled together, then himself.* **[Drawer 4]**

33. Four Evenings

There would be four.

The first night—
she took me to the park,
I bought her a strawberry tart in the grocery bakery,
I met Lilac and his dog Jesse,
and there was no toilet paper for her in the bathroom.

The second night—
I bought her a jacket,
 I took her to a Gershwin concert, and she was transfixed by
the beautiful young lady in the silver dress singing "Someone
to Watch Over Me."

The third—
we had sundaes at Dairy Queen,
she ran wildly around the baseball diamond,
she read to me from a book of nursery rhymes I bought
her from a secondhand bookstore.

The fourth—
she set me straight about her mother (as did Ruth),
she drew me a three-legged tiger,
and, with her mother, she did a sleepover.

To say there's anything sacred about four nights of babysitting is, I suppose, sacrilegious. The "sacred" should confine its realm to the pages of scriptures and the walls of cathedrals. To me, though, those four nights, the scriptures were the city streets, and the cathedral was Maheza's world.

I would not have used that word "sacred" in explaining to a colleague. No, I would have used the word "worthwhile." I would have replied, "Oh, it just seemed like the most worthwhile thing I could do on any of those four nights. Or for the year as a whole."

Of course, I kept it a secret. Such an explanation would not have satisfied a colleague's wondering why I wouldn't be outraged a student—no, ex-student—would so presume on a professor's time. A professor with a doctorate. A six-year-old girl he hardly knew. As though he had nothing else to do with his evenings. As though he wouldn't have preferred taking in a concert, a play, or just sharing a dinner at a Mediterranean restaurant and an indie film with a companion.

More "worthwhile"? How could that be?

Fortunately it was only one person who knew and asked me: "Wouldn't you rather be doing something else than this tonight?" And that was Silkie.

"This feels more worthwhile," I replied.

Because, as with the eerie phone call, it did partake of what, indeed, felt sacred to me. *Something I had to do. Something intended for me.*

I was feeling an almost spiritual compulsion to follow wherever Silkie led. I still could not shake the notion that whether or not it was a very conscious planned thing with her, she was *leading me*. Where? Or was she, too, being driven? Led? By someone else. *Something* else.

My decision, therefore, to watch Maheza was never personally an indication of some weakness or deficiency in me. Still, I feared I would fail in carrying it out. Feared Maheza wouldn't feel comfortable with me when it was one-on-one. The necessary result being her mother would think less of me.

"No," I told myself, "I am a father, I have been raising a daughter of my own, even if in recent years from a distance." I knew children. I could read to her. If she were shy, I would just leave her alone till she felt more comfortable. I would do nothing stupid that would cause her to be afraid of me. Very likely, Silkie's class being almost three hours long, Maheza would fall asleep before her mother returned. Perhaps fall asleep in my arms.

So naïve I was! I was visualizing my own house as the setting—or, if hers, something not that different from mine. There would be a living room. A rug. A couch and armchair to read to Maheza in. Children's books in some sort of bookcase. A TV. A kitchen. A bedroom with her own bed to put her into.

I had to remind myself about that first evening I'd gone searching for Silkie's house months earlier to tell her I'd let her into my class. Given Silkie's somewhat homeless existence, where would I be going? She'd nodded when I'd asked her if it would be the same place where I dropped them off a few days earlier, but she'd said she would call me. Let me know. Why couldn't she have told me right away? Was she not herself sure how or where this babysitting would happen?

"The obvious place is my own house," I said to myself. At least, I would offer.

But was it a good idea to bring her to my house? I looked around—the paintings on my wall, carvings I'd brought back from teaching in Africa, wall-to-wall carpeting, plants, a DVD player and TV, a stereo, a spacious kitchen, three bedrooms, shelves full of books. What, if any of this, did Maheza have? Would it be upsetting to Silkie for me to show Maheza what her mother could not provide?

I was in such consternation about all this, I became angry with myself, and said aloud, "Jesus. Just see what happens!"

Planning was wise, even so, so I threw into the backseat of my car some of Paul and Corrine's things left from years earlier—a handful of children's books, a Frisbee, and a midsize soccer ball—then scouted the neighborhood where I'd dropped Silkie and Maheza off. It was a part of town I was not familiar with. I parked the car a couple blocks away and walked. Most of her street and the cross streets were a mix of old shingle and wood-frame houses—small and run-down. On one corner was an auto repair shop, a small salon next to it. There had been a service station across the street but it was no longer open. Down a block was a small property management office and a small mom-and-pop grocery transformed into a convenience store. Just three or four blocks south was a city park that ran under a freeway. It had long been a haven for the homeless, who stretched out in sleeping bags under the trees and near some picnic tables and trash containers.

I found the note under my office door when my first class was finished. From Silkie, telling me she would meet me around 6:45 p.m. at a certain corner on the campus near where her class was. Did that mean I wouldn't be taking care of Maheza at her place but somewhere else? My house? If so, why couldn't I just read to her from Corrine's books, or let her watch some video on the TV? Old Disney videos were somewhere in the closet.

Afterwards I could take her to some fast-food restaurant for a late snack.

The first night—

Silkie and Maheza both had on old backpacks when they showed up. Maheza was wearing her overalls.

"I put a couple of her books and cassettes in her bag.

Some drawing paper too," Silkie explained.

"So should I just take her to my place?" I asked.

"Is that okay?"

"What time should we meet?"

"Oh, right. Class is supposed to let out at 9:50. It's a long one because it's only once a week. I wouldn't take it, but it's a requirement. Educational Psychology."

"Meet here?"

"Is that all right?"

"Sure."

She hugged Maheza, then left. Maheza stood watching her mother who, farther down the walkway, stopped, turned around, and gazed at us (or just Maheza) for a few seconds, and seemed to half wave, then hurried on. Maheza didn't move till her mother was out of sight.

I sat down on the curb and waited for her to acknowledge my presence.

She didn't.

"What shall we do?" I finally asked.

She turned to me and shrugged.

"The overalls. You look good in them," I said.

She looked down, opened her coat, and stared at them.

"Are you hungry?" I asked. "We can get a snack—cake or something—then you tell me what you want to do. We can go to my house later, if you like."

She seemed to think about it. "We can go to Marketplace?"

"The grocery? The one on Adams Street?"

316

She nodded.

"Why?"

"They have tarts. The bakery there."

As we drove to Marketplace, where I'd shopped only once or twice before, it struck me this babysitting might be a regular thing. Why would next week be any different? Meeting her on campus, taking Maheza to some place to have a treat, then to my house, then back to the campus to pick up Silkie.

Not that it mattered to me, but I doubted Silkie would offer to pay me—for my time—or reimburse me for any money I spent on Maheza. If she did, I wouldn't take it anyway.

We pulled into the store parking area.

"You come here a lot?"

She shook her head.

"So how do you know . . .?"

"I want to go back."

"Pardon?"

"Go back."

"Back where?"

She was looking off down the street, not at me.

"Mama didn't take her medicine."

"Medicine?"

"She forgot. It's in the room. We didn't go there . . . all day."

"Can't she just take it later?"

She stood there, rigidly, as though forced into some critical decision, and finally turned to me and shook her head.

Maheza had these very large, blue, determined eyes, which could, in moments of resolve, gather into a weapon. None of the mystery and vulnerability her mother's eyes had. I would learn over the next few weeks that her eyes spoke her strongest words. That there was no backing down with her. And it was because she took care of her mother as much as her mother took care of her.

"Don't you think . . . are you sure? Medicine for what?" I was hoping an across-the-counter medicine would work.

She didn't answer. Looked over at me anxiously, her somewhat unkempt brown hair hanging over her face.

"I can tell you how to get there," she insisted.

"It's the same place as before, no? Remember the time I dropped you off?"

She nodded.

"But . . . you know . . . your mother's in class. You can't really . . . give it to her. Right? I'm not even sure what building she's in."

She ignored me again.

I pictured a little girl walking into a large classroom with a bottle of pills and thrusting it into the face of her embarrassed mother.

"I think she's okay. Probably has them with her. So . . . don't worry."

"It's not far," she insisted, a tear forming in the corner of her left eye. There was no arguing her out of it.

"You don't want to get the tart first, since we're here?"

She thought that over, then shook her head again.

"All right. We can come back later, I guess."

When I pulled up in front of Silkie's apartment, Maheza jumped out of the car.

"Hold on!" I said. "I'll go in with you."

She was running up the side stairway, and I had to rush to keep up. The whole structure looked cheap—eight or nine large aluminum panels put together, easily taken apart. If once a motel, one for the down-and-out. The veranda flooring a sort of aluminum sheet, the outside paint peeling everywhere. At the fourth opening down, Maheza disappeared. When I got there she was rushing to the end of a hallway along which were numbered apartment doors on both sides. The linoleum on the floor was cracking and chewed away. Brown paper and plastic trash bags full of bottles and cans sat outside some of the apartments. A pungent marijuana smell hung in the air. One of the doors was open and I could see inside a heavy-set man in his undershirt bent over a small table on which were three or four dirty plates. He looked up, ignored us.

Maheza, at the end of the hall, was struggling with the door there—Room 24 (the metal "4" was dangling upside down). It was locked.

"You don't have a key? You forgot."

She stood there looking anxious, then tried again with

some desperation, rattling the doorknob till I thought it might break.

There were tears in her eyes.

"Listen, I'm sure your mother is okay."

She wiped her eyes and her nose. On the way back down the hallway, she pushed open a door with a sign taped to it that read "Toilet 2" and closed the door. I waited. After a while I heard her moving about, but she didn't come out. After too long, I finally called in.

"You okay?"

It was quiet. Then, "There's no . . . paper."

"Toilet paper? Wait, I'll see if . . . " Not seeing any closet that might have it, I went down the hall and knocked on the half-opened door where I'd seen the man. "Can we borrow some toilet paper? The little girl—she lives down the hall—Room 24—needs some. I'm taking care . . ." I anticipated a sarcastic retort such as "You don't *borrow* toilet paper," but he only scratched his very black greased hair, then, without saying a word, went back into his apartment, putting out his cigarette in an ashtray along the way. When he returned it was with a wad of toilet paper wrapped around his hand. "This enough?" I sensed he was trying to be pleasant but didn't know how.

"Yes, should be. Thanks." I was thinking to ask for more but decided against it.

"I have it. Here." I called in to Maheza. "Open the door a little."

She opened the door a crack, and I slipped it in.

When she came out, she didn't look at me.

"I guess we'll head back to get the tart," I said.

Even as we drove away she kept her head turned out the window.

"Your mother will be fine. She's in class. I was her a teacher, you know. She'll be okay."

We stood next to the car. The parking lot of Marketplace again. But she wasn't moving.

"She'll be okay," I said again. "Let's go in."

I started walking. She stood there. I stopped. Started up again. Finally she followed.

One whole side of the store was full of cakes and pies and rolls and various sorts of bread.

"Choose one," I said.

She stared into the long glass case. When she finally pointed at one of the strawberry tarts, it was as though she'd given the matter a great deal of thought, and that was the resulting conclusion she'd come to. "That one."

It struck me, in fact, that almost everything she said came out that way—sounding as though it had been preceded by lengthy deliberations in her mind.

She ate it very slowly and carefully at a nearby table. I shared a half-pint of milk with her and ate a biscotti.

"What now?" I asked. "We have two hours or so to kill."

"Can we go see Lilac?"

"Lilac? What's that? A movie?"

She smiled for the first time and giggled. "No, Lilac's a man."

"A man?"

"He's got Jesse. A big dog."

"Where is he?"

She hopped up from her chair.

"I'll show you."

"Where? Do you mean his house?"

She shook her head.

"What does that mean?"

"He doesn't have a house."

"So how do we . . . ? Does your mother know . . . ?"

"In the park."

"Park? Which park? It's dark."

"By the river."

I wasn't sure about this. "Why don't you do that some other time? Your mother knows about that. What if we just go to my place?"

She was silent.

"Do you want another tart?"

She stared at the crumbs on the napkin in front of her.

"I can get you another one and you can eat it later . . . or tomorrow."

As we walked back to the car, she carried the bag with the second tart in it.

"What if we head to my place now?"

"Can we take this to Lilac?"

"The tart?"

I took a deep breath. "You sure this will be okay with your mother? Is he a friend?"

She thought about it, then nodded.

"Okay. I guess we can go quickly. You know your mother gets out in a little over an hour. How long will this take?"

Before we reached the car, she stopped.

"Can we go back in and get something for Jesse?"

"Jesse? Oh, the dog?"

She reached into the front pouch of her backpack and produced a dollar bill.

When we exited the store a few minutes later with a large can of dog food that I paid for, I remembered the need for a can opener.

"We should have gotten two small cans," I said. "You can just pull off the tops. This can needs an opener."

"He has one." She seemed sure about it.

Ten minutes later, I pulled the car into the park road. There were, fortunately, lights in the lot for cars because no other vehicles were in sight, and beyond the lot it was completely dark.

"You sure you don't want to do this in the daytime? Tomorrow maybe?"

She ignored me.

"Do you know where to go?"

She grunted some sort of yes, and, carrying the bag with the tart and the can of dog food, cut across the grass, almost running, toward the river.

"Maheza, wait! How far is it? Let's stay on the sidewalk till we get closer. Slow down. It's dark."

Pines and firs lined the river, so it got even darker as we moved away from the picnic areas.

"There!"

She stopped and pointed to a group of what looked to be all men, cigarettes glowing, seated around a picnic table near where the park dropped off into the tangled brush along the water, from which I could hear a gurgle now and then but couldn't see because there was no moon. As we got closer, voices became audible—both men's and women's. They had a fire going. There were beer cans on the table as well as coffee cups. Bicycles packed with bags full of cans, blankets.

"How do you know if he's here?"

She stopped some distance away.

"Maheza, you're sure he's here now?"

By now they saw us and stopped talking. Someone in a hooded jacket got up and approached us—slow, hips betraying a kind of limp.

"Maisie, that you? Who's this?"

A woman's voice.

She was very short and her skin looked very rough, even in the dark. Little or no teeth. But it was the smile, the eyes, that stood out. "You remembered to come see me."

She hugged Maheza, then turned to me.

"I'm Jo Ann."

"Hi. Stephen. Taking care of her. She wanted to see . . . to bring something to . . . Do you know someone named . . . Lilac?"

"Where's her mama?"

"In class."

She nodded. "Her mother's good person." She smiled, and looked down at Maheza. "Lilac was here earlier, honey, but he wasn't feeling well. " She put her hand on Maheza's head. "I 'spect he's where he sleeps at night. You know where's that, don't you?"

Maheza nodded.

"They're friends," she explained to me. "Listen, you want me to show you? She likes his dog. Haven't seen him for a time, have you?"

"If he's not feeling well . . . "

"Oh, he won't mind. Make him feel good. Maisie here knows where it is."

"Yeh. Thanks. Nice to meet you." I smiled as I took Maheza's hand to leave.

"They call you Maisie?" I asked.

"That's okay," she responded, as though she'd pondered it a long time before this—the rightness or wrongness of the name they called her.

"Your mother call you that too?"

She shook her head.

"I bet a lot of people don't say it right."

She shrugged.

"You have to turn that way," she told me as we exited the park.

"Left?"

"Uh-huh."

We drove down several blocks.

"Can I ask you something, Maheza? You and your mother ever . . . sleep at night down there . . . by the river?"

"Sometimes. When it's not cold. Long time ago."

"But . . . not now?"

She shook her head.

"Once there was a raccoon. Mommy and a baby. A man was feeding them."

"Who?"

She shrugged. "Mama's friend."

We drove another block.

"Over there." She was pointing up ahead.

"Where?"

"Right there."

"That's an RV place . . . where they sell them, isn't it?"

"Uh-huh."

"Where am I going to park? Wait, I'll have to pull up to the next block."

I parked the car and locked it, and we walked back.

"Are you sure . . . ?"

"See!"

"See what?"

Under one of the RVs there was a movement.

"That's Jesse."

"I thought you said . . ."

The dog lifted its head, startled, and started growling. Looked to be brown with white stripes—mix of some kind. And fairly big.

"Hey, it's me, Jess," she called out. The dog lay its head back down and his tail came alive briefly.

"They let him stay here," she explained, standing back and pointing at something near the dog. Even with the streetlights, though, it was so dark along the side of the vehicle, I would not have seen him had she not walked me closer—to a form lying still. Someone wrapped up in a sleeping bag.

"Maybe we shouldn't bother him," I whispered.

She sat down next to Jesse and petted him.

"Brought you some food, Jess," she said.

"That you, Maisie?" The figure on the ground called out without moving. "Your mama too?" He struggled stiffly over on his back and raised his head slightly. "Who's there?"

"Sorry to bother you." I pointed to Maheza. " I'm watching her. For her mother. She insisted on bringing you something."

He rubbed his face and glanced at Maheza. "Maisie?"

I could see now behind the RV was a trailer packed with bulky plastic grocery bags tied to the back of a bicycle, with a blanket tossed over some of it. There was a faint smell of beer.

"I brought you a blueberry tart," Maheza said. "And some food for Jess."

He finally pulled himself up to a sitting position, so that some of the streetlight fell on his face now. He looked to be about my age—in his fifties. Long hair—graying now, but maybe light brown at one time—tied in a ponytail down the back. A mustache. Eyes perceptive in ways my eyes probably weren't.

"Thanks, hon. I'll just . . . eat it later. Leave it in the bag, 'kay?" His voice was hoarse, grainy, and he tried clearing his throat, but his attempt didn't do the job.

"The lady in the park—Jo Ann—said we could bring it to you," I said. "She told us you weren't feeling well and it would make you feel better."

"Yeah, she's . . . Sorry. Lester's the name. Or . . . Lilac. Anyway. Just here for couple nights. Maybe I'll have a place next week. You know? You her uncle or something?"

"No, no. A friend of her mother's. Actually her teacher. Used to be."

"Oh. College?"

He dredged up the phlegm in his throat once more, but again with no success.

I nodded.

"You want some coffee or something?" he asked, staring down at the ground. "Sorry, haven't been . . . Have a bad toothache, and can't get it fixed till there's one of those fairs

. . . health fairs. . . . It's free then."

"It's all right. We'll let you rest."

"No, it's . . . okay. You know . . . I took a course—couple of them—electronics . . . at the community college. Four years ago. Someone stole my Social Security number and charged a lot with it. I ended up owing so much . . . couldn't get it straightened out. No job at the time. The dog here costs too. But most places don't let you keep one. He's my friend. Jess." He petted him. "Tried to take him away once . . . because he attacked some old lady's mutt. Would have put him away. Lawyer friend helped me, but . . . anyway . . . that was in Oakland."

He rushed through that information, I gathered, to paint an entirely different picture of himself than I had most likely formed.

"Life's not fair," I said, feeling stupid for saying it.

"I'm always on a waiting list. Name never comes up."

"Listen, I have to get her back. Here." I handed him a $10 bill and a couple ones.

"No, man, that's okay."

"I can spare it. You're her friend."

He took it. "Sure you don't . . . need anything?"

"No, no."

"I can fix things. Electronic things. Sure?"

"Thank you. Oh, I'm . . uh . . . Stephen."

"Stephen. You got kids yourself?"

"Yeah. Yeah, I do. Boy and a girl. California."

He nodded. "Mine's in Montana. She's twenty-two. Living with some guy. We used to be close."

I didn't say anything. Just gave him a knowing look.

"Does she know?" I asked.

"Know? Oh . . . this? I don't tell her. It's not so bad. There are places when it gets too cold. Food stamps. An odd job now and then. Like I say, I can fix things. Even cars. Had my own for a time because the guy didn't want to pay to fix it. Said I could have it if I could. So I did. But I couldn't afford the insurance and . . . anyway . . . it was impounded. Couldn't pay to get it back."

I went over and petted the dog so I wouldn't have to respond in some way that didn't come close to meaning anything to him.

"Listen, I'm supposed to meet her mother at 9:50. So I'll have to go. Thanks for the chat."

"Thank you." He reached for the bag. "What is this again? A dessert. And something for Jesse too!"

"You want me to show you where I live?" I asked Maheza as we were driving back.

"Okay."

"How old are you?"

"Six. My birthday's February 28." She said it with pride.

"So you'll be going to school next year, won't you? First grade. Where?"

She shook her head.

"What does that mean?"

"Mama doesn't know yet."

"You'll get new friends when you do."

She nodded.

"You have friends now, don't you?"

"One."

"What's his name?"

"Lilac."

"I mean your age."

She shrugged.

"Here's where I live. If your mother asks again, maybe you can come over here." I pulled into the driveway. "We have a few minutes to kill. You want to take a look?"

She stood inside the door, staring at the large African tie-dye cloth I had hanging on the far wall.

"You need to use the bathroom?"

She shook her head. Now she was staring at the pictures of Paul and Corrine on the end table.

"Who are these?"

"My own children. They're older now. Pictures are from a few years ago. Paul. He's ten now. Corrine's 11."

"How come they don't live with you?"

"Sometimes they're here. But their mother and I live in different places."

She was walking in the direction of the bathroom.

"Right over there. If you want to use the toilet."

When she came out of the bathroom, she stopped in front of a black-and-white photo of the Mojave Desert. A play of chiaroscuro.

"Is this a flower?"

"That? No. It's a desert. It's just that the lines—the spirals and hills, and clouds—make a pattern. So it looks beautiful. Yeh, you're right . . . kind of like a flower."

"That's sand?"

"Yeh, sand. Sand dunes."

"Did you take the picture?"

"Wish I had. No, a photographer. A nature photographer. You know the kind that takes pictures of rivers and wildflowers and wild animals."

"Someday I want a camera. I'll take pictures like that."

We met her mother at ten and I drove them back toward her apartment.

"She was worried about you taking your medicine," I told her. "Went back to your room but didn't have a key."

Silkie turned to her daughter in the backseat. "I took it with me. You shouldn't worry."

"Do you forget sometimes? I mean, I was wondering why she was so worried."

"Sometimes."

"So . . . what . . . happens if . . . ?"

"I told you. How I am. Once they took her away from me."

"Really? Took her where?"

"A home."

"How long?"

"Weeks. Till I got that part-time job and into school. Till I had money to get a place to keep her."

"Wow!"

"What did you do tonight?"

"Took me everywhere," I said. "Very educational."

I pulled up to the curb in front of their apartment.

Silkie sat there silently.

"So, are you going to need me again . . . next week?"

Still she was silent.

"I have a ticket to a concert," I told her. "Gershwin. I guess you know his stuff. Heard of him anyway. Bought it a long time ago. At the Performing Arts Center. 'An American in Paris.' I've had a recording a long time—actually a record— but I've never seen a live performance. I've been . . . looking forward to it for a long time."

"Then you can't . . ."

"Well, I was thinking. . . . what if I take her with me? I'll buy another ticket. If I can't get the seat next to me, I'll exchange for two of them together. You know? I could pick her up early. Around five and take her to the mall first. So she can buy something new to wear. You come too, then I'll drop you off before class. If we have to leave the concert a little early to get back by ten, that's okay. Will that work?"

She nodded. "Five p.m. here?"
"Five p.m. here."

The second night—
Maheza, tomboyish though she was, glowed as she tried
on four different frilly dresses at the mall, and when she
stopped to admire a blue nylon ski jacket, I bought her that
too; and, wearing it over the dress, she didn't take it off even
though it was hot high up in the balcony, and she smiled
as the brass section of the orchestra playfully honked and
beeped its way through "An American in Paris." But it was
when those sounds got swept up into the pathos in the final
part evoking the loneliness of a man far from his home, and
when, later in the concert, a young beautiful dark-haired
woman in a glittering, silvery 1920s gown sang "Someone
to Watch Over Me" that she seemed to most

> forget I was sitting next to her,
> and I was most
> aware she was sitting next to me.

The third night—
I took her to a secondhand-book store, and she picked
out Wallace Tripp's nursery rhyme collection—*A Great Big
Ugly Man Came Up and Tied His Horse to Me* —because she
liked the doggerel and limericks and the clever drawings, and
later read from it so smoothly I wondered if she hadn't read
the book before and memorized many of the rhymes. And,

before meeting Silkie, we had sundaes at a Dairy Queen and then stopped at a neighborhood school yard, and Maheza, her face grim and determined, hit the third pitch I threw and ran around the bases seven or eight times without stopping, because running to wear herself out with exhilaration seemed to be more her thing than hitting.

I admit to feeling the giddiness of being able to play parent to a young child once again, a satisfaction of doing things for Silkie through Maheza.

I was in charge. If Maheza showed me her world the first Thursday, I showed her mine the next two.

Even in my teaching I felt a new buoyancy.

It seemed to me to be a settled thing. The routine of picking them up on campus, dropping off Silkie, entertaining Maheza at my house, then driving them back to their room.

The fourth night—

was anything but routine. Only minutes after I dropped off Silkie I saw that Maheza was looking anxious—as she had the first night when she'd been concerned Silkie hadn't taken her medicine.

"You feeling okay?" I asked.

Sitting in the seat next to me, she nodded. But I could tell something was wrong.

I'd discovered from Silkie that Maheza liked hot chocolate chip cookies (she'd gotten some, of all places, at the bank for free on Fridays), so I'd resolved to make some, with her helping, to take up much of the time.

I was using the recipe on the back of the Nestle Toll House chocolate chip bag and setting the ingredients on my kitchen counter while reading aloud, then showing her how to measure out the amounts. But I could see her mind wasn't with it.

"Sure nothing's bothering you?" I asked.

This time she didn't answer. She was staring down at the butter she'd been mushing down with a fork to make it soft.

I was just setting the oven at preheat when she went to the bathroom.

I turned behind me later to see her standing in the kitchen—staring at me.

"You want to help me stir this?" I said.

"We have to find Mama," she said. Again, in that way she had of sounding like it came after considerable consideration.

"What?" I stopped mixing the dough in the bowl.

"We have to go."

"Where?"

"Find Mama."

"She's in class."

Maheza shook her head.

"What do you mean?"

She shook her head.

"She's not in class?"

She appeared to be on the verge of crying.

"Why do you say that? Why don't we just finish up one batch—I've got the oven on and you can take her some cookies—then we'll go early with them."

"We have to go now." Quiet but firm.

"She won't be out for another hour. I'm not sure what classroom she's in. What's wrong?"

"Can we go? I want to go." Her concern had become almost a panic.

"All right."

I turned off the preheat.

As we drove, she was leaning forward intently in the front seat.

"Why are you . . . so afraid . . . about her? I mean, I'm not sure what you want me to do."

"Can we go back to the park?"

"The park? The one by the river? Sure. I guess."

The road into the park was only a little less dark than it had been three weeks earlier. There was a partial moon but it was covered by clouds. The parking lot lights shone only a few feet beyond the concrete.

Maheza jumped out and began looking all around.

"You know it's raining a little now," I called out. "What are you looking for?"

"Mama . . . " Her final words were clipped by the wind and her turning her head the other way.

"What? Does she? I thought you told me she doesn't come

here anymore. Besides, she's in class. Come on, let's go home."

She came back. Stood outside the car, with the door open, staring off toward the river. Then she jumped back into the car. Then got out again, closed the car door, and began walking along the edge of the park back toward the main street.

"Maheza. Hey! Where you going?"

She kept walking, faster and faster. I got out of the car. I almost had to run to catch up.

"Listen, why don't we just drive slowly this way so we don't get wet? Get back in the car. Why do you think she's . . . ?"

She finally stopped without turning around, maybe considering the sense in what I'd said. Then she faced me and began walking back slowly. That image of her—coming toward me, in the rain, her hair and face shiny under the lights from the parking lot, her head up, eyes on me as if in a daze, and looking so tired out, and so in need of an adult like me at that moment—will always stay with me.

I opened the car door for her and she got in without saying a word. Seeing she was still peering anxiously out the window toward the river, I drove very slowly as we exited the park.

As I turned right and down the street, she was studying every person who was walking alone.

"You want me to drive to the campus so you can see for yourself?" I asked.

She thought about it, then nodded.

We got only a little ways into the campus, though. As

I began looking for a place to park, wondering how I was going to satisfy her without disturbing Silkie, she pointed to my left. "Can we go that way?"

We were stopped at a red light, so I had time to decide to become more assertive.

"I think maybe I should just park and we'll go see if . . . "

"That street goes to the park too."

"Which one? That one? Yes. Right. But to the other side of the park."

"She'd go that way then."

"From her class, I suppose so. If she weren't going to wait for us to come."

"Can we go that way first?"

The light changed.

"Okay."

We passed several campus buildings on the right and restaurants and motels and a small bar on the left. Seeing she was still peering out the window, even turning around to look at the faces of some of the students on the sidewalk, I drove slow.

"So are we going all the way back to the park this way?" I asked.

"The other side."

"The other side, yes . . . she'd go this way probably. She might anyway. If she really did leave class."

Beyond the campus area it got very dark. The road was lit by only the corner streetlights, which were long blocks apart.

It began to feel like Maheza and I were separate—in some profound way, apart—from everything around us. A very conscious, even visceral feeling—the two of us bundled up in an invisible blanket of darkness, rain, anxiety, wonder.

I'd already concluded it didn't matter whether or not Maheza was making any sense. Something serious was going on here, and I would ask Silkie about it later when it came time to pick her up.

We drove in silence back toward the park, but to the other side, which required we cross a small bridge over a stream branching off from the river.

"There!" she called out.

"What?"

"Stop! Stop!" She was yelling.

I pulled over to the curb and looked back. A lone woman was sitting on the low concrete wall that served as a guardrail for the sidewalk and road on the bridge over the stream. It was too dark for me to make out who it was, but it was likely a student because she had on a backpack.

"What? You don't think that's your mother?"

"Stop!"

"Wait! I can't be stopping the car on the bridge. I'll pull up further." If I hadn't held on to her arm, she would have pushed open the door and jumped out.

By the time I'd parked the car and turned off the engine, Maheza was already running along the sidewalk back to the bridge.

"Wait! . . . Jesus . . . Maheza!"

In the distance I could see her scooting up next to the woman on the wall.

It was indeed Silkie.

But she wasn't responding as I would have expected—wasn't hugging Maheza or expressing surprise. Just sitting there gazing at me coming closer.

"Hi." That was all I could think to say. She would figure out all that was in it.

At first I thought her silence was embarrassment, but as I stood there waiting for some explanation, I could see she was very confused, even agitated. Was it possible she didn't know who I was?

"Silkie?"

"Hi."

"What . . . are you doing here?"

Maheza, her eyes closed, had slipped both her arms around Silkie's right arm, hugging it like it was a teddy bear.

"Are you okay?"

The whole mental illness thing I'd read about months before came back to me.

Not wanting Silkie to feel I was pressing upon her, I sat down with Maheza.

That feeling of separateness from everything else was stronger now.

I would go slowly here till I figured out what was

happening with her. Glancing down at the water below, which seemed unusually turbulent as it rushed under the bridge, I said, almost under my breath, "You don't really hear the river in the day, but you sure do at night."

She was silent, her mind elsewhere apparently.

In the very quiet and dark, I became suddenly much more aware of the rain—a fine rain but over time enough to get us wet if we stayed here.

"Do you want to get dry . . . come to my house?"

"I didn't go to class." She was looking off the other way, so I couldn't read her eyes. Where she was.

"It's okay," I said, in the same tone I'd used with her long ago to tell her that her daughter was more important than anything we were doing in that class. "We'll just go to my place." I'd already decided that not only would we have a good talk—a very good talk— but she and Maheza would stay the night.

She got up, took Maheza's hand.

We were walking back to the car when, still holding on to Maheza, Silkie stopped and gestured beyond the parking area.

"Do you mind if we talk here first?"

"The rain feels like it might get worse."

She shrugged to say it didn't matter. There was a look of exhaustion, of surrender about her.

I stood there, alarmed for her, and maybe for that reason thinking it wiser to do things her way.

"It's funny how you hear so clearly at night sounds you

don't pay any attention to in the day—the river, cars in the distance, the wind in the trees."

"I like it here," she said.

The partially lit walkway into this side of the park took us along the river and past the back of some university research facilities. I wondered how far she would want to walk. If it were an aimless stroll, whether she would finally want to sit down. Where was her mind? The three of us walked in complete silence for a good ten minutes

The lawns, trees, gardens, buildings, sidewalks, concrete circular trash receptacles in front of us and to both sides were cast in a crisscross pattern of darkness and light. We passed a small line of RV trailers which because of their decrepit condition and ragged curtains in the windows looked to be housing the semi-homeless, then through a roadway underpass that was covered with painted graffiti words and pictures.

Just beyond that, along both sides of the walkway, were neatly planted shrubs and ferns, which in turn led into the park proper and a lot of picnic tables and even a small playground. Silkie pointed to the table closest to the jungle gym.

"There."

"Okay."

She walked to the table, but instead of sitting, she looked over at Maheza, as though confused. Maheza seemed to be reading her mother's eyes, but said nothing. She hesitated, then went over to the jungle gym, climbed the ladder part, and plopped down at the top.

Silkie sat herself at the table, facing outward, her backpack dangling a little off her back to one side.

I sat a little ways from her, sideways so I could keep an eye on Maheza, who, sitting at the top of the slide, had half-heartedly taken hold of the raised circular rail and was peeking out at us from beneath. She was not playing. The whole of her attention was on us.

Maheza had her hood on, but her mother didn't. Silkie's hair was clinging to her cheeks, and her thin jacket starting to soak through. It appeared she had some sort of sweatshirt on beneath, but I could see it, too, was wet at the neckline and sleeves. Depending on how long she'd been sitting alone on the bridge, her jeans also might be damp and cold on her legs. Indeed, the rain was growing in strength now. She was oblivious to it though, apparently. And I was becoming so.

She began fumbling in one of the slots of her backpack and pulled out a sandwich bag that appeared to have in it small metal or wood animals—a penguin, a cheetah, and an elephant. Silkie took them out of the bag, then slipped them back in and returned them to the backpack.

"Maheza's," she said without looking up. "Don't want to lose them." She seemed to be talking to herself. It struck me she was using this bag of animals to reorient herself to her immediate surroundings—the park, Maheza, me.

I might have gone over and comforted her—put my arms around her—had her eyes conveyed to me only a sense of feeling lost. But there was as much *abandon* as loss in them—even some of the *feral* I'd seen that very first day she'd shown up in my office. And somewhat to my shock, I discovered the wildness in her eyes and in the setting itself—a park in the rain at night—had aroused me in the same way as when I'd come upon her in the hallway after thinking she was dead.

So, if I went over to her, comforted her, might not she sense the sexuality in me and pull back? And Maheza's being there too.

I felt no shame in this discovery about my feelings—only caution.

"There was this girl in a print dress," Silkie said. "Very resigned. To what the flood had done to their house. I didn't know her. But I saw her—even though she was way back in the crowd. Maybe because she kept staring at me."

"What . . . flood?" I asked. "Where?"

My question seemed to wake her from some reverie, and she stared at me and shook her head. "It was earlier. Tonight."

I couldn't figure out where to go next, and Silkie had now turned anxiously toward Maheza. "Are you okay?" she asked her.

Maheza nodded, her head still pressed up against the rail at the top of the ladder.

"How did she know?" I asked.

"Know?"

"That you'd be . . . here."

"Oh." Silkie turned to me and smiled. One of genuine

amusement that didn't seem to fit her strange behavior. (Had I ever seen her smile in so pleasant a way before?) "That's Maheza. She can read me. Maybe it was in my eyes. When I left. I don't know."

"Eyes," I thought. What was in them? Depression. Just tiredness. No, she was right. Something else. I'd always been fascinated by the way her eyes looked at me. Yes, sometimes expectant, certain, but, just as often, confused. Lost. Desperate. At other times, distant, ethereal. Quite frankly, all over the place, but always striking. Did she ever look at anyone with everyday normal eyes?

"So . . . you haven't been going to class?"

She shook her head. "I tried. I went the first two times. Third time too—last week—but I left at the break."

"It's not going well? What class is it again you're taking? Do you have to take it if you don't like it?"

She didn't answer. Her mind seemed to have gone off again somewhere, and we were quiet for almost a minute.

"What did you say?"

"It doesn't matter. You told me before. The class you're taking. Educational Psychology, right? For teaching, you have to take it?"

She nodded, and pulled out the bag of animals again, seeming to be checking once that it was still there.

"Maheza's," she repeated. "I don't want to lose them. They're her favorites. We try to get a new one every couple months."

She was looking very distracted, so I decided to not question her anymore. It was some time before she broke the silence.

"We had topics to choose from. I was doing the homeless."

"For? Oh, the class. Figures you'd do that."

"But . . . "

I waited and she didn't continue. "So something wasn't going right for you in the class?"

"Yes. I'm sorry. I should have told you."

"What? Are you giving up? Dropping it?"

She stared at me, saying nothing. "The girl in the print dress I was telling you about. I was trying to help her. The flood. I didn't know what I could do . . . just that I was like her . . . in that situation once."

She seemed to realize she was off topic and fiddled in her backpack again. She was fingering the animal bag in the pocket.

I decided to ignore the print dress girl and the flood and get her back on what was happening with her school.

"Is it a money thing? You don't have enough money for school? Are you worried about that? I mean . . . too much pressure?"

"No, that's not it."

"You have financial aid, don't you? And some hours at work, no?"

She shook her head. "I get only five or six hours a week, and that's going to end soon. Gina told me."

"Gina?"

"At the bead place."

"But the financial aid."

"No."

"Didn't you have financial aid last year when you were in my classes?"

She nodded. "But I didn't do that well."

"You did in my classes."

"Just yours."

"What was your G.P.A.?"

"I dropped half the classes during the year. I finished yours and two more. The whole year. That's all."

"I don't understand. Why? You can get A's easy enough, no?"

"Too small."

"What do you mean 'too small'?"

The wind suddenly gusted and Maheza called out gleefully something that seemed to celebrate its power.

Silkie turned to her, then back again and stared down at her hands.

"I can't keep doing . . . this."

"What?"

"I can't . . . find the center. Maybe because of the problem."

"What problem?" I was getting impatient, but hid it. Continued in the tone of a therapist. Wondering, though, if I shouldn't let her know I was getting exasperated and just break through it all with a sharper tone.

She shook her head enigmatically.

I glanced over at Maheza. She was seated on the lowest bar now and watching us, and not so far away that she couldn't pick up much of what we were saying, even with the sound of the wind and light rain cutting through it.

"She takes good care of you, doesn't she?"

She nodded, almost smiling as she thought about it.

"So you come down here a lot? By yourself. And she knows it?"

"I like the river."

I was beginning to feel more comfortable because she was staying on the topic now, seemed less distracted.

"She says you slept down here with her a few times."

She shook her head. "Not any more. Months ago and only when it was warm. I lost her for a while because of that. They took her away. I have to have a place for her to be warm every night. They check on me now and then."

"Who?"

"Agency."

"This place you have now—is it working out?"

"I'm going to find another place. Cassie—the one I share it with—has a boyfriend—Martin. Uses . . . stuff. Meth. I like him though. Very . . . delicate boy. We get along. He's good to Maheza and doesn't do it when she's around. But Cassie's gotten nasty to me. Because of Martin. She thinks he . . . has something for me—doesn't like the way he looks at me or something. I don't know. I'm going to move."

"Does he?" I didn't know why I felt the need to ask her that.

"Maybe. I don't know. I don't care."

"But if you stayed in school, so you'd have the financial aid . . . then you could afford something better, no?"

"Yes."

"Last year . . . when you were in my classes, and doing okay . . . where were you staying?"

"Small apartment. It was just Maheza and me. No one else with us. I didn't manage my money well, and I started . . . messing up, like I said, in some classes."

"What do you mean . . . not manage your money well?"

She shrugged. "I lent people money. Gave it to some people that helped me before. I felt bad."

"You mean other people—like you—homeless or whatever?"

"Just those who helped me . . . before. And others you meet. Need help. Not their fault. You have to. Especially women."

The rain gave no sign of slowing.

"I wonder . . . would you have finally told me?"

She looked up at me as if she wasn't sure what I meant, then seemed to figure it out. She nodded. "Maheza likes you."

I looked down at my lap, then over at Maheza.

"I would have. Told you. Tonight. Next week."

"I don't know what you want me to do. What are you going to do? You seem to have just dropped your class. Are you going back?"

"I can't."

"Why 'can't'?"

"Like I said. It's too . . . small."

"Small?"

She didn't say anything for almost a minute. I decided it was not so much ignoring the question as it was pondering how to answer. I waited.

"It's hard to explain."

I waited. She was silent.

"For my sake, will you try?" I said. "If . . . only for me. And what about this . . . girl in the print dress . . . and the flood. I'm sorry. I'm trying to follow. To be of help here."

She looked down at her lap. "She's. . . . she's in Pakistan . . . I think. I can't remember the place. Indus? Is that the river?"

"I don't know. I'm not sure what you're talking about. Pakistan?"

"Just now I was there."

"Come on, Silkie. You've got to explain." I wanted to add, "Stop talking crazy," but knew that not only would it be wrong to say it but wrong to see it that way.

Her hands began trembling and she began hunting through her backpack again and feeling for the bag of animals.

"Why are you worrying about them?"

"They're her favorite."

"I know but . . . anyway . . . what were you saying?"

She stared off to her left and seemed to become rigid.

"Silkie, listen . . . "

"Would you rather see an elephant in a zoo . . . or running in a herd in Africa? On some savannah."

"In a herd, of course."

"Even if you couldn't get close?"

I nodded.

She seemed to think about that. "I met a woman once who lived on a Pacific island. She said the waters in the lagoon on the island where she lived were very blue and beautiful. But if you dove down deep along the reef, that was a whole different thing. Not just a greater beauty but a whole different perception . . . different world."

"So you're saying that's the same thing. The elephant herd. The reef."

"It is, isn't it?"

I nodded. "Sure. Of course."

Silkie turned around.

"Are we going?" Maheza called.

"Just a few more minutes, okay?"

"Should we discuss this later?" I asked.

"Just a little longer. I have a serious problem."

"All right."

"You . . . you remember Ruth?"

"How can I forget?"

"Ruth . . . sees the whole herd . . . the entire reef. Me . . . . Silkie . . . I don't. I see mostly Maheza. I have to. I have to focus on her. Ruth cares about Maheza too . . . but in some other way . . . not the way Silkie has to. Maheza lives in Silkie's world. Not Ruth's. I have to be in that world with Maheza. So I have the medicine. To keep me from . . . being Ruth. Seeing everything that way. My psychiatrist is right. It has to be that way. Problem is, I can't give it up. It's hard to give it up. And the medicine doesn't even always work. Maybe because I don't want it to all the time. I'm not sure. I tried one time to explain it to him. The confusion in me. But he's right. 'Your job as a mother, as a student, is to function,' he said. 'Go to class. Work. Take care of Maheza.' So I can have a place and they won't take her away."

"So how doesn't it work? Because you forget to take it? Is that why Maheza was so worried?"

"She thinks I forget. Maybe once or twice. But not anymore. It just doesn't always work. She doesn't know. The doctor doesn't know for sure. I'm not . . . real open about it. I'm not sure what he'll do. I don't want more medicine. I'm already too drugged. It's working less and less. I'm less and less able to focus on Maheza . . . on being her mother . . . on being Silkie at all. I'm less in control. I'm scared. I'm . . . scared. You asked if I was going to tell you . . . that I wasn't going to class. That I was making you watch Maheza for no reason. I was. But I wanted to do it when I could tell you the whole thing. Or more of it."

"What whole thing?"

"The whole Ruth thing."

"Tell me again. Who is Ruth?"

"I told you who Ruth is . . . in that story. A great-aunt who looked a lot like me. That picture of her, and my aunt telling me about her and calling me by that name . . . left an impression on me. When I was . . . needing to be someone else . . . to get away from my life . . . when I was young."

I waited. "So?"

"Ruth drowned when she was a teenager. Younger than I am now."

"And you . . . what? . . . Become her now and then?"

"Yes . . . but it's not just . . . escape. . . . It's not just for escaping anymore."

I thought about that, but I waited because she too seemed to be trying to figure it out.

"That phone call you made . . ."

"What I'm saying is she's already dead. So that means . . . she knows more . . . because she sees more. And my becoming her . . . when it happens . . . is . . . big. And that makes almost everything else seem small. Everything. Like my class."

"What does the doctor say about that?"

"I told you, he doesn't know. I started to explain it . . . but it's part of the whole schizoaffective thing to him."

"It isn't?"

She shook her head. "Maybe long ago it was. But not . . . the last two or three years."

"Your journal . . . "

"Ruth goes anywhere she wants. Or places I've never been. You read some of that in my journal. Her understanding is always wider, bigger, fuller. You know what I mean? When I said the whole herd on the savannah . . . the whole reef."

"But . . . "

"That poem by Whitman about the sea birds—the one I read in class. Ruth . . . she's *both* the sea birds and the poet writing about them *at the same time*. She's *big* that way. Not *small*."

"And everything else . . . in your everyday life . . . is small?"

"Except Maheza. She herself. Not my having to focus on her but . . . she herself. . . she's never small. Nor are . . . you."

Up till this comment she hadn't been looking at me, just down at her lap. With that, though, she turned toward me.

Flattered though I was by the implications of her final allusion to me, I was more interested in driving to the heart of this peculiar bifurcated version of the universe. "So it's both wonderful and . . . frightening. But I would think this sort of . . . greater seeing . . . or whatever it is would make you feel . . . helpless?"

"Helpless? Yes. This girl in the printed dress. Pakistan . . . wherever. What if it's now? I think it is. Then the class is not . . . where my mind should be. But on her. No?"

"No. I mean yes, it shouldn't be. But what do you mean if it's 'now'? How can it be now?"

"I don't know. But even if it isn't, does it matter—if it's now or last year or twenty years ago? Or ten years into the future? It's now at the moment. No matter, it's always *now*."

I was tempted to ask, "Sorry, but what if it's all just in your head?" But it seemed to be an invalid or improper question. Even the cliché bothered me.

"I have dreams I am somewhere strange—and Maheza's not with me. She's not with me! So . . . yes, helpless. But it still seems . . . okay. How it's supposed to be. You see? You do understand."

"See . . . understand what?"

"You see what I mean. You *do* understand. You asked if I felt helpless. That's . . . right now . . . so much of it. The doctor didn't really understand. And I think that's why . . . when everything else is small . . . and Maheza isn't . . . you too . . aren't . . . aren't small. Why is that?"

"Where are we going with this?"

"I know."

"What?"

"Where it's going."

"Where?"

"That word . . . 'ineluctable' I asked you about. It's 'ineluctable.'"

"Ineluctable where? Sorry, I don't follow. More . . . ineffable."

She shrugged. "Both."

"That doesn't help me know what to do."

"Can I ask you something? If I were to ask you to watch Maheza next week while I just . . . pretend to go to class . . . and instead . . . walk down by the river . . . you would do it, wouldn't you?"

"Yes."

"Why?"

"I like Maheza. You're a friend."

"But that's not why . . . not the whole answer."

I wasn't sure how to respond to that. "I've gotten so I just go . . . where it feels right. Sometimes things . . . just feel right. It's not that hard. Just slide into it. What has a feeling of comfort. Deep . . . deep . . . comfort. Good. Rightness about it. When I slip into it, I know . . . it's what I'm supposed to do . . . where I'm supposed to go."

The rain was coming down too hard to ignore. Maheza had come over by now and sat down on the other side of her mother. "I'm getting all wet, Mama."

"Okay." Silkie shielded her with her arm.

"You stay in my house tonight," I said. I almost added, "Stay in my house as long as you want" or "Stay in my house from now on," but wouldn't know what I meant by it or how she would understand it. But . . . I almost said it anyway.

She was silent in the car. Maheza was too.

"I have an extra room," I said, as I pulled the car into my driveway.

"We were making cookies," Maheza whispered to her mother.

Once inside, Maheza threw off her wet jacket. To my surprise, though, Silkie didn't remove hers. Just sat down on the floor with her back against the wall in the living room.

"You want to sit there? Here give me your jacket. I can dry it. There's a chair."

She shook her head. I stood holding my hand out for her jacket anyway, and finally she slipped it off and gave it to me. But she continued sitting on the floor.

The sweatshirt beneath was loose and wet around the edges, leaving her shoulder bare, shimmering, and I discovered my arousal for her returning. The unnaturalness of all this. The abandon. The letting go.

"I can get you some dry clothes. One of my sweatshirts." I sensed I was a little too eager in asking.

She shook her head and smiled, "No."

"You want some tea or something?"

Maheza plopped down between her outstretched legs. Silkie was pulling the animals out of the backpack and bag for her.

I put on some hot water, then came out and sat on the floor across the room from her against the opposite wall, figuring it was best to let her decide whether to talk or not. After a while, I got up and poured the tea and held up a cup from the dining room.

"Is this going okay for you?" she asked, in the most normal way; it sounded like a whole different person from the one I'd been talking with in the park. She nodded to Maheza.

I answered, "Yes. With Maheza? Yes, fine."

I was thinking as I sat there that I would have preferred

to be drinking wine. I felt no guilt about the desire.

I wanted to talk more about what she'd opened up to me about, but I didn't think it wise with Maheza there listening.

"Can we finish the cookies?" Maheza asked.

"Sure. We can do some of the batch anyway. Gotta put the oven on again. You can give your mother a couple."

We spooned out globs of the dough on a cookie sheet and slipped them into the oven. The incongruousness of making chocolate chip cookies at this time did not escape me. I looked out at Silkie. She was sitting with a dazed expression like she'd been in a physical accident and was just becoming conscious.

"You okay?" I called out.

She didn't answer.

A few minutes later, Silkie asked me, "Did you like her picture?"

"Picture?"

"Didn't she give you the one she drew?"

"I forgot," Maheza said.

"Go get it."

She went to her bag of books in the corner and pulled out a drawing. It appeared to be a tiger with a dark green outline and yellow and black stripes.

"A tiger?" I asked. "Thanks."

She stood grinning up at me. "You have to find out what's wrong?"

"Wrong?"

"She always does it wrong. She likes to add one more something or take away something that's supposed to be there," Silkie explained, with a quiet smile not unlike the one that had pleased me so much earlier in the park.

"You made some mention of it in your journal, I remember."

"No matter what she draws. She thinks it's funny. Last week she drew this horse with two tails. And once . . . what was it, Maheza?. . . this very, very long dachshund that covered the whole length of the paper. She thinks it's a riot."

"I see. Okay. Well, one . . . two . . . three . . . legs. It's supposed to have four."

"Right!" Maheza exclaimed, suddenly animated.

"A three-legged tiger. Does he get around okay that way? Maybe you should draw him a cane to carry."

Maheza smirked and turned away. I poured her a glass of milk, which she drank with the cookies. Then I went back into the kitchen and washed the cookie sheet.

When I came out, I could see Silkie's eyes were glassy. Maybe there were tears. I'm not sure. Maheza had her head propped up against her mother's leg and seemed to be falling asleep.

"Do you know about vision quests?" I found myself asking. "Native American thing. That book on the reading list I gave your class—*Black Elk Speaks*—it's in there. Your description of how Ruth sees things. Reminds me of it. Nature or the universe as one big living thing. Blending one into another.

Trees, deer, spiders, water . . . probably even rocks. At least, that's how I remember it. But maybe yours . . . is different. I don't know. Point is, it wouldn't be a mental illness."

Silkie nodded and said, almost to herself, "Me—I'd still need my medicine. But when I don't, sometimes—not always--that's when it's most . . . beautiful. Because of Ruth."

Maheza was dozing off. Her mother laid her hand on her daughter's forehead and gently pulled back the hair that had fallen over it.

"About everything. I'm sorry. Don't want you to think I was lying. I'm just not . . . always the Silkie you know. The one I want to show you."

"Does she"—I nodded my head toward Maheza—"see it a lot? Ruth, I mean."

"All the time."

"She's almost asleep. You stay here tonight." Again I almost added, "as long as you need to." "There's a bedroom I don't use . . ."

"Can I just use the couch?"

"Yeah, sure, but Maheza . . ."

"You know what . . . she always sleeps on a blanket on the floor next to me wherever. Wherever we are. She's used to it."

"Will she be comfortable?"

"Always is."

"Anyway. I'll drive you back tomorrow. I have a guest speaker coming to my morning class, but you . . . stay at least till I get back."

Then Silkie said something very strange that I would

ponder all night. Because it was a real question she sought an answer to.

"It's good if you keep finding out things about her, isn't it?"

She meant "good for *you*"—not "good for Maheza." That's how I took it. Or at least good for *both of us*.

"Yes."

"When I get home from class tomorrow, we'll have dinner together. We can talk more. Maybe I can . . . lend you . . . I don't know . . . give you some money . . . for a while to get . . . I don't know . . . but tomorrow we should talk about it."

She seemed to ponder what I was saying, then just nodded.

I left and came back with two sheets and a couple of blankets, and took the cushions off two other chairs and put them beside the couch for Maheza to lie on.

"Are you sure you don't want to use the other bedroom?"

She shook her head.

I helped tuck the sheet around the cushions. Then I brought back two old sweatshirts and just set them in front of her.

Silkie got up and sat on the couch. Looking down at her, I felt like a father—to both of them. My earlier feelings of lust had gone away.

Still, if during the night, she decided to slip into my bed, it would feel very good.

"The bathroom is right there," I said and pointed down the hall.

She nodded.

ROSS. *Ross always sat in the back of my American Lit class. Hardly ever spoke. Wrote beautiful papers on Dickinson and Whitman—as no student has or will. Two years after leaving my class he called me, asked me to meet him for coffee in the university cafeteria. Wanted to talk to someone about his wife who was leaving him for another man. I did. But what could I say?* **[Drawer 3B]**

34. Gone

You have to go back to World One. To survive. You can't stray too far into World Two.

That meant going off to teach the next morning. Earning my salary. But it also meant doing something practical for Silkie and Maheza. And so as I lay in bed that night I decided that on the way to work I would stop off at the ATM and withdraw $200 to give them.

When I awoke, they were still asleep—Silkie wrapped in a blanket on the couch, Maheza in a blanket on the floor next to her. I left Silkie a note I would return for lunch and added: "We can talk some more when I get back."

It was not to be. When I got home, she was gone.

She had scrawled at the bottom of my note: "Thank you for <u>everything</u>. I will stop and see you at school later this week. I look forward to that dinner with you." I half expected it would be signed "Ruth," but it wasn't.

I drove back to school to teach my afternoon class, determined to go over to her place later in the evening to see how she was doing.

After class I returned to my office, only to discover that a yellow notebook paper folded haphazardly had been slipped under my door. Opening it, I saw at the bottom "SILKIE." It had apparently been written on the spot because the paper had been torn roughly from its pad.

> Dear Mr. M,
> I'm not making it in school anymore. I told you. My fault, I suppose. I don't know. It should matter to me but it doesn't. I do things like what I did the other night. Just go off by myself. Sometimes to the river. It's no good. Good for Ruth. No good for Maheza. Didn't mean to mislead you. Understand that. I'm going to California today to see Maheza's father. I've had a bus ticket for several months now. He'll give me the money to buy return ones. Didn't want you to think I was trying to get money from you. Don't think badly of me. When I come back, tell me what you want me to do. And I'll tell you too. And we'll have dinner.
> SILKIE

I set out for her apartment immediately but stopped by the bank again and withdrew an additional $300, for her trip—thinking she might actually have to take a hotel room for a couple of days and pay for her meals, and maybe something for Maheza, too, to entertain her on the bus trip down.

All too late. An emaciated, tired-looking girl, chewing gum, came to the door and said Silkie had left. I asked the girl if she was her friend, and she shrugged and muttered as she turned away, "I let her stay with me when she . . . you know . . . "

"Listen, I'm the one who has been taking care of her daughter—Maheza. Did she tell you the address in California? She left me a note saying she was going there. I may need to get hold of her."

"No, I don't think she knew exactly. That's what she said. She'd have to look when she got there. Call this guy or something."

The chewing gum girl didn't seem to want to be helpful.

For the next three weeks, I began spending each evening lying on the couch, sometimes with the TV on, till I finally fell asleep, often without removing my clothes. If I rose to go to my bed, sleep eluded me. Several times, Silkie appeared in my dreams. Once she was somewhere in my house and my mother came to visit. In another dream I was in my Catholic school classroom of long before, then I was walking home with some friend and found Silkie in what felt like my house but didn't look like it. I was happy she was there, but she said she was going home. The dream left me feeling helpless, hopeless. Another dream she was walking ahead of me inside a grocery and I called but she didn't answer. Then I got interrupted by other people I didn't know asking me about class assignments. That one left me feeling disturbed, anxious.

In a fourth dream, I was walking down a hallway in one of the classroom buildings and happened to pass a room in which Silkie was standing alone, and I felt a desperate need to go in and hug her. But I didn't.

In the last one, I was biking on a crowded street in the rain and came upon "Tabi Sahlei" of my Nigeria past. He had a closed umbrella in his left hand, and he raised it into the air and smiled at me as I went by—seeming to offer it to me.

Twice in my sleep I had seizures too. Because in neither case was there any motor effect, however, I could not be certain if the seizure had been triggered by the dream or if it had been part of the dream itself. In either case, I woke at the moment of the disruption of my brain waves.

The term ended. Then came June. July. August. September. No Silkie.

KIDNAPPED INTO PROSTITUTION IN INDIA *According to a documentary—The Day My God Died-- I saw yesterday, thousands of young women are kidnapped every day and sold into prostitution from Mumbai to Broadway. A friend (sometimes even a sibling) slips something into their drink and they wake up imprisoned in a brothel. When they resist they are tortured in various ways until they submit. Beaten, gang-*

raped, serving 15 or more clients a day. The moment they wake up is called by the women in India, "the day my God died." Some are as young as seven, many contract AIDS, and many commit suicide. [**Drawer 4**]

35. Strange Roots

In Hermann Hesse's novel *Demian*, two of the characters are mystically linked. Common sense was always there—reminding me of the absurdity of any notion of a *Demian*-like mystical relationship between Silkie and me. It was simply a matter of ripping out the roots of that fantasy one by one. The truth, though, was that that strategy had never entirely succeeded. There would always be one or two roots—roots that I shared with her--that insisted on living, and I couldn't find them. When I gave up and ignored them as perhaps just more of the fantasy, I discovered that they'd pushed up into me. Not just one or two, but many. So infested was I with them that, in the end, I just allowed them to sprout.

What was I to do, buy some sort of mystical weed-killer? Nor could I rid myself of the fear that were I to kill off those roots connecting us, *I would kill off myself.*

I continued to feel those roots. And with her disappearance, now, my moods became darker and darker. Only in rare moments—usually in the early morning hours when I was engaged in some very normal activity such as brushing my teeth or washing the breakfast dishes—would the whole experience take on a cast of, "Jesus, what was I doing? She was just a girl that I built into some mythical creature because I needed it." At such times, the ordinariness of her was so abundantly clear I couldn't understand how I could have seen it in any other light.

But then, at almost the exact moment I would enter the building in which my office was housed, I would begin to feel something alternating between a heaviness and a lightness, then a sickness that both enervated and alarmed me. Would I be able to get through the day? It became a daily phenomenon—this progression of moods slowly, inevitably wearing me down at the very moment I should most have been charging myself up for the teaching day.

By evenings, the deflation would emerge into a deep depression. Sometimes so strong it was a suffocating cloth or tarp being tightened over me. I would come home and lie on the couch for almost two hours, feeling a psychological ache that bordered on physical pain, then rise and eat a little, and go for a drive, relying more and more on music to soothe me.

My subconscious would not let it go: "Until she returns."

I longed for those morning moments when the proper state of mind—the saner perspective on the real situation— would return: the one in which Silkie was a normal student who had a daughter and who went to school for a while and who had a boyfriend who fathered the child and who now went to California and would most likely not be returning.

Every few nights, too, I would go looking in the park for Jo Ann—the woman who'd come out to meet me that night with Maheza.

And because she was never there, I would ask anyone in that area if they knew of Jo Ann or where I could find her.

Each time I struck out. Did they no longer frequent that part of the park?

One evening—around ten—I drove back to the RV dealership. Parked the car. Walked back to the one RV Lilac had been sleeping under. No one. I even called out "Jesse" because if he was there, then for sure Lilac would be back. No movement anywhere, no barking.

When I found Lilac, it was only by chance. One Saturday morning I saw a man standing on a street corner holding a Please Help sign. At his feet was a light brown mixed-breed dog. The man's face was somewhat covered by a baseball cap over a hood, but I was fairly certain the dog was Jesse.

As it was near a shopping plaza, just three blocks down from the RV lot, I pulled into a parking slot and walked out to the corner.

"Excuse me."

He turned but didn't seem to recognize me.

"You are . . . Lilac, right?"

"Right."

"And this is Jesse."

"Do I know you?"

"Some weeks ago—we were talking. You were staying over in the RV place. You know Maheza. Maisie. I was watching her that night. You were sleeping, but we woke you. And talked. Remember? It was a while ago, so you might not."

"Yes. Kind of. Maisie. [I wasn't sure he did.] Where is she?" I noted his voice was not as grainy as it had been that other night.

"Actually, I was hoping you could help me with that. Her mother. Silkie. Have you seen her anywhere recently?"

"No. Not for a time." He began scratching his head—an apologetic mannerism, perhaps.

"I think she might have gone to California. I was hoping you knew something about it."

He shook his head. "Sorry."

"Anyway, want me to pick up a meal for you? And for Jesse?"

He seemed to think about it. "Maybe just something . . . from the deli. Over there in the grocery."

A little later, I came back with a box full of chicken, some "jo-jo's," coleslaw, a piece of pie, a cup of coffee, and a couple cans of dog food.

He retreated to the side of a bush back from the street. His bicycle and attached trailer were leaning against it.

"I should've got some sort of dish for your dog," I said.

"No, no need," he said, yanking out from a bag tied to his bike seat a black plastic container—the bottom of some frozen food dinner. I sat down off to the side while he ate.

"Want some?" he asked, holding up a piece of chicken.

"No, no."

"You're looking for Silkie? I thought she was in school."

"She was. She . . . quit for a time. Like I said, she told me she was going to California. But told me she'd be back. Something to do with Maheza's father."

"Oh," he grunted.

"Tell me. You know anything about him—the father?"

He shook his head. "Never met him. She never talked about him."

"How long you known her?"

He stared down at his food. Was he suddenly getting suspicious of me? Maybe I was police or something or some agency rep?

"Look . . . I'm sorry. I'm her friend. I was her teacher. I don't know if you remember the conversation we had that night. It's been a while."

"So she's not in trouble?"

"No, not at all."

"Two years maybe. Saw her a lot at first. Then she had to get a place or she would've lost Maisie, so didn't see her much after that."

"Did she . . . sleep in the park . . . ever . . . before that?"

As he answered, his words were broken by his gnawing at the chicken—slowly, carefully.

"Her friend . . . had a tent. Not sure where she is now."

I wasn't getting any information that was helpful.

He nodded to the food in the Styrofoam on his lap: "She used to do this a lot."

"What?"

"Bring food. Not me . . . maybe once or twice . . . for some of the women. She had money when she was in school; they didn't. So she'd bring meals now and then."

"She paid for it."

"Most times. Had food stamps too, I think. One of them had money from a boyfriend, but she didn't. Later she had some money—from the college. I don't know what it was— the college money. Maybe loan. Government, you know."

"But you don't have any idea where I might find out about her now? Those women you mentioned . . . what were their names?"

"One was Tess. Tessie something. Don't know her last name. She's still around. And Jo Ann."

"Yeah, Jo Ann. Does she still hang around the park?"

"Maybe."

"So if I keep checking—down by the river . . ."

"You know what? Try the Mission too. There was this younger girl—real knockout beauty, but sickly. Some sort of hepatitis. Other things too. Silkie and she used to hang out together. But . . . it's a long while since . . . seen her. Her boyfriend—you know, he was into stuff pretty heavy—ended up in the river. About three years ago. Silkie took care of her—in a way—after that. I think this girl—Jenny or Janet

. . . something like that . . . was her name—had a mental problem of some kind too."

When I finally left Lilac, I gave him my phone number and asked him to call me if he heard anything about Silkie. He said he would. I gave him $20, thanked him, and left.

One of my park visits paid off. I found Jo Ann.

"Tessie? Long gone," she said, shaking her head enough that the gold earrings dangling heavy from her ears gleamed in the park lights. A bright Gypsy scarf was wrapped tightly around her head and gray hair and tied at the back. Except for the fire burning between the rocks and for the filmy light on the ground where the half-moon found its way between the branches, it was very dark.

It was in the same area of the park where she'd been months before when Maheza had taken me there. This time I sat with the whole group of seven or eight of them. On the table were a couple crushed cigarette packs, two or three beer cans, and a section of the daily newspaper. Under a tree off to the side was a stack of old backpacks and blankets and sleeping bags. Three or four magazines as well.

"Where gone?"

"Got a place. Even a job. Haven't seen her since last summer. She's not on the street anymore. They found her an apartment. Low income, you know."

"What about someone named Janet? Lilac said she was her friend? Silkie's friend."

"Janice, you mean. She's in that . . . what-you-call-it unit at the hospital."

"Psychiatric," a very tall man in the back with a long beard said. "Assaulted a police gal when they were taking her boy away." He had an air of someone who had settled into this life more successfully than the others "Way last year. Not sure where she is. Silkie—she got mixed in that."

"How?"

"Trying to help her," Jo Ann said. "Went down to the Children's Services and started spitting fire. Think they would've arrested her if she hadn't been in school and had a place."

"How do you know about that?"

"Bunch of us was there. With her. Waiting outside."

I smiled. "I've seen her get angry."

"Almost lost her daughter the same way," a tall, thin woman called out from the end of the table. She was wearing a black fur cap and looked a little less ragged than others. Although she was not young, she had a more youthful, healthy glow to her—reminding me of the upper-middle-class yuppies I'd see jogging in groups or pairs in my neighborhood. She looked happy, even ethereal. I wondered if she was new to the scene or wasn't part of it at all.

"Yes, I know how Silkie is," I said and looked away.

"And now you don't know where she is?" the young woman asked.

I shrugged. "California. Maybe. None of you know

Maisie's father?"

"Never saw any father," Jo Ann, sitting next to me, said quietly, "She came here with just her little girl from somewhere. San Francisco . . . or Sacramento. One of those."

"So you don't know who might have an address or anything?"

I was asking Jo Ann but turned to the rest of them. "Any of you know?"

"You tell us. She's a good girl. When she had extra money . . . those months she was in school . . . and the food stamps too . . . made sure she stopped by now and then. Brought us meals. Even after she moved into her friend's place. Had to get a place to stay at night."

"They would have taken away Maisie," Jo Ann confided. "Yeh."

"Find her . . . you come back and tell us."

"I will."

I thanked them and turned to leave, discouraged that my persistence was getting me nowhere.

As I was walking across the grass in a very dark part of the park far from where my car was, I heard someone call me from behind.

"Excuse me!"

I turned. The tall woman in the black fur cap.

"May I ask you something?"

"Hi. Yes. Sure."

I waited for her to come closer.

"My name is Allana. I'm just wondering, why do you want to find this Silkie so much?"

"I'm Stephen. Sorry—didn't introduce myself before. Silkie was my student. I taught her in a couple classes. At the university."

"You're a professor?"

"Close friend too. I took care of her daughter a few times."

"Why?"

"Why . . . did I?"

"Why—I'm sorry . . . I guess maybe it's not my business . . . but I'm curious. Why are you looking for her like this? I saw you out here once before—last week. You stopped and asked me if I knew a Jo Ann. I told you I didn't because I didn't know you. I was afraid she was in some trouble. You didn't look like you were one of her friends. You didn't say anything about Silkie. Maybe you don't remember?"

"No. Well, kinda."

"So, why are you looking . . . so hard? Is she lost in some way? Are you afraid something bad happened to her?"

"No. Not lost. Just to me." I suddenly realized from her expression that remark made her suspicious of my motives. "Silkie's . . . different."

She didn't respond to that, seeming to think about what it meant.

"Can I walk with you? To your car?"

"Sure. Do you know her?"

"Met her . . . just one time. One late night more than a year ago. She's young, right? Maybe twenty or so. Kind of skinny. Looks like a little girl. Blonde hair?"

I stopped. Faced her. I didn't want to get to the car too quickly. It struck me this Allana was herself different. None of the diffidence, hesitation, I felt from the others in talking to a professor. Most likely she was more educated.

Way off to my right were the lights of the city. To my left all darkness—except for the fire near the homeless group from which we'd walked some distance now. There was nothing for me either way. Just here. With this woman who wanted for some reason to talk to me about Silkie.

"What happened? How did you meet her. The one time?"

"I was having a bad week. Relationship thing. Especially that night. I'm not with him anymore. But I was for several years. I wasn't really homeless. I'm not now really. I'm a student. Left him and went back to school. I'm doing a project. On people who live in the park. Spending a few days with them. They know. Jo Ann and them. Nothing phony about it, you know." I nodded. "But, that night, I was out by myself . . . alone. Bad scene with this guy. Been going on a long time, like I said. I'd actually gone out and gotten myself a six-pack and drunk almost all of it, and vomited—in an alley. Never did anything like that before. Stupid, I guess. Like you'd picture it in a movie. A mess. It was cold and I was shaking both from that and the feeling sick. So I went into the bus station and sat in one of the chairs with my head in my hands—trying not to look too conspicuous. Didn't want them to kick me out. Went over and got a Coke out of the machine so it would look like I was waiting for a bus or someone to come in on one. I checked my bag to see if I had enough to take a bus somewhere. But I had only eight or nine dollars. I finally went outside and just leaned back against the wall, then went over to the curb and lay my head in my hands again. She was walking by. This girl. Saw me there. A mess. Asked if I was okay. No, I remember she just said, 'Hey!' I looked up. 'There's a small all-night café across the street,' she said.

"She had a little girl with her who stood back, so I didn't see her at first when I said okay.

"Anyway, the three of us sat there. In a booth. A couple hours. Her little girl fell asleep . . . head on her mother's lap. It was really late. At least eleven. I remember thinking, 'Why doesn't she just take her little girl home to sleep?'

"We just drank tea, and I picked at a muffin she got me. And I got through the night because of it. Later she walked me to her place. I'd told her I couldn't go back to mine. I remember it was quite a walk but the cold air made me feel good. Turned out it was in the back of someone else's house. I don't think I could find the place again. It was dark on that street, and there were a lot of houses just looked all the same to me. I was in bad shape. Not paying a lot of attention. When they were saying tonight—the others back there—how angry she gets, I couldn't picture it. That night, she was so . .

. I wouldn't say sweet, just . . . honestly concerned . . . about me. You know. In control. Focused on me and her daughter.

"I remember her name because it was so unusual. 'Silkie.' She said her mother had gotten it from some Joan Baez song about a sea creature. The Great Silkie of something or other."

"You know what? I never thought to ask her about it—her name."

"The next morning, she showed me where I could get help for a few days if I didn't have any place to stay. Said she'd get in trouble if she let me stay at hers. That she hadn't even been paying the rent. We walked out here. That's how I met Jo Ann and how I found out she—this Silkie—had been homeless for a long while."

"I think I know the place," I interjected. "I went there looking for her. That's another story. Why I did it. But she'd moved out already. An older woman and her son owned it."

"I don't know. That night I was a disaster. I did notice, though, she didn't have much. Her stuff . . . and her daughter's . . . were pretty . . . spare—almost looking like it was unpacked . . . in a hotel. . . . Like she wouldn't be there too long. She opened some cupboards looking for something, and there was almost nothing in them. A couple plastic plates and cereal. Not much of anything you'd expect. Yet I think she said she'd been there several weeks. Anyway, that's not what struck me most about her. Later. Not right away."

I waited for her to continue. "What?"

"Maybe it was just because my mind, my head was so

screwed up that night, but I can't recall she said much of anything the whole night. In the restaurant. Her apartment. Just the basic things like, 'Hey!" and 'You want a cup of tea?' and 'You can stay here' and 'I'll show you in the morning.' All the talking . . . I did. Since I was the one needing help, maybe that wasn't so strange except that . . . I had this feeling with her that . . . she wasn't going out of her way to say comforting things to me—the usual 'You'll see, it'll all be all right' or 'Things will be better in the morning.' Nothing like that. But she had this way of seeming . . . a lot . . . wiser. . . . Not 'old person' wise but . . . like she saw through things . . . in a way that made everything that was bothering me not so important . . . so . . . critical. I never forgot her. Younger than me but so much more . . . something. All in that silent way."

I smiled and nodded. "She's had a difficult life."

"At the time . . . that night . . . I didn't know she'd been homeless. I think she might have said it quickly, but it didn't register with me—how crappy her place and she looked. It wasn't till the next morning and she took me here that I figured it out."

"For many years. Started at age fourteen, I think she was."

"I hope you find her."

"I do too. What she did for you that night . . . over many weeks and months . . . me too."

"If I ever see her again, I'll tell her you were looking. What's your name, again?"

"Stephen. Stephen Mollgaard. But you can just say,

Stephen your teacher. She'll know."

"I will."

"And you're . . . Lana?"

"Allana."

On a hunch—it had worked for me before—I turned once more to the bead shop. The lady behind the counter was somebody new—a short girl reminding a little of a plump Goldie Hawn.

"Do you happen to know a girl who worked here—Silkie?"

"Yes, Silkie? Sure."

"Does she still work here?"

"No . . . actually, not sure. You need to ask the woman who owns this place. Gina . . . but she won't be back till closing."

"Do you have any idea when Silkie might be coming back?"

"No, as I said, you have to ask Gina. You know she only had a few hours a week though? She didn't come much."

"Yes. I knew that."

I thanked her and decided, for the third time that week, to drive by the apartment where Silkie and Maheza had been staying. I knocked on her door. No one was there.

I began to think of it as a disease—a kind of mental illness. I pictured my encounter with a psychologist.

PSYCHOLOGIST [Smiling knowingly]: Sounds to me like you just have feelings for this girl. Aren't those natural? Even in midlife and older. Quite common.

ME: *I think, believe it or not, Doc, it's more . . . existential?*

PSY: *Well, you can call it what you want.*

ME: *You don't understand. The phone call . . . she herself calling to tell me she was dead. The effect it had on me—that something was happening not just to her but to me too.*

PSY: *Isn't that possibly just some manifestation of her dissociative disorder? And your response to it some psychological need deep inside finding an outlet?*

ME: *No, it was more than that. It was a sort of "Listen, Stephen! Pay attention! Something meaningful is to follow. Something which will resurrect in you a purposefulness you've discarded along with your Baltimore Catechism and Siddhartha."*

PSY: *Doesn't some neurological aberration seem plausible?*

ME: *Silkie herself—she's an aberration. Of the ten thousand or so students I've taught over the previous twenty-five years, none has even come close. On my list of remembered students, she has her own page. Her own chapter.*

PSY: *I see.*

ME: *No, you don't. Nor do I.*

There were times, perhaps a sign my mind was deteriorating more than I would admit, that I wondered not only about her not ever coming back but about *who she was.*

JOURNAL *[September 28]*

Why her, God? Why her strange interruption into my life? Where did she come from?

You knew about me, didn't you, God? That I was in need of some very profound comfort. I'd been needing it for years. She came then because she knew my state of mind? Or you were bored . . . knew that, just like with Mercutio, my wound was mortal. "No, 'tis not so deep as a well, nor so wide as a church-door; but 'tis enough, 'twill serve: ask for me to-morrow, and you shall find me a grave man."

No one else knows of my wound. Just you, God, and Silkie.

The rub is only those who know you are wounded can help. And for some wounds even that is not enough. If it cannot be relieved by a pill, a doctor, a "power of positive living" book, or just sympathy, then how about a friend? Not likely. "I'm sorry about your affliction," my friend will say, "but I don't want to hear about your dying, only your living. If you have nothing to say about living—'How are you doing today?' 'Oh, fine. How are you?' 'Fine. I think I'm going to buy myself a new pair of shoes today. How about you?'—then I don't want to know."

It's best that way, I guess—if you are of the Mercutio mind—to not let people know about your mortal wounds.

And so we die. Mercutio and I.

Yet, here I am inexplicably reaching out to her.

Is it because she knew? Even then—that week of the phone call? Knew wherefore the dying came?

Knew of my obsessions. Knew that my wound—being "not so wide as a church-door"— was, even so, "deep as a well."

Let's see . . . how does it work? Obsessed with the plunge, I become equally obsessed with the one who provided the final push—the phone call.

I was falling and looking back up, and she was the only one looking down, the only one whose eyes were speaking to me with compassion. Silkie—the one who pushed me. Silkie—the one who can save me.

It was late September, the first week of fall term. I began thinking about visiting my children in California again. It had been almost two months since my last visit.

It had been more than four months since I'd last seen Silkie. Most likely, she too was in California.

36. Revelation in a Pharmacy

September 29, the first Thursday of fall term, was an uneventful day, but even so a very remarkable one. Because I came to a realization.

It happened in the least remarkable of places: a pharmacy. On the way home from work, I'd stopped to pick up my antiseizure pills. I'd tried earlier in the day but the prescription had run out, and the pharmacist hadn't yet heard back from the doctor. He said he would call the doctor again. As I was almost out of pills, I stopped by again two hours later.

"We're filling it right now. Sorry, there's been a backlog of orders. Can you wait just another few minutes?"

I sat off to the side next to a small table with magazines entitled *Diabetes* and *Health* and *Parents and Children*.

That's when it came to me—as the most commonsense revelation. I'd been anxious about the prospect for many weeks. But *now I knew.* Summer term had come and gone and fall term had started. If Silkie were going to return, as she had indicated she would, surely it would have been by now. Besides, her going to see Maheza's father in itself was so much an expected choice to make—mothers wanting their children to know their fathers—I should long ago have given up on any prospect of her return.

The realization was devastating to me, even so.

Any degree of mysticism I'd been clinging to and attributing to our peculiar relationship had been nothing but a dramatic fancy or emotional need. The eerie phone call, her strange talk of Ruth, my saying over and over again to her "I'm sorry"—all of this I had to put away as a child at some point puts away memories of a fun day at the circus or fantasies of traveling into space.

When I left the pharmacy that afternoon, I discovered, then, two warring urges in me.

One was to courageously (I gave it that much import) *confront the prospect of a future without Silkie*. That urge, unfortunately, necessitated some serious rationalization. Some "Did I really need her anyway?" And what kind of "need" was it? A romantic one? She was twenty-three. I was fifty-two. Perhaps a little of it was romance. Surely, yes. But the romantic feeling, whatever the percent, was not the essence of it. If there was truth in that need, it was not the key to the obsession. Rather, it was that she was a kind of antidote to the existential disease that had wracked my soul for months, years. Absurd as it was, inherent in it was *meaning* . . . because of how it had started, the way her eyes seemed to be . . . anticipating something I would do, sometimes admonishing me for not yet doing it. And what *doing* was that?

Now, her going, seemingly for good, and for the most understandable of reasons, had taken with it whatever remnant of the mystical I'd been hanging onto. And with the mystical gone, there was left in the myriad broken images of the previous months . . . only the *sensible*. And the sensible by its very nature had to cut off all the ragged edges, the tentacles reaching too far and too deep. The sensible meant excising what was too elusive, too disillusioning . . . too profoundly enigmatic.

Unfortunately, the *sensible* would not satisfy. Not who I'd become.

So ultimately I chose the second urge. To plunge into *whatever she was about. To substitute for "Silkie" other "World Two" experiences.*

What experiences? I didn't know, but I would *let them happen*. Perhaps, like Calvin, I would run wildly off the path into the forest and plunge my hands into the muck of the wet leaves. Or, like Mercutio, play-act as though mortally wounded with no one knowing I really was; or, like Little Big Man, lay my head in my hands and say nothing.

It was the better way to go. In that direction lay at least the prospect of comfort if not its ultimate realization.

I drove home, opened my front door, stepped inside, then . . . just stood there. Waiting.

I would write a letter to my children.

Searching through my own journal, I found three entries about them which I decided to copy for them to see. To share my longing for them. The entries were reflective by way of my memories.

When I'd started the journal years before, I'd done it traditionally—writing longhand on unlined paper in a small leather-bound diary, and later on lined paper in a larger bound journal. I had images of Jefferson and Hawthorne and Poe writing in similar kinds of journals.

It was impractical, however. The pages of each notebook were too quickly filled up, and my handwriting would become increasingly illegible as I wrote more feverishly. When I had a computer, it worked better. I could read what I wrote and easily correct it, or insert new ideas wherever I wished—even at a later time. Then I could print out the pages and put them in folders organized by year.

So when I decided to share some of what I'd written with Paul and Corrine it was easy to just fix up the entries as needed and print them out.

One was my rendering of an experience I'd had months earlier sitting in the waiting room of a medical clinic. A man had come in with his little daughter—maybe two or three years old. Her chin resting on his left shoulder, she was looking back. She was apparently the sick one, but even so she had a far-off dreamy look—so comfortable was she being held by her father. The look of infinite trust in not only her father but life itself—that all would be okay—struck me. But how to convey that expression to my children who had not been there? I decided against sending it.

Instead, I made copies of three poems: Roethke's "My Papa's Waltz," Whitman's "Noiseless Patient Spider," and the first few stanzas of Millay's "Renascence." I chose the last because when I had been their age I was caught up in the childlike rhythm, the rhyme, and that final terrible, wonderful "scream" of joy, which I came to equate, strangely, with the feeling one got when listening to the choral movement of Beethoven's "Ode to Joy."

> All I could see from where I stood
> Was three long mountains and a wood;
> I turned and looked another way,
> And saw three islands in a bay.
> So with my eyes I traced the line
> Of the horizon, thin and fine,
> Straight around till I was come
> Back to where I'd started from;
> And all I saw from where I stood
> Was three long mountains and a wood.
> Over these things I could not see;
> These were the things that bounded me;
> And I could touch them with my hand,
> Almost, I thought, from where I stand.
> And all at once things seemed so small
> [I thought here of Silkie's use of the word "small"

that night in the park.]
My breath came short, and scarce at all.
But, sure, the sky is big, I said;
Miles and miles above my head;
So here upon my back I'll lie
And look my fill into the sky.
And so I looked, and, after all,
The sky was not so very tall.
The sky, I said, must somewhere stop,
And — sure enough! — I see the top!
The sky, I thought, is not so grand;
I 'most could touch it with my hand!
And reaching up my hand to try,
I screamed to feel it touch the sky.
I screamed, and — lo! — Infinity
Came down and settled over me . . .

At first, I added a note about each poem, telling them why I'd chosen it, but in the end I decided to include only a brief cover letter and write below it, "These are some poems I've liked." I put all of it in an envelope, addressed it, and put on two stamps. I would mail it that evening.

I set about another, very different task now—cutting out the three newspaper articles I'd been planning to file but hadn't gotten to yet. I'd left the newspapers themselves in a pile in the corner of a bookcase, where I had the habit of keeping such things until I had time to get to them.

One article had to do with a woman whose only son, who had spoken out against the government in Indonesia, had been dragged away for his efforts and beaten to death. Another had to do with four volunteer hospital workers from various countries doing charity work who were gunned down in Sierra Leone.

Taking note of them specifically in this way meant I was not ignoring these events, indeed in some way doing something about them.

Performing these tasks—first, the selecting of journal entries and poems, the writing of a short letter to Paul and Corrine, the folding of all the pages in thirds, slipping them into the envelope and neatly addressing it, sealing it to send out, knowing they would touch the pages, read the words (my thoughts); then, second, laying out the newspapers and carefully clipping out the articles, making sure not to accidentally snip off any of the text in the corners, folding them neatly, taking them to my file cabinet, drawing out that one folder in the bottom drawer, slipping them in—left me with a certain peace.

But it was a precarious business I was about, I discovered—because it was one that required that I *keep going*. These were not discrete tasks I could perform, then feel satisfied. They were the beginning of something . . . holy.

I sat at the table, the envelope for my children in front of me. I pushed it aside, lay my head into my folded arms, and closed my eyes. I was very still, imbibing a silence which seemed to be almost tangible. Images came to me—a black-and-white photo of an alley in a busy marketplace with the silhouettes of figures bent over, stalls, trash cans; another of some men seated on a wagon emerging into an old man sitting on some rocks and another of a cave—a deep one—with a great mist like that of a waterfall shrouding it.

I rose. Very slowly. Put on my jacket, went outside, and walked.

A walk that would mesmerize. It was the nature of such walks. The kind that one took only at such times. The kind by which you shed the "anyone," the "everyone," and become—even if by illusion—some essence of who you are.

My walk turned into a hike of five or six miles, and at some point I discovered I had, once again, begun heading toward the park, the river. Might not Jo Ann be there again? Better yet, Allana?

The table where they sometimes gathered was vacant.

I walked some more and got home at 11:14. I know because I stared down at my watch for half a minute, as though the time were very important here. I smiled at that. Began to cry.

There, hunched over, I slipped into a deep sleep, eventually keeling sideways onto the floor, from which I would not awaken till almost three in the morning. Friday, September 30.

That's when I realized how quietly momentous the day before had been. What I had given life to.

Turning on one's right side, with a hand under the ear, one could easily have fallen asleep there. But one wanted to get up again with chin uplifted, only to roll into a deeper ditch. [Franz Kafka, "Children on a Country Road"] **[Drawer 3A]**

37. World One Infraction

That morning—Friday, September 30—the end of the first week of fall term, I knew the revelation of the previous day about Silkie would bear some very tangible fruit. Something was going to happen. And, in World One, it would take the form of some very unacceptable behavior. And I would be the perpetrator.

I woke feeling an odd mixture of discomfort and exhilaration. Frustration and anticipation. Discovered my breathing was uneven, heavier, from some piece of a dream in which I'd been trying to pull myself up into a bucket suspended by three ropes and which was itself being slowly pulled up the side of a very tall building. The sensuous details were unnerving. I could literally feel the coarseness of the ropes as I gripped them, feel the cutting into my fingers.

I didn't drive to school. I rode my bike, thinking it would do me some good, allowing me time to reflect, to gain some peace of mind before having to face twenty-five students in a classroom. I'd done it many times before—ridden the bike to the bus station and taken the bus from there. This time, though, I did it very early. It was only 5:30 and the streetlights and those from distant houses were glowing especially orange. It had rained briefly during the night and small pools of water along the concrete bikeway glimmered.

The ride took me down the back streets, then along the stream again—with the cranes, ducks, nutria, raccoons, cattails, blackberry bushes, and Scotch broom mixed into tall grasses. Across the way, in a large fenced-off construction site, were some thirty or forty abandoned cars, pushed unnaturally together and looking like scrap-metal sculptures of dying old men. In the darkness under one of the underpasses, curled up and immobile, was a homeless man wrapped so completely in his filthy dark sleeping bag I couldn't tell from which end his head protruded.

On several occasions when I'd chosen this path, I passed a homeless couple and once or twice given them $5. "Yes, I'm so humanitarian," I muttered aloud in self-derision when I was beyond their hearing. "Randy"—that's what the man said his name was. His girlfriend—"Melody"— was a Lakota who would walk directly behind Randy with her head down. Her face was very red and pock-marked. Randy seemed to be kind to her and so I could never figure out why Melody always walked behind him.

This morning, though, I did not see them, and it was disturbing because some brief exchange with them was a necessary component to this *new self*—which was the way I'd come to think of what was happening to me. Those other times—when I had chanced upon them— their appearance had been just interesting, something I wrote about in my journal, but this morning they would have played a different part in all this—gatekeepers to a world my everyday routine denied.

Exiting the bus at the college, I was disheartened to see that the buildings, the parking lot, the walkways, the trees, the fountain—everything—looked the same, then laughed that I'd harbored the notion the campus had any responsibility to costume itself for my play.

But once I'd unlocked the outside door, the back stairway and the third-floor hallway to my office cooperated. They were empty. I was alone. Separate.

This was not the first time I'd tried to transform my routine. Weeks before I'd begun closing my door halfway so my colleagues wouldn't stop by and chat. Younger teachers by several years—they still went to professional development conferences listening to published academes talk about issues like "Pedagogical Strategies in a Post-Modern World," and they were still looking for innovative ways to "integrate diversity into the classroom"—"diversity" alluding only to race, gender, and sexual orientation, and not the peculiar creature Silkie was and I had become. There was a time I'd been part of all this, regarding it as necessary to my profession. It *was*, of course, necessary. They were good teachers. Committed, conscientious. Indeed, I was ashamed to have lost my enthusiasm. The shape of their voices revealed superior teachers. Perhaps in the past I'd been a superior teacher—or striven to be one—but no longer. If I hadn't yet fully transformed myself from inspired teacher to paid bureaucrat, I felt like I had.

So, I'd been keeping my door nearly shut—open just enough to let students know I was in (there was still the business of assignments). To neither students nor colleagues, though, did I want to reveal my state of mind; nor to hide it by being forced into inanities, small talk, just to keep myself from becoming too intense.

This particular morning, I shut the door all the way. It was necessary if *this* was to work . . . if I was to succeed in committing whatever abominable act I was about to perform (though only vaguely aware of what that would be). I knew only that, in my new role, it was absolutely essential I execute it.

In my very first class, it happened. An entirely new disruption in the routine. One I'd often fantasized about. One which might signal soon a volcanic eruption. An extended seizure? A deliberate abandonment to "World Two."

I'd just had them read an editorial from the *New York Times* condemning the United States for its lack of a meaningful response to the genocide in Sudan. They were to write a journal entry critically analyzing the editorial.

"WHY?" I asked them. "Why haven't we stepped in?"— knowing there wasn't one damned answer that would satisfy the *me* that now stood before them.

Did I already know what was going to happen—where I was going with this? And did it have to do with *me myself* rather than the direction of the argument?

They had written their entries, and some had shared their responses.

"Our government intervenes," Troy said, his head down as he read his paper, "only when one of our companies or trans-national corporations is in danger . . . "

"But why is there such an unwritten policy?" I broke in, throwing it into not only Troy's face but all their faces, affecting an impatience with them not because of anything Troy had said (he was right!), but because they were all safe here in this classroom and we could discuss genocide as an academic issue—relevant only on the rhetorical level. "Why beyond even that? The big WHY. We have one editorial writer's vision for a meaningful response to inhumanity on a colossal scale—genocide. So what?"

Where was I going with this? I knew only that it would end up in some ditch. No clashing of ideas soaring upward to real enlightenment, in the way I'd been demanding of them in their argument papers. Instead, pitching them into a pit of "so what?"

Two more half responses—because I cut in both times—I challenged with "So what?" Was I teaching them? Or was I bullying them into submission to some perspective that was as invalid as anything they would or could offer?

"To whom is this writer writing?" I was sticking my nose

into their faces. "A newspaper-reading public? Us? Here we are reading the editorial . . . discussing it . . . in a class for journal entries and 'reaction papers' and 'free writes.' Comp 121. Three credits. Composition for skill development and career enhancement. Meantime, even as we enter our responses in our journals, another five hundred people may have been slaughtered. We—you and me—we are guilty of too much talk. Not much do."

This disrupting or confounding of their usual analytical process might have been more effective if I had expressed myself with more Ph.D. metaphysical eloquence. Instead, I'd ended up sounding ninth grade. I groped to push it up.

"We study philosophy but have no philosophers. That's what Thoreau said. No doers. Just . . . students sitting mindlessly around tables wanting to know what is the assignment for today. Teach compliance. That's all I do. Because that's what I'm expected to do."

I thought to say something more, but instead scanned the class searching for one set of eyes that spoke something more than astonishment at my demeaning of the process, bewilderment at my changing of the rules. Eyes that revealed some sort of empathy. Even challenge. Rebuttal. I didn't find it. All they heard was my seeming incoherence. My borderline madness. Hadn't Mick warned me I was going to crack someday?

"We can't do *it* anymore," I said quietly.

Astonishing me more than them, I grabbed my papers and

book and walked out. Walked away . . . out of the classroom . . . wondering what *it* meant.

They must've thought my sudden exit was some pedagogical strategy, and I would return. I'd done it once before.

This time, though, I kept walking. Feeling guilt and exhilaration at the same time. What the hell!

I didn't come back—rationalizing to my conscience that it was to make a powerful, memorable statement about learning.

Just left them there.

Waiting.

For what? The answers to my unanswerable questions.

It was an institutional crime, even if just a minor one.

You simply didn't do what I'd just done—in any school. A World One misdemeanor.

There was a need to *break from everything*. I articulated it that way and concluded it was as cliché in action as it was in words. *Find some opening somewhere*. I liked that better.

I was no different from my students if I didn't find one. An *opening*.

I imagined excusing myself to my colleagues for my inappropriate behavior: "Sorry, fellow higher education bureaucrats, but I need to get to the *other side*—this is the time—even if it means leaving my students with their mouths open in shock."

As I made my way out of the building and down the sidewalk, I thought back to the moment I'd exited the classroom. My eyes had fallen on Chloe, a thin, almost frail, dark-haired girl, older than most in the class though probably not yet thirty, who always had the exhausted, intense look of one who'd just gotten off work counseling rape victims. She who had several days earlier come into my office frustrated about her paper. Because it kept slipping into more, as she put it, "uncertainties." "Where am I going with this?" she'd asked as I read over her paper condemning the destruction of the Amazon rainforest and its wildlife, but found herself arguing equally for those poor of the region who, in their desperation to survive, were the destroyers. It was as though *it*—the real bedrock thesis—was there and she thought I could find it for her. "Going right where you should," I replied. "Hammer down the thesis too much and you cheapen the exploration. Simplify too much the complexity. Yes, search for an underlying principle, but acknowledge it may not be absolute."

I remembered telling Silkie something similar. Was this all I could offer then? Had I reached the limits of my rhetorical insight?

But, of course, Chloe was not Silkie—was a different human being. And probably had never till that moment been told how it really was with assigned compositions—that they were of *life itself*. That the thesis every writing teacher asked for could, by its very nature, its insistence on a certainty arising out of solid evidence, sabotage the search for the Truth it supposedly served. "Imagine a photograph of a man cutting down trees in the forest to provide for his family," I said. "What would the photo say? Would it have a 'point'? No. You force one in and it'll squirm and fight its way out again and dissipate into nothing. Writing is groping. Not finding."

Chloe had been surprised at my response then, if not as shocked as she was this morning—at the moment of my leaving the class. Both times, though, I could see it in her eyes: a recognition that seemed to at least comprehend, if not cheer on, my disruption to the usual pedagogical approach.

It was the encouragement I needed. To *not come back.*

It felt good. Very Mercutio—the street reveler, defiant in death, whatever form my demise would take. Something wild. Something sexual. Something irrelevant and irreverent . . . something . . . sacred.

"Infinity settled over me." The line from Millay was in my head suddenly. How did that happen? She reached up . . . *screamed to feel it touch the sky.*

"Touch the sky." Very adolescent, girlish vision. Still, the courage to do so . . . to reach out that way . . . if the metaphor kept going . . . to push beyond . . . beyond what it too easily meant—that was worthy of some admiration anyway.

But, to go with the impulse—the force—in me, I had to do *everything differently*. I could not, therefore, if one of my students complained about my walking out, stop by the department office and offer some explanation to the chairperson. "Listen, Dr. Stone, I suddenly didn't feel well and had to leave class. Going home. Will be back tomorrow, of course." That would have been heresy to my mission, if "mission" was indeed what it was. Nor could I take the bus back to my bike in town as was my custom—bike to bus, bus to campus, from campus by bus to bike, bike to home— because custom was what I had to break with.

I walked—

Off the road through the wooded area so no one would see me and ask if I needed to be picked up . . . some student in the class I'd just split from, wondering what was happening, asking out of concern if I was okay . . . and later mumbling, "The guy flipped."

I trudged the entire two or three miles to the bus station and stood staring at my bike. The fuzzy-headedness about all this should have cleared up during the walk, but it hadn't. In the end, I left the bike there, determined to resist the seduction of the habitual, its calming assurances. A compromise of that sort would mean *it* was over. My experience. I knew only that I had to be alone. But not for contemplation. That was what I'd done on late-night drives with music. It hadn't been enough. *This* had to be different.

The aloneness was nourishing the sweet recklessness. Slowly but inevitably. A high of some kind. Part dizziness, part anxiety, part inspiration.

I saw faces. My children. Silkie. Chloe. Couldn't be the everyday student. Someone, though. Others. Go find at least one of them. Maybe share a table with one. Coffee. A dinner. I'd pay if necessary.

Around 12:45 p.m., I called Mick.

No answer. Probably in class. It was still Friday, after all. I left a message.

"Mick? This is Stephen. If you're free around three I'll be at the Willow. If you can't, no problem."

I thought to add more, but it would have been too complicated. If he came, we could get into it then.

Still leaving my bike locked, I began walking the streets around the bus station to kill time. A costume shop with full, brocaded Victorian gowns displayed. Two hippies playing chess on a board on the sidewalk. A secondhand store of some kind with old *Playboy, Time,* and *Life* magazines and foreign trinkets in the window. A homeless man with a "God bless" sign. A Taco Time. Three Muslim girls in hijabs. An auto parts store. An old woman with a walker. Two high school girls laughing—one of them, slim and smartly dressed, very aware of her looks and of any eyes that might be on her; the other, a little chubby and more carelessly attired, just laughing. A homeless guy with a sign: "Anything helps. Veteran. God bless." Chinese restaurant that would most likely soon be out of business because through the window I could see only one table taken. I felt sorry for them. Struggling Chinese immigrants trying to make it. Was their food too Chinese or too American? Something profound to say there maybe.

If so, I didn't know at the moment what it was. Post office—American flag raised high. Then an anomaly: a modern office building crowded between a small café and a travel agency, both of which its very size and newness threatened to devour into oblivion.

Shouldn't I be deriving some sublime literary themes from this short excursion, these observations? "Okay, class, for assignment one, describe a scene—maybe a Chinese restaurant or an auto parts store—that says something to you. Or how about some homeless woman or whoever just happens to enter and leave the office building or the bookstore. Maybe both of them." Or, "Okay, class, today we'll write a 'comparison-contrast' paper comparing a derelict who holds up a 'Please help' sign with your grandmother who makes Christmas cookies."

"You in the back row, . . . God. Read us what you've written."

It was around 1 p.m. when I found myself in that old cemetery at the edge of town, a block from the university. Historical. Protected by the state. A moss-covered stone wall about two feet high fenced off the Civil War dead from the other markers. A little past the wall there was an older couple bending over one of the headstones and nearby a student sitting up against a tree studying. A girl with real dark straight hair. Asian.

"I know her," I said to myself. I'd briefly talked with her

in the university library about how to get two-sided copies on the copy machine. She was a grad student. A few days later we'd said hi to each other on the bus. She told me she was Chinese.

At this moment her head was down, studying, a pen in her hand and a book lying open on her upraised knees, her legs pressed close together. A quiet contemplation. "If I could fall in love with a girl in one moment, this is it," I said to myself. Acknowledging she might not even remember me—especially in a whole new setting like this—I still wondered, "Is this a sign?" Yes—my ticket to a transcendental moment. It was all for this. My leaving early, Mick's not being immediately available. My happening to head in this direction. A cemetery. Yes, I liked her, and if there was any moment in my life I needed someone, it was now.

She was very pretty. Long black shiny hair (though in this case it wouldn't have mattered what kind it was). Very smart and scholarly looking. Strolling in her direction in a most unaffected very Wordsworthian thoughtful way, I called out, "Hi."

I wished I knew Mandarin to impress her.

Stopping at a distance, briefly, to consider the possibilities, it struck me she would see me only as some strange man ogling her, so I kept walking, right up to her. As I did I imagined she was a violinist or classical singer, that she always studied here in the cemetery when she could, that she was very silent and sensitive, and in China used to walk through early-morning, dew-covered cabbage fields.

"Hello," she replied uncertainly, apparently not recognizing or remembering me and fearing perhaps I might be some pervert who habitually roamed the cemetery preying on lone coeds. I wouldn't push it. What was there to gain anyway?

"Oh, do I know . . . ?"

"We met at the copy machine, a few days ago," I interrupted, wanting to remove, immediately, any embarrassment. "Or longer ago. Maybe three weeks."

Still she couldn't seem to think of anything to say except "Oh."

"Is this where you do your studying?"

"Sometimes."

"No one you know here?"

"Pardon?"

"Anyone you know here?" I asked, motioning to the nearby headstones and smiling so she would catch the humor.

She laughed embarrassed. "No, no. You?"

"No, I'm just killing time." The "killing" sounded like a stupid joke.

"Me too," she said. "My husband doesn't get out of class till . . . [she glanced at her watch] . . . a little while." Warning me, I guessed, not to press this conversation the wrong way. I wondered if she even had a husband.

I hadn't wanted anything more than to talk with her. . . . No, not true. . . . I'd wanted to share a dinner or dessert with her. . . . Well, it didn't matter now. She'd cut it off . . .

though it was disturbing that it came so quickly—even if understandable.

"Have a good read," I replied and went on my way. I gave it an unfriendly edge.

As I surveyed a few more of the inscriptions on the headstones, I became alarmed that the brief encounter with this girl had in some insidious way sucked away whatever force had possessed me earlier. Perhaps to invade a worthier soul. The volcano in me was now sending forth a barely perceptible steam. The Mercutio in me was dying with a reluctant whimper rather than a raucous shout. The Prometheus in me wanted to just sit down and die.

Besides, what Promethean task could I perform except walking? Sluggishly. Aimlessly.

Still, the experience and its disappointing result had taught me something about this journey. I could not be alone for this whole day. Solitude was good perhaps for the journey's start, but not indefinitely. The prospect of company was essential.

I thought of Ombeni. And Camara, who'd translated Ombeni's letters. Camara. What if I visited her at her office?

On the way out of the cemetery, I came upon a World War I memorial with the names of some fifty or so from the county who "gave their lives in the Great War 1917–18." Reading over some of the names, looking for no one name in particular, of course, I began to feel agitated, discovering

I'd become desperate, anxious, unmoored. Very alone.

I left. Went into a 7-11 and picked up some Boston baked beans in a box and ate through half the box before I realized the anxiety within me was growing at an alarming rate. I stumbled and had to stop walking to right myself.

I needed to be with somebody.

Camara. I could stop by to just to say hi to her. She'd ask if I got any more letters. "No, I'd tell her, but I've been thinking about writing back. Could you translate for me when I'm done?"

Of course, there were other things we could talk about. After all, I'd once taught in Africa—even if it had been on the other side of the continent in Nigeria. I remembered—that time we'd been discussing Ombeni's letters at the student union cafeteria—we'd somehow gotten on to the colonial influence in both countries.

"You know, when I was in Zaria, I used to feel uneducated if I didn't talk British," I told her. "Those English with their 'boot,' 'bonnet,' 'petrol.' When I got back here, I kept calling trucks 'lorries' and nobody knew what I was talking about." I told her I still remembered fondly the little sayings painted on the back or side of the lorries. "Smile, everyone," "Love your God"—reminders of how to live life. I had taken a picture of one of them—piled high with old tires and used car parts, on top of which eight or nine people, sprawling and sitting back, were traveling to wherever. A twenty-plus-year-old truck still running on the skill of some uncle who'd learned mechanics from another mechanic's friend. The whole thing swaying like it was going to topple over at the next bump or rut in the deteriorating tarmac roads.

"My older sister used to ride that way," she said. "Bargain with someone to get a ride from my town. It spilled. Lorry swayed and tipped when the driver turned too sharply. Killed three passengers. Two children . . . including my sister."

She'd said it matter-of-factly and began fiddling with a paper napkin.

I imagined the whole scene again. There were things we could talk about. Even if for only ten minutes.

But . . . what if, when I got to her office, Camara wasn't there?

I crossed the street. Entered the Foreign Languages building. Knocked. It was a large shared office. Another African teacher—a male—said she was in class and would be back in a little over an hour. "For lab."

"Thanks. I may come back."

"Want to leave your name?"

"No. I'm not sure I'll be able to make it later." I left.

It was a disappointment. Camara was from what used to be called the "third world." I needed that now. Someone from some continent that wasn't this one. Where, yes, you had to struggle to even get an education. Especially if you were from some rural village.

But my disappointment in her not being there seemed all

out of proportion to what it could have yielded. She would, of course, be busy and have little time to talk. And there was no overt reason to be going to see her. To talk about our pasts?

It was absurd.

The truth was I wanted to sit down with someone and say, "You know what? I walked out of my class this morning." And if he or she asked "Why?" or why, for that matter, I even wanted to tell, I'd be forced to answer. To come up with a reason. The significance of my bizarre action was, I knew now, greater than I had yet comprehended. And part of it entailed being very afraid to be alone right now.

For sure, I needed to talk to someone.

About what?

About Silkie.

With whom?

With Silkie.

And, that being true, who would serve my purpose? Who could I sit across from and be understood? Or be made to understand what even *I* was struggling to grasp?

I'd left that message with Mick. If he were able to come, what would I say beyond "I walked out of my class this morning" that would not be a waste of his time? He was busy. He was not my counselor and might even resent being put in that position if he suspected that was my real motive in calling. He'd lived a lot more life than I had—but that didn't mean he had any more answers than I did. To what? To why I would walk out of my class if it had nothing to do with the students' performance. Might even scold me.

I pictured the scene. Mick, sitting across from me at a side booth at the Willow Café, all around us students with laptops, me staring down at my coffee.

What would be the key word? Confusion? Malaise? Mystery? Darkness? The one to get me started about complexity and too much to deal with. "Fractals!"

I wouldn't so much say it to him as mutter it to myself— across the table from him. It would be a kind of necessary rambling to get at the chaos of it all.

"Fractals. Nature's Escher. So many lines and patterns— crossing, spiraling, splintering out, piling on, pushing outward, sucking inward, indistinguishable ins and outs, overs and arounds—too intricate to fully grasp.

"Even if you could sort it out in some higher form of mathematics, some algorithms with discrete factors, there'd be too many. Because a lot of the 'what' factors become 'how' factors and ultimately 'why' factors. You have to figure in too many of them. I mean, if there is to be real validity. Any complete truth. Right? You can't just stand back and admire the imperfect perfection. Every building collapse or war atrocity, every dead possum or squirrel in the road, every stray dog, every ant washed down the drain . . . you begin to think about too much. Each one a new dimension to work into the mystery. The point is you can't just decide which ones to leave out. They're all part of it.

"For some insane, perverted reason, Mick, I've been fixating on the wrong ones. Analyzing too obsessively the sick factors. I've been collecting accounts of these things—newspaper clippings—and saving them in folders. A lot of my students' papers too—older women writing about how their ex-husbands beat them, younger women on how their stepfathers or older brothers sexually abused them. Argument papers about the treatment of chickens—forced to bump about in darkness their entire short lives—about the destruction of the forests.

"Yeah, they're just papers—not my life—but you start to lose your sense of the separation of their world from your own.

"Bewildered by it all, you slip into some malaise, and you don't know what to do about it. So you send a check to the Global Women's Fund, give a homeless guy a $10 bill, do your bi-monthly thing with your kids—and plunge ahead like it all didn't exist. As you get older . . . you give up. Too many factors to juggle. So many you just want to walk away and let 'em spill everywhere."

But isn't that what I'd be doing with this harangue—spilling it all over Mick?

And in the end, what could he say? What could anyone say?

Suddenly I knew. I knew where I would want all the little streams of conversation to empty—the river that took the form of one question: "So how's this student Silkie doing?"

Because I would have to answer, "She's gone. And I don't know if she's coming back."

It was with a sense of panic that I now realized that, as much as I didn't want to be alone, there was no one I wanted sitting across from me *except Silkie*. Why? Because when I told her, "I walked out of class today," *she was the only one who wouldn't ask why. She would remain silent.*

The aloneness had become panic, stark realization, horror: I had no place to go. No one to turn to. Mick, Camara, Asian girl, even my children, could bring only temporary relief.

An hour later, I was slipping dangerously back into the everyday mind. If I did, everything I'd done since walking out of class would be inexcusable, not only to others—as of course it already was–but to myself. Foolish.

My anxiety about it, my desperation to remain the person I'd become early in the morning, was now, in itself, becoming a new mania. How long could I sustain *him*? The new *me*.

I rode my bike home. Along the stream. Slowly, very slowly. Pondering what to do. Soaking in the high grass, ragweed, Queen Ann's Lace. The homeless man I'd come across beneath the overpass was no longer there.

My decision to plunge into World Two was as well a decision to plunge into near madness. If there was comfort to be found somewhere, I didn't know how to find it.

"Suicide," as not just a word but an intelligent alternative, slipped quietly into my consciousness, having invaded my psyche as some necessary and inevitable response to my developmental stage.

Once inside the warmth of my house, I set about making myself busy, microwaving some leftover chili and wolfing it down with French bread. When that failed to distract me, I put on the fourth movement of Beethoven's Ninth Symphony, turned up the volume, and, immersing myself in the heavenly chorus, commenced conducting both the orchestra and the choir. Then I ran it back to the first movement, lowered the volume, and tried to fall asleep on the couch.

Perhaps it was the profound peace of the adagio movement, or that I briefly dozed off, but an hour later the horror of the suicidal rapids had subsided and flowed into the spiritual calmness of a great ocean. And with the transformation came a sense of purpose. A journey.

I rose, got into my car, and for some time, drove—waiting for whatever was *meant to happen* to me. In the end, I returned to the city.

The heavy wooden doors to St. Thomas's Catholic Church called to me. Was there anything for me in the darkness by the flickering red lamps? It was about 10:00 p.m. It was something I'd done years before—whenever I'd been alone in a big city and needed comfort, solace. A carryover from my Catholic-school upbringing. Seek out a Catholic Church when there was no service being held. Walk in. Sit alone in the darkness. Gaze at the candle-lit statues of Joseph, Mary, Jesus, the stations of the cross.

The doors to St. Thomas were locked.

As much in defiance, delirium, and self-deprecation as in

despair, I went looking for another kind of quiet darkness—that of a late-night bar. In my seeker's journey state of mind, even a bar could be a transcendental experience. Hesse's Goldmund understood the need to take all of it in—the human and the spiritual—if you were to understand. A church, a bar—both could be the door to World Two.

I crossed the northernmost bridge over the river and headed up into the northeast side. Mill Avenue. The main streets near the freeway arteries were full of fast-food restaurants, service stations, motels; but farther down there were primarily older groceries, warehouses, carpet and furniture stores, with a lot of chain-link fences and whole blocks dark. The side streets were residential—brick houses built in the 1930s and '40s with driveways that were little more than two strips of concrete separated by worn grass, and serving an increasingly aging population that probably rarely got beyond their porches.

And now and then a tavern—usually with some sort of masculine theme. "Stan's Cave." "The Corral." The one I chose, though, was called El Dorado. It was a little after 11 p.m.

I hadn't been in an honest-to-goodness bar alone for years. To what purpose was I there? Company with a young beauty with a poet's soul. Not for sex, of course, but its possibility. Enveloped in intensity. Sex with a sacred accent. Touch, gazes that could turn into more—someday. Profound comfort *meant to be.*

Wasn't *all* of this *meant to be*—ever since walking out of that class?

Inside, though, were only men—four of them. Two of them together at the bar itself. Plaid shirts and open jackets, one young with very dark hair and the other older with a receding hairline. Who were they? Tool workers? Ex-ballplayers? They were chatting with the bartender who was too thoughtful and even delicate looking to fit my stereotype of the kind who made a living filling others' beer mugs and whiskey glasses. An old man, short with a head of very white hair, sat farther down at the end of the counter, staring into space, or maybe into his past, or some empty future. The fourth guy was sitting at a table far in the back, appearing to be studying me—maybe because I was a stranger and looked out of place in any bar. He had a suit on but one that looked as though he wore it every day.

It was then that I spied the woman–maybe about thirty-five— in the corner booth, so much in the dark I wouldn't have seen her except for the man's being turned toward her. As for the woman, I couldn't make out her expression, but there was something about her that suggested boredom born of some meaningless routine or pattern.

I sat down where I could seem to be facing the bar but still, by turning my head just a little, study the woman.

"What'll it be?" the young bartender called to me.

"You got Heineken?" I asked, trying to come off as someone who did know what sort of beers were available in bars. "Or on tap?"

He rattled off some brews. "You know," I said, "any beer's okay."

I sounded unsure of myself, and the guy must've picked up on it. Surprisingly, however, when he brought the beer, he was almost solicitous—perhaps recognizing my discomfort.

"Bud okay?"

I liked him.

Holding the beer mug to my lips, I looked over the rim, trying to assay her eyes, hoping they would reveal she was sensitive, lost. Like me. On her own off-the-path journey. It was too dark for that kind of reading, though. She had on a rather tight blouse—greenish, with cowgirl-style bangles—and jeans. The sexuality was there but too much paint.

She left just a few minutes later, and barely glanced at me as she did. Anyway, whatever lust I felt for her shapeliness couldn't get beyond the painted hardened face.

What was I doing anyway? Looking for an STD?

I could imagine some holy man asking, "What did you find on your soul's journey?"

"The clap."

"What of the eternal truths?"

"They don't seem to connect. If that one over there is eternal, how can this one over here too? So, you could be wrong about such a thing. Then what? If you're wrong."

I left after only thirty minutes or so—one beer. Back home.

38. The Journey

I napped on the couch and, when I woke around eight that night, lay there contemplating what I would do. For sure I would leave in the morning. But for how long? To where? Perhaps to see Paul and Corrine. Along the coast? And should I bring anything? A change of clothes. A snack.

I packed an extra pair of underwear and a second pullover shirt, a couple oranges, and a bag of Fritos. The previous visit I'd told my children about Ombeni. Maybe then I would bring along her two letters.

It was in retrieving those two letters that I made what would turn out to be a critical decision. They were in Drawer 4 of my file cabinet—the bottom drawer. Therein was the folder with the "rage" newspaper clippings. And the two letters to Gabriel.

Before this moment it had been just an image. When was the first time? Certainly years earlier. Perhaps one of those days when I'd been slipping a new account into that folder, that drawer. In any case, till this moment, that is all it had been. An image of me doing something. A poetic symbol.

No empirical shape. Not something I would *actually do.* Nothing that *anyone* would actually do.

I would put some of these clippings, these slips of paper—maybe twenty-five or so, at random—into a jar. To go on a journey.

Which ones? How many would fit?

I took out the folder and began reading through the clippings, some of them many years old now. Yellowing, frayed at the edges. Most were only a paragraph or two. But, yes, some were too long. Would jam up the jar. But couldn't I just substitute for them a strip of paper with a label on it making reference to the article? For sure, for the two letters. Two labeled strips: "Eagle in a Box" and "Norma Jean."

Then there was the question of the container to house them. I already decided it would be a jar. Glass. One that could be sealed. One that would float.

But what jar?

Of course, a special one. My mother had purchased a three-set (large, medium, and small) when I was still young. She broke the medium-sized one while washing it in the kitchen sink. Since the set was no longer complete she gave one to a neighbor child with candy in it. When she died I kept the largest one—as a memory because she had liked the whole set so much. It was hexagonal with a bright copper lid imprinted with a pattern of birds and clouds.

The lid had a rather noticeable dent near one edge—the result of a fall from the kitchen counter in the second year of my marriage.

And half the edge was tarnished either by the sun, when it had been too long on the windowsill, or from a spill.

Even with the dent and tarnish, however, the aesthetics were very pleasing to me. It was worthy of its purpose.

Its purpose? To house those Drawer 4 clippings, labels. At some point on my journey, perhaps after I visited my children, I would drive to the coast . . . walk out to the beach at night . . . set the jar near where the surf lapped at the sand just as the tide was going out. For the gods to take. An act of defiance to them. A prayer for those who suffered the tragedies that were chronicled in those accounts and alluded to with those labels: "Eagle in the Box," "Norma Jean," "Mary Turner," "Three Mexican Girls," and twenty-some more. For the jar a singular journey.

In the morning I awoke very late—close to 11. It was Saturday, October 1. I tossed into my overnight bag the snacks, the jar.

Already, though, the spiritual force that had driven me to behave in a way I'd never behaved before, with so much abandon, plunging into World Two, was gone. The morning before I'd been moved . . . inspired to walk out of my class and explore World Two, spurn all that meaninglessness that had become of my existence, and just leave. Everything.

Now, a day later, I stood staring at my Honda Civic parked in the driveway. It might just as well have been out of gas. I was. What had I decided? My children. The coast. The jar. Why in the end would it be anything more meaningful than what I'd done every morning for years? The day before I'd allowed myself to slip into some delusional state: surrender masking itself as some sort of seeker's journey. Since walking out on my class I'd accomplished nothing, experienced nothing that promised fulfillment. Seeing my children, yes, but I could do that anytime. As for the jar and its journey, nothing but a symbol of . . . what? Perhaps as much defeat as defiance.

And what of my classes Monday morning? Should I call in sick now—just in case—or would I be back to normal by then? "Back to normal"? In what sense was I not normal?

I knew the answer already. *I was unable to teach. At all.* For the remaining weeks of this term. Even worse, I was incapable of going to my office to prepare the necessary instructions to a substitute: where I was on the syllabus . . . what was to be accomplished in the remaining time . . . what papers still needed marking . . . special notes on particular students. For four classes! It would mean not only going back to the office but focusing, concentrating to a degree World One required and to which I was not capable at this time.

But to not teach the rest of the term meant going to a doctor, getting some official letter. Saying what? I had not had a stroke or a complete mental breakdown. It was just that in some way I was . . . unable to carry on as always. No real tangible diagnosis.

It was too much to think about now. Perhaps by Sunday

night or Monday morning, I would feel differently. As for this moment, I might not even get two blocks. Turn around. Come back.

I was in a state of disorientation—but one devoid of restless anxiety, of the reckless spirit that had driven me the day before.

I drove slowly. The world was as it always was late morning. Cars, stores, streets, houses, trees.

Maybe just go home. Turn on my brain by reading a book. Turn off my brain by switching on the TV. Or sleep it off. Sleep *what* off?

I crossed into the fringes of Chinatown and came upon a young muscular man—Asian, short hair, cut-off sleeves, jeans, smoking a cigarette—seated in the shade of a doorway and staring out into the street. He had the look of a high school dropout. I wondered that he wasn't cold because the temperature had gone into the low forties the night before.

I slid my car over to the curb, stopped, turned off the engine, and sat there, staring out the front window.

I got out. Walked.

Two blocks later I came upon a group of three transients on a street corner seated on the curb, one of them very old, white, gray-haired, tearing off a page from a local ads newspaper, the other two—both black, more middle-aged— talking with some animation about something. Each word was dragged out tediously.

"Like it was . . . like it was . . . the reeaal thing, you know?"

". . . believe it. She's a biiitch. I remember the bitch used to . . ."

The old white guy was reading to himself the page he'd torn off.

They didn't even look up when I passed.

Jesus, did I really want to mingle, even sit down, with any of these guys? Did they have anything to offer? Some inspiration? I continued shuffling around the block, pondering. I pictured them as babies. Adorable. Perfect faces. Smooth skin. Big eyes. And now? But maybe one of them actually had a master's or a Ph.D. and couldn't get a job except as a substitute ninth-grade social studies teacher, and then couldn't pay the bills, so his wife left him and he took a job as a security guard or a convenience store clerk or a real estate agent—all of which were so unsatisfying, he turned to the romantic call of the hobo, hopped a train or truck, and ended up on the street hoping for enough quarters to buy a drink. "Tell me," I'd say to him, "you've got a whole different perspective here. Do you perhaps have it all figured out? The universe, I mean. Purpose. I mean, you're down at the 'other' end. The people on top, even with all their studying, haven't got a clue. That's where I am. The other end. No clue."

Would they laugh? That would be worth it. The sharing of the absurdity. The wry cynical recognition of the human condition in the guise of four lost souls on a Saturday morning.

I kept walking. Up and down streets looking for something

to reignite whatever spark had set me off the previous morning.

It was a little after two when I stopped for a bite to eat at a small café. I ordered a Reuben sandwich and iced tea, and as I ate I noted across the street an old brick church on the corner. It was fairly sizable and had a white steeple whose paint had badly peeled. Perhaps it had been the center of this neighborhood at the turn of the century. Today you wouldn't take any more notice of the steeple than you would of a cigarette billboard.

When I'd finished eating, I crossed the street. The heavy wooden front doors were open. Once inside the vestibule, however, I discovered the entrance to the church proper was locked. I tried the long dark hallway running along the right side. At the end of it was a half-open door through which I could spy a handful of pews. There were only a few left, and, without the usual sheen I had grown used to in Catholic churches, they were no more impressive than the scattered card-table chairs in the back.

I went in. Hymn books strewn on a table and on some of the wooden chairs. Perhaps the church was still used then. Even if only as a meeting place. At the front was a raised platform and a pulpit. I sat down in the rear. It didn't have the feel of a church—too much light coming through the side windows. If I moved up nearer to the pulpit, it was considerably darker. Even so, there was no sense of God here now. God had most likely moved out long before.

I sat down anyway.

Silkie was on my mind.

Not the day's journey. Rather, the longer journey I'd begun years earlier. Because Silkie was part of it—the whole thing. She'd never been separate from it. *Even when I hadn't known her.*

It was essential I sort this out right away. For the legitimacy of what I was doing. Even for what I was. What if, after all, what I was doing now was nothing more than, in effect, getting drunk? I'd gotten myself obsessed with this young woman, this student no less, now gone away. Most likely for good. Call it what it was. Love lost.

Nothing else.

Yes, there'd been this other-worldly dimension to it all. But couldn't it have been my attraction for her that had caused all of it?

Which was it? And if it were *both*, what did that mean for what I was doing? Had I sunk to this depth *gradually* because of my need to get into some World Two, or *precipitously* because she'd taken off? And if the latter, was it because going to see an old boyfriend meant what such things always meant, and there was nothing mythic about her at all?

I let *it* settle all about me—the hopeless pondering—till *it* was no longer rational, no longer even thought. A sort of lifeless weeping.

Abruptly I rose from my seat. *It*—some purpose in what

I was up to—had, inexplicably, come back.

Was it spurious? No matter. You had to go with such impulses.

I left the old church.

When I was a kid, I sought to reach God through Gabriel. But here I was, an adult, trying to reach him by just walking away—from everything. Yes, I'd been searching in a church. But in a tavern too. Was I about to embark on something hallowed or something profane? The leaving class had been the beginning of it.

I looked up into the sky, which had turned very gray. I began to feel cold. And hungry. I explored six or seven other streets before settling on a second bar. Taverns still seemed to be the kind of place I needed to become one with. Maybe because it was as far out of my routine as robbing a bank. Besides, this bar was one in which I could get a sandwich as well as a drink.

I entered. The dim, spacious room was empty except for a man and a woman in a booth far to the back. The man, his back to me, looking surprisingly well dressed, was leaning over as though he didn't want to be heard by anyone.

I sat at a side table and ordered a beer and some peanuts ("If you have any") from a short, heavyset, red-haired waiter.

I turned my attention to the man and woman. The man, still bent over close to the woman, seemed to be tense and anxious, as though in a hurry to finish a deal. Once he called over to the guy who'd taken my order. "Hey, Caz, can I get a wet towel over here? It's shit stinky on this table." The red-haired waiter came out of the back, picked up a cloth from behind the bar, and wiped the table. The girl had her head down.

"Caz" came over to me then.

"Anything else?" he asked with a friendly smile (maybe because I was a contrast to the other guy).

"Would you have . . . some sort of hamburgers here?"

"Big one. Fat with lettuce, tomato, you name it." He smiled.

"Sounds all right."

I liked him. Small niceties can make a difference.

It was very dim in the corner where the man and woman were, but the lighted red Heineken sign above their table reflected in the girl's eyes. They were vacant, hurt. She was maybe thirty-five; the guy, I suspected from the thinness of his hair and fat of his torso, maybe forty or forty-five. A white collar peeked above a spiffy sports coat. One of those guys for whom shiny suits were the chief claim to success. The girl—who struck me as being from someplace like Guam or Manila—seemed to be tired. She was maybe a little overweight. Pretty? A little. But again, where she sat was too dimly lit to tell.

She gulped down the rest of her drink and then just sat there with a lost look. The guy glanced back over his shoulder apparently to make sure I wasn't paying too much attention, couldn't hear, then leaned over toward her again, whispering now in a tone of wanting to get something settled. Yeah, he was older than her. Considerably.

Finally he reached into his back pocket, pulled out his wallet, and deposited what appeared to be some bills on the table in front of her. She stared down at them but didn't seem interested. There was a kind of beseeching in the tone of his voice, then even a solicitousness for her. I didn't see her respond in any way. Her lips didn't move, so for sure she said nothing. Finally he just got up, went to the register and paid, then left, with an unfriendly glance toward me. She sat there staring down at the money. No good-bye to him.

I stole glances at her as I ate. After a while, she let her gaze fall on me, her hand grasping her empty glass. I turned away. Didn't want to invite anything here. At least . . . well . . . did it matter? A sort of malaise began to creep up through me from my chest, then gained in force and took hold of me roughly—not in the usual nature of malaise. What was I doing, anyway? I lay my head down on the table, thinking how curious that must look to her, to "Caz." My hand was half hooked around the handle of my mug.

I was going nowhere. The whole thing was absurd. Some foolish game mortals play to give themselves hope for an eternal life—a hope which stops at the edge of a table in a bar, and which ceases to exist altogether when one closes one's eyes and presses them against one's arm.

I was seeking enlightenment in some woman at another

table who meant nothing to me as a prospect. For whom I had no attraction.

I shifted my head upward without lifting it from my arms so she wouldn't be able to see I was studying her. Yes, she was thirty-five or so but trying for a young face with considerable makeup to cover the lines that were probably alcohol and cigarette deepened. Life worn. And yes, a little overweight, the excess being pushed into place. I found all of *it* repulsive, but, oddly, not *her*.

I smothered my face again. Wanting to sleep.

A minute or two later I heard a movement near my table.

Assuming it was the waiter, I lifted my head. "Yes, I'll have another . . ."

It was her. She was already pulling out the chair and seating herself across from me. Her eyes were apologizing for the intrusion into my rest. She had long glossy hair, making her look younger, even with the lines in her face. "What are you eating?"

Maybe it was because during the minutes with my head down, I'd shed every last trace of my short-lived transformed spirit, whoever or whatever it drew upon . . . avatar, seeker, Rasputin, Lothario . . . or because the way in which she'd asked was that of a sister asking her brother, or because she looked like a woman who would much rather have been with a brother than a boyfriend—whatever—I could not help but regard her as if I were truly that brother.

"Pardon?" I was surprised how tender my voice was.

"Eating. What are you eating?"

This time it sounded more like a little girl, naive and wary.

Up close now I realized that while her skin was dark, her features were a little European. Maybe a generation back the product of a GI and a Filipino or some such mix.

"Oh, just a hamburger. Already finished it."

She sat down. Didn't ask with words or gestures if I would allow her to do that. Just sat down and set her purse on her lap and stared off to her left, looking at nothing in particular. Now and then an inquisitive glance at me. Finally I spoke. "You want one?"

She shrugged, then shook her head. I pointed to her empty glass, which she'd carried over from the other table and was still for some reason holding in her hand. "What was that?" I asked.

She lifted her head as if confused, then saw where I was pointing. "This? Ginger ale."

Where to go next? She had this inquisitive look, like a shy little girl whose mother had pushed her forward to meet me. But now that I'd begun to talk, I'd have to lead, despite her boldness in sitting down in the first place. Lead where? What was this about anyway? She didn't fit the image or scenario my fancy had been playing with since I'd first walked out of the class the day before. Why couldn't it have been that other one—the girl from the cemetery, perhaps on some soul journey of her own—seated across from me?

Well, I had this one instead, and right now she was just

sitting there quietly, expecting me to say whatever had to be said. Was I supposed to know? Was there a classic script?

So I did. For the next half hour I asked her everything and she asked me nothing except my name. I found out her name was Selena (she made sure I didn't spell it "Celina") and the man was a boyfriend named Manny whom she had an apartment with but he was leaving her. Which she seemed to be somewhat sad about, but that was all—taking it in the course of life. She had a sister in Boise and a brother in Knoxville. The brother was a manager of a restaurant. Because Knoxville was too far, she was planning to go to Boise.

Her answers were brief, and it began to dawn on me that it wasn't so much from shyness as from a lack of perception of the complexity, the nuance, of anything. She was a little slow.

Deciding it was best to extricate myself from an experience I feared was going to be more tiresome than transcendent, I glanced down at my watch to let her know I had to go somewhere, and got up to leave. She sat there gazing at me like I was walking away from my own children.

"You have any place to go?" I asked. For some reason I was beginning to think fate was playing with me. That she was the reason I'd cut out of my class.

She shook her head right away. Was this where she'd been going all along with this?

"But you said your sister . . ."

The scene of the boyfriend giving her money flashed in my mind. "That money your boyfriend gave you. You can use that to get to . . . where? . . . Boise, no? You have a way to get there, right?" She didn't say anything again—just stared at me.

Jesus, what did she want? Was I *supposed* to do this? What "this"? Take her to Boise?

"Fated" and "destined" till now had been appealing to me, but not in this form. Was she the one? The one to do what? Why THE ONE, you fool—the catalyst to a greater understanding. God has a sense of humor. First it was you, Gabe. The whole scene of the nuns and that picture card of you in glorious garb. Now this. God's idea of a joke. "You're a seeker? I'll give you something for your troubles, Bub." I wondered if these seekers were a source of insufferable tedium to God. Well then, I would see what God's joke was all about. Or would I? I suddenly had visions of a packed rear seat and a U-Haul trailer. No way. That was not what I'd bargained for. Besides, maybe the boyfriend wasn't entirely gone. Some kind of jealous sort who'd have no problem driving his Mustang faster than I could drag a U-Haul.

No way would I take on this Selena.

"You . . . want me to take you . . . home . . . to your apartment?" I heard myself asking. I could do at least that much. After that . . . she must have friends. People who knew more of what she was all about.

My subconscious visions of a one-night stand with some muse or siren had completely evaporated.

What if I just left her a few dollars after I dropped her off?

She looked very lost.

"Listen, where do you live?" I congratulated myself on how I'd hit upon the perfect response to both her need and my conscience. "I mean, it's not too far, is it?"

She shook her head.

"Okay."

"Is this where I turn?" I asked.

"Here, yes, right. Two more blocks . . . past that big sign and that store . . . the one with those old mannequins in it. Closed years ago. Strange, isn't it, those things still in there collecting dust like that? Spooky. Listen, I have things I have to bring with me. Like my engraved jewelry box. Okay?"

"Take where? I'm just dropping you off, right?"

"Okay, that's all right. I know. But I'm just saying I want to make sure I take it with us."

"Why . . . that box?" (What was I doing? Why did I care if I didn't have any plans to . . . ?)

"My mother when I was really small back in Umatilla. She gave it to me."

The jewelry box must have been the most important thing in her entire life because she talked about it for the next few minutes. Its entire history, like it belonged in the Smithsonian. "I have to get it. It's an heirloom."

In the meantime I was trying to figure out just exactly how mentally challenged she was. Enough that her response to her apparent plight didn't seem adequate.

"You better not think of me as your savior because I'm more lost than you are," I said to myself. "I'm in seeker mode—just split out on my job. I've cut myself loose and I can't let myself get all entangled again. Need to keep loose. *Unless, it—the "seeking"—is in the being entangled.* . . . Oh shit. Whatever. Just keep going."

I glanced over at her, wondering if this slowness of her mind had a mood side to it too. The way she jumped from that "I don't care anymore" look in the bar—head down, staring straight ahead—to this "This will be fun" look of anticipation, excitement in the car. New life for her.

As for me, I knew already where my experiment in seekership was going. Before it was over I'd probably be—figuratively speaking—dangling a million-dollar bill in front of her so I could eventually tear it up. Jesus!

On the other hand, this Selena was really lost too. Not like me. Not the same way. But . . . surely . . . lost.

While we drove she stared straight ahead. "He wants me to go. He gave me some money." ("To do what?" I wondered.) "He says I should go to my sister's."

"Your sister. Where is she?"

"She lives in Boise. I told you, remember?" ("Yeah, that's right, that's what you told me, although at the time I wasn't thinking.")

"So he gave you enough . . . you have enough money then to take the bus? To Boise."

She shrugged.

"Do you know how much it is?"

She opened her purse and answered at the same time. "Thirty-nine . . . forty-nine dollars, I think. It used to be."

"How much do you have there?"

She began fingering some bills and then some change. "I don't know. Sixty. No, sixty-two something."

"That's all? What if I give you some more? Fifty dollars maybe."

She shrugged, and looked like she was going to cry.

"Look, Boise's a long drive for me. I can take you to your apartment, then to the bus station. Can you tell her . . . your sister . . . you're coming?"

She nodded.

"That's okay, isn't it. I've got something I've got to be doing tonight. Boise . . . it'll be three in the morning or later. Besides, your sister won't be up then."

That meant motel before then. Tomorrow morning. Yep, that settled it. Not only was I not packed for such a thing but how was I going to handle sharing a room with her? A motel room with this Selena.

But by the time we'd reached her apartment, I had a surprising change of heart about it all. "Oh, well, I'll just make it clear this isn't anything more. Just make it clear. Don't want her accusing me of rape or giving me the clap. Who knows how many guys she's been sleeping with . . . or her boyfriend, for that matter. This whole thing isn't my thing.

I'm a teacher, a professor. Derelict though I might be at this moment, that's who I am. Then again—why not just cohabit the room innocently? Well, two rooms won't break me, I guess. Now that I think about it, the drive itself is maybe just what I need. A quiet drive there, and a very long quiet one home. Will fill up the weekend. Fact is, this frightened-to-be-alone feeling is still with me. Suicidal thoughts taking over. Need the company. And then—there's this *fate* thing. . . .

"Off we go . . . "

The apartment she'd shared with her boyfriend wasn't in a residential area. (I recalled the clothes the guy was wearing. What a phony.) It was upstairs in an old house on a side street just off another street on the corner of which was a tire center.

"Do you want help?" I asked, leery of going inside for fear the man was there. She nodded.

I followed her in. It was surprisingly very neat inside. Probably compliments of her alone—some sincere commitment to future domestic bliss with this prick. (I'd already decided that's what he was, though maybe before this next day or two was over I'd be a greater one. Maybe that's just how it was in this whole scene I'd never experienced. People get screwed and expect to.)

There was, however, a pile of clothes—women's stuff—in a corner of the entranceway. Somebody had already prepared her for leaving. She gathered up some of it, went inside, threw a lot of bathroom stuff into a box, and retrieved her jewelry box. (I have to admit, it was an impressive one. Covered in red leather with gold embroidery and with several compartments and tiny drawers. But from her chance remarks I suspected the real value of it for her was who had given it to her years before—some young man who'd loved her.) Then she started carefully putting the clothes and a few odds and ends into a large red suitcase. She wasn't really crying or even looking thoughtful. Just put the stuff in like it was a job she did in a store every morning. She carried it over, piece by piece, to the front door, stood staring down at it like she was sure to be forgetting something, nodding her head in an odd sort of way that meant either she was counting items or recounting memories of the place, then, with an apology, remembered she had to go to the bathroom.

When she came out she had a plastic bag full of toiletries.

We were on I-84 to Boise. No World Two in sight. Late Saturday, October 1. I'd been drugged. Forced by conscience to walk down some long road at the end of which was not enlightenment but shame. It triggered a memory when I was literally led down a long hallway to the principal's office by a nun who had accused me of "taking the Lord's name in vain" on the playground. A friend did, not me, but I didn't want to get him in trouble. I was innocent then and just as innocent now. This was where a weekend of seeking had left me. The principal's office. God as principal?

I-84. I'd done this before. Along the breathtaking Columbia Gorge with all its many waterfalls—here rushing, here trickling—over high cliffs. The same ones that hung frozen in the winter. But I looked to neither side, feeling more and more oppressed with the prospect of the long drive ahead and the unpleasant burden of it all. I needed to sleep. Or just the peace of being alone in a bed in a motel. Or on the grass under a tree at one of the rest areas. Wherever I could draw upon the serenity of night.

I'd remembered how eastern Oregon was so dry and western Idaho even worse because the highways were not properly painted. But to my surprise, the setting sun was bathing the landscape in a golden glow, and the black shapes of the mountains in the distance cutting into the darkening blue sky rendered this part of the drive quite pleasant.

Farther and farther into Idaho, however, meant farther and farther from where I needed to be. Had expected to be. Paul and Corrine. The coast. Farther and farther from anything sacred. Farther and farther from Silkie.

There was no way this could be World Two.

She began sobbing . . . noticeably. Little attempt to smother it. "What's wrong?" I asked her. She shook her head, and I wasn't sure I wanted to pry anymore. A couple minutes later, though, she was excitedly talking as though she were a little girl entering a big city for the first time. Explaining to me, for some reason, about the boyfriend who had just dumped her, about her sister, even about the restaurants she'd been to on I-84. The details she provided were all superfluous. "He likes to wear his red shirt," she reported. "Two days a week at least. Usually Monday and Tuesday after I wash it." And "My father had a shirt just like it." "My sister's husband doesn't like me. Yells at me and uses bad words. You know, mean words."

At one point, she began jabbering about everything—what she used to do long ago in Boise and Umatilla. Some girlfriends of hers. Then about her pets. A gerbil named Harriet. Not knowing how to cut in, I let her go. Then inexplicably she started telling me about her sexual escapades, as if I wanted to hear about them. Some guy named Ben. Ben liked to "do it outside." Ben was real tall and liked the rodeo.

On and on. It brought to mind Sandy's tedious ramblings in Twain's *Connecticut Yankee*. But this was today in the real world and I was deciding she must be manic-depressive or something close to it. They're very sexual, I was told once by a colleague who had a student in common with me—a student who, to my shock but not altogether displeasure because it was certainly flattering for one my age—came on to me in my office. Autumn was her name. A strange name. A very good writer. Was this Selena then like Autumn? And if so, was that good news or bad? I leaned toward the bad.

It was about 1:45 a.m., Sunday, October 2, when we got to Nampa. "We'll have to get some rest here," I told her with some dread. She'd already fallen asleep against the door, and I really didn't want to waste another $60 on a second room. She was sleepy. We'd just both collapse. It would work out okay.

I got a room with two beds.

Unfortunately, it turned out the sleep in the car left her rested—a little too rested, I suspected, and I became wary of what she was going to put me through. "This is it," I thought, while at the same moment wishing it was the Asian girl in the cemetery with me on this trip. We'd have intelligent discussions about college, books, whatever country she was from. We'd go to a good movie first (well, if it weren't so late), then dinner. Maybe a Chinese restaurant and she'd tell me things I didn't know about the food. After that, because of what preceded it, the sex would have a kind of beauty about it.

Of course, the cemetery girl wouldn't have gone for any motel business. As my fantasy, though . . .

Selena was standing next to the car, waiting for me to open the trunk and unload her bag. She was surveying the street a little too wide-eyed for me.

That's when it happened. Maybe it was the way she not only accepted me, but seemed to want to make herself enjoyable to me. Even if she wasn't bright enough, deep enough, to grasp what state of mind I was in—existential despair—she seemed to have some woman's sense of how relationships become meaningful in a world without much meaning.

Fact was, I had started to like her. And she didn't look that bad. Pretty in a way I'd never thought attractive before. An appealing shape too.

I needed time to think. Deposit her in the room. Let her sleep. I would go get a beer. Or two. Then . . . I would know. If there was something wrong in even allowing it to go that far in my conscience, I didn't care. After all, it had been God's sense of humor that got me here. Well, I could play the game too.

The recklessness of this behavior—the Mercutio—had become immoral. Bullshit to you, God!

Still the guilt was there. I felt it. I was smothering it, but feeling it. God had deposited her in front of me. God damn it all!

She was sitting on the bed, eating a piece of chocolate from a large bar she'd been carrying in her bag.

"I . . . need to get something," I told her. I didn't want her going along. "There was a convenience store back a little way. Maybe it's 24/7. You just sleep. You're tired, aren't you?" She shrugged. "Get me some cigarettes, will you?"

"What kind?" I hadn't bought cigarettes for over twenty years probably, and then just once for a friend. Did they still have Philip Morris and Pall Mall?

"Marlboro," she told me.

I was off. An all-night grocery. Walking. Down the road away. Cigarettes for her. Beer for me. Play it safe—a condom too. I hadn't bought one for some time. A little embarrassing. Revealing. Oh well! The beer would help. I was going to get myself into the right state. If it seemed like it was *supposed* to happen, then it had to feel that way. Natural. Not forced. I didn't want to be feeling guilt. Get all hung up on STDs and babies and accusations of rape. This was something I needed to do: give it a chance for . . . the *supposed* to *be*.

I could not help but smile at the way I was making a potential one-night stand sound like the redemption of humanity.

Just didn't want to be thinking too much. It had always been my undoing. Not this weekend.

I bought three Buds. Considered more to make sure I'd get to the right state of mind, which in this case would be out of my mind. Where to drink it? It was quite a walk to a kind of coppice of trees way back from the road. Probably somebody's backyard. Dark enough, hidden. Didn't want to be mistaken for someone breaking in. No, there appeared to be a stream there.

 She would be sleeping by now (I hoped).

That lurking guilt. Just needed to stave it off. My guilt. God's fun. Sin as the necessary doorway to cosmic enlightenment. St. Augustine's sexual exploits . . . St. Francis Assisi's wealth . . . I was trying to remember from my Catholic school days. . . . weren't they sinners first then?

The trees were just on the edge of a car dealership but hid me enough. I drank the cans down—two did it. I wasn't much of a drinker and the abandonment carried me well enough downstream.

Problem was I felt sleepier, not braver.

I got there with the assistance of the cool air. Moral confusion. Reckless seeking. Who gave a shit anymore?

I unlocked the door. She was curled up on the bed watching TV. Some stupid old sitcom. The laugh track found idiocy hysterical.

I would have undressed to my underwear in the bathroom, but that would have meant, afterwards, crossing over in front of her to the other bed, and I hadn't brought pajamas or a bathrobe. So, noting that she was lying so as to look off the other way, I slipped under the sheet and worked down to my underwear as best I could.

Unfortunately, I was exhausted—effect of the beer, the long drive, my mental state. What if I just cascaded into sleep? First, though, there was the necessity of letting some of that beer out of me. I dressed again (under the sheets), climbed out, and went to the bathroom. When I came out, she was slipping what looked like a birth control container back into her purse. I wasn't sure whether to be relieved or panicked. She'd taken off her sweater. Looking a little bored. But also, letting her bra straps slip off, a little playful. This was probably different for her because I wasn't her boyfriend— couldn't make sense of me and that was enough to pique her curiosity. Besides, I was a guy, she figured, and probably I'd be expecting it. For helping her.

I just sat there on the other bed, gazing almost sadly, resignedly, at her.

The beer was working. I had to admit that.

But did I really want this? Her breasts were really full. Still young. She slipped off the bra. Waited. Stared down at the floor. Then at me because I wasn't moving.

I was actually excited. I'd begun to doubt it—that it was possible under the circumstances. Which circumstances? The ones going all the way back to my walking out of that class. Those circumstances. "Sorry, class, but I need to drive to Boise to meet this girl named Selena in a hotel room. I've never met her, but . . ." Maybe it was the taking the bra off just for me that moved me. "Just for me?" Who was I kidding? It must have been for many others in other apartments . . . other motels.

No, that wasn't fair either. Anyway—now it was just for me.

I turned away. "Stop this!" I said to myself and thrust the spread fingers of my right hand through my hair. I'd make her think I really did want to do it but that I'd already decided I didn't want to take advantage of her. My guilt working. My fear of insulting her working. Both with that one gesture.

No way I was going to go through with this. All these doubts rushing in to rescue me. Conscience. Fear of clap. I'd had a couple condoms break. Fear of producing some unwanted child nine months down the road. Birth control pills worked 99 percent of the time, didn't they? If you didn't forget to take them. After all, I'd be protecting her too if I turned the offer down.

But, still sensitive enough to know she had to think I wanted to, I did the act up. "Yeah, I'd like to," I told her, "but listen, if it's okay with you, we'll just skip that. I'm very tired. And I wouldn't feel . . . right to do it now. Okay?"

Jesus, was I her father?

She actually looked more hurt than surprised. She kept sitting there. Staring down at her hands clasped on her lap. Didn't even crawl under the sheets or put on a sexy nightgown like in the movies. At least she'd brushed out her hair.

I turned off the light and plopped down on the bed. Closed my eyes. That was that. "See you in the morning" sort of thing. Seconds later I heard the TV set get louder, blare way too loud. Done in anger. She came up behind me in the bed and began pushing against me.

Okay. I'd done my best.

The beer worked. I turned loose. Other fears be damned. God seemed to be in on this one. If he wasn't, what did it matter? What did the whole damned weekend matter?

I got excited. Guilt was gone. Went for it. She seemed to get swallowed up in it. A half hour later, she was all over the room. Literally. On and off the bed like a crazy woman. Screaming with excitement and crying at the same time. She was naked and her long hair was flying in all directions. Her body snapping, contorting. Lasciviously. Getting out the poison. Bursting out of prison into the clean air. Opening the boil. She was making so much noise, I panicked she would hurt herself or alarm some tenant in the next room who would call the front desk.

"Selena . . . okay?"

To keep her from hurting herself I finally took hold of her shoulders and pressed her forcibly back into the bed. She was strong and spun away. Some demon in her needing to be exorcised. Or maybe it was just a goddamned seizure. What was happening with her?

Whatever initial satisfaction I'd felt at helping her to expel that lifelong pain or anguish deep inside her quickly turned to guilt. Had I yanked it from the unconscious into the conscious?

"Selena, you okay?" But holding her down, pressing so close, I found myself excited again. It was like some violent turn-on. Comforting her and ravaging her at the same time. I actually felt like getting inside her again. If someone came in at this moment they'd call the police. Forcible rape. But it wouldn't be. Instead some cosmic form of orgasm. "Seeker Attains Highest Buddhist State in Sleazy Idaho Motel!" the headline would say. Besides, a second time might produce a show exponentially magnified. (I was a math minor. In fact, it seemed like on this trip I'd gone from existentialist philosopher, to bar sociologist, to moral pervert, to mathematician.)

"I'm sick, twisted," I said to myself. "This is the *supposed?*"

She settled down. I held her. She was shaking but not crying. Unless the crying was inside.

In the morning—still Sunday—we drove on. She slept late so I had to wake her with a breakfast of scrambled eggs from McDonald's down the road. A road lined with the flat nothing of southwestern Idaho. Dull greens mixed into large patches of brown. You don't look left or right. Just at the road. Especially when you want to be coming back as soon as possible.

All the rest of the way she was crying quietly. Instinctively I knew it wasn't going to stop. I'd opened some repressed agony in her and if it came out explosively at first, the rest of it was still leaking out.

An hour later we pulled into a long gravel driveway to a small half newly painted shabby shingle house a long way back from the road. Her sister came out immediately. She was obviously older than Selena and one of those run-down, too-thin-from-hard-work, not-very-happy women. Existence hadn't turned out to be what she'd expected the day she got married. Selena got out. I stayed in the car. She talked a long time, and then the sister walked over to me still sitting in the car. Lines in her face. A cigarette in her mouth, her hair still trying to wake up for the day. (Reminded me of the woman pumping gas at the "eagle in a box" road stop years earlier.) She glared at me with disgust. "You can at least help her carry her stuff in."

"Listen, I'm just . . ." But, of course, I wasn't "just."

"Shut up, you prick!" she said and turned away. "Prick!" The very word I'd applied to her ex. Selena stood there near the car. Her sister stomped back into the house and I could hear a man's voice shouting. "Fuck . . . Christ! . . . What the fuck! Is she back?"

I decided I would just leave her bags and boxes near the doorstep and go. "I'm going. I . . . hope it turns out well," I said quietly to her. She didn't reply. Just stood there.

I drove away.

I'd opened her up to something new. Then just left her there.

I'd committed a serious crime. A World Two crime. Drawer 4 headline: "Poor Girl Dumped." My own label for it: "Ditched Selena."

For a while I told myself there was some great significance to the events of that weekend. The crossing of Selena's life with mine. Two lost souls. Lost in different ways but ultimately seeking the same thing. Except that I could articulate it better than she—or maybe just more philosophically, pedantically. Happiness. Not happiness. She could understand that. Why give it any other name?

Ultimately I decided that if there were any revelations to be gained, I'd missed them entirely. The only truth learned was the story of trying to find that truth. Should I carry it back to my students? "We have two Truths. Truth 1: Not only do I not have the answer but you never will either; nor will anyone. Truth 2: In seeking to be kind, good, compassionate, we—all of us—will hurt others along the way. Terribly."

I drove to California. To see my children. Knowing that unless I didn't sleep at all, I'd have no chance of making it there by the following morning—Monday, October 3. And while I had no classes to teach till Tuesday, getting back to Oregon from Los Angeles on time would be equally impossible.

I kept going anyway. Slept an hour at a rest area on I-5 near Medford in Oregon. Another two hours at a rest area near Orland in California. Drove on. It was Monday early afternoon, October 3, when I reached Los Angeles. And then had to kill time till my children were out of school.

"Remember that Ombeni I told you about last time. The girl in Tanzania. She wrote me these letters. See?" I held them up. "I send money to her each month. For food. Her school books. She's nine. Or maybe ten."

Paul and Corrine were seated across the table from me at Denny's. Being with them helped erase the guilt, ugliness, and embarrassment of the Selena experience.

"Her eyes . . . she looks much older," Corrine said. "Like fifteen or sixteen."

"She's had a rough time. Takes care of her little sister."

"The way her eyes look out at you. Like she's . . . really . . . you know . . . right into you."

"Yeah." I slipped the picture back into the envelope.

We didn't have much time that day. Just that meal and a short walk later. Again I hadn't called in advance. Just showed up. This time driving. They had homework to do. Corrine was Sacajawea in her school play about the settling of the West and needed to finish her costume. There was a glow in her eyes. Paul had had a soccer practice. His hair was uncut, he'd gained a little weight. He was still wearing whatever he'd practiced in, which turned out to be a sloppy sweatshirt with "Sequoia National Park" and the outline of a tall tree imprinted on it. (I should have been the one taking them there.) So here we were at Denny's at 5:10 p.m., Monday, and I had two hours at most to tell them what I wanted to tell them.

Which was what? It had to start with Ombeni. I wanted them to know that about me. That I would take on the responsibility for a little girl in Tanzania who had no money.

Maybe that would get me where I needed to go with them.

When evening came we had that strange conversation.

It was normal enough in most respects, but they didn't know what was in my mind.

It went something like this:

ME: What's that play about? Your mother says you're Sacajawea.

CORRINE. Just a little role. Everybody's got just a little role.

ME: You must have to say something. To Lewis and Clark, right?

CORRINE: Not much. My teacher just wrote in a couple

lines for all of us. Sacajawea doesn't say much. I get to talk more with . . . my eyes, I think.

ME: Let me know when it is. The play. I'll try to make it.

CORRINE: It's not till the end of next month.

ME: Still . . . I'll see. . . . [Glancing over at Paul] Sorry I haven't been to any of your soccer games, Paul. You got one this weekend?

PAUL: We had one yesterday. Won't be another one till next week.

[We got our food about then.]

PAUL: How come you're here like this? I mean with the car. How will you get back in time to teach?

ME: Just felt like it. Got tired of teaching. Just needed to go somewhere. Here I am.

[They looked at me like they knew something was wrong but didn't know how to ask me.]

ME: Sometimes you have to do that.

PAUL: What?

ME: Go looking.

PAUL: For what?

ME: [Shaking my head] I don't know. [They looked confused, concerned. I wanted that.] Someday you'll feel the need to do that.

[They went back to their food.]

ME: Sorry, I don't want to get . . . what do you guys say. . . all heavy on you. I'm doing okay. It's good seeing you.

[How do you tell your kids you've just picked up a girl in

a bar? That killing yourself didn't seem like such an irrational possibility anymore? That except for them I didn't feel there was much substance to anything I did, especially because it was less and less with them? I did the best I could. Showed them the picture of Ombeni. Reminded them who she was. Told them that I'd just needed to go somewhere. Go looking. Gave them a glimpse of World Two. That was enough for now.]

ME: I bet your mother and Doug take you to nicer, more interesting places than Denny's all the time. Chinese or Italian? You like Mexican food?

CORRINE: We don't go out that much.

ME: Still, I'd like to be the one taking you to Sequoia, Yosemite.

I hope they will remember that night. That Monday, October 3. When I'm finally able to tell them all that was happening with me.

I dropped them off. Hugged them. Paul was starting to get embarrassed by that hugging. Not Corrine. Then again, girls hug everyone.

"Next time," I said, "we'll just walk in an enormous circle around the entire city and come back here."

They both almost smiled. I think.

They made me responsible. Reminded me what I should have been doing. That night I called the office and left a message on my department head's voice mail. "This is Stephen.

Stephen Mollgaard. I'm sorry to tell you this, but . . . I'm not well. I'm not going to be able to teach the rest of this term. I'll be bringing you in a letter from a doctor about it. I guess you'll have to get a substitute. Sorry it's so last minute. I guess I was thinking I'd be able to get through this term. But . . . I'm just not. I messed up. Should have called earlier. Last week. It's just that . . . I've not been feeling . . . right. But I should have called. I know. I'm not even sure why I didn't. But I'm okay. I'll call again. Soon. I'm very, very sorry. Oh, my syllabus is, as you know, on file in the office. My grade book is in my office on the top shelf above my desk. You can ask the students where we are. In each class. I'm not even up to that—to preparing a substitute. But I guess one of the adjunct professors will appreciate the extra money filling in. I'll . . . call again." I did not mention where I was, where I'd been.

I took a motel on the highway, then, in the morning of Tuesday, October 4, drove on to San Francisco, without thinking why I was doing it. Closer to Silkie? How would I know? So maybe it was just because I'd always liked San Francisco—the Bay and all—its mentality—young, bohemian.

In the center of the city—some five blocks from the cable-car line—I parked my car in an all-day garage and took in a movie. One of those art theaters that show classic films. They were showing *Midnight Cowboy* and *The Graduate*. I watched all of the first and half of the second, then returned to the car, sat myself on the passenger side, scrunched up against the door, and dozed off.

When I woke, around 4:30 p.m., I panicked.

Panicked, it seemed to me, as I had never panicked before.

Here I was sleeping in my own car in a city I didn't know and didn't even care to explore. My seeker's journey was not only naive but moronic. I'd found nothing, and when I returned would be lucky to reclaim my job.

The panic, though, was of a more fundamental species. Having sought real meaning and not having found it, I'd discovered *I no longer could even count on what had masqueraded as meaning.*

I scrunched up and held myself tightly, feeling cold, though I knew it was not cold—in the seventies, in fact.

Not knowing what to do about it, this panic that was almost wracking my body and soul, I allowed myself to slip quietly into sleep again. A deep sleep.

When I woke about seven, I reran the film of the previous few days since leaving class—analyzing, reviewing the decisions that drove the events one by one. I traced the journey: taking my bike, walking out of the class, going home, driving, the church, the bar, Selena, sensing there would be some treasure in it that might still save me. What did "save" mean here anyway? I could find nothing in it that might invigorate any sense of purpose in me anymore, and, failing by searching within, I let my eyes search without. A very professional-looking woman with a briefcase was unlocking the door to her car parked down three spots. Other than her, there was no movement on this level of the garage. I glanced into the backseat—and saw my bag there, half open, some of the contents spilled out. I'd been pulling things from it haphazardly to the point it was in disarray. Did it matter? I'd just tossed things in when I'd first packed—a change of underwear, an extra shirt, a paperback of collected African stories, the . . . jar. The jar with the clippings.

There it was. I'd pushed it into the back of my mind. My plan . . . to set it on a beach to be swept away . . . a challenge to the gods . . . to God . . . was, after all, meaningless. Like the priest telling me that little piece of bread he put on my tongue was really the body of Christ. Why was this any different? Something ritualistic and therefore, in the rational world, absurd.

The sea whisper'd me. [Walt Whitman, "Out of the Cradle Endlessly Rocking"] [**Drawer 3A**]

39. The Sea

I drove all that night of October 4 and into the morning of October 5, Wednesday, stopping only to grab a hot dog and chips at a convenience store. A couple of hours later, I picked up three bananas, a wrapped deli sandwich, and a thermos (which I filled with hot coffee) at a grocery. At a rest area I fell asleep for several hours.

When I arrived on the Oregon coast, it was early evening, and the portion of the beach I chose had only one or two visitors who were plodding over the loose sand, apparently on their way back to the one hotel or the beach houses that sat farther down and high above the shoreline. I parked my car nearby on a once-paved area covered now with blown sand and high grass. It didn't appear to be a popular section of beach, but the parking area was big enough to hold a dozen cars.

I turned off the engine, sat there in the car. How long would I stay? Just a brief walk? An overnight? Maybe just long enough to recognize the senselessness of it. An ocean provided no more meaning than a Pizza Hut.

Still, I was here.

After fifteen minutes or so, I locked the car and set out, searching for a perfect spot—back a little from the tide, but hidden from both beach walkers and from the beach houses up the hill behind me.

I knew it was crucial that I find my own place. I did—a little cove, with an accommodating rotted out drift-log emerging from the rising hill behind it—and made myself comfortable. Thermos, blanket, jacket. Leftover snacks— banana, deli sandwich. The jar.

I was about fifteen miles north of the nearest coastal town.

How long did I expect to be sitting there? A few hours. All night if I fell asleep. Certainly not too late into the next day. Too many people.

Two days earlier I'd wanted to be with someone. Now I wanted to be alone.

A fine rain began to fall—not enough to disrupt my plan, if it really could be called such. I sat there with my back rigid against that log half-buried into the hillside where the beach rose up precipitously to become a grass-infested rocky sea wall over my head, forming a cave-like protection from the wind and rain.

I dozed off, woke, then lay down with my blanket wrapped around me and fell into a deep sleep.

Somewhere close to midnight, I opened my eyes and discovered the light rain had ceased, but the beach had transformed itself. The driftwood which was just that during the day took on a definite shape at night. My two closest driftwood companions were a giant gecko rising from its hind legs upward, its mouth open, and a large fat snake with the head of a cow. And those who chanced to walk in the distance along the beach near the surf—three children walking hand in hand, a teenage boy and his little sister, an old man and a woman, two teenage lovers—were only far-away silhouettes. Metaphors for the ephemeral. Emerging from the darkness of the far right, disappearing into the darkness of the far left. Just those three or four minutes of silhouette. Here, then gone. Unlike the ocean.

"Would-be writers like me love these kinds of images," I thought. "So fraught with symbolism they are." I smiled.

Laying my head on the sand, I began to hear the ocean as two very distinct sounds. The one close up, that of the surf, like the sound of the wind through a willow tree; the other, that of the whole sea, like the roar of a thousand far-off jet engines.

I slept, and when I awoke again and needed to relieve myself, I walked out into the surf.

I took one step at a time, staring down at my feet to be certain the water did not come above the rubber part of my shoes. But with each step I felt the darkness swallowing more and more of me. Heard the roar of the ocean getting louder and louder. I was alone, entering deeper and deeper into a cosmic cave fed by an indifferent sea.

This ocean offered no comfort.

I was frightened.

I was not powerful.

My seeking gave me no special status in the universe. Here . . . on this beach . . . at one or two in the morning . . . I was the only one in the universe, but not, thereby, more significant; instead, less significant, a puny nothing . . . to an ocean so massive, so indifferent to who I was.

I'd sought the ocean's peace and gotten its terror.

I lay down in my cove again. "What day is it?" I asked myself aloud. "Thursday, right? October 6 now." I checked my watch to corroborate that fact, but it was too dark to see.

Periodically I would fall forward and to the side, curling up and pulling the blanket around myself a little tighter. My jacket and jeans, both of which were crusty from having dried after the light rain, were not enough. Next to me was the thermos of coffee, but it was almost empty and no longer hot.

At some point, I found myself reflecting on my coming here. I'd gone beyond the initial spark of desperation, which had blossomed temporarily into an inspired search for World Two, but then found myself mired in useless wandering leading to the Selena experience—ugly and demoralizing in every way—and then to that panic of the parking garage. Panic that needed alleviating. I needed comfort. The beach. The sea as I thought it would be.

I was waiting. For something.

No. I was not waiting for anything. I just felt comfortable

sitting here. To do so was to ward off the panic I knew I would feel if I returned to my previous life. Back to the car. Back to school. Back to teaching. No Silkie. No World Two. No anything. Except Paul and Corrine, and they were far away now. Ombeni—even farther away.

Earlier I'd taken out the jar with the clippings in it, and now I stared down at it in front of me on the sand.

While I was in California, parked at a rest area, I'd even taken the time to stick in two more slips of paper—one labeled "Selena" and another "Ombeni."

But would I really do it? Set the jar out near where the waves were lapping onto the sand. Let the tide take it out. With all those clippings. To whatever god would deal with them.

I would. Even if it was only ritual.

Five a.m. . . . Six a.m. I could see the faintest trace of where the water met the sky.

Yes, as I lay there on the beach, the ocean could reach and grab me and pull me in as easily as it did a starfish, a barnacle. But just as easily could it snatch at that jar. The jar into which I'd placed the clippings. A message for God.

The Mexican girls. Norma Jean. The eagle in the box. Mary Turner. Selena. Ombeni. Brief news accounts. Labels on slips of paper.

The second night, the night of Friday, October 7, I set it out there—the jar. Where there was no driftwood to impede its journey, for the tide to take out. And perhaps some hours later, early into the next morning of October 8, someone, some sea creature, some goddess of the ocean, some ghost out of some opening to another realm of understanding, did pick it up and rewrite it for some other universe.

But if something so wonderful did happen, I didn't see it. So it did not happen. More likely, as I lay there asleep, the jar of clippings was, indeed, gently lifted up and spirited out to sea, but only to be washed up on some distant shore for some fisherman to find and wonder at its strange contents of newspaper clippings of human and animal tragedies that, like the jar itself and its wanderings, ultimately had no significance beyond the journey, beyond whatever laws of nature came into play to ultimately decide its fate, beyond the moment when the two minds—mine and the fisherman's—were drawn to them. Normalcy as useless wonder.

The morning of the third day—Saturday, October 8—I began checking my watch periodically—odd behavior considering that here it had no significance.

Being very weak and hungry, I got up, took a glance far down to where my car was parked to be sure it was still there, walked the half mile to the town, bought myself a sandwich, a Coke, a bag of chips and another banana, and then trudged back down the beach.

In my beach cove once again, I was struck with a startling fact. *I had no intention of getting up, leaving.* At least for some time. I had no place I wanted to go. Except here. The idea of a "center" suggested itself to me. Wasn't that the word Silkie had used that night in the park? Something about not being able to find her center. One of those moments of complete contentment, satisfaction, peace, that you imagine one experiences just before dying. What if I died right here? Somebody would come by, see me sitting there seemingly immobile, say "hi," and discover I was stiff. Dead. Just like those frozen grotesquely shaped bodies, stark and black in the snow of Wounded Knee, South Dakota.

Sitting there gazing off into ocean that extended into infinity, I found myself dozing off again.

I tried sipping coffee to rouse myself to some more reasonable action, but found the most rational one suggesting itself to me was still to just sit there. There was nothing for me to do anywhere else. I was not going back to see my children. Silkie was somewhere in California, and what did it matter if she wasn't? There was for me only eating at restaurants and relieving myself at rest stops on the way home, then sitting alone in my apartment.

That awful *normalcy.*

Several times in the course of the day I got myself up to stretch and tried walking back and forth, but never left the cove area where I'd situated myself—afraid maybe that

I'd lose it to some intruder or squatter—because now there were a number of people farther down the beach.

I'd gotten possessive about this spot.

The other startling fact was that I was not very hungry. The bag of chips was only half-eaten, and I still had one of the two bananas.

To find purpose again I pulled out my notebook and began to write. It was a journal entry—that was all I meant it to be—but I discovered the form it took was a letter—to Silkie, or maybe to myself because, of course, Silkie was never going to see it:

> *You don't drive, do you, Silkie? But let me tell you, there's a state of mind you get into when you're driving late, alone, and you're sleepy. It happens when you tell yourself you'll stay awake, that you won't fall asleep because you're hanging your head out the window or aiming the fan in your face. But there is this in-between state when you think you're awake but you really aren't, when you realize you can't remember the last minute or two. You're sure you were awake because here you are on the road, but somehow you can't recall what it was you saw or were thinking in those two minutes.*
>
> *That's the state of mind I've slipped into on this beach, and I'm going on more than two days here. I've slipped into and out of these images when I doze—the ocean changing colors, people passing—and me sitting*

here stranded, as though the car has run out of gas, and there is no more gas to be found. The present is no more empirical or tangible than the past. And it's this surrealistic state that defines me right now. Not sleep so much as one long giant dream that seems to have some existence apart from my sleep.

There's this "normalcy" thing. No other way to think about it. You're normal after all. Believe it or not, I was beginning to think you weren't. Absurd as it was. But then—off to California you go like any woman with a daughter who needs a father. All beyond me. Whatever those looks at me, that expecting me to take care of Maheza, like you had some special power and divine expectation—all silly. First-order delusions.

I stopped writing. Went to sleep. All bundled up in my sleeping bag. When I awoke, it was very early in the morning. Sunday, October 9.

I picked up the pen again.

Let me tell you, Silkie, the danger of telling yourself (or anyone) anything at 5 in the morning or when you're drunk is that you might just tell the truth. It comes at you at such times in its quintessential, undeniable form. And what it is that cannot be denied is the normal. That in the end no matter what fantastic aura you've cast over events and possibilities, it's all normal. No matter how you want to see a thing, it is what it is.

The implacability of the normal.

It was the chimney swifts I saw one time that taught me this, and the revelation was so devastating it left me nowhere to go. I'd been walking by myself in the evening when I came upon them. Thousands of them forming a magnificent tornado-like funnel. Soaring upward, then spiraling, swooping, downward in smaller and smaller circles in groups of 30 or 40 into the chimney. A spectacle of some 25 minutes until all of them—maybe 2,000—seemed to be sucked into one stone cylinder that looked to be able to hold no more than 50 of them. I stood there in awe of what must have been as daily a ritual as the sunset. It was one of those scenes that the soul draws upon for its aspirations, inspirations, and most sacred beliefs.

But it wasn't till the following morning as I chanced to wake around 5 that the image came, sharp and lucid, and revealed its secret. The truth of the spectacle, the ritual of the swifts, was that there was no more to it. That was its all. The beautiful and the meaningless. A pattern of behavior the swifts obeyed for hundreds of years probably and continue today. I could not transform it into a belief system or a transcendent moment except by my own fantasy. In the end, it was the normal that held sway. Birds diving into a chimney and out again. Day after day. In season.

All is just normal. All is just what it is.

On the other hand, "normalcy" can be good right now, no? That is, whatever my motives for this "journey," everything is still the same in the world I was living before the journey. Nothing has changed for the worse. Omayra is still in her picture on my wall. I still have my children, and my job, and I can very consciously improve my relationships with both if I put my mind, my heart into it. You're gone, but you were just a student who temporarily took over my psyche by way of a freakish, bizarre phone call. Whatever I plan to do with my life now—whether I quit teaching and explore other lands, take new jobs—I don't, in the absolute sense, need you.

So why do I want so desperately for you to be sitting next to me right now?
Why?

At this moment when I feel my thinking has gone from somnolent, drunken, surrealistic, delirious, to acutely clear, rationally lucid, that one fact continues to haunt me. Why do I need this person whom I've never needed before and who no doubt would not long be a part of my life?

It's like all that's been noble in my past efforts, my thoughts, my determination, has been not so much phony or hypocritical, as doomed to failure, and I just need a moment to be comforted. A haven. A Beethoven symphony. A poem by Roethke. A quiet stream. A place by the ocean with no one around. Someone to love.

Why am I just sitting here?

Because I don't know what else to do.

I'm too far away from events over which I have no control. Horrible events whose newspaper accounts I have shrunk into labels and inserted into a jar.

And you—what are you doing right now? Will I ever see you again? I picture you—first on the sand, then at some apartment somewhere, Maheza lying asleep on your lap, or on the floor near you. There is only one light on—from the kitchen. I picture myself there with you sitting on the floor up against the wall. Quiet.

Maybe you're sleeping with Maheza's father this very night? In a real house. Unless Maheza—to whom this house is still strange—cries at 2 in the morning to be with her mother, so you would have to sleep with her instead.

I'd like her to do that. To want to go out to the park. With you and me.

But then, what if it doesn't work out for you and

this guy? Where would you be? Point is . . . I want to be sitting with you at this very moment. On this beach. You—holding Maheza. Me—holding both of you. Silkie as Silkie. Maheza as your own Paul and Corrine.

What kind of family is this? Almost like a real one. Mother, stepfather, daughter. I certainly don't want that. I'm beyond that. I'm too old. Too tired for that prospect and the life it means. But just one night, on that beach, the three of us . . . that would be okay.

You were a student. My student. Will you ever return to school again? My classroom. Perhaps you too are feeling very lonely. You don't know that at this very moment I'm sitting alone on a beach. In fact, you most likely ceased to care. That I've staked out this place by the ocean. That I'm goddamned afraid to leave. If I get up to wander wherever, won't I just end up back home a dangerously distraught human being? It's better to stay here. I need someone to direct me into some purposeful behavior that's of World Two. But that won't happen. So . . . what it all comes down to is . . . I need . . . someone to hold me. Even in fantasy. Now. Before that other certain moment of despair comes.

Omayra's eyes in the picture. Your eyes the last time you visited me in my office.

Whatever else my journey is about, it's also, because

of the phone call, as much about you.

I put down my pen, dozed a while, then rose to write some more because it was a weapon to keep myself going. Defiance meant my journey, my possibilities, even my surrender to what was happening, had significance.

Dear God,

I'm a dreary fellow, aren't I? A little too dreary for your joke.

Why, God? I wonder. Why the journey? The bigger one. Why if it was going to end here? More alone than ever. Pondering in some phony literary way the final act. The one decisive act where you don't weigh the pros and cons. Because there are no such things.

Silkie promised me some kind of redemption. Or did I promise it for myself?

You were both guilty. Not just me. It wasn't me who brought me here. Well, now that I think about it, it was. From long ago. Needing a Silkie. Needing a divine act.

The truth is, haven't I often made a decision in my life, a critical one, because forces, circumstances seemed to be driving me that way? That I was supposed to be doing that. Perhaps that is the same thing as "fate" or "destiny" but, in this—our—case, I choose not to interpret it so definitively. Whatever cosmic forces there may or may not be in our universe, the fact remains that some of those forces I feel in advance. True, after the fact, I claim it was a feeling I had that made me do what I did, and someone more scientific, more rational, will tell me that's absurd—that I take whatever ensues and say that was it. I don't dispute that reading. But I will say this: going with such compelling forces within me has served me well in life.

The logic must amuse you, God.

And yet—

The joke. Your joke.

Make him obsessed with her. Then whisk her away. And then . . . bring her back. Tease him a second time.

So why, God, does it, still—in fleeting moments only, in remembering the journey and its promise, even the Selena portion—have a sacredness in it for me as I sit on this beach? Fate or no fate, fulfillment or no fulfillment, I have, at least, the memory. I retrace the events over and over again to discover their meaning.

Till normalcy once again takes over.

It had been more than three days since I first deposited myself there. Huddled with my back up against the sea wall in a little cave-like niche, thinking these things.

I rose, very suddenly—though I didn't know to what

purpose—put together my things, and walked to the car.

It wasn't there.

Turned out it had been towed by the state's park service, and I had to thumb a ride and then pay $100 to get it released.

I must have been some sight to the police when I had to prove I was indeed its owner. Clothes I'd been sleeping in all night—crusty, sandy, wrinkled. "The car appeared to be abandoned," they told me, not as an apology for what they'd done, but as a warning that staying on the beach for almost three days was a stupidity beyond comprehension. They were right.

I drove. Back home.

At first I felt no hunger. But once I'd reestablished myself with the reality of driving home, I slipped into a sort of movie, which was how, for some reason, I'd begun to see the "before-beach" part of my journey—the sitting in the church, the driving Selena to Idaho, the visit to my children. I drove slowly. A highway, but with only a narrow lane on either side and almost no shoulder, through a heavily forested area broken only by two or three very small towns, each made up of a store or two—complete with gas pumps—at an intersection, and a few houses off side roads. It was a pleasant day. Blue sky. In the low sixties.

I stopped at a small café in one of the towns in order to bring myself back to this world. I had a butterhorn and a cup of coffee. The waitress seemed concerned about me. I didn't look good. How could I, with my state of mind and having slept on the beach two nights? When I stood at the register to pay, a woman waiting to be seated drew back—away from me.

Whatever mysticism I'd found in my three-day vigil on the beach at the Oregon coast, it didn't last. Sipping a steaming cup of coffee, cutting through a hot, soft, frosted butterhorn, gassing up at a Chevron, slapping a wet paper towel on my face in the restroom, deciding whether or not to buy a pack of gum to chew—these were the crucial acts, the crucial decisions. I performed them because I had to. To remind me where and who I was.

I wanted to cry but it wouldn't come. Or I was too tired.

Even before I drove to my house, I drove to Silkie's. Knocked on the door. No answer. I sat in the car I don't know how long, but when I left it was early evening. For sure, she hadn't returned yet from California. If she ever would.

When I finally opened the door to my apartment I found myself welcoming its comfort, but not its sameness. I slept.

At night we were . . . shamed into pettiness by the innumerable silences of stars. [T.E. Lawrence, Seven Pillars of Wisdom] **[Drawer 3A]**

MEDICAL PROFESSOR. *A medical professor at the University of Washington went to Botswana for a new purpose in life. He began training health workers to work with AIDS victims, and he himself worked in remote clinics. Yesterday a crocodile pulled him from his canoe and killed him.* [**Drawer 4**]

40. Unexpected Visitor

When I awoke the next morning, it was Monday, October 10. If I had known what would occur just five days later—on Saturday, October 15—I would have scrupulously recorded the details of my actions and decisions during that period— especially as they would reveal my state of mind. *Verifiable empirical details.* Experiences of a tangible nature that I shared with someone.

But I didn't. I did not enter anything in my journal. The days blended one into another. They had separate calendar dates, but other than that they were indistinguishable. So what I can tell you is at best the result of a very foggy memory.

What I recall most clearly is my intention to work myself back into a psychological state conducive to teaching—in essence, to reenter World One. Unfortunately, I discovered I could do that only gradually. Which meant that, most of those five days, I was alone, doing little more than going through the motions.

The very first day I did not even leave my house. The phone rang several times, but I didn't answer it for fear it would be the college, and I'd have to explain what was going on with me—something I did not fully have control over yet. No, one time I did answer. It was a woman's voice—asking me to contribute to the fire-medical emergency services again this year. I told her yes. She confirmed my address. I said "Thank you" and put the phone down.

I heard the doorbell, peaked out, and saw it wasn't anyone I knew—an eager-looking young man, probably selling religion. I didn't answer it.

Yes, there's no way I can verify the phone call, the man at the door, but I recall them clearly enough, I see no reason to question they happened.

I also recall that when I sorted through the bills and letters stuffed into my mailbox, I came across another letter from Ombeni. I opened it. One page, yellow ruled, in Kiswahili. I stared at it for some time because it reminded me how artificial had been my supposed World Two journey. Ombeni's World Two was an everyday thing. She didn't have to go looking for it. Mine was phony. It had produced no enlightenment. No satisfaction of the soul.

A feeling of guilt overtook me. I set the letter aside.

As I said, I was determined that week to immerse myself once again in World One. Drive to the school. Open my office and see how I left it. Visit with the dean to see who it was had replaced me after my unannounced exit. Fill out whatever "sick leave" forms had to be filled out. Attach a letter from a doctor certifying my state of mind. Check my schedule for the next term. Reacquaint myself with my colleagues.

And that was what I did the very next day. That must have been the second day. October 11, Tuesday. But as I drove to school that morning it was with increasing panic. Was I ready yet? And if not, what then? Back home? Alone?

I drove around most of the morning, then almost mindlessly headed to the college.

I must've looked like a zombie to my colleagues. Jack Millwood, seeing me pass his door, came out of his office.

He was younger than me by more than ten years, much less intense, and thus understandably uncertain about how to approach me, a very taciturn colleague even when not disappearing for weeks at a time.

"Stephen, you're back. How you feeling?"

"Okay. Better." I wasn't sure if my "illness" had been reported or rumored as physical or mental. I thought it best to change the subject. "Is the dean in? I'll need to . . . get things going again."

"He was here earlier. I guess you'll have to check. Listen, what, if you don't mind my asking, was wrong? I mean were you in the hospital?"

"No, no . . . a kind of . . . exhaustion. I wasn't teaching well. Some kind of sudden burnout. Not good for the students."

"Yeah, it happens. So you're feeling better. Teaching again next term?"

"Unless you guys cut me out." I smiled and started to walk away—not wanting to encourage a lengthy conversation about a psycho-mystic phenomenon so elusive, and thus so unacceptable, to those firmly rooted in World One. Jack must've sensed my reluctance and let me go with a "See you." I wasn't up to it and dreaded seeing the dean for fear he'd ask me too much, and I would break down if I veered too much into honesty.

That brief exchange with Jack Millwood is, of course, verifiable. A shared experience I could corroborate. I didn't. But I could.

I unlocked my office door, stood in the doorway, feeling weak, panicky. Then, realizing it wasn't good for anyone to see, I shut the door and discovered that entering had made it worse rather than better, and I was shaking so much I pushed against the wall with my back. It was a kind of seizure, I knew, because I was pushing too forcefully, rigidly, and grimacing, unable to release myself. It was a full minute at least before I let my muscles relax.

I wasn't ready yet. Maybe wouldn't be ever again. Therein lay the panic.

I slipped down to the floor, sat there, my legs sprawled out, for some time, starting to feel good—just because I was alone and sitting there. At some point my eyes got moist and that too felt good. But the despair—from whatever source—did not go away.

I got up, peeked out the door to be sure no one else would see me and question me, and quickly slipped onto the back stairway.

That episode, of course, I cannot verify. Could I have imagined it? Imagined having a seizure? As in a dream? I suppose so.

I would see the dean next week, perhaps have to meet with the Grievance Committee about my exiting classes and making no provision for substitutes. Although I assumed, given my many years of service, there would be no serious consequences, at the very least I could expect a reprimand, even loss of pay for the period I'd left without notifying the department.

I had no idea whether I would make some sort of defense—other than "I was burned out." Something they could accept, understand. I'd make an appointment with a doctor and get a letter corroborating it.

For most of the rest of the day, I drove around listening to music, stopping once to buy a falafel at an outside kiosk from a young man with a shaved head. I could go back now . . . ask him if he remembered me. Most likely, so many days later, he would not.

It was still Tuesday, I believe. Early evening. When I remembered. The Bead Game. It was the closest I could come.

Besides, I might learn something. Whom else could I ask?

A little after six I knocked. It was closed but I could see someone was inside. It wasn't Silkie. Still, if it was the one who'd been there the last time I'd come, she might recognize me.

I knocked on the window. It was the same one—the plump Goldie Hawn—but she gave no indication she remembered me and gestured that it was closed. I persisted, so she finally came to the door with a smile and opened it.

"Yes? We just . . . "

"Actually, I just need to ask a question. I'm wondering about someone. If she still works here. Silkie."

"Silkie? No, it's been . . . several months since she's worked here. Business was slow then. She only had a couple days a week."

I apologized for coming late and said I might call back in the morning.

Another shared experience. Verifiable.

The next day—the third after my return, so it had to be Wednesday—I did not leave the house.

My uncomfortable exchange with Jack Millwood, my office seizure, the overall panic I felt, the day before, had convinced me I could not yet face my colleagues. At the same time I knew I needed to prepare my lessons for the next term, thereby working myself back into the routine and regaining my more stable emotional state.

Realizing this, I determined to now and then go to my office but very early before my colleagues showed up. I did that the next morning—Thursday. But not the following morning. Friday. Or was it the other way around?

By Saturday, the 15th, I had lost all track of time. I didn't even know it was Saturday and need not have gone to the university so early. What if I had slept in and gone later? What if I had not gone at all?

I will ponder the rest of my life the decision to go.
Would it have made any difference? Would what occurred have occurred someplace else at some later time?

I left for the college a little after 5 a.m., remembering only when I was almost there that it was, indeed, Saturday and I need not have gone so early. I'd very likely be the only teacher in the whole building.

Being so alone reminded me of my early mornings on the beach. It was about 5:30 and the sky was just beginning to turn a glowing orange behind the inky-black mountains which cut a stark presence in the dawn. The campus itself was in that dreamy state just between night and morning when the ordinary becomes fascinating—when the three or four cars parked there through the night take on the nobility of solitude and the walkways go on forever.

Those few cars, probably those of the security and food services staff, were scattered over the lot, each claiming its own place. The lights along the walkways were lit, but the shadows hugging the sides of the buildings and spreading outward from under the trees were so dark, you couldn't make out even the large trash receptacles and shrubs until you were just feet away.

Because I believe now it's significant for me to say this, I will note here that, needing the fresh air to wake up, I took the long way around to my building. That's not to suggest I was in some sense "sleep-walking," but that I wanted to be certain I was alert to do my work. I remember, for example, that I passed where the top of the facilities building protruded from the ground, from which, deep down, I could hear the whirr and grinding of the infrastructure machinery of the campus—heating, plumbing. I passed the bike racks—virtually empty this early. And construction cones set off to the side of the walkway. And sculptures—a statue of the pioneer woman, and one of three children hugging one another. I remember peering closely at some honeysuckle vines coiled around gates. I passed straight-edged hedges. And, looking up, saw the ornately framed arched windows of the library and other older buildings. And the rectangular office-shaped windows of the newer buildings.

I felt a peace I hadn't felt in some time.

And so, when about to go up the front steps lined on both sides by a low brick wall which wrapped around to the right, I happened to catch sight of someone a few steps further up and against the wall, I stopped and wondered if I were just imagining it—as I had imagined in the driftwood on the beach strange creatures. Was it a sleeping dog? A dead raccoon? No, it was a person, curled up between sitting and lying and seemingly sleeping.

I was at first annoyed I might have to deal with a homeless person if he or she were awake because my conscience would not allow me to just pass.

Still, if he (I assumed it would be a "he") was asleep I could just slip by (as I had days before the man sleeping under the overpass when I'd biked to the school) and not disturb him. Security would deal with it.

Just then, though, the figure moved slightly, sat up, but not like someone startled but rather as waiting for me to come closer.

He . . . or she . . . was smaller, thinner than I had thought. She looked right at me.

Silkie.

"My God, is that you?" It was something like that I said. I was too shocked to remember. It's her exact words that are crucial here and that I must recall as best I can.

What I'm sure about is that, despite the strangeness of the circumstances and my astonishment at seeing her, what I was feeling most was a boundless joy at her sudden reappearance in my life at a time when I'd descended into such an appalling despair about everything.

I suppose my so easily accepting her being there—that fact in itself—puts in doubt my rationality. Still, it was not an unqualified acceptance. Nothing was right about this.

Whatever joy there was in her return to my life, in my seeing her once again gazing up at me, I remember saying to myself, "Something is horribly wrong here."

"What in God's name are you doing here at this hour?"

"Waiting for you."

I took in the spectacle. How long had she been there? It was very early and still chilly. Indeed, it had been very cold. She was wearing her parka—her hood up—over a long thin dress of the kind much older women wore. Her hair was uncombed, and I wondered if she hadn't been sleeping here all night.

"How long have you been here?"

"Not long."

"But you must have been . . . "

"Not very long."

"I don't understand how you knew I'd . . . What are you doing? Why are you here? I thought you were . . ."

She looked off toward the mountains to her left and said nothing.

"Let's go to my office and talk. You're cold."

She shook her head and whispered, "Can't we just sit here?"

"Here? Are you sure? We'll be alone in the building . . . "

"We're alone here. This is better."

There it was again—that quiet stubbornness I'd become used to. Certain, in fact, this was to be no normal exchange of questions and answers, I sat down near but facing her.

She leaned away from me and began dragging a large

piece of broken tree bark over the stone step. (Why do I remember this? If I went back, could I find that piece of bark? A meaningful verifiable empirical piece of it all.)

"I thought you were in California," I said.

"No."

"I mean . . . you did go, didn't you?"

She turned to me but didn't answer, as though it didn't matter. Then she nodded thoughtfully.

"So when did you come back?"

"A few days . . . weeks ago. I don't really . . . "

"I don't understand. How could you know I'd be here?"

She shrugged and half smiled. "You are."

I smiled at the logic of her response.

"Aren't you cold? Are you sure you don't want to go inside?"

"I like it here."

She was still playing with the bark, making a spiral motion now. Abruptly she raised it up.

"See this. I picked it up over there. See . . . it's got deep-cut lines. I like the lines."

This inordinate attention to the piece of bark was, surely, just so she wouldn't have to explain herself—her being there.

"When I got back . . . wait, you don't even know I left. I . . . took off for a few days."

I expected her to look up in surprise, but she didn't. Continued to thoughtfully play with the bark.

"I checked back at your friend's apartment and where you worked. Did you move?"

She shook her head.

So where's Maheza?

She did not answer right away—and when she did answer her voice was quavering.

"She's okay. With someone, but . . ."

"But?"

"You'll be seeing her, won't you? I mean, you want to?"

"Of course. Are you going back to school?"

She shook her head again, almost imperceptibly—more to mean it didn't matter than to say no.

"So, is it money? What about working again? I actually can help you out. I should have offered before. It's just that you took off so suddenly. I tried to get your address."

"No. I'm okay. Maybe . . . I . . ." but then she closed her eyes in a way that I decided meant she didn't know how to answer my offer.

Surely something was very wrong with her—her silence hiding something. If I were to be silent too maybe it would be awkward enough she would finally explain herself.

Why she was here like this.

If only someone had walked by about this time . . . someone I knew and could follow up with. But it was too early.

She'd stopped playing with the piece of bark and scrunched herself up—pressing her knees together, holding herself tightly, bending over and slowly rocking. I imagined this would be the sign of a silent weeping, but it wasn't. Indeed, sad though they were, her eyes exuded strength. Acceptance, peace, even surrender.

The expectation and admonishment I'd grown accustomed to in her eyes when she looked at me wasn't there. Rather, a quiet fire that maybe she wanted me to see because she'd now fixed them on me unwaveringly. Holding me.

In thinking back on that morning, I realize now how significant that was—her way of being. Until now she'd been an enigma to me. Explosions in class, words spilling over the edge of the papers, quiet transformations into some mysterious "Ruth," eyes which seemed to demand, expect something from me, strange requests students simply did not make of teachers.

But at this moment she was inscrutable to the point I was unable to speak. How was I to explain her sudden appearance at five in the morning on the steps of the college? As though she knew I'd be coming that early. And to my commonsense, to-be-expected questions—about where she was now staying, whether she was working, returning to school, her seeing or not seeing Maheza's father or, for that matter, even going to California—giving me no real answers.

Should I have insisted she explain herself? Surely I had that right. She'd come here to see me. About what?

It was then I noticed the paper sack next to her. A possible handle because it was so tangible a thing. Right there in front of both of us. "Is that your breakfast?"

She looked up at me, then followed my eyes to the sack.

"No. It's something for you."

"Me?"

She nodded, pulled the bag closer, opened it very carefully, and pulled out something glass.

"Here. You remember the jar of chocolates you gave me a while ago?" She set it next to her without getting up. "We ate them all. Mostly Maheza. She liked them too much. Anyway, she told me I should give you something back. I thought of nuts. Once you told me you liked nuts. Different kinds."

I reached for it and held it up to look at. It was three-quarters full of peanuts.

"Maybe I should have gotten you chocolates again," she added.

I smiled. "No, peanuts—they're my favorite. Healthier too."

"I brought it for you . . . your coming back."

"So then . . . you knew I was gone."

"Yes."

"How? Did you come by my house?"

She half-shrugged in a way that didn't tell me yes or no.

Again we sat in silence, both of us with our heads down. But when I lifted my head to peek at her, I saw that she'd already raised hers and was gazing at me as she had always done before. Without blinking. Seeming to read me. Puzzled now in some different way.

Abruptly she rose, looking right and left in the way of one anxious about where she'd left something. "Listen, I'm sorry . . . you'll have to take care of Maheza again."

Then, as abruptly as she'd risen, she sat down, hunching over again and holding herself tightly.

I liked hearing that request. "I can do that." It hit me then, it hadn't been a request, but a statement of what I would do. Once again, it was settled.

I began now to feel more comfortable. Some of the old connection was coming back. I picked up the jar of nuts. "Thanks for this."

She nodded.

"Thank you for coming," I said, very quietly, proud of myself for keeping it simple. "How did you get here?"

"I like to walk."

"In the dark you walked? Alone? Was that safe?"

She didn't answer.

"You seem very tired. I'll drive you back. To wherever you're going."

"No. I'll walk."

"No. I'll drive you. You're tired. It's dangerous."

She didn't move.

I wondered how long we would sit there. I didn't care. No one would be coming for a long time if at all. It was Saturday. Perhaps the longer I sat there the more she would open up about her strange behavior.

I picked up the jar of peanuts to open it and grab a few. "You hungry? Want some?"

"No. Thank you."

It was then that I saw it. The dent. The deep scratch.

Because of the nuts in it, I hadn't noticed immediately. It was not the jar I'd given her, so she hadn't just refilled it. For sure . . . yes . . . not the one I'd given her. More significantly, it looked not just a little like . . . no, a lot like, the one I'd had on the beach. From my mother's collection. The only difference was a thin almost imperceptible brownish stain—a smear—near and over the bottom edge of the jar. I slid my thumb over it and tried scratching it off. It worked.

It was a remarkable coincidence. The jar that I'd left on the beach. This one. Size (large). Shape (hexagonal). The dent. The copper lid.

I sat there examining it. Drew the lid closer to my eyes to see if I could make out the pattern. I'd need to look more closely later, but, yes, some pattern of the same sort—birds, clouds. But perhaps that was a common one. I remembered, too, around half of the edge it had been tarnished from use. I would check that later too when there was more light.

Did she know? Was that why she was here? A student leading a teacher to discover for himself. Discover what?

As quickly as I'd asked myself, though, I smiled at the absurdity of what it meant. But then I was also certain this was not the one I'd given her. If that's what she thought it was. That once the chocolates were gone, she'd filled it with nuts. The one I'd given her wasn't hexagonal like this. It was round. Cylindrical. A little smaller too. And the dent . . . did she drop it? Maheza maybe?

"Can I ask you something?"

She didn't look up.

"Did you . . . or Maheza . . . drop it—the jar, I mean? I'm just looking at the little dent here in the lid."

"No. Maybe Maheza. I don't know. Does it bother you?"

Was she playing some game with me? Were we both *being played with*?

"This is crazy," I muttered, shaking my head.

"Yes."

It was a queer response. Not "What is?" but "Yes."

She had fixed her eyes on me. Without blinking. Seeming to read me again. Then as quickly not reading me. I was losing her. Back into the inscrutable. Puzzled now in some different way. She about me. Me about her. I don't know. About even more than that—a bigger something. Was it just because of the confusion in her eyes? Because I was needlessly concerned about the dent when she'd taken the time to fill it with nuts and bring it to me? *Or something else?*

"Do you suppose . . . water . . . sea water could have left it . . . the deposit?" I asked, as though she would know why I was asking, but so low it was more to myself than her.

"What?"

"Nothing . . . really. I just happened to see a little deposit on the bottom. It's gone. I rubbed it off. So . . . nothing."

We were silent for maybe a minute when she finally spoke. "Maybe I do need a drive. Can you take me . . . a few blocks? I have some errands."

"It's too early and dark, no? Why don't we go to my

office till then?"

She nodded.

As I worked at my desk, she sat quietly in the chair against the wall to my right.

"What if I got you a cup of coffee from the vending machine downstairs?"

"I'm okay."

In actuality my mind was completely on her and not on what I was doing, which was of little value to my preparations for fall. I was unable to concentrate.

I picked up the jar. Examined it in the light of the office.

Shape was the same.

Pattern on the lid close if not identical.

There was a tarnish too, for sure. Very evident.

Where the smear had been there was still a sliver of brown—reflection rather than stain. Could the deposit I'd scratched off have been some acidic mineral that worked itself into the glass? Probably not in just a few days in the sun and ocean.

Surely, though, there were other jars similar to mine—old ones like this—in the world, so . . .

"You didn't say this was the same jar I gave you, did you? This is your own jar, right, so I'll need to give it back."

"It's yours."

"No, it . . ."

"Does it matter?"

"I suppose not."

"I don't want it back. It's yours."

I set the jar back down and studied Silkie. She had her eyes closed, her head tilted slightly downward, almost as if praying. Something was wrong, and after only a few minutes, I got up and left my work on the desk.

"I don't feel like working," I said. "I wish we could talk. I wish you hadn't left my house that morning. I thought when I returned, we could . . . clear up some things. Where are you staying now? The same friend?"

"No, a different one."

"Where? Who?"

"It's hard to explain."

"Why?"

She shook her head.

I was frustrated, almost angry, with her, but smothered it.

"I'm confused," I said.

Not knowing where to go from there, I was, once again, silent, and stared at her in a way to let her know how perplexed I was.

"Do you mind if we don't talk?" she said.

"No," I nodded and smiled affectionately, "but I'm going to stay with you today. For a while anyway. Do your errands with you." I didn't give her a choice.

As we walked to my car, I continued to ponder the mystery of the jar. "I need to think about this. The possibilities. Two jars the same. Nothing unusual about that or startling. Still—the dent, the size, the pattern, the smear or stain. She never said it was the same one I gave her. So . . . just by a coincidence. There was no way she could have found it. Some other beach? What an absurd idea! Must be many such jars in this world."

I had no answers except that it was completely irrational to think this could be the same jar I'd left to be taken away by the tide. Even if the odds were against the two being identical.

What were the odds? The exact size and hexagonal shape. The tarnish. The dent. The pattern.

The timing.

She asked to be dropped off at a certain corner, against my objections, insisting she would be okay, telling me she "had errands."

No, I told her, we would have breakfast together first. And we would pick up Maheza too.

"She is with other children," she replied. Those were her precise words.

It was so early only donut shops were open, and we were forced to drive out to the highway to find an all-night restaurant.

But though I insisted she have something solid to eat, when the waitress came over, she said softly, "Just a cup of tea."

I stared disapprovingly at her, then gave in. "Maybe then just tea and an English muffin for me."

Well before we arrived at the restaurant, I was going over in my mind all that I wanted to ask her: What had happened in California? What now? Would she be going back to school? If not, then what? Where in actual fact was she living? What money did she have? And about that jar . . .

"Do you mind if I get some things clear?" That's how I started. Something like that. She could be mysterious. She was always reluctant to reveal details to me. But this time, I would be persistent. *I needed to know. I could not ever again go through what I'd been through.*

I tossed some of those questions to her. All at once. So she would understand my frustration with her. I wanted to get them all out there for her to respond to in some meaningful way.

She was staring down at her cup of tea. She wasn't drinking it. Not even holding it. Later, in fact, I noticed she was still fiddling with the piece of bark—on her lap.

She listened silently, then cut me off.

"Please . . . I have something to say . . . to you." She said it slowly, quietly but firmly. A mother explaining to her child why he cannot do something for reasons he will understand only when he gets older.

Thinking back on it—that slow, careful way of speaking, in that quiet sonorous voice—I wonder if I'm not coloring it to accord with what I would learn later.

But, no. She was silencing me, assuring me in a way that transcended my questions.

"You have to listen to me," she said with that gentle firmness, and looked right at me. I almost imagine she was grasping my head in her hands, but, of course, she wasn't. "All that . . . all you're asking . . . you'll find out. You'll be seeing Maheza. She's okay. I wouldn't . . . ever really leave her." I wondered why she had to say that, since none of my questions had even hinted at that concern. "And I'm . . . all right. You too. All of it . . . will be okay. But . . . just wait. Just a few more days. Is that okay? I don't . . . understand . . . in a way I can explain. Just the feeling. It's not because I don't want to. But you must tell me you understand. When I say it will all be okay . . . I mean it. Mean it . . . in a very, very big way. Do you remember when I said my classes seemed 'small'? That I know more now. Because of Ruth. It's . . . in a way . . . very big. Much bigger than . . . this. So . . . trust me . . . for now. Will you? And if I don't answer your questions it's because . . . I can't."

"So . . . if I . . . "

"Wait. There's something else. In the jar. Maheza and I put something else in there for you."

"What?"

"A drawing. We both drew it. A bird. Remember the fractals. That was my part. For you. You'll see."

"A picture?"

She watched me carefully as I pulled the jar out of the bag.

"I want to tell you something," she said. "There was a room. I was walking alone down a hallway. A kind of school, but it was too small to be a classroom. I went in. I thought I was alone because it was so quiet. Then I realized there were some people because there were voices. I heard them—the voices. I didn't say anything. Just stood back, listening. I got it in my head they were talking about you. Although I don't know why I thought that. I almost remember, but not quite. Just a piece of it."

"You've lost me. What does the . . . room . . . have to do with the drawing?"

"Something. It was while I was in the room I remembered . . . to put the drawing in the jar. Because then you would know . . . it would be okay. I really don't know why. But . . . I do want you . . . to know. More than anything I've ever told you. "

I took a deep breath. Was this just more of her mental illness? I remembered her references to a "girl in a print dress" and a "flood" that night in the park. "Can I look now then? The jar?"

She nodded.

I opened the jar. There were three wire catches that held the lid in place. Then I took hold of a paper napkin on the table and lay it out and began pouring some of the nuts onto it. A piece of paper emerged from the jar. It was folded into fourths. I opened it. The paper was the size of a small square envelope. On it was a pencil drawing. A large bird. "Looks like a hawk . . . or an eagle," I said. "Yes, an eagle," she answered. The wing was huge in proportion to the bird's head, and the wavy lines of the feathers in its wing had the look of her fractal drawings. There was only that one wing, but it was so large the feathers could have been the waves of a miniature ocean or the wind-blown sand of a miniature desert.

"Why . . . this?" I asked.

She stood gazing at the picture. "The nuts were not enough."

"Thanks. Still . . . "

"In that room . . . the one I told you about . . . there were no words. Just voices."

She folded up the paper, slipped it into the jar for me. Then began folding the nuts back in.

"I'm sorry. But . . . I have to go," she said, avoiding looking at me.

"Okay. But I want to be able to find you. To know where you are, instead of it being by way of some note. You understand? I don't want you doing this stuff . . . this way . . . anymore. This time it will be different."

She stood there with her eyes fixed on me, as though once again I would or should understand. Then she turned away.

As for her request that I ask no more questions, I had no choice but to give in, and, a few minutes later I dropped her off on the corner of the street that led from the campus down to the park.

Sitting there in the car, confused, watching her go down the sidewalk in the other direction, I let my mind trace back to the whole Ruth thing. The phone call. I wondered if, once again, she didn't explain not because she was hiding the truth but because *she didn't know herself*. I almost followed her but decided against it for fear of the embarrassment if she caught me doing so.

Should I, when I saw her again (when would that be?) invite her and Maheza to stay with me? But where would that lead? What would it be saying to her?

I would tuck away this idea for now.

In some panic I realized she was once again gone, and I had no way to be sure, despite what she'd said, I would see her again. No apartment. Not working probably. Not in school.

Pondering this, my mind flashed back to the message on the phone that morning months before: "My daughter . . . she has to be fed."

The message is still on my phone. It's verifiable. The drawing of the eagle with the expansive wing. I have it. It's in my possession.

I could not have gotten it in any other way. It could not, therefore, have been just my own personal madness.

SERBIAN MENTAL INSTITUTION. *A Mental Disability Rights International worker, investigating an institution in a Serbian village, reported: "I looked at the crib and saw a child who looked to be seven or eight years old. The nurse told me he was 21 and had been at the institution for eleven years. He has never been taken out of the crib in eleven years." [Time]*

41. Questions

Questions—about the jar, about the strange story describing "a room" and "voices," about her insertion of the drawing, and about her showing up in so peculiar a way—they kept me awake through most of the night, and I was determined the next time I saw her, to get them resolved.

There was nothing more important in the world to me at that moment than to speak with Silkie again.

For the rest of that day, I did a lot of walking. Wondering where she was living. Wondering about the jar. Wondering how the college, the department, would deal with me for my delinquent behavior over the previous weeks. For sure I would have to get a letter from my doctor which corroborated to some degree my state of mind which made it impossible for me to teach.

I slept poorly that night. Not any more than an hour total, and that in short stretches.

Early the next morning, I sat on a bench near the university library, closed my eyes, and let my head drop onto my chest.

My only comfort at that moment was the memory of the previous morning. Silkie . . . waiting for me at 5:30. To give me a jar of nuts? Surely there had been another reason.

When I raised my head I saw that a middle-aged woman, with long hair and dressed in a khaki jacket and jeans like a student, was poring over a large paperback book across the way on another bench. There was a backpack at her feet from which she slipped out a spiral notebook and began to write down something from the book. She glanced at me and started as though to say something, but then smiled and returned to her studying or reading. I lay my head down once again and was slipping into a doze when I heard a voice next to me.

"Sorry, but are you all right?" It was the same woman. Looked to me like a very outdoorsy sort. Hiking, bird-watching, yoga. Exulting in life.

"Aren't you a teacher? I mean a professor?" She didn't wait for an answer. "I took your class. You probably don't remember me. It was . . . six, seven years ago. I'm Tracy. I didn't mean to bother you, but it looked like you might be sick. I'm sorry . . . maybe I shouldn't have disturbed you."

I didn't know if it was because she was nervous in addressing me that she went on in this rambling way or if it was just her personality to be so friendly. In any case, she had seated herself next to me—not as my former pupil but as a mother might with her child.

"Well, I kind of remember—your face. Not your name."

I didn't remember her at all. "What class was it?"

"Just a freshman writing class. I got an A."

"So are you still in school ?" That was always the safe question.

"Last term. I graduate in June. Marine Resources."

I nodded.

"Sorry, I shouldn't have bothered you. You looked like maybe you weren't feeling well."

"No, just tired. Too much . . . to think about. Have a problem I'm working through."

It hit me then—her field of study.

"Actually . . . you said you're in Marine Resources? . . . Maybe you can answer something for me."

"What's that?"

"Do you have any idea if . . . let's say a glass container . . . a jar . . . if it floated ten or eleven days in the ocean, in the sun . . . and it had gotten some mineral deposits on it . . . the deposit would or might somehow eat a kind of stain into the glass?"

I saw right away she didn't know. Or even why I'd be asking such a strange question.

"Probably not easy to answer, eh?"

"I don't know. Seems reasonable. Maybe if you ask one of the professors in the department, they might know."

"I suppose. Good suggestion."

She left.

Once again I began to feel very alone, cold—the image of Silkie huddled up on the steps the previous morning coming at me again and again.

> *Though nothing can bring back the hour*
> *Of splendour in the grass, of glory in the flower;*
> *We will grieve not, rather find*
> *Strength in what remains behind;*
> *In the primal sympathy*
> *Which having been must ever be;*
> *In the soothing thoughts that spring*
> *Out of human suffering [William Wordsworth,*
> *"Ode on Intimations of Immortality."]* [**Drawer 3A**]

> **NGAWANG SANGDROL** *Ngawang Sangdrol is seriously ill after ten years in prison in China. She is twenty-five and was recently released on parole. She had been jailed at the age of fifteen and was mistreated in prison. Her crime? She had participated in demonstrations against the Chinese in Tibet.* [**Drawer 4**]

42. Grim News (Again)

Whatever perplexity the strange reappearance of Silkie into my life had caused me, whatever nagging questions I had about her plans and the jar, I was a man risen from the dead. There would be time to work through the mystery of it all. Silkie had been a mystery to me from the first day she had shown up in my office asking to be put into my class. It was merely a new chapter.

Rejuvenated, the very next morning—Monday—I made an appointment with my doctor to request a letter officially confirming my state of mind, so that I could claim sick leave for the time I'd taken off. I would make an appointment with the dean as well to follow through on whatever procedures were necessary to teaching classes next term.

I picked up some groceries and planned in the afternoon to clean my refrigerator.

Late morning, I checked my mailbox. There was mail from CARE, the Global Women's Fund, a bank statement, a utility bill, and a catalog. Sandwiched somewhere in the middle of those was the letter that would change my life.

The return address was:

Department of Police and Safety
Division of Special Investigations
Sacramento County
Sacramento, CA

"ATTN: Gillingham" was handwritten in pen at the top.

Any correspondence from a court or police department was alarming to me, but especially so because my children lived in California—albeit not Sacramento. In some panic, wondering who else I knew in the way of old friends or relatives who might live in that area, I opened the envelope immediately.

It was formal in appearance, but brief and personal in style. A "Sgt. Craig Gillingham" was requesting for me to call "as soon as possible" the Sacramento Police Department (phone number followed) regarding Case No. __. That it had to do with the "death" of a "possible acquaintance" of mine and papers found relating to the care of the deceased's child. I was to call between 9 and 5 p.m. on weekdays, ask for the Division of Special Investigations, provide them with the case number, and they would explain.

It was Monday around 11 a.m.

I called.

An answering message said, "If this is an emergency, hang up and call 911. Otherwise, wait on the line."

Seconds later, a woman's voice—businesslike, but not

cold. "Police Department. How can I help you?"

"Uh, Department of Special Investigations." Even though I was more curious than alarmed, I noticed my voice was quavering.

"What is the reason for the call?"

"I have a letter here . . . with a case number. Signed by a Sergeant Gillingham. He says to call about the death of some acquaintance."

"What is the case number?"

I told her. She put me through.

"Investigations."

It was a man's voice this time.

"I need to speak to a Sergeant Gillingham about a letter I got.

"He's out on assignment right now. Do you have a case number?"

I repeated it.

"Can you hold? I'll see what I can find out. What's your name?"

"Stephen Mollgaard. I'm calling from Oregon."

"How do you spell your last name?"

"M-O-L-L-G-A-A-R-D."

"Is 'Stephen' with a 'ph'?"

"Yes."

"Hold please. I'll pull it up—case number—on the computer."

After a couple minutes, I heard his voice again. "Are you still there?"

"Yes."

"It'll be just another minute."

I heard talking in the background, then a different voice. "Mr. Mollgaard? Stephen Mollgaard? That how you pronounce it?"

"Yes."

"This is Sergeant Gillingham. I'm the one sent you the letter. Hoping you can help us. A woman—apparently homeless—was found dead last month. Near the American River. A lot of homeless live together along one section of it. She apparently drowned in the night. The point is, she had . . . has a daughter . . . who got temporarily put in a foster home. The deal is, recently, a letter was found in the little girl's belongings. Backpack, says here. The letter has your name and address in it. It seems to say that you should be the guardian of the child if anything happens to the mother. It's signed by the woman whose body was found. Somehow figured it was (or most likely) her signature. She must've had some other document to match it with. So, what I need to find out is if you . . . know this woman. We're wondering if you're a relative and if you could help us find where this little girl should go. We can't come up with any relatives at all. Like I say, she was probably—according to the other people that were with her the night before—sharing a tent with a couple other homeless women. They're the ones who identified her."

"Sorry, doesn't sound like anyone I know. What's her name?"

"Well, even that's not certain. They found an unofficial identification card of some sort. The name on it was 'Marian Sanders.' S-A-N-D-E-R-S. The one woman witness that seemed to know her best, though, said she went by another name—'Silky' or something. Not sure how that's spelled."

"Silkie? No," I said. "I just saw her. A couple days ago. Here. You said 'last month.' Right?"

"Who? Saw who?"

"Silkie."

Silence at the other end. Then: "Are you sure?"

"I was talking with her."

Silence again. Then: "So . . . the one you were talking with . . . what is her name? Could there be two Silkies?"

"No, you said . . . Marian Sanders. That's the one. She's called Silkie."

I looked down at my left hand—it was shaking.

"I suppose there could be some misidentification," he said.

"How . . . long ago . . . did this happen? The drowning. This woman."

"Wait. Let me read this. Can you hold?"

I sat down. Clearly there had been a mistake, but how was such a ghastly mistake possible?

My hand was shaking more forcefully.

The voice came on the phone again. "The date is September 27. The report says the body of a woman was found . . . by a homeless man . . . snagged in the branches and tree roots along the edge of the river—American River."

"September? Couldn't be. Wait, what's the name of the

child? How old is she?"

"Hold on."

I could hear him rattling papers and breathing heavy. "Unusual name. If it's spelled right. It says her name is . . . it's spelled M-A-H-E-Z-A. They were unsure, but the little girl wrote it out for them. She's says she's six. Or was at that time. So all we need to know from you . . . "

"My God!"

"Sir?"

"Yes."

"Yes, what?"

"Maheza. That's Silkie's daughter's name. My God! Sorry . . . I'm trying to figure what's going on here."

"Pardon?"

"Where is Maheza?"

"I have the name of the temporary foster home where they've placed her."

"But . . . Silkie . . . I just spoke with her. So it can't be . . ."

"Is there any way you can come down here. Identify the body then? The letter this Marian Sanders wrote. I have a copy. Do you want me to read it to you. It's in the file here."

"Yes. Yes, please." The shaking was now not just in my hand, but in my voice as well. I realized I was barely audible.

"I'm looking at it here—on the screen. It's just a copy. It's not addressed to anyone. It says:

> *I am afraid. What will happen. If it does, something happens to me, I want my professor Stephen Mollgaard*

to take care of my daughter. Maheza is her name. He is her good friend and has taken care of her many times. She knows him. He knows her and what to do with her. He should be the one. No one else. The official paper is at the Office of Woodside and Boyd, Attorneys-at-Law. I signed it. Marian Sanders. June 14, 20—

"You know anything about this? The letter. The document at the office of her attorney?"

"No. But . . . it's right. I did take care of her. Maheza. I . . . need to come down there. I'll fly down there. Today. As soon as I can."

"If you could. Yeah. That would help us a lot. Do you need our address?"

"Yes . . . hold it . . . here."

"Anything you can tell us."

"Yes."

"You know . . . with homeless . . . these things happen all the time. The police don't have the time to follow up when there's so little information to go on. No living relatives or friends to call. So, if you can come down here . . . "

"Yes."

Once again, as on that day two years earlier, I'd gotten that grim message. Once again, I froze. Because once again it was a report of the death of Silkie, and once again it made no sense. Then it had turned out she was indeed very much alive. Now . . . would she just show up—again—and reveal the truth?

Still . . . Maheza—there could be no mistake with that

name—was in their custody. Silkie wouldn't have left Maheza down there. A letter found?

As in the case of that long-ago phone call, I finally forced myself to think clearly, rationally. This time, though, the horror—fueled by a smothering guilt that I'd let her walk away, and by the image of her in the darkness of early morning on the steps of the campus—clogged both my brain and my throat, causing me to literally choke.

"No, that can't be her. I . . . just saw her . . .I can just go find her," I heard myself saying over the phone--almost adding, "Besides, that could be Ruth."

"Sir?"

"Yes?"

"It's probably best if you come down here."

"Tell me," said Ivan earnestly, "I challenge you— answer. Imagine that you are creating a fabric of human destiny with the object of making men happy in the end, giving them peace and rest at last, but that it was essential and inevitable to torture to death only one tiny creature—a baby beating its breast with its fist, for instance—and to found that edifice on its unavenged tears, would you consent to be the architect on those conditions? Tell me, and tell the truth." [Fyodor Dostoyevsky, The Brothers Karamazov.] [Drawer 3A]

43. World of Facts

When Ralph Waldo Emerson lost his son, he wrote in his journal nothing but this: "Last night at 8 p.m., Little Waldo died." When the young Vietnamese girl in Tim O'Brien's "Style" lost her whole family in the burning of her village, she danced.

In the face of death, you put down your pencil because you have nothing to say, and you find your own place to go.

But because I was not sure Silkie was indeed lost to me forever, I didn't know where my own place to go was. It should have been of World Two, but there was the world of "verifiable facts" to deal with first. And they were in World One.

This world then was the one I plunged into. The one I'd tried to extricate myself from weeks earlier. The world of what had really—empirically—happened to Silkie. The world of official documents and witness accounts and coroner's reports.

Part of that world, however, involved reexamining my state of mind. Could I have—given my bizarre behavior, my depression, my visions on the beach—in my desperation to see Silkie, simply imagined her? Had I, because of the three days on the beach, crossed over into madness of some sort? Surely the strange circumstances of her knowing I'd be there . . . so early in the morning . . . all alone . . . no explanation . . . Maheza not with her. It was, to be sure, eerily disturbing. More so than the phone call. Way more. And if I had been rational, shouldn't the circumstances themselves have told me it was all a hallucination?

But then there was the jar! I latched onto that. It didn't matter whether or not the jar was the same one, what mattered was that there *was a jar*—a physical glass jar with a copper top. *She* had given me that. Stuck in it a drawing.

I went to my bedroom half expecting it would have vanished as she had. But it hadn't. The jar was there. *She* had given it to me. Or *someone* had. I could check out the restaurant. The waitress, would she remember us? A key empirical shared experience. Or would she just barely recall I was there and that I was with *someone*?

The mystery was too much for me. The jar seemingly being the same one. Silkie—present or not?

And those mysteries gradually surrendered to the greater issue—Maheza. She was in a foster home. Alone.

Before the day was over I made reservations for a round-trip to Sacramento. I called the police department again to get the address of the foster home. A woman helped me. Looked it up from somewhere, gave it to me, then added:

"You know, in cases like these—homeless mothers with children, no other family involved—we don't have the staff to . . . investigate causes . . . thoroughly, beyond what's obvious . . . you know? The report says she, from the two witnesses questioned, was living in a homeless camp . . . for . . . for several days, or weeks. It might even have been a suicide. Or mixed in with a mugging. Drugs or alcohol involved. These things . . . among those people . . . is pretty common. Not easy to follow up on. Did you know her well?"

"Yes. Very well."

"I'm sorry."

In my mind, until I saw Maheza, there was still hope. Maybe someone had stolen her ID. And Silkie was alive. Some horrible mistake compounded several times over in some incomprehensible way. Once I got down there, it would become clear how the mistake was made.

I set up appointments for the next two days with all of the involved agencies and departments within the agencies— ensuring that one of the first of them was the foster home. I needed to see Maheza. How was she doing? Did she have a story to tell? Certainly she could clear it up. Enough of it anyway. Did Silkie ever make it to Maheza's father's house? Why had she been living with other homeless people? Why this letter they found in Maheza's bag that Silkie had never spoken to me about? Why, if I'd actually been speaking to Silkie that morning on the campus steps, had she not told me about it? She'd said something to the effect that I "would know."

It turned out she was right. But wouldn't I have found out anyway even had she not shown up? So . . . did that mean the whole strange visit from her that morning was about . . . the jar . . . only the jar? And to say good-bye? From a ghost?

Unfortunately, I hadn't been able to get a plane out with the right connections without being overnight somewhere. So I elected to take an early morning direct flight. My plane was scheduled to leave at 6 a.m.

> *My life closed twice before its close—*
> *It yet remains to see*
> *If Immortality unveil*
> *A third event to me*
> *[Emily Dickinson, # 1732]*
> **[Drawer 3A]**

44. A Stark Dream

Through the night I slipped in and out of a state of semiconsciousness. But, for an hour or so, I must have fallen into a deep sleep, one that was not restful, because it was afflicted with an unusually long starkly detailed nightmare.

It went like this:

I was waiting in my office for something to happen. A feeling of utter aloneness. I'd been, it seemed, sitting there for hours. A colleague I couldn't recognize came to the door. "They're ready," she said.

I was ushered into some room that had desks—like a classroom—but they turned into a large oval table around which sat several of my fellow faculty. I didn't recognize them at first, then some I did. Ray Reller—dark beard, swarthy, looking particularly imposing. Elma Martin—thin, scholarly, close to retirement, looking especially academic. Alice Summers—older version of a flower child.

In the dream they seemed to embody my alienation from the whole department. Over the previous year it was true. I'd begun shunning social events, missing meetings.

I found myself in a chair at the far end of the table, and I listened quietly as Ray Reller announced apologetically (though it hit me as insincere) something about the purpose of the hearing: "You understand why we have to have this hearing . . . to get the facts correct here." Then something about "a copy of the letter and a necessary procedure."

I didn't know what letter he was talking about but when I looked down there was a letter in front of me, and I don't know if I was reading from it or hearing Reller speaking it, but I heard in my mind, "walked out on his class on three separate occasions [*No, I thought, only two!*] . . . and failed to report expected absence from classes and arrange for substitutes."

All the faces in the room were staring at me.

"I was sick," I said.

I looked down in confusion and discovered in place of the letter now was Silkie's journal and the jar next to it. And in my lap the photo of Omayra I'd had on my wall.

Now I was showing them these items and actually handing the picture of Omayra to someone on my right to pass around the circle.

Then I thought I heard Elma ask, "So who is this Silkie?"— in effect, accusing me of having an affair with a student.

A defiance welled up in me. I began to see my own colleagues as enemies. They wanted me either to get it over with—a simple "I should have taken sick leave" explanation— or dig into a juicy affair to make the meeting worth their while.

A powerful feeling of anger—a refusal to cooperate with them—began to dominate the nightmare. I would not give them either.

In confusion I began flipping through the pages of Silkie's journal, looking for a part I might read that would help. But I couldn't decipher her writing. I noticed the picture of Omayra was now hanging on the far wall behind them. I fixed my eyes on it. For comfort. Omayra was the only one in the room with any sympathy for me.

Somehow I was now back in my office because my bookshelves were to my right. I got up and stood in front of the wall of books and fastened on a shelf of paperback American Literature works (expecting one to speak to me?): *Huckleberry Finn. The Scarlet Letter. Walden. The Awakening.* When I took down a copy of *Maggie, Girl of the Streets*—in my mind to give it to Silkie—an almost sacred feeling came over me as I held it in my hand. Why hadn't I bought her a book now and then? As a gift.

Back in the hearing room, the table had become student desks. I announced to the committee that I was going to the restroom, but instead I went to a vending machine and got myself some coffee.

"Just get it over with," I said to myself. "Make it easy on me. On them."

I closed my eyes, and when I opened them I was back at the hearing and noticed for the first time a committee member not of our department. Jamil Hollins. Physics. Had he been there all along? And why was he seated back a little from the table?

I glanced over at Jamil. Our eyes met. There was something honest, direct, not institutional about how he was looking at me.

And perhaps it was that recognition that there was something not institutional about all this, something beyond the script we were all to play, that hardened my defiance—*I would not read my lines.* I would not make it easy on them. Nor on myself.

I think I had it in my mind that I was some enlightened being—like the professor in Plato's "Allegory of the Cave." That I knew reality in a way they didn't. They saw only shadows and I saw the real thing.

I looked down at the journal in front of me, then out the window to my left. A lot of rain clouds. A dark afternoon. Ominous. Still I gazed that way. I needed for them to see I was pondering how to begin.

How did one say something existential without coming off pretentious? *Maybe by expressing the momentous as though it were nothing. Apologetic. With awkward mannerisms.*

"The . . . the order in here . . . you know, the tables arranged as they are in here [the desks were once again tables] . . . the sameness of the chairs . . . " I became confused. Unsure why I was talking about tables and chairs.

This wasn't working. Wasn't coming off as I'd hoped. My voice was shaky. I began to feel dizzy. The aura!

There was anger in their expressions. I was wasting their time. Acting superior.

"What is this? This is just a hearing." I thought it came from all of them. In chorus almost. (I recall tossing in my bed during this part of the nightmare.)

I searched their faces, then stopped, fixed my eyes on Jamil Hollins. He was the only one who just might comprehend: that whatever I was doing would be more than just a *departure from* routine. It would be a *disturbance through* it. I, Stephen Mollgaard, would take no other course. This was the true one.

They were moving uncomfortably in their seats, clearly bewildered about the relevance of what I'd said to anything they were supposed to be accomplishing at this hearing. I felt certain of myself but uncertain about what any of this hearing meant.

It hit me I was avoiding their eyes in order to sever myself from any of it.

I heard myself talking again, but it seemed to be just inside my head. That they were straining to hear. "Listen, a long time ago there was this eagle. It was in a box."

I had my head down. I didn't want to see their response to where I was going. Despite my faltering, I was determined to keep going. At the same time I was beginning to doubt I could. Not all the way to where it needed to end.

I paused to master myself.

I heard their annoyance, impatience in the slight movement of chairs and the smothered sighs—clearly a response to why this "eagle" business was in any way germane to this case.

The eagle . . . it was *too far away*, I realized. It would take too long . . . to . . . get to the journey . . . the jar . . . to Silkie. If I could get to Silkie right away, it would silence them.

"I'm sorry," I said, my voice quavering noticeably. "It doesn't matter. The eagle . . . was in a box . . . and . . . I had a seizure."

I was breathing heavier and looked up at the ceiling, like it was the sky, then down again. My mouth was twitching, my hands trembling. For some reason, I stood up again. (Was I actually awake, not sleeping, in this part of the nightmare?)

They were staring up at me, confused.

I had two choices. One was to stop. The other was to jump.

I jumped. "There was this phone call I should tell you about. And the jar here." I looked for the jar that had been on the table in front of me and discovered it was gone.

I was becoming more agitated—shaking my head and turning right and left nervously, as a teacher would who could not make his students understand because it was beyond them. In exasperation, desperation, I tried digging down inside myself to find the necessary something that the learning situation called for to enlighten them.

I began to feel tired. Very tired.

"I need time to think. There's nothing sordid here. Just . . . the opposite."

I took a very deep breath and threw my hands up to express frustration—their frustration to understand, mine to say what I needed to say clearly. "Listen, it's in her journal. What you really want to know. What's most interesting here. What you probably think of as the more sensational part. The part you're not allowed to ask me about. Silkie. That was her name. Silkie. You . . . the school . . . know her by another name. Marian. It's in the journal."

I was lost again. Had I somehow gotten on the wrong train and needed to get off, maybe even go back to the station and get on another one? I smiled, half laughed, shook my head . . . but not in a reflective way. More in a way to say I just didn't care anymore.

"It's all absurd to you, I think. So it doesn't matter what evidence I bring. There it is—a journal. Exhibit A, but you won't read it, and I can't ask you to, and I don't even want you to. My journal too. I should have brought that too. That's where it is. What you want to know. The authentic truth with all the juicy parts in it. The point is, though . . . *you don't know how to read it. I myself don't even know*. But it is . . . there."

"Excuse me, Stephen, we . . . I mean, are you going to . . . ?"

It was Jamil.

I looked directly at him and waited for what he would say. Not moving, my eyes focused on him.

I knew the role he was playing had nothing to do with the question he'd asked. That he—the one participant not of this department—was also not part of World One, and was, therefore, trying to save me. From the others who didn't know *where I was.* Who saw me not only as seriously distracted and therefore mentally ill, but as condescending as well.

"No, no, it's okay," he said solicitously. "I'm sorry I interrupted. I'm beginning to see."

He actually said that. *I'm beginning to see.*

I stood up in front of my jury . . . I'm not sure why . . . and to everyone's alarm began to shake. My hands fumbled with the journal. Searching for something inside myself that could be found only by playing with this object in front of me. Then, I stopped. Sat down. Looked up and around the room . . . only briefly—perhaps just long enough to let them know I was aware of their presence after all.

"Silkie," I said. "I need to tell you about her. She's the one you want to hear about. I know that. I know the rumors. You've been afraid to ask me. Maybe thinking it's part of all this. It is. That's where it is. Silkie. And World Two. The part about me and the student. Silkie's her name. In the journal. Silkie. World Two."

Now no one was moving. I knew it—I had them. Their impatience was on hold. Who was this Silkie? The student, right? They'd all heard the rumor. And it allowed them the higher ground.

But where to go next?

"Can we just postpone this?" I asked. "Till next week, when I'll be more ready?" I began breathing heavily. "One morning there was this phone call. Saying she was . . . but even before then, I found out . . . there was something wrong . . . "

I fell violently into the table. A seizure.

"I'm okay!" I called out as I woke up.

But, I wondered if the dream had only been partially that, and had been filled out in brief awake moments by very real concerns of my conscious mind taking hold in a world that allowed for the surreal.

45. Still Questions

I tried to nap on the plane, but was besieged by too many questions, by visions of what horror I would see in Sacramento.

Silkie had alluded to an attorney in the letter they found. A guardianship would have necessitated that. I remembered her mentioning off-hand one time her considering getting a disability status to help her with her finances, but she hadn't followed up on it. So was that how she had the services of a lawyer? I would have to look up that attorney . . . call on him or her. Later.

In one of my phone calls to the police the day before, I'd asked what effects had been found. One was "a notebook with a lot of hard-to-read stuff—writing—in it. Like a journal or diary." Silkie was still keeping one. What was in it? News of Maheza's father. Comments about me—regarding Maheza?

Did they have pictures of the body? Did Maheza in any way take part in the identification? And if indeed the one they found was Silkie, where was Maheza when it happened?

Was it murder? Suicide? An accident? The police had a maddening lack of curiosity about it. Big-city homeless deaths.

Not a priority, obviously. Too difficult to get meaningful facts about causes, motives, family. Nobody to care or push the investigation. Quite often drugs involved. The policewoman had admitted that's how it was.

Maheza had worried about how Silkie would just wander off. How she couldn't always afford her medicine. How Silkie admitted liking to walk alone by the river. Silkie's mental state, period. Even a six-year-old knew she wasn't normal.

Had anyone seen me with Silkie that morning? I should have, yes, gone back to the all-night restaurant and asked the waitress if she remembered me and that I was sitting with a young woman. Or with *anyone*. That would at least mean I didn't imagine the whole thing. It wasn't all a hallucination.

As for the jar? Yes, there could conceivably, I supposed, be two exactly alike. Did she know more about that? "She?" What "she" had I spoken with? Silkie? The other Silkie—Ruth?

Was I mad? For real? Not just metaphorically speaking.

And if I went down there and said I saw Silkie so she couldn't be dead, wouldn't that argue against my being a guardian for Maheza? "He's in a questionable state of mind." Might there be some court hearing about this apparently crazy guy being given a very young child to raise?

There were questions about Silkie too. The whole Ruth thing. The phone call. The peculiar journal entries about other countries.

Was this her expectation for me, then? To save her? Was that the reason for the admonishment and anticipation that her gaze had communicated to me for so long? If so, my stupidity, my insensitivity were appalling. In my failure, did she in the end kill herself? Or had it been just an accident resulting from the strange way she had of wandering off? That last night with Maheza. "We have to go find her."

Either way I should have been more perceptive.

A personal failure. A cosmic betrayal. Where was the *something happening* of that long-ago phone call now? A meaningless death in a river. How could anything be *happening* if she was now dead? Accident or suicide—it didn't matter. A bewildering relationship ended in the denial of its even being bewildering.

Homeless mentally ill woman. Dead. Drowned. Happens all the time.

God's joke! World Two, after all, wasn't moral. It could, in fact, be monstrous. A world, a universe, of clumsy chance. We save a starfish, as did Loren Eiseley, fling it out beyond the breaking surf, while around us millions of other starfish drown in tide pool silt. Is the wonder of a living Silkie different from the wonder of a dead barnacle?

But then . . . I saw her!

I was on the short flight from San Francisco to Sacramento when I was struck with a realization. Having *seemingly lost* Silkie, I had embarked on a long journey of utter despondency and irrational behavior. Yet, now that it was possible Silkie was, for sure, *irretrievably lost* from my life, I was feeling no such depression, despair. Feeling, instead, a peace.

Something akin to World Two.

It did not last.

On the ground—in the Sacramento airport—it was gone. I had to accept the truth. It was in World One that the necessary decisions and conclusions would be made.

My own personal investigation into *something happening*—the stain on the jar, the seeing of Silkie (talking with her several days after she should have been dead)—was over. At least for now. For these next few days, I could take it as I wished. Either a jar full of newspaper clippings sent out to sea as a complaint to the gods, and then returned by a ghost. Or, more likely, a jar that never came back, a girl who drowned, a daughter who "needed to be fed." Period.

The rental car line. "Medium-sized or full-sized?" "Will you be needing collision coverage?" "If you gas it up before returning it, you'll pay the going price—much cheaper . . ."

"Do you have a map of the city? Or maybe you can tell me how to get to the main police station. I think it's near the courthouse on ___ Street?"

"Out to the left, then left again. You'll need to get to the freeway . . ."

Ended up on a one-way street, not going the way I needed to get. Circled back to the freeway . . .

A very large brick building. Parked two streets down for fear of parking in a restricted lot. A main door. Listing of county and municipal offices. I was told the main floor. Room 101-103. At the main desk, give the clerk the case number.

Hallways. A small room to the rear past some desks.

A nice-looking young man in his thirties with a neat dark mustache—Sergeant Craig Gillingham. He had pictures. Some from the scene. Some of the body. Face. Several angles. Sharper images than I'd imagined. Yes, yes—

Silkie. A body. Silkie. A body.

My God!

As ghastly as these photos were, I was reminded of the "Los Angelitos" photos of dead children. A migration to a sacred place.

No witnesses of what happened. Only finding her the next morning. She'd been staying with them in the camp. Had a tent from someplace. Shared with her daughter and another woman. Apparently went off in the middle of the night. Had only a little money. Friend—an older woman—said Silkie had been planning to take the bus trip back to Oregon but needed another $56. Had been there only ten or eleven days.

I made an appointment with Children's Services.

"Can you direct me how to get there?"

Provided them my paperwork. A passport identifying me. My birth certificate. My university I.D. My driver's license. Filled out papers.

"How far is the place. The foster home?"

Got lost. Missed a turn off the freeway. When I got back on couldn't get back to other street where I was supposed to turn.

The frustration became too much. I pulled over at a convenience store. Bought a hot dog and a Pepsi. Sat down on the walkway in front of the store. As I sat there, I remembered some short story I'd taught once. In it, a poor woman, unable to feed her baby, shoves it wrapped in a blanket into the arms of a total stranger passing.

I got up, went back into the store. Asked for directions. "What street is it you want again?"

"It's out a ways but if you can tell me how to get to this street here on the paper . . . I should be able to find it . . ."

Made another wrong turn. Almost began to cry from the stress of the trip, the photos, the meaning of all that I was about in this strange city. Seeing Maheza again—but in these circumstances.

Through it all, six words kept sounding in my head—the phrase you fall back on—"could not believe she was gone." Words that every grieving human has appropriated for his own personal tragedy. Like the lines of a catchy song refusing to go away even in sleep. Six words describing the incomprehension of death. ". . . could not believe she was dead." A meaningless phrase because one *did* believe. Even in such cases as mine. No choice. The photos.

"Damn!" I shouted aloud in the car. If I could not deny the meaning of the words, I would, even so, not use them so casually, so dishonestly. The images came—not only that of the final time I'd seen her on the campus steps, but her stumbling into my office . . . into my life . . . out of the rain . . . and the way she seemed to study me the morning I confronted her with the phone call. These were images, though, that did not testify to her still being alive. Rather to *another and perhaps greater death. Was a greater death possible?*

It was the death of the *something is happening*, of her eyes—gazing at me with so much anticipation, admonishment. If, indeed, *something had been happening to me,* what was I, therefore, supposed to be doing now? Just this? Driving to a foster home. To find whom? What form would Maheza take? Who was she now?

I pulled into the parking lot. Trembling. I picked up the photocopy of Silkie's letter and reread it.

> *I am afraid. What will happen. If it does, something happens to me, I want my professor Stephen Mollgaard to take care of my daughter. Maheza is her name. He is her good friend and has taken care of her many times. She knows him. He knows her and what to do with her. He should be the one. No one else. The official paper is at the Office of Woodside and Boyd, Attorneys-at-Law. I signed it. Marian Sanders. June 14, 20—*

The policewoman had appended an official note introducing me and the circumstances.

The "home" the state was using to care for children who'd been left abandoned or homeless by parents killed, arrested, or taken away, was an old structure which looked to have been converted from an early twentieth-century mansion and in that conversion lost its charm.

The somewhat matronly lady who answered the door led me into a side office where I provided my introductions and papers and asked to see Maheza.

"Yes, of course. She's probably out back. They're playing. This is their playtime. She'll be finished soon. Just wait here."

"Listen, can't I go out there? To the yard?"

She seemed reluctant. "Well, I suppose so. That's not usually the way, but I guess it's okay. You've come so far."

I followed her through the "house." Unimaginative dime-store pictures of dull landscapes, an absence of bookshelves or real plants anywhere, and the lone large wooden box of assorted broken toys that must long ago have lost any interest for the children—that all gave the home as cold an appearance as I might have imagined such homes to have, and with little suggesting the primary tenants were children.

The backyard was spacious, but the lawn was worn mostly brown, and there appeared to be too many children for the play area available.

"She's over there. Behind the others," the woman said, pointing to the far corner of the open area, well beyond where the other children were playing and down over a hill near an aluminum fence marking the back boundary.

I could see from the way the hill sloped down to the left that just on the other side was a stream with trees along it affording some shade.

46. Running in Circles

Maheza was there, running in an ever-widening circle that carried her for some distance close to and along the stream. She was by herself, paying no attention to the other children, nor to anyone for that matter.

To get there, I had to take the long way around the swings, slide, and a field where three older children were playing some form of tag. I stopped. Stood back about twenty yards from her, then sat on one of the two swings.

She was so occupied with her running that she didn't seem to know I was there. Her circling took her around the crown of the hill so that as she reached the far side, near the stream, I would lose sight of her until she reappeared at the other end. Her brown hair was falling all over her face in a way she seemed to want it to as she ran because she allowed it to cover her eyes. She was not smiling. Her lips were pressed together, her eyes intense—those of someone trying to win a race. She had on a jacket but the jeans she was wearing could have been the bottom of the overalls I'd bought her.

I was content to just watch her, not to call out or disturb

her in any way. I'd always thought it wise to not reach out to young children so obviously that it revealed the intent. All the overbearing aunts and new stepmothers who would smother you with kisses almost before they got through the door.

She kept circling—but now more like a sea bird or an eagle who'd become part of the very air currents buoying her. Finally, at a point behind the hill where I could see just the upper portion of her body, she stopped and turned toward me. Did she even recognize me? It had been several months. And considering what had happened during those months . . .

She began running again. This time faster and faster in a large circle, reminding me of the time she had run around the bases that night long before. Finally she stopped, to catch her breath.

She seemed to think a while, then began walking slowly in my direction—over the top of the hill—but with her head down. When she got to me, she looked up quickly then down again, and grasped my right arm with both hands, tugging somewhat on the sleeve of my jacket. She pressed her face into the cloth, the way she had that night with her mother sitting on the wall over the river.

I hugged her. She held my arm more tightly. It was a full minute or more before she quietly pulled away.

She didn't seem to know what to do then.

"I like how you run," I said. She turned to her left and, surprisingly, began running once more, this time very slowly and at a steady pace. But by the time she'd reappeared at the other end I could see she'd sped up and was gradually accelerating to where she was running so fast, so wildly, I was certain sooner or later she'd be forced to let go, stumble and fall so hard she'd be hurt. Indeed, just as she circled around to my right, she sprawled onto the dirt near the fence.

She lay there awhile then, apparently exhausted, got up and came back to the swings and sat in the one next to me.

"Am I going with you?"

"Do you want to?"

She looked away, then nodded. "I don't like it here."

"Why?"

She shrugged, but didn't answer.

"Do you think you . . . could like it with me?"

She nodded again. "Do you have children? You showed me . . . those pictures."

"Right . . . but . . . they don't live with me. But . . . yes."

"Why don't they live with you?"

"They come sometimes. They live . . . like you did—with their mother."

We didn't say anything for some time. I couldn't tell if she was crying, because she was staring out toward the field, but I thought she might be.

"Do you want to talk about it? About . . . what happened . . . or what is happening?"

I was hoping, without directly asking about her mother, she would tell me something which would confirm whether Silkie really was—yes or no—dead.

She shook her head, but I could see there were tears in her eyes. I remained silent, giving it some time. Perhaps she would open up. Tell me something that would make it all clear. But she didn't.

"I'm going to stay here with you for a while. But then I have to go. Tomorrow, though . . . I'll be back. It may be a few days before they'll let you go with me."

"How many days?"

"I'm not sure. Maybe tomorrow I can tell you. Hopefully not too long. That . . . letter. The one your mother gave you. Did you give it to them?"

She nodded.

"Do you know what was in it?"

"Mama told me."

"I know you can read . . . remember at my house. Could you read the letter?"

"She didn't print the letters. I can't read the other way. Just my name."

"I forgot. She used cursive." I was talking more to myself than Maheza then. "I don't know if they'll let me bring anything to you tomorrow. But . . . if they do . . . what might you want?"

She shrugged.

I wasn't sure where to go next. What she asked me then startled me. As she did, she stared straight ahead.

"Do you take medicine too?"

"Yes, why?"

"Mama says you take medicine too."

"It's different. Not what she was taking. I don't have the same problem she . . . did. Besides, I always remember to take them."

"Can I see them?"

"I guess so. Here." I withdrew from my pocket a little plastic box in which I kept a spare pill for my seizures and one for migraines. "I always keep one with me. See, it's probably different from your mother's, no?"

She glanced at it then away.

"Can I ask you a question, Maheza? Did you and your mother visit your . . . father? While you were . . ."

She suddenly screwed up her lips with hatred and seemed to almost bite at my question before I could finish it. "He's . . . "

She didn't finish, and I dropped the subject. "We stayed with . . . a lady. She had a tent."

"Was that by the river?"

She didn't answer. Her lips were pressed together and trembling. Her eyes were full of anger, hatred. If she'd tried to answer it would have come out in a sob, I suspected.

"So, were you going to come back? To . . . where you used to be. Oregon."

"Mama didn't have enough money."

"I wish . . . I wish . . . she had written me. Called me. I would have given her what she needed . . . to get back."

Maheza started to lower her head, but then turned toward me. She had that same look in her eyes she'd had that night in the park, walking back toward me in the rain—the night she'd insisted on going to find her mother, insisting she was not in class.

It was only an hour or so later, when I was driving back to the hotel, that I remembered where I had seen eyes like that before. The picture on the wall. Omayra's eyes. Very strong. Stronger than mine. It made me wonder if Maheza wasn't much stronger than me. I would be taking care of her, but, in the same way she looked after her mother, she'd be looking after me. Making sure I took my medicine.

Still in the play yard, I showed her the drawing.

"Maheza, did you draw this? For me?"

It was almost imperceptible. Her "Uh . . . huh."

"Thank you. When did you . . . ?"

"Mama helped me."

"I like it. Do you remember when . . . you drew it?"

She sat there, her head rigid. Saying nothing. I saw her eyes moistening.

"That's okay."

"That . . . night. She had it . . . I think."

"Thank you. I like it."

"It's not wet."

"No, it's not."

It was a strange thing to say for sure. "It's not wet." Even more strange than her not asking me how I'd come to have the drawing at all. And immediately my mind conjoined "wet" . . . "ocean" . . . "jar"—though everything argued against

Maheza's making any such connection (she knew nothing of my "journey" nor of the early-morning visit, which had, in fact, occurred well after the drowning). In any case, I did not ask her what she meant by "It's not wet."

At that moment, I thought it was for her sake. I did not want to recall for her what must have been horrible scenes. Her mother's body in the water, perhaps the drawing in her pocket—the one they had worked on together to send to me or give me.

And perhaps it was--for her.

But it was as much, if not more, for me. The threat of that awful *normalcy*. World One rearing its head at the moment there was the possibility I'd escaped it. Crossed over.

What if Maheza were to say her mother had spilled some water on the drawing just after they'd finished it? And that led to her memory of Silkie mailing it to me at some post office days before? The jar too.

Common sense, rational World One explanations. Whatever the beauty, the elegant order of the spiraling chimney swifts, however exotic their seasonal journeys, they were in the end *Chaetura pelagica*—birds of the "swift" family which commonly nest in chimneys in North America and migrate to northwestern South America in the winter. The phantasmagorically-shaped driftwood I'd marveled at as I drifted off to sleep on the Oregon coast was just that—wood. Trees. Pine. Fir. Perhaps here and there one that found its way to these shores from far off—a guarico from Ecuador (the kind Silkie spoke of in her journal), an Acacia from Peru, a cinnamon tree from Korea, even a baobab from West Africa. But still . . . trees. And any poetic rendering of the meeting of World One and World Two as a shoreline or a horizon had, in the end, to draw upon a mere mixing of chemicals: atmospheric gases—nitrogen and oxygen infused with a water vapor that empties into a vast saline sea of oxygen and hydrogen; which in turn mixes with long gleaming stretches of silicon dioxide we call sand. World Two itself was no more than a penciled number to the right of a vertical line on a piece of paper. The eagle was long dead, never having broken through the screening, the plywood. Ruth was a delusional disorder—neatly defined in the psychiatric textbooks. The file cabinet was a file cabinet. The clippings and labels just paper. The jar just a jar. In this case two jars that were made by the same company at the same time and happened to cross in the most bizarre of ways.

All those inexplicable tragedies I'd raged at and housed in the bottom drawer. They happened. Returned empty jars do not make them go away. Future wonders cannot undo past horrors.

To whom could I talk about any of this and not leave them in doubt? Mick, Rafael, Paul and Corrine. They would listen quietly. Offer no answers. Marvel at my passion. The intensity of how I told the tale. What more could I expect of them?

"Oh, but Ombeni. Her second letter. Her dead brother came back. What about that?"

Even I could not accept that. She was so young. Had to take the word of others.

She was so young.

Me, I wasn't young. I was . . . mad? For those few weeks. Those last few days, anyway.

And so I did not question Maheza any further. Not as I sat there with her. Maybe later. Now she *needed to be fed.*

FINI

[In memory of Erik Kraven]

Note to the Reader

The characters and events in this novel are a creation of the author's imagination: fiction. Any resemblance to real people or events is coincidental.

The "File Cabinet" is the only exception. The newspaper accounts it contains ("Drawer 4") are of actual historical events and people. The students described ("Drawer 3B") were my students, though I changed their names. The literary quotes ("Drawer 3A") are, of course, those of the writers to whom they are attributed.

News Article Sources

Anastasijevic, Dejan. "Disabled Serbians in Harsh Conitions." *Time* Nov. 14, 2007.*
http://content.time.com/time/world/article/0,8599,1683763,00.html

Bjornstad, Randi. "Animal Lover Out of Time, Money." [from *The Register Guard*, September 4, 2002] *The Free Library*. http://www.thefreelibrary.com/Animal+lover+out+of+time,+money.

Chernos, Saul. "Ken Saro-Wiwa's Body Being Exhumed." February 1, 2000
http://www.ens-newswire.com/ens/feb2000/2000-02-01-01.asp

Ewoldt, Delbert. "A Single Pair of Stockinged . . . " ZoomInfo. www.zoominfo.com/p/Delbert-Ewoldt/277000868 "Fire Kills Mother and Children at Home." *New York Times* October 17, 2002.
www.nytimes.com/2002/10/.../fire-kills-mother-and-children-at-home.html

Morrow, Lance. "When Hope Is the Enemy." *Time*. October 25, 2002.
http://content.time.com/time/magazine/article/0,9171,366332,00.html

"Ngawang Sangdrol released." FreeTibet. October 17, 2002.
http://www.freetibet.org/news-media/pr/ngawang-sangdrol-released

"Saartjie (Sarah) Baartman's Story." www.saartjiezfreerepublic.com/focus/f-news/920916/posts
Spillius, Alex. "We Are Unarmed Bait, Said UN Victim of Mob." September 8, 2000
http://www.telegraph.co.uk/news/worldnews/asia/indonesia/1354603/We

"UW Medical Professor Killed by Crocodile in Africa." KOMO News, March 21, 2006.* http://www.komonews.com/news/archive/4180496.html

Weisskopf, Michael. "Civilian Deaths." *Time*. May 3, 2003.
http://content.time.com/time/magazine/article/0,9171,449440,00.html

*Date modified in story to fit timeline.

Acknowledgments

A lot of people helped me in the writing of this book. I especially want to thank: Anthea Ferguson, Michael Skupsky, and Andrew Rothgery (my son), all of whom contributed many hours of their time. Special thanks, as well, to Joshua Daniels, who took the cover photograph, and Makayla Ries, the model for "Silkie" in that photo.

Stephen Mathys, Cynthia Kallenbach, and Hugh Kent contributed passages to the "student index cards," and Rachel Rothgery (my daughter) contributed two of the entries to Silkie's journal. Erik Kraven, who died in 2001, authored the beautiful short story "Seffner," from which the "Darky" passage comes.

Lenana Faraj and Happines Bulugu did the Kiswahili translations for me.

I must also thank my wife, Hsiao-Ching, whose encouragement has kept me writing.

But there were many more, among whom I must not fail to mention Naomi Grace, Patricia Sandoval, Hannah Wheeler, Sonja Anise, Shelly St. Clair, and James McCarty.

David Rothgery teaches English at Lane Community College in Eugene, Oregon.

CPSIA information can be obtained at www.ICGtesting.com
Printed in the USA
BVOW02s0848120314

347380BV00002B/31/P

9 781626 527591